SICK AS A PARROT

Liz Evans

An Orion paperback

First published in Great Britain in 2004
by Orion
This paperback edition published in 2005
by Orion Books Ltd,
Orion House, 5 Upper St Martin's Lane,
London WC2H 9EA

A CIP catalogue record for this book
is available from the British Library.

ISBN 0 75286 531 5

Typeset by Deltatype Ltd, Birkenhead, Merseyside

Printed and bound in Great Britain by
Clays Ltd, St Ives plc

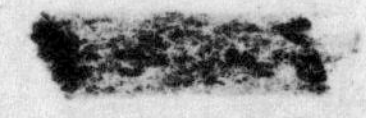

www.orionbooks.co.uk

1

There is a moment in every case when you realize things aren't going as planned; in this case it was being perched half-naked up an oak tree with a drop-dead sexy murder suspect a few feet away.

The job had started with me sitting behind the reception desk of Vetch (International) Investigations Inc freezing my butt off. It was just gone two o'clock and I was tempted to call it a day. It wasn't like I had to be there. All the investigators in Vetch's were self-employed. We paid a monthly fee to the company for the use of office space and 'shared facilities' (a fax machine and a bolshie receptionist guaranteed to insult every client with impartial stroppiness).

It was a long time since I'd sat in the building for hours on my own. I'm not usually the over-imaginative sort, but I was beginning to feel spooked by the combination of the dark afternoon and the wind howling around the building as if it were auditioning for a featured appearance in *Dracula – The Seaside Years.*

Once my ears had tuned out the wind, I started to hear other things. Claws rustling way above my head. Just the birds scrabbling for a foothold on the roof I told myself. A low moan in the empty cellar beneath my feet. Definitely a draught finding its way through a gap in that warped window-frame.

'Get a grip,' I said aloud. 'Nothing nasty from another dimension will be dropping in today.'

The front door was flung open by an unseen hand. The wind moaned into the hall with an unearthly shriek. And a faceless figure in an ankle-length black cape swept into the building. Paralysed I watched it close the door then glide swiftly towards me, arms crossed over its chest like an effigy carved on the top of an old tomb. I scanned the desk surface; hole punch, two pencils, notebook and used mug. There's never a stake or a bunch of garlic around when you need one. The thing stopped before me and I looked up into the black oval of the hood, half expecting to see devilish red eyes or the glint of pointed incisors.

The voice took me by surprise. It was light, soft – and female. 'I'd like to see a private investigator please.' Flicking back the fur-trimmed cape hood, she revealed hazel eyes in a pale oval face.

'Yes?'

'Yes.'

We stared at each other. I sensed there had already been a breakdown in communication here. 'How can I help you?'

She gave a soft 'oh' and frowned. 'Do I have to tell you about it before I can see an investigator?'

'I am an investigator. Don't I look like one?'

I did a quick check. I was wearing a pair of navy fleecy men's thermal pants, two sweaters (one pink, one russet), thick socks (striped red, cream and blue) stuffed into short brown boots, a mauve padded jacket, knitted black gloves and one of those woolly hats with ear-flaps that are the last word in chic if you happen to be a Peruvian peasant.

'I thought you were the receptionist,' the cloaked one said.

'She's off sick. There's a flu bug going around.'

Knowing Jan, we might have suspected her of pulling a sickie, but since she passed out in reception and you could have fried eggs on her forehead when we checked, we decided she was genuine this time.

'Aren't there any other investigators working here?' the cloak asked.

Boy, this girl really knew how to make you feel wanted. I gave her my best professional smile and the good news.

'There were six. But one left last year and we haven't replaced him. Two work across the Channel a lot. They really only use the office as a mail drop and answering service. They did pop in a couple of days ago.' I saw hope lighten her features and let her enjoy it for a few seconds before going for the jugular. 'Flu. Hit them in twenty-four hours. They're both in bed. Not together.' (Well, possibly together actually – I've never been quite sure with those two.)

'What about the others?'

'Vetch the Le . . . the owner is ill as well and Annie . . . the *other* Miss Smith is on holiday, in Barbados.'

'You must charge top dollar if your investigators can afford to holiday in the Caribbean at this time of year. When Daddy took us, we had to go in May because it was half the price of the peak season rates.'

I processed this information. Daddy had money. The cloak looked like designer gear. Who cared if she had no confidence in me? My integrity was for sale. Which was more than could be said for the plumbers in a fifty-mile radius of Seatoun. The office boiler had broken down a few days ago and I couldn't get anyone to repair it. It was either spend money heating my own flat, or find a reason not to sit around here.

I used this lack of facilities as an excuse for my eccentric wardrobe and promised that we charged only professional rates and mutually agreed expenses. At that moment, to my relief, the computer screen 'pinged' as a small envelope icon appeared in the bottom toolbar. 'That'll be Annie. I'll just get it and then we'll move somewhere warmer for a chat.'

Annie had gone on holiday with her new boyfriend, Stuart, and her new WAP phone. I had no idea how Stuart was doing, but I knew that damn phone worked. It took still photos and video images, it sent emails, it received emails . . . for all I knew it sang and played flaming Dixie. An image appeared on the screen; two chairs around a table covered with the remains of a meal. Beyond it you could make out golden sands and brilliant blue sea through the bars of the balcony rail. A sheet of white paper was propped against the coffee pot: 'BREAKFAST ON THE TERRACE AGAIN. TEMPERATURE 24°C. WATER-SKIING LATER. ANY NEWS?'

'It looks banging, doesn't it?' the cloak said wistfully. 'Like you want to jump on a plane and go right there. But I have to keep my inheritance for more important things.'

I added that 'inheritance' to the hints about Daddy's bank balance as I grabbed the keyboard and banged out a reply: 'No news, no cases, no heating, no plumbers.'

Resetting the answering service and security alarms, I led Ms Cloak down to the end of the street and turned along the road to the front promenade. The beach at Seatoun was wide and shallow so even in extreme conditions the sea never came in far enough for waves to break over the balustrade and pavements. But the gales skimming over the grey rollers scooped up salty droplets, mixed them with grains of sand and flung them inland to scour the rusty shutters pulled down over the ice-cream and novelty shops that were closed until Easter, and test the guy ropes lashing down the deckchair stacks for any hint of weaknesses.

Hoping the cloak was following, I struggled along past the entrance to the amusement park and string of arcades with their flashing neon lights before turning down a side street. My goal was in sight. And its windows were deliciously fugged up. Warmth. Food. Hot drinks. I plunged straight through the door.

Pepi's was my favourite greasy spoon café – and at present it was pretty much everyone else's. Anyone who didn't want to – or couldn't – pay for heating was taking advantage of the warmth. Shane, the owner, was flipping pancakes on the griddle behind the counter and swaying to the sound of Freddie Cannon belting out the attractions of being 'Way Down Yonder in New Orleans' on the jukebox.

I bagged the last empty table, ditched the padded jacket and Peruvian cap, and ran my fingers through my hair to unplaster it from my head. I keep it cut short and blonde (from a bottle) so that's about all the styling it ever needs. Slipping into a chair, I watched my would-be client settling herself opposite. The reason for the carved effigy pose became obvious when she disentangled a pink transparent file that she'd been hugging to her chest under the cloak and laid it next to the large red plastic tomato on the table. Unclipping a neck clasp, she shrugged the cloak off and flung it over the chair.

I revised my assessment of her height. I'd pegged it at around five feet, eight inches, a couple of inches less than mine. But now it became obvious that about four inches of that was being provided by the heels on her boots. She was all in white under that cloak. Knee-length boots, tight trousers and a loose fluffy cowl-necked sweater.

Shane delivered the pancakes and sashayed over to our table. 'So what'll it be, girls?'

I ordered two coffees.

'Lattes?' Shane asked.

'You do lattes?' Pepi's was the original chips-with-everything establishment. I loved it. It was cholesterol heaven.

Shane leant over the table and lowered his voice. 'It's the stuff out of the cappuccino machine. Only I don't put chocolate on it. And I charge 'em thirty pence more a mug.'

'For not putting chocolate on it?'

'Supply and demand, Smithie. Everyone wants latte these days. You eating?'

I ordered a cheese and onion toastie and Whitey had bacon on wholemeal.

Once Shane had squeezed his way back through seats and pushchairs to the counter, Whitey said, 'Smithie? Is that what you're called?'

'Grace Smith. I'll answer to Grace or Smithie. And you are . . . ?'

'Hannah Conti.'

'Italian?' Oddly enough I'd thought of Italy as soon as

she'd pushed back her cloak hood. Not the olive-skinned brunettes that that word usually brings to mind, but the auburns and pale translucent skins of the women in some Renaissance paintings.

'My paternal grandparents were. My mother's are Scottish. At least . . . that's what I want to see an investigator about. I'm adopted.'

A birth-family trace then. Probably dull and routine but reasonably well paid. Aloud I said, 'I'll need a copy of your original birth certificate if you want me to find your family. Although I should tell you there are specialist agencies that—'

'I've *done* all that.' The unspoken 'dummy' hung in the air between us.

I looked into the hazel eyes flecked with green and thought that this was a girl who wouldn't be fobbed off until she'd got whatever it was she'd set her sights on.

Apparently she was aware that her tone wasn't exactly going to make us contract-long buddies. 'Sorry. I didn't mean to sound rude. It's just that it's been really hard getting all this stuff . . .' She indicated the pink folder. 'Everyone kept trying to put me off. I can see why now, of course. But they still didn't have the right, did they?'

Before I could reply, Shane arrived with the toasties and chocolate-free cappuccinos. He slid cutlery wrapped in red paper napkins in front of us. I made a half-hearted show of searching in the jacket pockets. I always preferred clients to pay for meals. It showed commitment.

Hannah was fumbling around the cloak, apparently looking for a pocket, when Shane said, 'On the house girls. Enjoy.' And headed back to the jukebox to feed it with the pre-decimal shillings that drove it. Roy Orbison serenaded that 'Pretty Woman'. In case I missed the point, Shane made a pointing gesture with both forefingers . . . at me?

It was a mirror gesture of the pose in one of the dozen black-and-white framed photos around the café walls. They were all Shane – but just after he'd changed his name from

'Hubert' and become the lean, mean and moody rock singer in tight jeans and T-shirt, his hair greased back like Elvis's, and his upper lip curled in a contemptuous sneer. The lean and mean had long disappeared behind the pot belly, and the hair was confined to a tonsure around a bonce that gleamed like polished marble, but the sneer was still in full working order. I got it every time I tried to bum free meals in Pepi's (i.e. practically every day). And now he was *giving* me nosh ... without my grovelling or begging. Could the after-effects of recreational drugs take thirty years to kick in? I was so shaken that I nearly missed what Hannah was saying.

'... anyway I had to see a counsellor. I didn't want to, I mean, what were they going to say? That it could be a big disruption to my birth parents' lives? That I shouldn't expect some fairytale reunion? I could figure all that out for myself. He was asking me things like what I would do if my mother completely rejected me, or if I turned out to be the result of rape ...' And then, seeing my reaction (rapist-tracking is not an appealing activity – for obvious reasons), she added hastily, 'It's not that.'

So 'it' was definitely something then.

'*Damn!*' Reaching to pick up her mug, she'd managed to tip it over. Hastily she dammed the fawn rivulets with her napkin before they could cascade over the table edge. 'Sorry. I'm always knocking stuff. Anyway he finally handed over my birth certificate.' She wiped greasy fingers on the red napkin and popped the flap on the plastic folder. Extracting the top document, she passed it across to me. 'I brought photocopies, not originals.'

Hannah Conti had been born in Seatoun nineteen years ago on 1 December. Birth name: Flora Wynne-Ellis. Mother: Alison Wynne-Ellis, aged sixteen years, home address 21 Hinton Road. Father: unknown.

Hinton Road was on the council estate up by the North Bay area, blocks of identical red-brick and concrete housing that had been plonked in the area between the older

Edwardian terraces near the front and the farm fields that still encircled Seatoun.

'I went there,' Hannah explained. 'The people in the house have only been there three years. It's changed owners loads of times since my . . . mother . . . lived there. But I'd got these.' She removed two more photocopied documents from the pink folder.

Sheets of paper stapled together. I scanned the first sheet. 'Electoral lists?'

'One recent and the other twenty years ago. They keep copies of the old ones at the county historical records office. I got the whole area in case there were other relatives.'

'And are there?'

'No. At least, there are no other Wynne-Ellises listed. But look . . .' She flicked both lists, folding them open at the third sheet, and pointed to an underlined entry on each. Twenty years ago, 19 Hinton Road had been occupied by Kenneth and Lucia Darrowfield. Now it was home to Kenneth and Philip Darrowfield.

'So has Lucia started shaving or has Kenneth come out of the closet?'

Hannah smiled for the first time. She had the kind of smile that lit up her whole face. I felt scruffier than normal. 'Neither. Mrs Darrowfield, Lucia, died. Philip is their son. I guess he was too young to be on the electoral list twenty years ago.'

'And they knew your mum?'

'They must have done, mustn't they?' Her tone had hardened. It was obviously an encounter that hadn't gone well. 'Philip has something wrong with him. He can't walk and he can barely talk. It's really difficult to make out what he's saying. He's got a sort of monitor thing he types on, but I didn't get a chance to ask him anything because Mr Darrowfield just lost it as soon as I told him who I was. He practically threw me out. But I was just *determined* to get some kind of information out of him.'

And she had. She'd got her maternal grandparents' new

address from him by standing outside his front window and crying copiously (aided by an onion hidden in her handkerchief) until he'd thrust it at her just to get rid of her. Triumphantly she showed me the Thamesmead address scrawled on the back of a torn flyer for a pizza chain.

'I went there. And they were *gross.* I mean, totally, *gross.* They didn't even want to let me in the *door.*'

'So how did you . . . ?'

'I threatened to make a big placard saying who I was and sit outside their front door.'

'And that worked?'

'They still wouldn't talk to me about my mother. But they gave me this.' *This* was an information leaflet for a garden centre.

'She's the restaurant manager. She calls herself Alison Brown now. I was going to get to know her a bit before I told her. But it all went wrong. I blurted it all out, almost as soon as I saw her. She said . . .' Drawing a deep breath, Hannah pronounced each word flatly but clearly: ' "I didn't want to see you when you were born. I don't want to see you now. Go away and never contact me again." So I went. I wrote to her afterwards. I thought she might just need a bit of time to get used to the idea. But she never wrote back.'

We were nearing the end of the folder's contents. 'And then a few days later this came in the post.'

A newspaper page dated nineteen years ago:

SCHOOLGIRL GUILTY OF MURDER

> This afternoon, schoolgirl Alison Wynne-Ellis (16) was found guilty of the vicious murder of school-teacher, Trudy Hepburn . . .

'Came from where?'

Hannah produced the envelope: plain brown self-seal, address printed in black ink, posted in Central London.

'Any note enclosed?'
'No. Just that.'
'And you want me to . . . ?'
The green flecks sparkled in her wide eyes. 'Prove that my mother didn't do it, of course.'

2

It wouldn't work out. These cases rarely do. If they didn't find out the truth when the evidence was fresh, it was unlikely that someone blundering around two decades later was going to overturn the original verdict. I tried to persuade Hannah of that fact. But not very hard. The final sheet in the folder was a copy of a letter from a solicitor, confirming that now Hannah had reached her eighteenth birthday she was entitled to draw on the monies held in trust for her under the will of the late Mr Alistair McRae. The capital and accrued interest amounted to just under thirty thousand pounds.

'He was my maternal grandfather. He died when I was twelve.'

'He was plainly very fond of you.'

She got the point of the unspoken question immediately. 'He was. *All* my adoptive family are totally brilliant. I'm not looking to replace anyone.' She nibbled a corner of sandwich. 'Have you ever looked at any of the websites for genealogy? They've got millions of members. People want to know where they've come from.'

I knew that. Whenever I've had to do a trace at the Family Records Centre, the place has always been packed with intense punters browsing ledgers of birth, death and marriage certificates.

'I don't mean the places, I mean the kind of people that created them.' Hannah struggled to put into words whatever need was driving her. 'I want to know whether I like sewing because she did. Or if my dad sucked his thumb too when he was a kid. When I have children I want to look at them and think, "That's her grandmother's nose" or "He's musical, just like his grandfather." And if there are bad things, I want to know as well.' She looked me directly in the eyes. 'Could you kill someone?'

It was a question I'd asked myself several times. Normally when I was backed into a corner by someone who wanted to inflict extreme pain. 'If I thought they were going to kill me I guess I could.'

'Anybody could then.' Hannah dismissed my reply with a flick of her fork. 'Or by accident. Like drinking too much and then trying to drive. But they say whoever did it put the knife in a dozen times. The killer must have watched as she got weaker. Fell down in her own blood and tried to crawl away, slipping and slithering in her own gore. Could you have gone on putting the knife in after that?'

'Probably not.'

(Although when I thought of a couple of past clients and their acquaintances who had wanted to do exactly that to me, I reckoned I could have stretched a point. But admitting you have a slight inclination to homicidal mania can be a deal breaker in the client/investigator relationship, I find.)

Hannah said, 'Me neither. It takes a special kind of person. And it's no good telling me you can't inherit a murderous trait. If you can inherit a talent for painting, say, why can't you pass on the lack of whatever . . . call it the conscience gene?'

'Do you feel a lack?'

'No. But perhaps it skips generations. Anyway, she didn't do it.'

'How do you know?'

'I just do. Soon as I met her, I sort of knew she couldn't do something like that.'

That didn't exactly square with her description of her meeting with her mum, but I'd done my best to dissuade her from channelling some of Granddaddy McRae's cash in my direction. There's only so much altruism a girl can put out. I quoted her for ten full days' work to be spread over the next month and asked for £500 expenses up-front.

She gave me a cheque without protest and wrote down her phone number and address so that I could send a formal contract. I'd assumed she lived locally, but she turned out to be a London girl. 'I thought since it all happened here it would be best to employ a local investigator. And Vetch's is the only one in the book.'

Boosted by that vote of confidence, I walked her to the door. Shane charged through the packed tables in a welter of elbowed backs, slopped coffees (sorry – lattes) and yells of protest from his customers.

'Smithie! Not leaving already? How about another coffee?'

(The jukebox switched to one of its few slow numbers 'Do Not Forsake Me Oh My Darling'. Sometimes I got the odd feeling that it had established a telepathic link with Shane.)

'Hannah's going.' I opened the door a crack, allowing her to slip out and a blast of freezing salt-tanged air to rush in. 'I, however, would love another coffee.'

'Coming right up. Em . . .' He threw a look towards the counter where several customers were queuing to order or pay. 'You couldn't give us a hand, could you?'

I'd noticed he seemed to be rushing between the front counter and the back kitchen. Normally his wife, Marlene, would have been manning the hot-plates out back and stacking the dishwasher. When I asked after her, Shane informed me she was sickening from something.

He licked his lips. 'Smithie . . . ? Can I, like, ask a favour?'

I prayed he wasn't going to ask me to do my ministering angel act with Marlene. I was crap at the ministering and after a few hours of dealing with sick people, I tend to favour euthanasia.

Luckily he didn't. It turned out he needed someone to petsit his brother's parrot for a few days. In return I'd get to eat at the café for free whenever I liked. It sounded like an easy gig. What could possibly go wrong? All I had to do was slip a handful of sunflower seeds in each day.

'Magic.' A huge grin spread over Shane's face. 'I'll bring her round.'

'Looking forward to it already.'

I helped out at the café until Shane shut up at five-thirty, then I climbed back into the layers of clothing, retrieved Hannah's file and headed out. The temperature seemed to have plunged even further. At this rate we'd have ice-bergs drifting off the coast and penguins perched in the bird baths.

I stank of eau-de-chip-pan and needed a bath. It would take about an hour for the water and room temperature to become bearable, so instead of undressing, I added the duvet to my ensemble to form a padded tepee and opened the newspaper account of Alison Wynne-Ellis's trial.

3

This afternoon, schoolgirl Alison Wynne-Ellis (16) was found guilty of the vicious murder of school-teacher, Trudy Hepburn.

The judge, Mr Justice Vickers, lifted reporting restrictions, allowing the press to name 'Miss X' as Alison Wynne-Ellis, a sixteen-year-old schoolgirl from Seatoun, as the killer of Miss Hepburn, a science teacher at St Martin's Comprehensive School.

The photograph looked like an official school mugshot. She was a pleasant enough looking kid; even-featured with blue eyes and long light brown hair tied back from an oval face. Her smile looked a little forced, as if she was uncomfortable being photographed.

There was a picture captioned 'Alison's parents leave court with her solicitor, Indira Patel', but there was nothing to be seen of the Wynne-Ellises. Her father had kept his head down, giving the photographer the top of thinning dark hair. Alison's mother had a hand raised to fend off the lens, allowing a glimpse of startled eyes through outstretched fingers.

In another shot two young men in police constable uniforms were walking towards the photographer. One was blond, his suit, even in a photo, showing signs of sharp creases and he had highly polished shoes and buttons. The other was dark, his eyes on something beyond the lens. Apparently these were 'PCs O'Hara and Pennington who were called to the scene of the murder'.

The victim was pictured in the lower right-hand corner.

Once again it was a posed studio shot. Graduation day this time; the gown and mortar board coming from the one-size-fits-all loan store for the day. Round-faced, too much dark hair and make-up that looked as though it had been applied by someone who only used it for special occasions. I looked into Trudy Hepburn's wide eyes behind eyelashes mascaraed into rigor mortis, and found nothing of any help.

It was warm enough to discard the duvet. Shrugging it off, I examined the rest of the pictures. A long shot of the main gate of St Martin's Comprehensive. An ordinary brick council semi that I knew even before I read the caption was 'Alison's home'. The other property – a substantial country cottage – was, more surprisingly, labelled 'the murder scene'. Until then I'd been toying with the scenario of an enraged pupil losing it on the school premises and lashing out after class. I read on.

> Trudy's body was discovered by a friend, Gina Gibbs, who returned to the house they shared late on the evening of 13 April. Miss Hepburn had been attacked in a manner described by prosecuting counsel in his opening address as 'sustained and frenzied'. More than two dozen knife wounds had been inflicted on the body.
>
> Describing her horror at what she'd found, Gina (31) said the scene in the kitchen looked 'like a slaughter house'. 'I don't think I'll ever forget what I saw that night,' Miss Gibbs, an attractive blonde, said. 'Even when I was standing in the middle of it, I felt as if I was dreaming. I'm just grateful that the police officers arrived so quickly. Trudy was a dear friend and I miss her dreadfully.'
>
> The case against Alison was based largely on forensic evidence. Expert witnesses testified that her clothes were heavily soaked with Trudy Hepburn's blood and the knife found in her possession was likewise covered in the victim's blood. Further testimony matched the wounds

on the body to the weapon recovered by the police within half an hour of the attack in what Mr Peter Corbin, the prosecuting counsel, described as 'exemplary quick-thinking by the officers on the scene'.

Mr Vaughan Greives, the defence counsel, had already indicated at the beginning of the trial that his client would not be taking the stand so the court were unable to hear her explanation for the wealth of evidence against her. Mr Greives suggested that Alison had stumbled on the body after the murderer had left and had failed to call for help due to her profound shock at the sight of her teacher bleeding to death. This scenario was rejected by the jury who took just two hours to find Alison guilty of murder.

The motive for the attack remains a mystery. Alison was said to be a 'quiet and sensible girl' by friends and neighbours. Her parents have refused to be interviewed but their solicitor issued a statement saying they were bewildered by their daughter's actions and sent their heartfelt sympathies to the victim's family.

Pupils at St Martin's said that Alison had never been involved with drugs.

[Like they're going to tell a reporter when the next question would be 'And how do you know?']

One pupil described her as 'a bit of a sad case, she didn't have a lot of mates'.

Miss Hepburn (25) is believed to have come from Norfolk originally. Her parents are reported to have died in a boating accident when she was a child. Staff at Nottingham University where she obtained her degree described her as a bright and conscientious student. She had joined St Martin's two years ago following a spell teaching at an Inner London comprehensive.

Mr Justice Vickers thanked the jury for their efforts during this distressing case and adjourned proceedings for four weeks to allow pre-sentencing reports. He warned Alison that she should expect a substantial custodial sentence.

[She'd got a life sentence of course and been released on licence after a suitably redeeming period. Hannah had already checked that out.]

Alison, a pale-faced, slightly overweight girl with lank brown hair showed no reaction to this statement. Throughout her court appearance she has evinced little emotion, instead staring blankly ahead, and only occasionally fidgeting with the pleats of her blue tartan skirt or pulling the sleeves of her over-large sweater down over her fingers in a repetitive gesture.

A spokesperson for 'Victims against Violent Crime . . .'

I scanned the rest quickly. It was largely spokespersons advising that it wasn't a good idea to go around sticking knives in people, and if you did there was a fair chance other people would think you were not a very nice person. There was a final paragraph advising readers that Alison would probably start her sentence in a secure young offenders unit.

We were practically at flesh-baring temperature. Ditching the jacket and jumpers, I pulled out a sheet of paper and jotted down 'Things to Do':

1. Interview the Wynne-Ellises' neighbours.
2. Interview Alison's parents.
3. Find if Miss Nearly No-Mates had any friends who were still around.
4. Check out the scene of the crime.
5. Locate Trudy's former housemate, Gina Gibbs.
6. Locate any police officers who worked on the case.
7. Locate Alison's solicitor.
8. Locate prosecuting and defence counsels.
9. Find out some more about the victim – any enemies?

10. Locate teachers who were at St Martin's twenty years ago.
11. Find what evidence was available.
12. Talk to Alison.

I ran a bath and added a big dollop of some crème bath I'd got from the Help the Aged shop. As it hit the steam, I couldn't help but wonder if the scent of chips might have been preferable. I splashed around until the water cooled, then rough-dried myself. Something had occurred to me while I wallowed. Dialling the number that Hannah had given me, I got through to her mobile. By the sounds of it, she was in a bar.

'Have you found something?' she asked.

Absolutely. Superwoman, that's me. Your money back if we fail to deliver a solution in three hours. 'No. I forgot to ask you if you want me to tell people who I'm working for?'

'If you have to. I'm not ashamed of it.'

'OK. Be in touch soon.'

'There is one more thing, Grace. I was wondering . . . well, if you could find out who my father was, that would be cool.'

'Wouldn't your mother be the best person . . .' I stopped.

'She won't tell me. It's not important, not as important as the other thing. But if anyone were to say something . . . ?'

'I'll keep my ears open. Bye for now.'

As I was talking to her, I'd been aware of a scuffling outside. The flat was a basement with its own access via a flight of metal steps from the pavement. Someone appeared to be coming down them, dragging something heavy. I hefted an iron frying pan and whipped the door open.

Shane was staggering backwards down the steps with his arms clasped around an enormous cage that was resting on his stomach. He looked over his shoulder at me.

'Here we are then, Smithie. One parrot.'

The thing barely cleared the door frame. Inside it was fully furnished: perches, toys, mirror, feed tray, water dispenser. Everything but the parrot. 'Where is it?'

'In the car. Back in a mo.' He returned with a small box, a bit like a cat carrier, and a plastic bag. 'Here you go. Meet Tallulah. Her diet sheet's in there. You can collect fresh food from the café when you need it. This is her travelling box. You put her in here if you want to take her anywhere.'

Like where? Did he think we were going to go clubbing together? Tallulah and I took stock of each other. She was about twenty inches long, mostly grey with a white patch over her face and some scarlet feathers on her rump.

'Does she talk?'

'Er . . . yeah. She sings a bit too. I've got to get back. Marlene.'

'Do you want to stick her in the big cage before you go?'

I sensed he wasn't keen on the idea. Maybe the thing bit. But she seemed docile enough when Shane opened the door in the side of the large cage and coaxed her across. Sidling along a perch, she ruffled her feathers and started rearranging them. She looked a bit moth-eaten to be honest. Tapping the wire bars, I said hello. Tallulah cocked her head on one side, considering me with one bright black eye.

'Well, must go. See you, Smithie.'

Shane had already got the front door open. The icy wind was finding gaps in my towelling robe. Drawing it closer, I followed him out into the basement area. 'Give Marlene my love. Hope she's feeling better soon.'

'Will do. She likes a fly around most days.'

'Marlene?'

'Tallulah.' Shane shot up the iron staircase, jumped into his car and leant across to wind down the passenger window. 'Oh, by the way,' he shouted 'don't let her near booze and . . .' A motor-cyclist roared down the road, his motor screaming out 'look-at-me-I've-got-a-big-engine'. Whatever Shane was saying was lost under its macho-blast.

Hugging the robe, I trotted up the steps and caught him as he was pulling away. In response to my mime, he lowered the window again.

'I didn't get that last bit. What did you say?'

'I said you can't let her get too cold. And she suffers from errymeeophobia.'

He accelerated away before I could ask for details. Turning back to the steps, I caught a movement out of the corner of my eye.

It was a jogger. He staggered towards me, his body rocking with each step as if he were going to keel over at any moment. There was something about the shape that nudged a memory. I knew this guy, but from where? He got closer and the lights from the neighbouring windows illuminated hairy legs, muscular arms, a square-jawed face that was starting to run to fleshy, and dark hair dripping sweat into his eyes. No wonder I hadn't recognized him right away. PC Terry Rosco in his underwear only featured in my nightmares.

'Hi, Terry. Fighting the flab? I gotta tell you – it's winning.'

He came to a halt in front of me. His breathing sounded like a rusty buzz-saw that had jammed on slow. His mouth opened and closed as he tried to say something. There had to be a woman behind this. And given that Terry thought he was God's gift to anything with a vagina, she must have a serious phwoar-factor to convince him he needed to get in shape to impress.

He drew in an enormous breath. Tried to speak. And passed out cold.

Dragging him down the iron staircase meant his legs banged against each tread and would leave some painful bruises on his calves. There's a bright side to most things.

Once I'd got us both inside, I did a quick check. He didn't seem to have broken anything. His pulse was rather slow and his skin was freezing. I diagnosed mild hypothermia. Which served the idiot right for running around the streets in his underwear.

I took a closer look at his outfit and cautiously investigated the shorts (there was no way I wanted Terry to

find me groping around his crotch area). I was right. These *were* his underpants. Why hadn't the idiot bought a tracksuit? Probably wanted to impress Ms Phwoar with his manly physique. If I'd known where she lived, I'd have arranged a special delivery.

He moaned and started to shiver. I pulled a spare blanket from the pantry cupboard that now served as my wardrobe and flung it over him.

Tallulah burst into song. '*Always Look on the Bright Side of Life*'.

'Better save it until he's conscious, kid.' I dropped a peeled banana in her dish and put the kettle on.

When it had boiled, Terry was still moaning and shivering, but his colour was coming back. By the time I'd made coffee he was able to sit up with the blanket clutched around him. 'Where am I? What happened?' he managed between chattering teeth.

'My flat. You fainted.'

'I don't faint. Woofters and pansies faint.'

'Why are you running around in your underwear?'

'I have to stay in shape.'

'You mean you *work* at looking like that?'

'Heh, there's nothing soft about me. Solid muscle.' He balled a fist into his stomach, and expelled a 'whoof' of surprise. A tear oozed from his eye.

'Well, now you're awake, you can shift that honed bod back outside.'

He hugged the blanket tighter. 'Is that coffee?'

'It's my coffee. Shall I give Linda a ring? Get her to pick you up?'

'No!'

There was alarm in those piggy eyes. A suspicion formed.

'She's chucked you out, hasn't she?'

'No. No way. I walked.'

'In your underwear?'

'Jogging kit.'

'Right.'

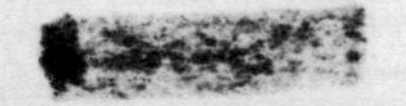

Terry not only suffered from the delusion that he was irresistible to women, but occasionally he stumbled across the white stick of a female who was prepared to go along with this fantasy. Everyone else at Seatoun nick had known about his playing away for years. Now it seemed that Linda Rosco had finally found him out.

'Well, soon as you're ready, Terry.' I jerked a thumb towards the door.

'I couldn't stop here for the night, could I?'

'No. Go to a hotel.'

'I can't. I've got nothing in these pants.'

'I know. I peeked.'

A scowl twisted the fat lips. Then he forced them back into a smile. 'Yeah, good one. I mean, no pockets. No cash. You couldn't lend us some, could you?'

I nearly choked on the coffee. It was an unwritten rule that I bummed money and others gave. 'No, I flaming well could not! Can't you go round a mate's?'

'I did. He's out.'

'What about the station? You could bed down in a cell?'

I knew he wouldn't go for that one. Let everyone at Seatoun nick know that not only had Terry Rosco – superstud – been locked out in his underwear but there was no queue of panting females fighting to offer him bed and bonking for the night.

'It's against regs,' he mumbled.

'When has that ever bothered you? A guy who lives on the edge? A maverick who laughs in the face of danger?'

I should have remembered Terry didn't do sarcasm. His ego swelled.

'I wouldn't be any trouble. I could kip down here on the floor.'

I was lumbered. If it had been summer, I'd have left him to camp out in a beach shelter, but with the temperature at brass monkey castrating level, I had no choice unless I wanted to find him stretched out in the basement like a deep frozen frankfurter come the morning.

My flat had once been the kitchen and pantry areas of the original boarding house. Now it was largely just one big room that I used for cooking, eating, sitting and sleeping. The only other areas were two small rooms at the rear. One was the bathroom and the other was a very narrow, windowless space that I'd christened the guest bedroom. Its sole furnishing was one fold-up bed.

Dragging some more spare bedding from the ex-pantry cupboard that was now my wardrobe, I told Terry that he wasn't to leave the room until morning.

'Supposing I want a slash?'

'Turn right outside this door. Do not even consider turning left towards my bed.'

'No problem. Skinny birds aren't my type. Aren't I getting anything to eat?'

'Not here you're not. Night.'

There were no locks on either of the internal doors. I'd never felt the need for them because I don't like sharing my space. I waited until the sounds of grunting, rustling and thumping had stopped inside the guest shoebox before I scrambled into the flannel pyjamas and bed socks I was sleeping in during the current freeze, dived under the duvet and switched the lamp out.

An unearthly shriek and crash sent me bolt upright with my heart trying to find the route back from my throat to my chest.

I flicked the light on. Tallulah smashed into the cage bars, bounced back to the floor, picked herself up and clambered on to a perch. Half a dozen downy pale-grey feathers were drifting in the air around the cage.

Shivering, she launched into a chorus of 'Oklahoma'. After the twenty repetitions of the same word ('*Oooooo-kla-hoooomA!*'), she shook herself, grabbed a wing feather in her beak and started grooming.

I switched the light out and lay down again. The din was even worse this time. It sounded like someone was feeding her tail-first into a crusher with the squawk being forced out at the beak end. The cage started rocking on its base.

Banging the light back on, I scrambled out and across to her. More curled feathers were swirling in the room. 'What the hell's the matter with you?'

I remembered pictures of parrot cages with covers over them. Maybe she needed to feel secure or something. I dug out a couple of old jumpers and swaddled the cage. Tallulah stopped serenading me and pattered up and down the floor, muttering and cracking her beak. Problem solved. I went back to bed and clicked the lamp off.

The impact of her hitting the cage bars was so loud I was sure I'd find her concussed on the base when I whipped the covers off. Instead she was cowered low, her wings spread out on a bed of dislodged feathers. More floated out to tickle my nose.

In the end I had to sleep with the lights on. Which was hard enough, but it wasn't helped by Tallulah nattering non-stop. She seemed to have learnt to talk and sing by listening to movies. Bizarrely, although she spoke whole sentences, when she started singing she stuck on the same two or three words – presumably the sounds she liked the best – like a demented tape recorder set on a loop mode.

Wondering what roasted parrot tasted like was the last thing I remember, until I woke suddenly with a warning alarm banging away in my head telling me I'd heard something – someone.

'*Mmmm . . . great bod. Let's bump pelvis.*'

The voice was male – low and throaty, and coming from near my ear. Flaming Terry!

Without moving, I tried to work out exactly how he was standing so I could lash out and cause some serious personal injury.

Then, across the other side of the room, I heard the click of the bathroom pull-cord. And Terry swear as his toe hit the bath.

'*Oh, luscious, are we going to have some fun tonight!*'

The short hairs on the back of my neck were standing on end and ants with legs tipped in frost were dancing down my spine. There was somebody else in the flat. How the hell had they got in? If they'd broken in via the front I'd have heard them. Had I left the back door to the yard unlocked?

He was right next to the bed so far as I could tell. If I turned to look I'd lose the small advantage I had. He wasn't expecting an attack.

I erupted up, throwing the duvet high. The plan was to get it over his head and blind him for a few seconds. Whilst he was working out what had happened, I was hoping to put both feet into where I judged his stomach to be – or lower if possible.

There was no one there. The duvet had landed on the floor beside the bed.

I looked around wildly: there were few places he could have hidden. The spare room? The pantry-wardrobe? In the bathroom with Terry? He must have moved like lightning and I hadn't heard a thing.

I glanced at the duvet. And the ice-boot ants did an entire chorus routine up and down my spine. The centre of the material was slowly rising from the floor. I scuffed back on my bottom and grabbed the nearest weapon. A pillow.

Terry wandered back into the room. 'What you doing?'

I ignored him. The ooze-lump had reached the edge of the duvet. I braced myself, pillow in attack position.

'*Hot totty*!'

'How the hell did she get out? Did you open the cage?'

'What the bloody hell would I do that for?'

Tallulah fluffed out her coat. '*Phwoar . . . hot chick . . . dive in and enjoy, sister.*'

It appeared that Tallulah's film viewing included the late night adult channels.

Terry chuckled. 'Heh, he's a good talker, isn't he?'

'She,' I corrected. 'Tallulah.'

'That's a girl saying them things? That's disgusting!'

Tallulah launched at him and landed on his shoulder.

Before he could react, she crapped down his vest. It was a pretty impressive poop. Maybe I'd overdone the bananas. I felt myself warming to the feathered bundle.

4

After I'd slung Terry out next morning, I drove around to Pepi's, intending to return the parrot to Shane. Free food was poor compensation for no sleep.

There was a printed notice stuck on the inside of the café door which hadn't been there last night:

CLOSED DUE TO
UNFORESEEN CIRCUMSTANCES
(Smithie – cash behind the counter at
the Happy Burger Bun)

I got egg brunch and coffee to go at the Burger Bun and headed out for Shane's house with Tallulah warbling her way through her one-word encore of 'Oklahoma'.

Shane and Marlene lived out on one of the approach roads to Seatoun. It was a long wide street bordered by rows of near identical bungalows like pieces on a monopoly board. Leaning on the bell-push that was shaped like a gold disc, I listened to 'You Keep On Knocking But You Can't Come In' playing in the rooms beyond. After a dozen plays I admitted to myself that there was nobody home. I was stuck with the ever-singing parrot.

I'd left her on the back seat of the car. When I returned to it she was spinning inside the narrow confines of the travelling box and shrieking something unintelligible. A small drift of breast feathers swirled in the Micra's interior.

'Bloody hell, Tallulah, what *is* your problem?' Perhaps the condition Shane had mentioned caused her to moult? I'd have to look it up.

The office boiler had not self-repaired unfortunately. It was still freezing inside the offices of Vetch (International) Investigations Inc. I put Tallulah's box on the reception counter. She promptly sneezed violently.

'Bless you. Shan't be long. Lay an egg or something.'

There was nothing of interest on the phone box. The world was still frozen out there. The emails had a few requests from local solicitors and one insurance company, but nothing that couldn't wait so I printed them out, stuck them in the pending trays and took out the 'to do' list from Hannah's file. In theory, talking to Alison Wynne-Ellis should have been my first step, but she didn't live in this area and I had an important appointment this afternoon that I had no intention of missing. So on that basis I decided to fill in a bit of background on the case before I tackled the alleged murderess in person.

The front of the Wynne-Ellises' old house at 21 Hinton Road had been covered with tarmac to form a car port; two large grooves had subsided under the vehicle weight and were filled with frozen rainwater. Beyond it, under the front window, was a strip of land choked with overgrown weeds. There was no point in knocking if the present owners were the last in a line of occupiers that had changed every few years. There was nothing of the Wynne-Ellises left here. No clue to tell me anything about her parents' personalities or the type of environment that Alison had grown up in.

I moved fractionally to stand in front of number 19. The Darrowfields' house was marginally less unkempt than its neighbour, but it was a close call. Was this what Alison had seen when she looked out of her bedroom window, or had the deterioration set in later? After Mrs Darrowfield had died perhaps? Interviewing the neighbours was number one on the 'to do' list. I leant over to unlatch the gate.

They were out. How come this never happens to those really cool detectives? They turn up, exchange a few wisecracks with the suspects, get the information they want and move on. Recalling Hannah's description of her reception by the Darrowfields, I figured it would be best not to alert them to the fact I was calling. I slid them down the 'to-do' list and headed back to the office to check messages again before preparing for my afternoon date.

Apart from a few work-related items for Vetch and Annie, there was just one email for me. The next bulletin from Annie had arrived. This one had a shot of the hotel's candlelit Caribbean buffet with a limbo dancer wriggling his torso under a bar that had been set on fire: 'THEY HOLD THIS EVERY WEEK. TRADITIONAL ISLAND CUISINE (PLUS LOTS OF AMERICAN DISHES).'

I banged back: 'THAT KEBAB'S A HELL OF A SIZE. BY THE WAY, DO YOU KNOW WHAT ERRYMEEOPHOBIA IS?'

Annie's head is full of the kind of obscure facts that win pub quizzes. She replied immediately with: 'IF YOU MEAN EREMIOPHOBIA, IT'S A MORBID FEAR OF BEING ALONE.'

Great. I'd been lumbered with a parrot who needed a shrink. I logged off and dragged the psychosis-ridden feathered one back to the flat.

My conception of christenings said floaty chiffon and big hats. But since I had neither, I decided I'd have to wear my only good suit: it was black with a choice of trousers or skirt to go with the jacket. I went for trousers, collected Tallulah's cage and headed out.

I was determined to be the perfect guest. I wanted Jerry Jackson to be glad he'd invited me. A few years ago I'd been bounced out of the police owing to a slight misunderstanding involving a fake alibi and a large sum of money appearing in my bank account shortly thereafter. A lot of the local force had me marked down as being a lowlife who'd taken a bribe to sell out and treated me accordingly (Terry Rosco was their club secretary). But not Detective Chief Inspector Jerry Jackson. Jerry liked me. In fact, he liked me enough to invite me to the christening of his new daughter.

There was a short queue at the front door of the Jacksons' house waiting to be greeted by Kathy Jackson. As each guest shuffled over the doormat they exchanged smiles, thank-you-for-comings and queries with Kathy.

'Where can I put this box? It needs to be kept cold.'

'What should I do with the wine?'

'Where shall I hang our coats?'

'Where can I leave my parrot?'

I'll say one thing for Kathy – she was the perfect hostess. Not one word of the 'are you totally mad?' variety. She just led me straight upstairs to the back room. A small jumble of furniture had been pushed into a heap in the centre of the room. The floor was bare boards and the walls had been stripped back to the plaster. 'We're redecorating the spare bedroom. Will he be all right in here?'

'She. Tallulah. And this is great, thank you.' It was heated so she wouldn't catch cold. And in response to a request, Kathy brought in a small portable radio and switched it on behind the box (I figured that way Tallulah would think someone was in the room with her).

There was a scuffle in the doorway and we were joined by a five-year-old with Jerry's face and Kathy's green eyes.

'Say hello to Grace, Max. Max has a new pet too. Why don't you show Grace?'

The kid held out a small box with a glass top. His new pet seemed to be a large ball of straw.

'Wow, that's really . . . amazing.'

'You can't *see* him yet.' He tilted the box and a nose appeared, followed by whiskers and eyes. 'It's a hamster.'

'He's got a big cage in Max's room. With tunnels and a wheel. Hasn't he, Max?' Kathy's tone was cheerily bright, underscored with an edge of desperation.

'S'pose.' Max's eyes were on Tallulah. 'Is that *another* present for Josephine?'

'*No!*'

In response to the alarm in Kathy's eyes I shook my head fractionally.

'No,' his mum repeated in a more relaxed key. 'She belongs to Grace. She's just brought her because . . .' She looked at me for enlightenment.

'She keeps knocking herself out on the cage bars if I leave her alone.'

'I see. Well, time for the christening, I think. Shall we go down?'

She ushered me and Max through the kitchen and into the living room where the rest of the guests were standing around. The star player was in her pink carrying basket down the other end of the room, surrounded by people making inane coochy-cooing sounds. Max scowled.

I sympathized. One rotten hamster was poor compensation for 50 per cent of your parents' attention.

With one hand on her first-born's back, Kathy steered him to the front of the crowd where his dad was waiting for them. Scanning the other guests, I was pleased to see there was only one other police officer present so far as I could tell; and I only spotted him because it was hard to miss the light flashing off all those shiny stars on his uniform. Jerry caught my eye through the mass of people and nodded. I gave him a half-smile.

I also started to recognize some of the backs of heads I was looking at from my position at the rear of the group. Right down the front was an iron-grey pudding-basin trim that belonged to December Drysdale, owner of the donkey troupe that trod the beaches of Seatoun in the summer season, and secret silent partner in the local nightclub, several cinemas and quite a few other businesses in the area. Seeing him solved a problem that had been bothering me: why weren't we in church?

Rumour had it December was a member of some obscure religious sect and I'd guessed some time ago that Jerry was too. It appeared from the preparations going on now that they didn't use a church. Instead the godparents gathered around and read out pledges promising to love and protect little Josephine and keep her on the path of righteousness and truth. After that Jerry invited us all to pray silently. That suited me fine. I don't really do organized religion, but a quick chat with God while we sorted out where we'd both screwed up in my life-plan this month was perfectly acceptable.

The praying came to an end and everyone let out their breath in a sort of collective 'whoosh'. Time for the serious partying.

Drinks were served and a help-yourself-buffet was laid out in the kitchen. Normally I'd have headed the dash for the buffet, but in my perfect-guest guise I snagged a glass of wine spritzer, edged my way down to the kid and made the right complimentary coos over the pink moppet.

Once the first rush for food was over, I wandered in the direction of the buffet, trying to keep it casual. Kathy was behind the counter helping to dish up. At present there were only two other customers – the shiny-starred one and a thin woman dressed in a blue-grey trouser suit. I had a niggling feeling I ought to know the bloke, although I couldn't think from where. I didn't think I'd come across him in my not-so-glorious police career. He had the kind of looks you'd remember: well-chiselled and lined in a way that made him look distinguished. His hand was resting on the trouser suit's back in a proprietorial gesture. Like him she was a blonde, although he was pale straw lined with silver and she was more Scandinavian frost. Frosty was oozing compliments on the baby.

'She's just so adorable.'

'Thank you. Some warm salmon pasta?'

'Just a spoonful. Did you make it yourself? With a new baby to look after? I really admire your organizational skills. I was just saying to Clive it seems only yesterday that our two were that tiny. And now Jarvis is at St Andrews. He's on the same course as Prince William, you know.'

'How nice. More salad, Mr Pennington?'

'Oh, Clive, please. I have a sufficiency for now, thank you. It all looks quite delicious. Shall we go and find a seat, Georgie?'

Pennington? Where had I heard that name recently?

The look Kathy threw at their departing backs was chillier than the frozen lemon pudding. Her smile for me was warmer. 'Hello, Grace. Do you want to help yourself?'

'Sure.' I piled my plate while Kathy took some rolls from the oven and started flicking them into a napkin-lined bread-basket. 'Part-cooked from the supermarket, but I don't suppose anyone will know. Have you heard from Annie?'

'Emails. She's having a great time.'

'Oh good.' Kathy started spooning lemon pud into individual dishes. 'It's a pity she missed the christening. We'd agreed not to invite police colleagues generally because it was hard to know who to leave out. But since Annie is ex like you, we were looking forward to seeing her.'

It was tactful of her to put it that way. Annie was 'ex' because she'd chosen to leave the service. As opposed to my departure with 'grass' apparently stamped on my forehead. 'You invited one. And the big cheese at that.'

'Yes.' Her tone was arctic again. As were her eyes, which were fixed on something behind me.

I swung round and found Jerry had returned from working the room. He waved an empty bottle and exchanged it for a full one. 'Hello, Grace. I hear you brought a parrot.'

'It's a casual thing. You know . . . I'm a girl, she's a parrot . . . we can never agree between hitting the wine bar or pecking a few seed bells.'

'I was telling Grace that we didn't invite police officers because we didn't want to offend anyone by leaving them off the list.' Kathy handed him the corkscrew.

Jerry started opening the bottle. 'There are a couple of retired sergeants I worked with years ago out there, but that's it.'

'And ACC Pennington.' Kathy's tone said he was as welcome as a viper.

'He invited himself.'

'So you said. Although why an assistant chief constable should want to come to the christening of a family he barely knows is hard to understand.'

'I explained that. He's dedicating a tree in the area and decided to drop in.'

Plainly this was an argument that had started some time before the christening. I started to leave. Kathy called me back. 'Do you want to sort out your suit? I've got some sticky tape in the drawer.'

Suit? I looked down. I was covered from knees to shoulders in pale, downy parrot feathers. Why do people never *tell* you these things? Spooling tape around my hand I patted myself down. The maker's name on the reel was Ellis Manufacturing Ltd., which triggered a sequence of thoughts back to the Wynne-Ellises.

A few more little sparks fired amongst the synapses in my brain. A live connection hit the bullseye. Pennington! Of course!

5

There's something about a man in uniform.

In this case it was a group of half a dozen other guests. ACC Pennington seemed to be holding his listeners' attention with no discernible effort. This was a man who'd addressed a lot of conferences, team-building exercises and focus groups in his career, I decided.

I tagged on to the back of the group. It's one of the advantages of being five foot, ten inches in my stocking feet: the low heels I'd put on with the suit boosted me to six feet and let me look over heads and straight into his eyes. I smiled and he responded with something between a smile and a preen. He thought I was coming on to him. No sense in letting the opportunity pass. I stepped between two plump elderly sherry-sippers and put myself a few inches from his shining tunic buttons.

'Hello.'

He extended a hand. 'Hello again. I think we met briefly over the cold meats, didn't we? Clive Pennington.'

'Grace Smith.'

'It's very nice to meet you, Grace. Friend or relative of the lady of the moment?' He gestured down to the cot.

'Friend.'

He was looking me over. Instead of freezing him off I took a sip of wine and held his eyes. 'I saw a picture of you in an old newspaper the other day.'

'Really? What was that about?'

'A murder case. Alison Wynne-Ellis.'

'Goodness me, that was a time ago! I'm flattered you could even recognize me.'

Well, his name under the picture had been a bit of a giveaway, but to be fair he had aged well.

'Twenty years, at least,' he continued, breaking the eye contact with me to include the rest of the group in the discussion. 'It was my first big case.'

I tried hard not to choke on the Chablis. His first case! He was a uniformed PC. His contact with the investigation would have been minimal and would have consisted of pure grunt work like crawling around in the mud looking for forensic evidence and ferrying suspects and witnesses in a squad car. His tone implied he'd overseen the whole operation.

He drew the other listeners in again. 'Tragic case. A young school-teacher brutally stabbed to death by one of her pupils.'

There were murmurings of 'no', 'how dreadful' and 'it's so common nowadays' behind me. I'd made sure I kept the spot directly in front of him. I wanted to judge his reaction to my next question.

'Did she do it?'

He blinked and reared back slightly. 'The jury said she did.'

And we all know juries are never wrong, don't we? Instead of pointing this out I put on my best hero-worshipping expression. 'Yes, but you were in a unique position. Right at the centre of the investigation. You must have insights that aren't available to outsiders. What was your gut instinct? As a professional.'

His ego went into overdrive. 'Well, I don't usually discuss cases, but since it was a guilty verdict, I think I'm safe in saying that I believe justice was served that day.'

'No other suspects?' I laid a hand lightly on his arm.

'Not that I recall. And overwhelming forensic evidence.'

'Did your partner think so, too?'

'Sorry?' His confused gaze went to Frosty Georgie who was chatting to Jerry Jackson by the crib.

'No, I meant the other constable in the picture.' I

struggled for the name of the dark-haired PC in the newspaper photo. 'O'Hara.'

'Declan? Yes, I'm sure he did.'

I sensed he was withdrawing from me. Metaphorically speaking. He couldn't do it literally without backing into the Jacksons' fireplace. Another warm oil massage of his ego was called for. 'Did he do as amazingly well as you in the police?'

The ego purred and rolled over to have its tummy tickled. 'Well . . . no. Declan left some years ago. In fact, confidentially . . .' He included the circling admirers in his confidential chat. 'I did hear that Declan had gone over to the *dark side.*'

Before I could ask him where I could locate Darth Vader, Georgie Pennington joined the circle. I took my hand from the sleeve of the ACC's jacket.

'We were just talking about Alison Wynne-Ellis,' her husband informed her. 'Miss Smith here saw an old newspaper photo of me at the time.'

'He's hardly changed at all, has he?' I tried charm on Frosty.

She responded with a glittering smile. 'Indeed he hasn't.' She slipped her right hand into the crook of her husband's arm, leant the left lightly on his forearm. The wedding and engagement rings sparkled against the dark-blue material and flashed out the unmistakable message: *Hands off, he's mine.*

'Clive, there's somebody over here who wants to meet you . . .' She steered him firmly out of the circle and towards an older man, who I'd already pegged as one of the retired sergeants that Jerry had mentioned.

Jerry himself was threading his way through the throng with baby Josephine. She'd had enough of socializing for one day and was letting the world know with some impressive lung power.

'Can I help?' I asked.

'No thanks, Grace. I'm going to take her up to the nursery. I think it's getting too warm in here for her. Why don't you get something to eat?'

I'd got something to eat, hadn't I? Then I remembered I'd left the plate on the buffet counter when I'd suddenly recalled why I'd recognized the name Pennington and charged through to try out some of those red-hot interrogation skills on him.

It had gone. Reloading another plate with what was left, I went back into the living room. The chattering groups had settled into fixed clumps. The Penningtons were still in a threesome with the retired sergeant. As I came in, their eyes went towards me. I guessed from the cooling of their expressions that I'd been pointed out as the low-life who'd been dumped from the service for taking a bribe.

Well, stuff them. I wedged myself in a corner where I could rest the plate on a side table. The other half of the semi-circular walnut top was taken by an older woman who was sipping what looked like a triple shot of neat whisky. She'd already cleared her own lunch – apart from a slice of broccoli quiche.

'Can't stand this muck, can you?' She poked the soggy pastry. 'Are you on Jerry's side or Kathy's?'

'I'm sort of neutral. How about you?'

'I puppy-walked Jerry when he was a probationer.'

Great. I'd picked the seat next to the other retired sergeant.

'Rosie Wilmott.' She extended a hand that was dry and leathery with the stained fingertips of a chain-smoker.

'Grace . . .' I hesitated. I'd had enough of those looks for one party. '. . . Jones.'

'I thought she was a big black singer.'

'I'm her paler, tone-deaf cousin.'

I'd been doing a few quick calculations. Jerry was in his mid-thirties so Rosie would have been still serving about twelve years ago when he'd joined up. And presumably also twenty years back when Trudy Hepburn had been murdered. I knew Jerry had done his probationary period in another area but . . .

'I was never officially stationed at Seatoun,' she said in answer to my question on her location. 'But I was there on a temporary placement for a few months around the time you're talking about. It was a rum time; all the usual ungodliness, bag-snatches, muggings, burglaries and then some bizarre cases, cows left on the beach and some joker dressed as a highwayman sticking up cars. I left just before the teacher's murder. It was a clean arrest from what I heard. No loose ends. What's your interest?'

Golden rule of this job: get as much information as you can and give out as little as you need to. 'Somebody was showing me a newspaper report about it a few days ago. There was a picture of ACC Pennington. When he was a constable. I guess you must have known him then?'

Rosie snorted. 'Oh yes. A right know-it-all, our little Clive. Graduate-entry. Couldn't teach him a thing. He was a lucky little bastard by all accounts. Got the right breaks at the right time.'

'And PC O'Hara?'

'Declan? He was a wild one. Had something about him though. Never any shortage of female officers wanting to go undercover with O'Hara. He got himself into trouble more than once by thinking with his todger did our Declan.'

'What about the investigating officers? Can you remember who was on the case?'

'Frank Broughton would have been the super in charge. Now who else was there?' Rosie swigged back her whisky in one long swallow and appeared to be searching for inspiration in the bottom of the glass. 'Joey Spencer . . . Spender, that's it. He was a sergeant in CID back then. And Neil Lambert was the inspector.'

'Any idea where I can find them?'

'Blowing in the wind.'

'They're *all* dead?'

'Hardly got a chance to enjoy their pensions. In Joey's case he never even made it that far. Keeled over on an observation. Heart attack. I blame all those cop shows in the 1970s. The plainclothes police spent their time knocking back fags and booze in between bursts of tearing around in dodgy Cortinas, wearing leather jackets and kicking down doors. They all started to think you had to behave like that to be a "real" copper. It's no way for middle-aged, overweight blokes to act. They were dropping like flies until *Morse* took off and they ditched the leather jackets and door kicking.'

'Is there anyone left alive who worked on the Wynne-Ellis case?'

'Bound to be. I just can't recall any name at present. I was only there a few months, remember. Been a lot of coppers come and gone in my life since then.'

'What about PC O'Hara? Is he dead?'

'He left the job. Used to hear a few things sometimes. Not for a while though. Oh shit, he's coming over.' For a moment I thought I'd got it wrong and Declan O'Hara was at the party. But it was Clive Pennington who was heading for our corner. 'Must dash,' Rosie said loudly. 'Bladder trouble. Peril of age.'

She headed for the door and the ACC settled himself in her vacated chair. The cold expression of ten minutes ago had disappeared. 'Grace, hello again. A little bird tells me you're a private investigator.'

His tone was neutral. I wasn't sure whether to get defensive about my profession or preen. I went for an equally non-committal 'Yep.'

'Fascinating. May I steal a little more of that delicious quiche, do you think?'

I held out the plate and he helped himself. Very intimate that – sharing food from the same plate. I waited to be told why we were having this bonding moment.

'Are you working on some case connected to the Trudy Hepburn murder?'

'Sort of. Did you know Alison Wynne-Ellis had a baby?'

'When she was paroled, I assume?'

'Much earlier. When she was on remand, I think.'

'I had no idea.'

He was probably telling the truth. Alison would have been swallowed up in the system and he wouldn't have had any contact with her until she reappeared in the dock a long time later.

'The baby was adopted. It's come as a bit of a shock to her to find out her real mum is a murderer. She wants to understand exactly how it happened.' I figured there was no need to mention she also expected me to prove her mum was innocent.

'Yes. I can see that would be important to her. Well, if there's anything I can do to help . . . I'd be happy to talk her through the case if she'd like that?'

Was it my imagination or was there a hint of relief in his voice?

'I'll mention it to her. Thanks. What about talking me through it while I've got you here?'

'Surely it would be better if I spoke to the young lady herself?' 'I really can't see there's anything to be gained from picking over the bones of the whole messy business twice. And this girl, what is her name by the way?'

'She was registered as Flora Wynne-Ellis. Excuse me, I must follow Rosie up . . .' I pointed to the ceiling.

There was a queue outside the bathroom. I wandered onwards. The door to the nursery was open. Jerry was leaning with both arms on the cot, staring down at his daughter. His expression was a mixture of love and wonder. I stood watching for a moment. And found myself wondering if I'd ever have a bloke looking at our child like that.

I pulled my thoughts up with a sharp tug on their lead. Who needed a bloke and babies? I was a foster mum to a parrot. What more could a girl ask for?

I must have moved. Jerry looked up and smiled. 'Hi, Grace. Come for a hug?'

For a moment I weighed up the offer. I'd never been one for poaching. Then I realized I was being invited to cuddle the moppet.

'No, thanks. I won't disturb her. She's probably had enough of strangers jigging her around. Thanks for inviting me to all this.'

'Our pleasure.'

'I'm just going to check on my parrot.'

There was no sign of her. The radio was playing to an empty box. On the floor were more downy feathers plus two long dark-grey ones and four brilliant scarlet ones. The catch on the box fastening seemed secure, but then I'd thought that about her larger cage. Figuring she was hiding amongst the pile of furniture in the centre of the room, I moved it cautiously to flush her out. Except there was nothing to flush. I checked the radiator just in case she'd slipped down behind it and ended up as lightly griddled bird. Nothing. Putting a hand against the window, I pushed in case it had a faulty catch. It hadn't. There was only one explanation: somebody had let her out.

I know I could have just gone downstairs and explained the problem, but I still wanted them to think of me as Miss Perfect Guest. Normal people didn't bring parrots to christenings; perfect guests certainly didn't lose them.

I listened carefully in the hope she was singing, but the only sounds up here seemed to be coming from the room at the end of the landing. It was a kind of whirr-whirr-whirr.

Pushing the door open cautiously, I peeked in, ready to slam it if Tallulah tried to fly out. Max was on the floor, watching the hamster running round on his wheel.

'Neat pet, what's he called?'

'Rover.'

'Interesting name.'

'My grandma says it's a dog's name. She says it's silly calling a hamster a dog's name.'

'Change it.'

'He keeps going to sleep. He's boring.'

'Listen, my parrot seems to be missing.'

Max's eyes slid away from mine. 'It wasn't me.'

OK, that solved the 'who'. That just left the 'where'.

I searched Max's room quickly and then moved on to the nursery. Once I was certain that was a feather-free zone too, I shut the door to prevent her getting in. I checked out the loo and bathroom and came up Tallulah-less. That just left Jerry and Kathy's bedroom.

It was pretty: yellow and white. Kathy's choice, I assumed. There was a vase of early daffodils on the cabinet. A wedding photograph stood beside it. Watched by Jerry in his morning suit and Kathy in her veil, I snooped around their room, looking down the backs of the bedhead and dressing table, behind the curtains and on top of the wardrobe. The last place to look was under the bed. Lying down, I squinted into the narrow gap.

From my position – nose to the carpet – I could look right through to the other side of the room and the door. When it opened I recognized the grey-blue trouser bottoms immediately. I was tempted to stay quiet, but as she got nearer to the bed she was going to see my legs sticking out.

I knelt up. 'Hi. I dropped something. It rolled.'

Frosty Georgie smiled politely. 'How irritating for you. I came for our coats.'

Instead of doing so, she sat herself on the end of the bed. 'Clive was telling me about this poor girl you're working for. Such a shock, to find out something like that about your mother.' I gave a non-committal mumble. 'How on earth would you start to investigate a case like that? It's a lifetime ago.'

'The police open old case files. Doesn't your husband talk about work?'

'Oh, I know how the police would approach such an investigation. I was just wondering how a private investigator would brief their staff.'

My staff consisted of a part-share in the bolshie receptionist and anyone with whom I cared to split the client's fee. But loyalty to Vetch's (International) Investigations Inc. made me say airily, 'The victim is usually the key in a murder investigation.' (That was good. I made a note to remember it.) 'I guess we'll start by looking into Trudy's life. Her family. Friends. Enemies. The kind of world she was living in at the time. You'd be surprised what facts can be uncovered by a bit of determined digging.' (So would I if I found any.) 'It's often the apparently unrelated fact that leads to the truth.'

'Really?' Georgie's elegant eyebrows rose. 'You sound very organized.'

Didn't I just. I was impressing myself here. Since I was on a roll, I asked Georgie if she and Clive had been together at the time of the murder. Who knows, perhaps he'd mentioned something he'd seen that night.

'No. We became involved after that.' I had one hand on the corner of the duvet. She leant over and wrapped her fingers around my wrist. 'Perhaps it would be best to tell the girl no more than what is available in the newspapers. Delving into all the unpleasant details could be a mistake. You could uncover things she doesn't need to know.'

'That's up to my client.'

'She's still very young. She must be what . . . nineteen? At that age we don't necessarily know what's best for us. I'm sure I didn't. Did you?'

'Probably not. But that didn't mean I hadn't the right to make my own mistakes.'

'And do you regret them now?'

'Some.'

'Most, I suspect, although we don't admit it.'

I was literally sitting at her feet. She was giving me a pain in the neck. And for more than one reason. What the hell business was it of hers anyway?

She released my wrist and tapped on the back of it with two fingers to emphasize her words. 'You seem like a sensible woman, Grace. Take my advice, tell this girl to stop looking back and to look to the future. Stirring up the past isn't—'

What it wasn't I never found out. A shriek from outside made us both scramble to our feet.

6

'*Eat dirt!*'

Clinging to a branch that was barely supporting her weight, Tallulah was using her wings to keep her balance as she dipped up and down and screamed defiance.

It was the kind of suburban garden that you can find in thousands of homes with small kids. The quarter nearest the house had been laid with large stone slabs to form a patio, the rest was lawn bounded by narrow flowerbeds that were currently bare earth studded with leafless shrubs and bushes. The grassy areas were dotted with a red and yellow climbing frame and slide, a miniature football net and a swing.

It would seem that some of the guests had spotted Tallulah loose in the garden and tried to catch her. And Tallulah had no intention of being caught. Another futile snatch sent her swooping around the garden, screeching her annoyance. She landed on the hedge, apparently decided she didn't like the texture, fluttered across to the swing cross-bar, missed it and ended up on the seat. She was plainly agitated at the crowds. If she flew out of the garden I might never get her back.

'Can everybody get back and leave her to me?'

They all obediently drifted towards the house. I approached Tallulah with a segment of apple from the fruit salad. She considered me with her head on one side.

'Come on, girl.'

'*You talking to me*?'

Somebody behind me laughed loudly. Tallulah swooped away, perched on the climbing frame, fell off and tried dragging herself up the base section. Time for some tough love.

The garden hose was wound on a hook above the outside tap. Coupling it up, I spun the water full on and directed the stream high so it fell on the parrot. The idea was to drench Tallulah so that her feathers were too water-logged for her to fly away, and then pick her up. Before I could get her wet enough, she launched and flew in a low arc.

Spinning and adjusting the angle of the stream, I shadowed her along the hedge, on to the patio and . . . the fact that she was now heading for the kitchen dawned on me just as the spectators jumped backwards to get out of my range and the full blast of the water caught Tallulah – and someone who'd just come through the back door.

I was vaguely aware of the muffled giggles and snorts of laughter from the audience who'd managed to avoid a drenching, and the sound of the water splattering the patio, but mostly I was focused on ACC Pennington. He looked like he'd been wading thigh-deep in a river. Little rivulets of water were draining off the bottom of his trousers. The up-spray when the jet had hit him had sent a finer backwash upwards, spotting his shiny buttons and misting his face. As I watched, a couple of drops slid down his nose and hung together like a dew-drop on his nostril.

He had to force a smile and pretend to join in the joke. It was that or look like a petulant prat. Jerry took him off to find a dry pair of trousers. I went into the kitchen and found Rosie Wilmott soothing Tallulah, who looked like a half-plucked chicken with bald skin showing through the soaking feathers.

She responded to my appearance by baring her beak and issuing a 'you talking to me, dog-breath' hiss. I figured she was unlikely to die of fright in the near future. I put her on the counter. She took a couple of wobbling steps, her legs crossed and her beak hit the deck.

'Oh hell, she's hurt. Where can I find a vet?'

Rosie laughed. 'I don't think she needs a vet. Just an AA

meeting. She's drunk. She must have been at the dregs in the glasses somewhere.'

Rosie moved to the open back door and lit up a cigarette. The freezing air was raising goosebumps but nobody liked to suggest she go all the way out and close the door behind her. As Kathy came into the kitchen, Rosie blew the smoke out into the back garden.

I tried to apologize again. Kathy dismissed it. 'Don't worry about it. Serves him right for gate-crashing. He heard Jerry talking about the christening at some meeting on crime statistics and suddenly it's "we'll be in the area on that day, we'll pop in and wet the baby's head". In the area – hah!'

'Well, we all know why he's doing it, don't we?' Rosie called from her position, half in, half out of the door.

'I don't,' I pointed out.

'The chief constable's on his way out. Autumn sometime, they reckon,' Rosie explained. 'Got a borderline medical report and decided to go watch vines grow in Spain while he still can. Clever Clive is after the job. Even if they don't admit it publicly, appointment boards tend to take notice of the message coming from the ground troops these days. At least at inspector level and above. Clive is networking. Letting everyone know he's just a regular bloke with a family like you and me. Did you notice how often the loving wife mentioned their sons?'

I hadn't. But then I'd been avoiding her for a large part of the time. Tallulah heaved herself more or less upright. Hunched on the counter with feathers plastered to her body, she looked a sorry sight.

'I'll get my hair-dryer,' Kathy said.

By the time Jerry reappeared, Tallulah was fluffing herself in the jet of warm air and rearranging the odd feather that wasn't lying just as she liked, with just the odd list to right or left, as the world rocked around her little hungover eyes.

'ACC Pennington and his wife wanted me to say their

goodbyes to everyone.' His lips were twitching. 'They said to say it was a pleasure to meet you all.'

'Blimey,' Rosie said. 'He *really* wants that job.' She pinched out the cigarette butt between her fingers and closed the door.

Splaying the warm air over Tallulah's rump, I said, 'Jerry I'm really sorry . . .'

Jerry burst out laughing. 'Don't be. Everyone else thought it was the highlight of the afternoon. It will be all round the stations by tomorrow morning.'

Great, I was the cabaret again. Why did other people manage these occasions with style while I just screwed up? 'Well, I think I'll be going now anyway. Things to do. Dumb creatures to sober up. Thanks again for inviting me.'

'I'm going to make a move too, Jerry.' Rosie ran the cigarette end under the tap before throwing it into the bin. 'Lovely to see you again, dear. I don't see nearly enough of the old faces these days.'

The mention of old faces reminded me of something. 'I'd really like to talk to Declan O'Hara. Is there any chance you might be able to get me a contact number?'

ACC Pennington hadn't shown much enthusiasm for discussing his past arrests with me before I'd half-drowned him. Maybe his ex-partner would be more forthcoming about the night of Alison's arrest.

'Grace is a private investigator,' Jerry explained.

'I know,' Rosie said. She'd seen through my disguise as Grace Jones's cousin then. 'I'll see what I can do about Declan. I haven't heard a whisper for a few years now. Maybe the pension people have an address.'

I gave her my phone number and got out of there with as much style as you can when you're clutching a parrot.

7

I woke up next morning wanting physical exercise of some kind. Parrot-strangling was way up there on the list. Tallulah had spent the night shrieking from an impressive repertoire of songs. I'd tried switching the television on to keep her company while I shut myself in the spare room, but she'd gone beserk, shrieking, squawking and flying at full speed into the cage bars. I fell asleep sometime around dawn – with '*Big Spender* . . . *Spender* . . . *Spender* . . . *Spender*' playing over and over in my head.

Whenever I want to think I go to the beach. In Seatoun when the tide goes out, it goes all out. At its fullest ebb the sea is just a silver streak out on the horizon. Normally I walk right down at the water's edge where the dirty-grey, cream-frilled waves break just inches from my trainers, but today I'd only got halfway across the flats before I knew I wasn't going to be able to get any further. The iciness literally took my breath away.

Turning, I started to trudge along parallel with the sea, my feet finding paths around the small channels of shallow water left behind by the retreating tide. My arms were aching from the weight of the travel cage. I'd wrapped it in a blanket to keep Tallullah warm, but had to keep up a running commentary all the time to let her know I was here.

I tried to analyse what was bothering me about this case. I knew my chances of finding out the truth about a twenty-year murder were somewhere between the parameters of 'nil' and 'snowball-in-hell'. In order to get anywhere I needed access to the original police files on the investigation.

'And what are my chances of getting my hands on *them*?' I shouted over the wind into the blanket muffler.

ACC Pennington might be a big, shiny-buttoned pain in the butt, but his attitude was probably typical of every other officer who'd been involved with Trudy Hepburn's murder. Nobody was going to talk to an outsider. I stood still, staring out towards the horizon. You can't hear any town noise down here, just the howling of the wind and crash and 'shooosh' of the ocean. It's like being on the edge of the world.

It occurred to me that Alison must have walked along this beach often as a kid. What did she imagine for her future? Not years banged up, I'll bet. It was decision time. To investigate – or return the deposit? No contest really.

I checked out Pepi's on my way back to the flat. It was still closed. I had to breakfast on double cheeseburger and coffee from the Happy Burger Bun and swallow it in record time after they figured out the blanket parcel contained a parrot (not many double-wool Whitneys tend to burst into 'All that Jazz').

Back at the flat I changed, then rang the number I had for Alison. It was a garden centre in Hertfordshire and my plan was to drive up there this morning, but I figured it would be smart to see if she was working today before I made the trip. An automated message informed me that the centre closed on Wednesdays from 1 November to 1 March. Okay, back to plan B – check out the background to the case. I called the receptionist from hell. She sounded OK to me.

'When are you coming back to work?'

'Is anyone else back?'

'No.'

'Don't need a receptionist then, do you? That all?'

'You went to St Martin's Comp, didn't you?'

'Yeah, why?'

'I need to talk to someone who was there twenty years ago. Have any of the teachers been there that long?'

'Mrs Anderson, the headteacher, has been there yonks. And Beattie Root. Is this about a case?'

'Yes. It's confidential.'

'I can do confidential.'

'No, you can't. Anyway you're off sick.'

'If I come back, can I work on it? It's dead boring just sitting in that reception.'

'Not this case. But there are several others outstanding.'

'I'll think about it then. That it?'

'Yep. Unless you happen to know any plumbers who aren't booked up for the next three months?'

'Well he might be. But he'll come out if I ask him to.'

Unlimited free hot water. Rooms that I wasn't paying to heat. Bliss! 'Ask him, whoever he is. Immediately.'

Getting hold of Mrs Anderson was easy enough. Getting to see her was more difficult when I mentioned the name Alison Wynne-Ellis.

'If you're a journalist, Miss Smith, I have nothing to say to you.'

'I'm not. I'm a private investigator.'

There was a long pause. I could hear her breathing on the other end of the line. Then she said, 'And what exactly are you investigating?'

'I'd rather explain face to face.' I could sense her hesitation and knew I'd have to throw in a little more. 'I've been employed by Alison's daughter. She was adopted at birth.'

There was another brief pause. And then she finally agreed to see me. 'This afternoon, four o'clock.'

Which left me with several hours to kill. I opened the pink plastic file and selected one of the sheets. Time to visit the neighbours.

8

'Mr Kenneth Darrowfield?'

He was in his sixties, I guessed. Round-faced, pink scalp showing as the last strands of grey hair fought a losing battle to hide his baldness. He was wearing a chequered shirt with the sleeves rolled up to his elbows under a sleeveless Fair Isle pullover and grey trousers that drooped over his slippers. His eyeline was on a level with mine so that I could see the wariness in the dark-brown irises.

'Yes?'

'I've been employed by Miss Hannah Conti. Can I come in?' I stepped forward, forcing him to back up. As soon as there was sufficient clearance, I put my hand on the door and started to close it. He went with the flow.

'I don't know a Hannah—'

'Shall we talk inside? In here, is it?'

I marched into the room on the right. Hannah had already warned me that Philip Darrowfield was disabled and only able to communicate by typing into a monitor so I was prepared for the cot bed which took up most of the space with a pulley system fixed to the ceiling above it.

The rest of the room was a leftover from the original lounge. There was an old armchair that had probably been part of a three-piece suite, a long sideboard against one wall which held a collection of china ornaments, the family photos and a crucifix; a wheeled unit for the TV and video; and striped wallpaper on all the walls except the one facing the window which was largely taken up by a sliding door.

They'd been watching some kind of make-over programme on the TV. Kenneth Darrowfield used the remote to mute the sound before saying: 'Now, Miss . . . ?'

'Grace Smith. I'm a private investigator. Hannah Conti has retained me to look into the case of Trudy Hepburn's murder. She's Alison Wynne-Ellis's daughter. You gave her the Wynne-Ellises' address,' I prompted, since he was looking at me as if I was speaking fluent incomprehensible.

Philip's head jerked upright. 'A . . . eee. A . . . eee's dor . . . er . . .' His mouth couldn't form the words. I could see the frustration in his eyes as he struggled to make his body do what he wanted. He was bigger than I'd expected somehow; a large round face with a mop of dark hair on a broad-shouldered body that was oddly angled. It was as if someone had broken him at the waist then stuck the top half back on again without lining it up correctly so that he now had a permanent bend to the right.

'My son's not well, as you can see. I don't want him upset. So I'd like you to get out right now, missie.'

'I'm not trying to upset your son, Mr Darrowfield. I'd just like to talk to you for few minutes. Why is that such a problem for you? Hannah just wants to find out a little background on her family.'

'Family!' He sneered. His face wasn't made for sneering; he looked like a kid pulling faces. 'I don't know what story she's fed you, but Alison never had a daughter. At least, she's not got one who's as old as that. That little missie must have been seventeen or eighteen.'

'Hannah is nineteen.'

'That proves it then. There's only ten months between Alison and Philip. She'd've had to have had that girl when she was no more than sixteen. And she was in prison then,' he finished triumphantly. 'So there's no way that girl can be Ally's daughter. She'll be some student. We used to get them round sometimes after the trial. Doing theses on teenagers who kill or some-such. They talked like we were laboratory rats. They upset my wife. She wasn't well.'

To some extent, I guess that explained his hostility to Hannah. 'She is Alison's daughter, Mr Darrowfield. I've seen her birth certificate. Alison gave birth when she was on remand, before the trial. I'm guessing the Wynne-Ellises didn't tell anyone here about their granddaughter's arrival?'

'Not a word. But we weren't . . . well, never mind that. Ally had a baby?' He stared at me. '*Psittacus erithacus.*'

I wasn't sure if he was swearing or he'd lost the power of coherent speech. 'Right. So about Alison . . .'

'*Psittacus erithacus,*' he repeated. He reached over and plucked something from the collar of my coat. It was one of Tallulah's feathers. 'African Grey, am I right?'

'Spot on, Mr Darrowfield.'

Tallulah had seemed a bit calmer so I'd decided to leave her in the car. I'd blasted the heater up high all the way here and covered the cage before starting a small portable tape recorder into which I'd previously chattered inanely for half an hour (harder than you might think).

Ken's body language relaxed. 'I used to keep exotics. How many have you got?'

'Just the one, Tallulah.'

Philip made more unintelligible sounds. His father used the remote to increase the television volume. 'I'll just get the lady a drink, Philip. Through here.' He urged me before him out of the lounge and along to the kitchen at the back.

The narrow room was lit by a glass door at the far end. I guessed that the sliding door in the lounge led to a downstairs bathroom that had been created by partitioning off a large chunk of the original kitchen.

'I don't like to talk about Alison in front of Philip. It gets him worked up and that's not good for his breathing.'

'Were they close?'

'Grew up together. Like brother and sister. Emlyn and Moira moved here when little Ally was two and she was in and out of this house from then. She was like a daughter to us. My Lucia loved her like her own. She started sinking after that business with Alison. It was a turning point, you could say.'

'Sinking?'

'She was ill,' Ken said shortly. 'Had been for years, although we were managing up until then. But after Alison went . . .' He filled the kettle. It was an automatic gesture.

I invited him to tell me about the Wynne-Ellises.

'Have you seen the state of next door? It would have broken Moira's heart to see it like that. She kept the house beautifully. Not a speck of dirt and everything in its place. Same with Emlyn and Alison. She turned them out lovely. Their clothes were always washed, pressed, mended. You never saw them in anything with missing buttons or frayed collars.'

'That doesn't sound like a lot of fun – for a kid.'

'No. Don't misunderstand me, I'm not saying Moira didn't love Alison, course she did, but she wasn't close to her. Alison used to come in here to make a bit of mess. My Lucia taught her to make little cakes when she was three years old; them chocolate ones where you crush up the cornflakes and mix them up with melted chocolate bars, they were her favourites.'

They'd been mine too. I'd made them with my mum and my sister. We'd always ended up with more chocolate smeared over fingers, faces and work-surfaces than ever went in the cakes.

'And it was Lucia told her about,' Ken lowered his voice in case the kitchen appliances were eavesdropping, 'womanly things, you know?'

'What about her dad? How was she with him?'

'Emlyn? They got on well enough. They didn't do a lot together. Not just the two of them, I mean. They always did things as a family, or Moira and Emlyn went out together.'

I asked about Alison's friends.

'She never seemed to have many. There was one girl used to call round for her. She moved away, I think.'

'What about boyfriends?'

'She never had one.'

'She must have had at least one, Mr Darrowfield. Hannah wasn't a virgin birth.'

'Well, I don't know about that. She never brought one to the house, I'm sure of that.' The kettle was boiling. He stared at it as if he couldn't remember why he'd switched it on.

'Do you remember the night of the murder, Mr Darrowfield?'

'Call me Ken. And of course I remember it. Not likely to forget it. Friday the thirteenth it was. We saw the police car come for Moira and Emlyn. It set off one of Lucia's attacks. I had to call out the ambulance. She was convinced it was the end. Wouldn't go to the hospital until I'd sworn to look after Philip. It wasn't, thank heavens. We had a good few years together before she finally went. Although perhaps it might have been better if she hadn't lived so long.' He shook himself out of the reflective mood and looked directly at me. 'Emlyn told me about the arrest. I never believed it. Never believed Ally could do that. I'll show you something.'

Removing a key that hung by the back door, he opened it and stepped through into the garden, beckoning me after him. It was laid to paving slabs near the house with a badly kept lawn over the rest. The far end of the garden was occupied by a large aviary with a wooden housing area and a wire-caged flying area. 'Had to bring them in in the winter,' Ken said. 'But they all enjoyed a fly around in summer. Course, you had to be careful who you put in with who. They're like people Take against another for no good reason. I had all sorts: Amazons, Pionus, macaws.'

'What happened to them all?'

'Had to get rid of them. After she started going downhill, Lucia thought they were making her breathing worse. Doctors said they weren't, but she'd got it into her head.' He shot me a look that dared me to criticize. 'It wasn't her fault. It was a symptom: depression and irrational behaviour. I always meant to get some more after she went . . . but by that time Philip was getting worse. Maybe one day. But that's what I really wanted to show you.'

He pointed at a large shed in the neighbouring garden. It was painted dark green and felt roofing was hanging off in patches. 'That was Alison's. *They*,' he directed a dirty look at the rear of number 21, 'keep motorbikes. Alison used to have her cages in there.'

'She kept birds too?'

'Kept all sorts. Birds, rabbits, hedgehogs. Not pets. Wild ones. She'd nurse them if they were injured then set them free. There's always creatures caught up in wires in the farm fields around here or covered in tar or oil around the shores. She had a real way with them. They trusted her.'

So Alison was the Florence Nightingale of the wildlife world. It didn't preclude her being a murderer. It wasn't unknown for someone to stab their grannie then cry because their kitten died.

'She used to look after my birds for me if I was out. Lucia couldn't manage it and Philip was always heavy-handed. But Alison was gentle as you like. She'd spend hours in there with those animals. She used to earn the money for them herself, paper round. Bought everything at the car boot sales; she'd a knack for stretching money until it squeaked.' I asked if her parents shared her interest in animal welfare? 'No. Moira wouldn't have animals in the house. Thought they were dirty. She'd never even go in the shed. When Alison was away – school field trips, that kind of thing – I'd go round and see to her animals.'

'Not her father?'

'I think he would have but for Moira. She was a good woman Moira, but she could be . . . it sounds bad but I sometimes got the impression she was perhaps a bit jealous. She didn't like Emlyn to spend time with other females. Not even her own daughter. Or maybe Alison just thought I'd be able to manage the animals better.' He said, trying to back-track. 'I tried to keep them going after she was arrested. Thought they'd discover it was all a mistake and send her home. But after a few weeks, I had to take them to an animal sanctuary. I wrote to Alison, told her what I'd done. Emlyn said he'd see she got the letter, but I don't know if he did. Never heard from her again. I was going to go to the trial, see if I could speak to her then, but Lucia had another bad attack.'

'What about her parents? They moved away, when?'

'Just after the trial. They did one of those council swaps with someone who wanted a house by the seaside.'

'Why did they go? Because of the murder?'

'I suppose so. And it wasn't as if they had family round here or close friends.'

'Not even you?'

He avoided my eye and muttered, 'Lucia had become . . . difficult. Made me and Philip swear not to speak to them. Wouldn't have them in the house. I told her it didn't make sense but . . . she was ill.'

'But you kept in touch? You had their address.'

'They sent us a Christmas card, first year they moved. Lucia tore it up.'

'And you remembered the address all those years?'

'I've always had a good memory,' Ken said. 'I gave it to her to get rid of her. She was upsetting Philip. But if she really is Alison's little girl, then I'm glad I did.' A buzzer sounded inside the house. 'That's Philip.'

He hurried inside, leaving me to follow more slowly. On the face of it, Alison did sound an unlikely murderer. I realized I'd been half-expecting to hear about some teenage jailbait whose daughter was viewing her through a twenty-year rosy mist.

Ken was wiping spittle from his son's face when I came in.

'A . .ee . . .' Philip said as soon as he saw me. '. . Eee. A . .ee.' His head jerked and he appeared to be fighting his father's attempts to clean him, although I think the movements were involuntary.

'Tell you what,' I said. 'If I see Alison, I'll tell her you said hi. OK?'

He seemed to relax as far as it was possible for him to do so. 'Yeth . . . tell . . . A'ee.'

'OK.' I browsed whilst Ken finished what he had to do. A silver frame decorated with silver bells held the Darrowfields' wedding photo and told me that thirty-eight years ago Kenneth Darrowfield had married Lucia Bonnini.

'That's my Lucia.' He picked up the photo and ran his finger-tips over the woman's features, gently tracing a smile that was frozen for ever.

'She was very beautiful.'

Actually she was averagely pretty, so far as I could tell under the stiff hairstyle and heavy make-up, but she did have a dark and vaguely exotic look about her that lifted her out of the ordinary.

'It must be difficult, looking after Philip on your own.'

'I promised her.' His tone sharpened. 'I gave Lucia my word I'd take care of our Philip at home, and I will.'

Even before I unlocked the car door I could see the cage rocking and hear Tallulah's shrieks. The tape hadn't fooled her. She was alone, she was abandoned . . . she was . . . kind of bald in places. When I shifted the cage, another pile of feathers fell across the upholstery.

I had time to kill before my meeting with Mrs Anderson at the school. On an impulse I drove through the Downs Estate and out along a narrow road that snaked between the flat farm fields that encircled Seatoun. During the early hours of the morning (and the 300th chorus of '*a dame . . . a dame . . . dame . . . dame*') I'd remembered where I'd seen that 'murder scene' country cottage before.

It had probably been a medium-sized farmhouse once. And by the looks of its thick walls and the way the front door had sunk below ground level, it had to be several centuries old. I parked up on the grass verge and walked up to the front gate. The front garden was bisected by a concrete path, the beds either side planted with shrubs and bushes. There was a wide unmade track at the right side of the garden, that ended in a barred gate into a small grassy field complete with a brick building that looked like a stable.

Glancing back the way I'd driven, I could see the first houses of the Downs Council Estate. There was no lighting out here and the nearest neighbours were . . . I turned around trying to find them. There was a huddle of about three houses about a mile away. Even from this distance the brickwork looked clean. They may not have been there twenty years ago.

This wasn't a main road, traffic would be light outside the rush-hours and school-run slots. It would have been easy enough for anyone to walk out here unobserved from Seatoun. I explored the track beside the house. It was bordered by a wooden fence that looked old enough to have been there at the time. It was too high to see over, but there was a small door a few feet from where it joined the side wall of the house. Cautiously, I tried the latch.

It led into a largish back garden that could have been a clone of the Jacksons': patio, grass, flowerbeds, kids' assorted playthings. The other side of the space was bordered by fencing too, but at the far end, where it joined the field, was a lower planting of thick hedging. Two ponies, ears pricked, were watching me curiously over the bushes. I was about to take a look in the windows, when I caught a movement behind the glass. Gently shutting the door, I moved on towards the field gate. Looking back, I could see the upper windows of the house, but not the lower. Even if the garden gate had been locked, it would be simple enough to climb over the hedge from the field.

If Alison didn't kill Trudy Hepburn, then someone else did. The three most likely motives for murder were money, sex and revenge. 'Which,' I informed Tallulah, 'means all I've got to do is find out who benefited from Trudy's death, if she had the hots for someone, or they had them for her. And if either of those two – or anything else she did – hacked somebody off to such an extent that they decided to do the same with lumps of Trudy. How do you figure I should approach that?'

'*Tomorrow is another day.*'

A parrot that gave career advice. Every girl should have one.

9

'Gillian Anderson. And before you ask, I have no idea if the truth is out there and I have absolutely nothing filed under X.'

I accepted a seat from the one who didn't hang out with Fox Mulder, and tried to squash the sensation that I hadn't done my French homework. Gillian re-read the business card I'd handed over and slipped it in the top drawer of her desk.

'So, you wanted to ask me about Alison Wynne-Ellis?' She interleaved long, slender fingers tipped with perfectly manicured nails and rested them on the desktop.

From Jan's description of her time at school as 'yonks', I'd been expecting an ancient, grey-haired crone. Gillian Anderson was in her early fifties. Her glossy black hair might owe something to colourants, but it had been cut into a sleek bob by experts. It was the same with her make-up, which sat lightly on her heart-shaped face with a delicacy that said it was way too expensive to need plastering on. She was wearing a pale grey suit over a white blouse; plain but chic. If I'd had to guess at her profession, I'd have put her down as an investment banker or corporate lawyer.

'And the woman who died, the teacher, Trudy Hepburn,' I said in answer to her question. I kept thinking of it as 'The Alison Wynne-Ellis Murder'. But really the case was about Trudy. Few people are murdered for no reason. What had there been about Trudy Hepburn that caused her to become a victim? I accepted Gillian's offer of tea.

'And for the parrot?'

'*A martini. Shaken not stirred.*'

'She's fine.'

Gillian opened a small cupboard and took out a kettle, teapot, cups, saucers and a tin of teabags. She flicked open a matching cupboard, revealing a small fridge, and removed a carton of milk. Even her office exuded the 'successful exec' aura. It was furnished in pale wood, the filing cabinets, cupboards and bookcases all fitted around the walls rather than pushed together in the haphazard manner I remembered from my school's interior decoration. The occasional snatches of high voices, running feet and slammed doors indicated that there were after-school activities.

'Perhaps before we speak,' Gillian said, pouring boiling water on to the teabags, 'you could explain what you're hoping to gain from this interview?'

'Hannah, my client, is having problems coming to terms with the fact that her mother is a murderer. She needs to understand what happened. She also needs to discover her mother's family – and if possible her father's – and where all that fits into her own life.' (Once again I deliberately omitted the prime motive – proving Alison's innocence.)

Gillian poured two cups of tea, handed one to me and took the other. This time she took the other visitor's chair, swinging it so she was facing me and we could both rest our cups on the edge of the desk. Once again I had the slight sensation of being manoeuvred. This, I was sure, was the technique she used when interviewing the parents of a problem kid. 'The child, your client, how old is she?'

'Nineteen.'

Gillian's immaculately plucked eyebrows rose. 'But that would mean Alison became pregnant while she was at St Martin's. Or shortly afterwards.'

'While.'

'I see. I'd been assuming she'd given birth after being let out on licence and that "working for Alison's daughter" was a euphemism for the adoptive parents having doubts about taking on the child of a murderer.'

I took out the copy of Hannah's birth certificate. 'I'm on the level, Mrs Anderson. My client is Alison's daughter.'

'Gillian, please. How bizarre.'

She didn't elaborate on this comment so I asked, 'What kind of girl was Alison?'

'The sort you don't notice,' Gillian said promptly. She took a sip of tea and seemed to be collecting her thoughts. 'Since you telephoned I've been trying to recall what I knew about her. I was her form teacher. Not the year of the murder, the previous one. And I'm sorry to say my strongest memory is that she was no trouble.'

'You said that as if others were?'

'Oh yes,' she said. There was a glimpse behind the professional face for a second. 'There was a lot of trouble. Both in school and out. Petty crime and vandalism mostly. Visits from the police were a regular occurrence.' She replaced her cup on the desk, but not before I'd noticed the slight rattle of cup against saucer. Even over the span of twenty years, the memories could still cause tension. 'The headmaster was near to retirement and just hanging on for his pension. So far as he was concerned, providing he didn't see it and it didn't get into the papers, anything went.'

'But Alison wasn't one of the wild bunch?'

'No, as I said, she was unmemorable. Not one of the brightest but not one of the hopeless cases either. Alison hovered in mid-stream. She needed to work to keep up, but she was conscientious about doing so. This sounds a little naive, but she wasn't the kind of girl you'd expect to become a teenage mother.'

'Doesn't sound like a potential slasher, does she? What was her personality like?'

'It's hard to say really. As I said she was quiet, but reserved rather than shy, I'd say. At least, she had the confidence to stand up for her own opinions.'

'In what way?'

Gillian crossed her ankles and slipped into an effortlessly elegant pose. 'Alison's best friend, her only real friend in point of fact, a girl called Cheryl Wright, left during the year she was in my form. Her parents moved, I think. The rest of them had paired off, or had formed their own little gangs, so Alison was left on her own. Anyway, as I said, there were a lot of troublemakers in the school at that time and their leading light was a boy called Orlando Roles.'

'As in Roles Motors out on the Fieldcross Road?'

'Exactly the same. It belonged to Orlando's father. Still does, I think. Orlando couldn't be bothered to work. He preferred to coast through school life on money and charm. Orlando initiated trouble, but he always made sure someone else carried it out. He hung around in his own group – all boys – although they did associate with a particular group of girls, the prettiest ones.'

'Alpha males and alpha females?'

'Exactly so.'

I remembered similar cliques from my own school. I'd secretly wanted to be one of those girls, but I wasn't 'girlie' enough to be admitted to those circles, I didn't know (or care) how to do cool make-up and I didn't want to cruise the clothes shops on Saturday morning picking out stuff to wear that evening. So instead I'd been the bolshie kid who hung out behind the school, smoking and drinking. Word quickly got round that I may not be able to blend cream eyeshadow but I could deliver a mean right hook. I wasn't popular, but I wasn't bullied either.

Gillian explained that twenty years ago there was no sixth form. 'There was a shortage of teachers and we didn't have sufficient pupils staying on to make it worthwhile. Anyone taking A levels transferred to a sixth form college. Which meant that when he reached the fifth year, Orlando was top dog at St Martin's. He led a charmed life. His father seemed prepared to supply unlimited cash and unlimited alibis. But one afternoon I caught him out. I got a call to say one of my children was ill, so I left earlier than expected. When I got to my car, it was full of smoke. Someone had forced the window down and dropped a lighted cigarette inside.

Orlando and his friends were there. I could tell by their expressions they hadn't intended to be seen. Orlando took control. He told me, with his usual self-satisfied smirk, that they'd *just* been about to call the fire brigade and he would advise me to check that I'd put out all cigarette butts before I left the car. He knew perfectly well that I didn't smoke. What he hadn't allowed for was Alison. I'd seen her as I came downstairs. She was setting up a science project in a room overlooking the car park, and she had a clear view through the window. I went and brought her down. Which, now I look back on it, was an unfair thing to do. Unfair on her I mean. But at the time I didn't think, I was just so angry. I needed that car, and I couldn't afford repairs or increased insurance.'

'And Alison snitched on Orlando Roles?'

'He'd obviously briefed some of the girls while I went to get Alison. Suddenly she was their best friend. All she had to do was say she'd seen nothing and she could have been part of that group; and by association popular and in demand. Instead she told me he'd done it. I don't think he could believe it himself. Later, after I'd calmed down, I actually asked her why she'd told me. She said, "Because it was right, people *should* take responsibility for their actions." '

'What happened to Orlando?' I asked curiously.

'Very little. The headmaster wanted to pretend it hadn't happened. In the end Orlando's father made good the damage to the car. More tea?' Without waiting for an answer, she collected up the cups and moved across to the cabinet.

'Did you meet Alison's parents?'

'Several times.' Gillian spoke over her shoulder. 'They were amongst the sadly small group of parents who attended teacher-parent evenings.'

'What were they like?'

'Apologists. At least, she was. He didn't speak much. Mrs Wynne-Ellis was all "if it's not too much trouble" and "I hope you don't mind my asking". On one occasion, another father turned up drunk at some evening do. He was making a nuisance of himself with the women guests. He pinned Mrs Wynne-Ellis against the wall and groped her. I mean he pulled buttons off her blouse and got right inside her bra. Some of the other mothers told her to report it to the police. But she just kept saying it didn't matter. "Don't make a fuss" was her motto. The headmaster loved her.'

'Why did you stay here,' I asked curiously, 'if it was that bad?'

'I lost my husband.' She resettled herself opposite me, placing the refilled cups on the desk. 'Lost as in he went out for a takeaway Chinese one evening and surfaced six months later with a takeaway blonde. I moved back here to be near my parents. The working mother's godsend – totally flexible child-care. And all it cost was endless sessions from the "I told you not to marry him" song-sheet.'

'Sorry, I didn't mean to pry. It's an occupational hazard.'

'It's all right. I don't mind speaking about it now. And it all turned out well in the end.' She waved her hands around the office. 'My chicks have flown and St Martin's had some of the best SATs in the county last year. We have a waiting list of pupils wanting to come here.'

I murmured vague congratulations. 'What about Trudy Hepburn? The newspaper said she was a science teacher?'

'General science.'

'Was she any good at it?'

'Not particularly. I daresay she knew her subjects well enough. We didn't have any budding Einsteins; providing she could drill enough into their heads to get through the exams, it would have been acceptable. But she couldn't control the classes. We – the other teachers, I mean – were constantly going in to complain about the amount of noise they were making. To make it worse, she couldn't even be consistent in her approach to discipline. One week she's applying the rules with the enthusiasm of a Visigoth, the next she's trying to be one of the gang. It was a disaster. The children bullied her. They locked her in a cupboard and left her there overnight on one occasion. Quite often she was physically sick before taking a class. I was always surprised when she returned at the beginning of each term.'

'Why do you think she did?'

'Depression perhaps. I think she was so demoralized it had drained her of any energy to look for another job. And she had no family to run to. She was brought up by a great-aunt I think. She died while Trudy was at university.'

'Did auntie leave her any money?'

'I have no idea. Why?'

'People sometimes kill for inheritances.'

Gillian caught the point of the question immediately. 'People other than Alison, you mean? Do you think she was wrongly convicted?'

'I haven't a clue,' I admitted. 'I was just fishing. Do you think so?'

'I never heard anything to suggest so, then or since. So far as Trudy is concerned, I doubt she had money. Or jealous relatives who wanted to kill her for it. I seem to recall that there were problems in raising the money for her funeral.' Gillian tapped some keys on her computer, scrolling through a list of files until she found the one she wanted. She hit the print key.

'Why did the school keep Trudy on?' I asked. 'If she was hopeless?'

'They had no choice. Literally. Science and maths are the hardest positions to fill. Fewer students take degrees in them. We'd already struggled through one term with other teachers covering those subjects; when Trudy's CV arrived I would guess that the headmaster fell on it with delight.'

She took two sheets from the printer and passed one to me.

'That's Trudy.'

If she hadn't been the only female in the group picture, I wouldn't have recognized Trudy Hepburn. I was looking for the lumpish female with the mass of dark hair from the newspaper's graduation shot in Hannah's pink folder. But this Trudy was slimmer and her hair had been thinned down to fall in blonde flicks and curls to her shoulders. She was casually dressed in a red-and-white striped, long-sleeved sweater, jeans and canvas lace-ups. It was hard to make out her expression because she was looking into sunlight, but she seemed to be smiling. In fact, her whole stance suggested someone relaxed.

'It's probably the last photo of her,' Gillian said. 'It was taken a few weeks before her death. She took some of her class on a field trip to Winstanton to study the biology of the seashore.'

The kids were all in fashionable outfits rather than school uniforms. Plainly it had been more of a jolly than a serious educational outing.

'She doesn't look ... well ... like the person you described.'

'That was the most tragic part of it, I suppose. Towards the end of that last term she seemed to be getting a grip; she was more confident, more in charge of her classes.'

'What brought that on?'

'I don't know. It could have been Gina's influence, I guess.'

'The housemate?'

'Yes. Gina had *no* problems with self-confidence. One way or another Gina Gibbs got what she wanted.'

'They seem unlikely friends?'

'That's because they weren't.'

I waited for her to elaborate, but when she showed no signs of doing so, I asked how she would describe Gina and Trudy's relationship.

'I'm almost tempted to say dominatrix and slave.'

'Were they gay?'

'No. At least, I'm sure Gina wasn't. If Trudy was there was never any sign of it. I simply meant that Gina had a very forceful personality and I've little doubt that things at home ran along the lines that Gina dictated. The reason they ended up together was because the cottage that Gina rented was too expensive for her to manage on a single salary. It had stabling at the rear—'

'I've seen it.'

'Gina kept a horse. She rode every day and she wanted that house. She needed someone to share. Once she was asked, I doubt Trudy would have known how to say no even if she'd wanted to.'

'Did she seem unhappy with the arrangement?'

'On the contrary, she admired Gina. She even started to sound a little like her. Some of Gina's teaching style may have started to rub off too, I suppose. I can't deny that the school had some excellent exam results in modern languages during Gina's time.'

'What about Alison and Trudy Hepburn? Did she teach Alison? Did they have any history of problems?'

'Yes. And no. Quite the reverse. After Cheryl, Alison's best friend left, Trudy and Alison rather drifted together, despite the difference in age.'

'Could there have been a relationship there?' I was already toying with the rejected lover scenario.

'Sexual, you mean? I doubt it. I think it was just a case of two square pegs coming together because they couldn't find a round hole.' Her lips twitched again. 'Given your question that's an unfortunate analogy, isn't it? But no, I truly believe there wasn't anything of that nature.'

'Perhaps Alison had developed a crush and Trudy knocked her back? How was their relationship just before the murder?'

'Cooler, I think. But that was probably down to Trudy's growing self-confidence. A woman in her mid-twenties doesn't usually want a fifteen-year-old hanging around.'

Rejection, my demon was whispering. *Puberty pique. Acne anger.* Damn and blast. I'd just come up with another motive for Alison. 'It said she was sixteen in the trial report.'

'She was by then. But she was only fifteen at the time of

the killing. Alison was one of the youngest children in the year. She'd have had her sixteenth birthday in the August summer holiday. I only happen to remember that because she shares the same date as my own daughter.'

'What about Alison's boyfriend?' I asked. 'Any candidates?'

'I don't recall ever seeing her with a boy, but you're more likely to get that kind of information from her classmates. They usually pick up on who fancies who. Particularly if who is trying to keep it secret.'

I flapped the print she'd given me. 'Can you put a name to these for me?'

She pointed to a boy to the right of Trudy; dark-haired, casually handsome, already taller than the teacher. 'That's Orlando Roles.' I'd have made him even without Gillian's help. Orlando faced the camera with the arrogant self-confidence that said he knew the world was a better place for him being in it. 'Mark Boscombe, Graham Knight, Laurence Sorensson, Sean Inchbeck.' She paused on the next two. Their faces were heavily shaded by something out of camera, making it impossible to make out their features clearly. 'I'm pretty certain those will be Andrew Lee and Michael Forbes, they were always in that crowd at that time . . .'

I recognized the last one of the group myself. He was sitting on the ground in front of Trudy, propped between Graham and Sean. His head, which had lolled oddly when I'd seen him earlier, was held erect as he smiled into the camera. His condition must have deteriorated over the years. 'Philip Darrowfield?'

'Do you know him?'

'I met him briefly this morning. He lived next door to Alison.'

'He was never really part of this little clique. He should have been in a special needs school really, but the fad had started for integrating them into normal classes. It never worked. Either they were neglected or the rest of the class was. I did try to get his parents to push the council for a place at a special needs, but it would have meant boarding away during the week and his mother wouldn't hear of him leaving home. But we still haven't got to Alison, have we?'

She fired up the computer file again. Thumbnail photos filled the screen. 'I had all the old school photos filed on disc.' She started clicking rapidly on the tiny squares. Full-sized pictures expanded on to the monitor and then disappeared again. I caught a glimpse of another familiar face amongst the ranks.

'That's Terry Rosco!'

It seemed to be a school play. The kids were in costume and make-up. Terry's gear consisted of green tights worn under a short green tunic, green facepaint, wings and some kind of gel that had been used to coax his hair into two stiff horns. He looked about twelve.

'He was my Peaseblossom,' Gillian said.

'Your what?'

Gillian gave a small but audible sigh. 'Peaseblossom. Often played by a girl, but we decided fairies should be asexual.'

Terry Rosco as a fairy! 'Can I get a copy of that picture?'

'If you wish.' She tapped the print key again and then continued through the scenes of school life. Despite what looked like an extensive collection, the only one with Alison in the scene was a large group shot; she was no more than a blurred face in the back row. I asked if they kept records of past pupils or class lists. Gillian shook her head. 'I'm sorry. I'm allowed to give out the photos because people sometimes ask for them to illustrate articles about school life in the past or such, but I can't give out any written records without the permission of the Education Department.'

She handed the picture of Fairy Terry to me and looked at a slim wrist watch. It was an obvious hint. Luckily I'm not a girl to take one.

'Do you have any idea why Alison would have wanted to kill Trudy?'

'None at all. If I had I would have told the police at the time.' She made a hopeless gesture. 'It was a mystery then and it's a mystery now.'

Great, just what the red hot investigator wants to hear. 'Do you remember much about the day of the murder?'

'It was the last day of term. Same as any other last day really; trying to take lessons as normal in the morning when all the children wanted to do was get out. It was good weather, sunny, exceptional weather for Easter. I'm afraid I don't even remember seeing Alison on that day.'

'She wasn't in school?' Maybe there was a clue there?

Gillian promptly trampled my little fledging clue into the ground. 'Yes. She was. The police checked.'

'When did you hear about the murder?'

'The following Monday. I heard people talking in the shops, saying someone had been killed and there were police cars up on Millrun Lane. But I didn't realize it was Trudy. I eventually found out when I ran into Gina Gibbs going into the Rock Hotel. She was in a state. Not, as it turned out, because she'd found the body, but because the police had sealed off the cottage as a crime scene, wouldn't pay for her hotel bill, and she'd had to have a row with them before they'd agreed to let her back in to see to the horse.'

'She wasn't upset by Trudy's death?'

'Oh, she was furious. But only insofar as it affected her. Although in the end it turned out well for her. Gina always did have a well defined set of priorities – Gina first, last and in-between.'

'Do you have any idea what happened to her?'

'Usual story. She got married. Transferred to a better school. Had a baby. Moved on. I think they were living in London the last I heard. But that was ages ago.'

I flapped the picture she'd given me of Trudy and asked if any of the boys in it were still around.

A small 'v' appeared over Gillian's nose as she considered the grinning faces. 'Orlando is. I've seen him cruising in some flashy car. And Graham Knight is a postman locally. I don't know about the others, I'm afraid. The two on the end, Andrew and Michael, were related in some way, cousins, I think. They were very good-looking boys; tall, dark-haired, blue eyes. And they were brighter than the rest of this lot. I'm almost sure they went on to sixth form college and university. Now I really do have to get this work finished . . .'

This time she stood up and moved towards the door. The interview with the head was at an end. I was dismissed.

I collected my parrot and headed out. Gillian showed me to the outer doors. There were more framed photos along the corridor walls: St Martin's from its opening in the 1930s to the present. I scanned for more pictures of the major players in the case. But these all seemed to be celebrating specific events; there were football and netball teams clutching cups, little groups waving certificates, people holding improbably large cheques made out to local charities. I'd have missed the only relevant photo if Gillian hadn't pointed it out. 'There's Trudy.'

Two men – one short and broad with a grey beard and wearing a formal grey suit, the other slightly taller, his thinning ginger hair brushed into a comb-over and wearing a double-breasted, brass-buttoned blazer in a bilious shade of pea-green – were clutching the handle of a zinc bucket and offering it to the camera with matching self-satisfied leers. There was a label plastered on the side reading 'Cancer Hospice Appeal.' The 'old' Trudy was hovering in the background: chubby, dark-haired, skirt to her shins and a bulky, wrap-around cardigan.

'We held a sponsored silence,' Gillian said. 'It suited her since she scarcely opened her mouth anyway. That's the headmaster.' She ran a fingernail over the grey suit. I had the distinct impression she'd have like to have done the same thing to the original. 'I could get you a copy of this picture if it would help?'

I decided it probably wouldn't. 'I'll stick with Trudy, the Barbie years, thanks.'

As I was stepping out into the playground, I asked what she'd meant by the murder turning out all right for Gina.

'She met her husband during the investigation. He was one of the policemen.'

'Can you remember his name?'

'Pennington.'

'Georgie Pennington?'

'Georgina.'

'I can't believe she didn't mention at the christening she shared that cottage with Trudy Hepburn. I mean, if you'd spent time shacked up with a corpse, or a future corpse anyway, wouldn't you mention it?'

'*What we've got here is a failure to communicate.*'

'I need to check that out, but it could be tough getting to see her. Particularly if there's a hose around.'

'*Life sucks.*'

'Couldn't agree more. We must talk like this more often.'

Tallulah sneezed. She was in her travel cage on the front seat of the car. I was running the heater to keep her warm but she still looked pretty sorry for herself. Steering out of the gate and back on to the road I passed the school's name board. In gold lettering it gave the school's name under a heraldic shield, told me Mrs G.A. Anderson was the headteacher and the premises manager was one 'Mr B.T. Root' – the second name Jan had given me. Not the ancient teaching crone I'd assumed either.

A passing sprog in the school uniform directed me to a house next door to the school playground where the caretaker (sorry – premises manager) lived. There was no answer to my ring. I added him to my list of people to see in the future.

Where to now? Evening darkness had started falling

while I was talking to Gillian Anderson. It made the working day seem finished somehow. Annie was away; Pepi's was closed; you could flash-freeze boiling lava in Vetch's offices. I had nowhere to go but home.

10

Hertfordshire is like most of the Home Counties. Busy towns and ugly industrial estates within sight of the main roads, but turn off and drive for a few miles and you're in the middle of networks of smaller lanes connecting villages that lost their public transport and local shops years ago and are only viable now if you have a car. The one I wanted was in the north of the county where it approached the borders with Cambridgeshire and the contours of the countryside became flatter as they melded into the plains of the fen country. I followed the signs off the A1, turning left in obedience to a signpost, and along a single lane that wandered through three villages, until I saw the entrance: Longmeadow Garden Centre & Children's Farm.

Tallulah and I walked around a bit first rather than heading directly into the restaurant. The place was dominated by rows of huge greenhouses. I kept circling. The kids' farm housed cute, cuddly animals that were presumably amenable to being poked, stroked and overfed. There was an outdoor play area too, with swings and slides. A picnic area. A large stone barn that was labelled 'Soft Play Den'. The whole place was well laid-out and maintained.

In order to get to the restaurant, I had to go through the shop, which was full of plant-related items like weedkiller and wheelbarrows, and things that had no connection at all with horticulture that I could see, such as greetings cards and scented candles. Beyond sliding doors, I tramped around stands full of shrubs, trees and bushes, and negotiated an enormous cavern dedicated to every blessed flowerpot you could possibly want (or in my case – not). Eventually I made the restaurant.

It had been converted from an old house – the original Longmeadow Farm, I guessed. The flagstoned floor, big open fire, and exposed wooden beams were all reflected in the copper items gleaming around the brick walls. It looked inviting on a cold late-February day. Which was doubtless why a lot of people were dawdling over lunch in here. That was a pain. Alison was hardly going to want to chat about her murderous past with so many ears within flapping distance.

A woman bustled out from the back carrying two dishes of apple pie and cream. She was way too old to be Alison.

'Just take a seat, pet. I'll be with you in a minute.'

'I'm looking for Alison Brown?'

'She only sees reps by appointment. Unless . . . is that bird for the children's farm?'

'*In your dreams, sweetheart.*'

'No. She's not. And I'm not a rep. Tell her it's about Trudy.'

There was no instant recognition on the plump face. Plainly the restuarant manager's history wasn't generally known hereabouts.

Alison came out from the back almost immediately, drawing on a jacket over her dress. 'Come outside.' She led me through a side door in the building that opened on to the space in front of the play barn. 'Now, who are you and what do you want?'

There was no point in giving her a cover story. I told her the truth. Her reaction wasn't what I'd expected. 'Oh God, you haven't been charging around trying to prove my innocence, have you?'

'Why? Aren't you?'

'I have accepted my own guilt and taken responsibility for actions which I now deeply regret.'

'That's the stock response for the parole board.'

'I deeply regret what I did,' Alison repeated. 'But I don't want to discuss it with you. Please leave, Miss Smith.'

'Call me Grace. Was the children's farm your idea?'

'Yes,' she admitted reluctantly.

So she still cared about small animals. Stupidly, even though I knew it was impossible, I'd been picturing her as the fifteen-year-old in those old photos. But this woman was five years older than me. She was small, slim and blue-eyed, the gleaming copper hair cut to just touch her chin. The icy containment of her expression slipped for a moment at Tallulah's attempt at 'Old MacDonald Had a Farm.'

'Do you always travel with your parrot?'

'We're kind of joined at the wing at present. Ken Darrowfield took your animals to a rescue centre. He wrote to you. He never knew whether you received the letter?'

'I did.'

I tried again. 'He had to get rid of his own birds.'

'I remember.'

OK, so much for social chit-chat. 'Look, I totally get that admitting guilt was the only way to get out on licence, but I'm not going to run snitching to anyone if you tell me what you really remember. Don't you want to clear your name?'

'It's not my name any more, I changed it. Will you go, please? And tell that girl to stop stirring things up.'

'That girl is your daughter.'

'No. She's someone else's daughter. I want nothing to do with her.'

'I can understand that there might be things you don't want to tell Hannah, but all she wants is—'

Alison spun round, catching at her hair which the wind was whipping into her eyes. 'I don't care what she wants. Just *go away*.'

I'd been told to push off by experts. She didn't come close. 'It's cold out here. Can we go in the barn?' I headed for it before she could say no. Inside it was huge and dark.

The light from the open doors let me see the playpit full of coloured balls, climbing ropes, rope ladders, frames and hammocks. The floor area and lower walls were covered with blown-up cushions like those used in bouncy castles. When the lights were switched on, I could see the high-raftered roof of the original barn soaring above me. When I tried to climb on the cushions, Alison told me sharply to take my shoes off. She slipped off her own black courts and joined me. It was like being on a ship; bouncing and swaying to keep our balance with our legs stretched out straight. The light and heat perked up Tallulah, who promptly launched into a chorus of '*A Life on the Ocean Wave, a Life on the Rolling Sea . . .*'

Alison smiled, and for a moment the fifteen-year-old school-kid peeked out from behind the hard-faced woman.

Hoping to take advantage of this chink in the armour, I said, 'You must have wanted the baby. Otherwise why not have an abortion?'

'I don't believe in abortion. It's wrong to kill a baby. They're innocent.'

'Was Trudy Hepburn guilty of something?'

'I don't remember.'

'Why did you go up to her cottage that night?'

'I can't remember.'

'I have this theory. I think you found Trudy bleeding to death and went into shock. You blamed yourself for not being able to save her. You had no motive to kill her. She was your friend.'

'I really would like you to go now. I'm sorry if that girl is disappointed with her family background, but I can't take responsibility for that.'

'That girl has a name: Hannah. Had she grown up as you'd imagined?'

'I never imagined.'

'Oh, come on, you must have felt something for her. You chose a name for her: Flora.'

'I chose nothing. I think one of the nurses picked it.' She

slid off the edge of the cusions and started chasing her shoes with her toes. 'And I don't wish to see her again – ever.'

Something that should have been obvious occurred to me. 'You sent her the cuttings about your trial, didn't you?'

'I thought it would discourage her from making further contact. Having a murderess as a mother would discourage most girls.'

'Not Hannah. She's a stubborn little cookie. When she makes up her mind, I'd guess she hangs in there no matter how many punches you sling at her.'

The opening of the barn door startled both of us. It let in cold air, daylight and a rush of outside noises that had been muffled by the cushioned walls.

'Is everything OK, Ally? They said over the restaurant you'd got a visitor?'

Forty-something. Tall and lean. Lines etched in long face. He placed himself behind Alison, laying a hand lightly on her shoulder. She reached backwards to cover his fingers. 'It's fine, David. Grace was trying to sell us a refit for the barn.'

He offered a hand. 'David Wright. I'm the owner.'

'Any relation to Cheryl Wright?'

'Brother. Do you know Cheryl?'

'Not really. She came up in my investigation.' I wasn't going along with her cover story. David must surely know about the prison sentence if his sister had been Alison's best friend.

'What are you investigating?' He shot a suspicious look at Alison and read the answer. 'Right. Clear off, whoever you are. I don't want you on my property.'

'It's all right, David. Grace was just leaving.'

David Wright escorted me to my car. As I was unlocking, he said in a low voice, 'Just a moment.' I expected another rocket for cornering Alison, but David said, 'Alison wants to put that entire murder business behind her and I have to respect that, but I want you to understand that Alison is one of the most honest and caring people I've ever met. She could never have done what they say she did.'

'That's what I'm trying to prove, David. But I'm not getting a lot of co-operation here. Does she ever talk about that night to you?'

'No. I've never asked her and I never will. As I said, we've put it all behind us. It's what makes Alison happy, but . . .' He cast a quick look behind; Alison was standing by the entrance to the barn, one hand holding back the wind-blown red locks from her face. 'If it's ever a question of more money to help you prove it, you can always reach me here.'

I drove home, aware that I had not only failed to gather any new evidence on the case, but that I'd also managed to get up Hannah's mum's nose and probably ensured she never wanted to see her again (OK, she hadn't wanted to see her anyway, so maybe that last one wasn't such a downer). Something Alison said had struck me as odd, however; she 'remembered' Ken Darrowfield getting rid of his parrots. I'd gained the impression that had happened after the murder, but if he'd never seen Alison after her arrest, that meant she'd never returned to Hinton Drive after that night. Hence the parrots must have gone before. 'Is that important?' I said aloud.

'*There are more things in heaven and earth, Horatio, than are dreamt of in your philosophy.*'

'You could well be right, but the name is Grace, beaky.'

11

A pile-up shut two lanes of the motorway, resulting in queues that crawled at four miles an hour. It was early evening by the time Tallulah and I finally reached Seatoun and I was tempted to head straight home, but conscious of a lack of progress on Hannah's case, I took a detour via Fieldcross Road.

Roles Motors occupied a large plot surrounded by a substantial wooden fence that had once been painted blue. It was entered via a set of big double doors. Since they were still ajar, I took it that Roles (motto: 'Why drive an Ordinary Motor when you can drive a Roles?') was still looking to trade. I parked near the gates and stared at the scene in front of me. There were about two hundred second-hand cars scattered around. I assumed they were for sale although there was nothing to indicate it.

In the midst of the yard was a pre-fabricated cabin, which was a lot smarter than you might have expected from the state of the surrounding perimeter fence. The internal lights were on, so I headed for the small flight of metal steps leading to the door. Halfway between the car and the front door, something that looked like a werewolf's larger, meaner cousin hurled itself from behind the building.

I froze, trying to decide whether I should sprint for the car or the office. The brain said car, but the legs weren't receiving the message. The werewolf kept coming, jaws drooling in anticipation of fresh human buttock. Then, just as suddenly, it jerked to a stop as it reached the end of its chain. Frustrated at the loss of a free meal, the thing started snarling at ear-bashing level.

'Cleopatra, shut your noise! Come on in, darling, she won't hurt you.'

The thing dropped its head, whined its disappointment and trotted back around behind the cabin, dragging a chain that looked substantial enough to anchor a battleship. Her owner was back-lit by the lights spilling from the open cabin door, until he got within a few feet of me. Then his features hardened to a sharp face with graphite-shaded eyes and deep-cut lines from nose to mouth and around his eyes. He was dressed in a dark-grey suit and shirt, the collar unbuttoned far enough to reveal a few curling white hairs on his chest. His tie was hanging like two ends of a deflated snake with the left side nearly touching his waistband and the right disappearing behind his neck. A trilby was pushed low over a thick head of light-grey curls.

'Billy Roles, proprietor.' He stuttered on the p's. The reason was tickling my nose. Mr Roles wasn't totally smashed, but the cracks were definitely starting to join up. 'Looking for something special, are you, darling?'

I was actually looking for his son, Orlando, in the hopes that he'd be able to give me some background on the students at St Martin's Comprehensive during Alison's last year.

Billy Roles hadn't really expected an answer from me anyway. He was already moving towards the cars with just the slightest sway as he put one foot in front of the other. 'Here you are, darling. Isn't she a peach? Soon as I laid eyes on you, I said these two were made for each other. Like a pair of lovers. It would be cruel to keep them apart. Go on, tell me you're not already in love.' He patted the glossy wing with affectionate strokes.

I couldn't identify the model, but it was a sports car of some kind. Red bodywork, long bonnet, wire-wheels. I yearned for something turbo-charged and shiny. But Annie had insisted I needed a vehicle that wouldn't attract attention when we were doing tailing jobs. Hence the very dull blue Micra.

Either Billy wasn't as drunk as I thought, or more likely a lifetime of motor-trade reflexes cut in. Correctly identifying the drool-mode I'd slipped into, he said, 'I'll just get the keys from the office and you can have a sit in her. Fire her up, feel the power.' He was heading in a wavering route through the other cars towards the office, but he suddenly changed direction towards the yard gates. 'Part exchange, is it? I'll take a look at what you've got. We'll make a good deal, don't you worry, darling.'

Despite being half-cut, he could still move faster than me. He ran a professional eye over the Micra. 'Not everyone's taste, but we can work out a decent price.' He produced a roll of fifties from his pocket, peeled off the elastic band and started thumbing the greasy notes. 'Now you call when, darling.'

'No. I mean, I'd like to think about it, Mr Roles.' I gave an involuntary shiver.

'You're chilled. And there's me keeping you talking out in this wind. Come into the office.'

'I can't!' I could feel my will power draining away. If he got me in that office there was a danger I'd come out the owner of a red shiny motor – and Annie would kill me when she got back. 'It's the parrot. I should get her home. She's too cold.'

'A parrot?' Billy peered through the window. 'So it is. Well, bring her into the office, darling. There's a heater in there.' Before I could refuse, he'd opened the passenger door. Once he'd got Tallulah I had to follow him to the office or try to wrest the cage away from him.

I wasn't in a wresting mood. Anyway the cocoon of warmth that surrounded me once I stepped through the door was wonderfully welcome. The inside was shorter than the outside. I guessed the left-hand side of the building held a washroom reached by the internal door behind the desk. The rest of the room was furnished with filing cabinets, easy chairs, a low table and a large radiator. Gratefully I held my hands over the latter and admired the pictures decorating the walls: one calendar with models who had less covering than the parrot, and a series of photos of gravestones.

Billy lowered the cage on to his desk, between a model ship and the open litre bottle of vodka. The bottle was 90 per cent full, but I could see another one lying empty in the wastepaper basket. 'Have a drink with me, darling?'

'No thanks. I'm driving.'

He seemed to find this excuse hilarious. Chuckling to himself, he took a glass from the desk, polished it on his jacket and poured two shots. He gestured to the ship model. 'My old man was a steward on that: Dover, Cherbourg, Cape Town. Only thing he left me. What you reckon then? Marble or granite?'

The abrupt change of subject confused me. Then I realized Billy was now looking at the wall photos.

'Most say black polished granite, but I've a hankering towards black marble myself. With maybe a thread of grey weaving through it?'

'Depends on your preference, I guess.'

'An angel, I thought.' He took a file from the drawer. Scrabbling through a pile of loose photos and brochures, he handed me a picture of a stone angel. 'I wanted a car, Rolls-Royce, sculptured to go on top of the grave, with me name on the number plate, but they say I can't have that. Not dignified.'

'Angels are very dignified.'

'They are that. Dignity's important. I did think about cars for the funeral procession. Go to me resting place in something that reflects me life.'

'Could they get the coffin on the roof rack of a clapped-out Ford Anglia?'

Billy laughed so hard he couldn't get his breath. Finally he gasped out, 'Oh, for two pins I'd do it, darling. But I've already got me carriage booked. Six black horses with full harness and dressings for Billy Roles.'

'Can't do better than that.' I was wondering how to bring up the subject of his son, when I caught the sound of car wheels scrunching over the surface outside and the brief sweep of headlights passing across the outside of the windows. The driver came to a halt, got out and slammed the door shut.

He came in on a rush of cold air and a flash of white teeth. The tall, skinny kid in the old school photo had grown a few more inches and filled out, giving him broader shoulders, but he still had the curly brown hair and deep toffee-brown eyes.

'Can I help you?'

'Lady's interested in the Interceptor.'

'Surely not? The steering's shot. Now I'd say you were . . . what?' His eyes assessed me. Right through my clothes. 'Stylish. Sleek lines. Fast. Sophisticated. Let me get you a brochure. Show you what you could get for your money, Miss? Mrs?'

'Grace Smith.'

'Orlando Roles.' He'd moved to a filing cabinet and opened a drawer. I caught a glimpse of stacked brochures. One was handed to me.

'Quixsilver Autos,' I read from the glossy top.

'That's us.' Orlando reached over and turned the page for me. Inside were more glossy sheets with pictures of happy motorists taking the keys of new cars. 'We source your new car from the Continent. Right-hand drive. Same warranties. But at a fraction of the price you'd pay if you bought it in this country.'

There was a business card tucked into a slot, which told me Orlando Roles was the managing director of Quixsilver Autos.

'So you're not Roles Motors any more?'

'I never was. This is my father's . . . business.' There was a note of scorn behind the description. I guess Billy caught it too.

'It kept you in clover for enough years, sonny.' As soon as his son had hijacked me, Billy had slumped back behind the desk and applied himself to the vodka. His glass was now empty. He reached for the bottle again. Orlando intercepted.

'I think you've had enough for one day.'

'I'll say when I've had enough. I'm going for a slash.'

He wobbled unsteadily through the rear door, leaving me and Orlando to exchange the tight smiles of the embarrassed.

'Sorry about that. The old boy's past it.'

'No problem.'

There were lavatorial sounds coming from the bathroom. We both pretended we couldn't hear them. Tallulah told us she was just singing in the rain.

'Nice parrot. Had her long?'

'Couple of days.' He was plainly wondering why I didn't leave. And I was wondering how to subtly slide into an interrogation on life at St Martin's twenty years ago. 'I saw a picture of you recently. An old school photo. I remembered because of the name.'

'Roles?'

'Orlando.'

'I knew that really.' He used that flashing smile again. 'My dad's choice. Mum wanted Wayne.'

'Orlando sounds more managing directorish.' Bad move. It was the cue he needed to launch into his sales pitch again. At the same time he was trying to sweep me towards the door. I side-stepped him. Subtle was going to have to go. 'We were discussing Alison Wynne-Ellis.'

Instead of asking why, he said, 'Who's "we"?'

'Mrs Anderson. The headteacher at St Martin's?'

'Oh yeah, Andy. She took me for English.'

'And fire drill.'

He burst out laughing. 'The car! God, I was a little shit back then. But I guess most of us were. I bet you were a foxy little pain in the butt to your teachers.'

Did he really think this chat-up technique was a come-on? 'Alison Wynne-Ellis wasn't. A pain, I mean.'

'No? I didn't really know her.'

'She gave you up for setting fire to that car.'

'Yeah, she did. Not quite the little mouse she appeared, I guess.'

'Do you think she killed that teacher?'

'Heartburn? How would I know?'

'According to Mrs Anderson, you knew most things that were happening at St Martin's back then. Most bad things anyway. Mainly because you were behind them.'

I thought I might needle him into blurting out something a tad less considered, but he just spread his hands, palms up, and shrugged. 'Heh, I was sixteen, what can I say? It was no worse than what most kids get up to. And I never stuck a teacher. Alison got one up on me there.'

'Did you ever hear any rumours that maybe she didn't do it?'

'Nope, can't say I did.' The sounds from the bathroom were becoming grosser. Tallulah was now accompanying them with one-word selections from South Pacific. 'What's your interest anyway?'

'I've been hired by . . . a relative . . . of Alison's to look into the case.'

'You a detective?'

'Private. Did Alison have a boyfriend?'

'Couldn't say. Like I said, I didn't know her.'

'Are you still in contact with anyone from the school? Old mates?'

He frowned and pursed his lips. 'Not really. I see a couple of them sometimes. I could ask around. What is it you want to know exactly?'

'Anything about Alison's relationship with Trudy Hepburn. And Alison's boyfriend.'

'OK. I'll see what I can do. Where can I find you?'

'Vetch's Investigations. We're in the book.' Tallulah came to a temporary break in her repertoire. We both became aware how quiet it was. Orlando stepped across and rapped on the bathroom door with one balled fist. 'Dad? You all right?'

The door opened slowly and Billy Roles leant in the gap, supporting himself against the handle and door jamb. I'd seen healthier looking corpses.

Orlando took an arm. 'Come on, Dad, you're going home.'

'Don't tell me what to do. I was running this place when you were in bloody nappies, don't you forget. I made sacrifices for you.'

'Yeah, I know you did. Now come on.' He forced Billy's other hand off the door handle. The old man swung round and managed to capture the vodka bottle on his arc. Orlando took it off him and handed it to me. Getting a firmer grip on his father, he half pushed, half carried him to the door. I picked up Tallulah and followed, as Billy was dragged down the steps and pushed into the back of a waiting Lexus. The werewolf let rip with the howls again.

'Shut up!' Orlando came back to lock the office door. 'I'm going to lock the gates so . . .'

'Sure. Just one thing. Do *you* think Alison did it?'

'I already said. I don't know. Is that what you're trying to prove? That she was innocent?'

'Or that she wasn't.'

'Can't help you, I'm afraid.'

'No rumours in the playground? No one boasting how they got away with it?'

'Nope.'

'Any guesses on why she did it?'

The shadow of the office cabin lay across him, but a faint beam of light was glancing from the metal strengthening bars where the two corners of the building joined. His eyes were partially hidden but his mouth was visible. I know I didn't imagine the hestitation before he said, 'No. None at all.'

12

Back at the flat, I opened the cage to give Tallulah a chance to stretch her wings and went through to use the bathroom. I re-emerged to the distinct smell of alcohol. Billy Roles's vodka bottle was lying on its side with the top off and a pint sloshing around the floor. There was a small groan from under the bed. Tallulah waddled out, legs crossing over each other until she reached the table leg and propped herself against it.

'You're drunk again, you feathered lush!'

'*Frankly, my dear, I don't give a damn.*'

I pushed the pissed parrot into her travel cage and headed out for the Happy Burger Bun. At the end of the road I nearly stepped into something large and nasty. At least he had his clothes on this time.

'Hi, Terry. Back in the bosom of Linda and mutants . . . er, kids?'

He scowled. 'No way. I'm making her sweat. Nobody tells Terry Rosco where to go. The bitch should learn she can only push me so far. She's cleaned out the bank account. And reported me credit card stolen.'

'Terry, I think you may be confusing me with someone who gives a damn.'

I stepped around him. Even above the roar of wind howling in from the breakers, I could hear his heavy breathing just behind me. It was like being tagged by an asthmatic warthog with acute depression.

As I neared Pepi's my heart skipped; the lights were throwing an oblong of illumination over the pavement. Goodbye, Happy Burger Bun; hello, Shane! The café was gloriously fugged up, Elvis was Vivaring Las Vegas on the jukebox, the scents of fried food were so thick on the air they tasted on your lips. With a sense of coming home, I headed straight for the counter and dumped Tallulah next to a display case of cheesecakes and fruit slices.

'Smithie. What can I get you?'

'Where have you been?'

'I had to pick up Marlene from her sister's place.'

'Where does she live? Poland? You've been gone for days.'

'Two. I had to talk her into coming back. Marlene's not been herself lately.'

'You mean this parrot has driven her nuts?'

He blushed under the rich red colour the kitchen heat had raised in his cheeks. 'Well, yeah, sort of. Marlene's had to be with her. Tallulah can't be left alone.'

'I've discovered that. Thanks a lot, Shane. You can have her back now.'

'I can't. Marlene will walk out again.'

'Keep the bird here with you.'

'Environmental health would close me down. You can't keep livestock in a café.'

'Yes, you can. They have fish tanks in restaurants.'

'They're not really livestock, just dishes that aren't as far down the cooking process as the stuff in the ovens. I can't pretend parrot's on the menu.'

'Don't see why not, mate,' Terry chimed in. 'She's half-plucked already.'

'Her feathers kept coming out,' I said defensively.

'It's stress,' Shane said gloomily. 'Don't worry, they always grow back.'

'And she's pinched half a bottle of vodka.'

'I told you not to let her near alcohol. She can unscrew caps. Please, Smithie. It's only for a couple more days. The monastery's nearly finished.'

'What monastery?'

'Me brother's a monk, didn't I say? They've all had to go

to a retreat while the monastery's being refurbished and it doesn't take pets. Look, I'll pay you.' He opened the till and drew out two tenners.

'A couple of days?' Shane nodded. 'I have to run my heating for her. The boiler at Vetch's is on the blink.' Shane extracted another tenner. I waited. Number four joined the pile. Then five. 'And I still get fed for free.' I twitched the notes from his fingers before I could have second thoughts, and ordered the evening special.

'I'll have the same,' Terry said. 'Her tab. I'll pay you back later, Smithie.'

'You've got to be joking.'

He looked like he might plead, then the old macho Terry reasserted himself. Straightening his shoulders and lifting his jaw, he eyeballed Shane. 'Right, I'm a police officer and I'm commandeering some food.'

I told him to get real. 'When was the last time you heard The Flying Squad flagging down a rump steak and yelling, "Follow that plate of chips!" Which reminds me, Shane, I'll take a side order of fries with that. And the parrot stays behind the counter until I've finished eating.'

'I'll bring the food over.' Shane duck-walked his way down to the hot plates along with Chuck Berry serenading Nadine. 'And you owe me one, mate, next time the car's parked on double yellow lines.'

Delight sparkled over Terry's fleshy face. He barrelled along behind me and slid behind the table.

The food arrived and since I was stuck with the sight of PC Rosco hoovering up mashed potato like a snow-plough on 'suck', I figured I'd make use of him. 'I was up at St Martin's Comp. It's got a really good record now. Not like in the old days. I hear it was a bit rough?'

Terry slurped and swallowed. 'Nothing I couldn't deal with. I knew how to handle myself in the playground.'

Of course you did, Peaseblossom. I saved that little gem for later. 'Do you remember the teacher who got murdered?'

'The jellyfish, yeah. We used to call her Heartburn.' A smile spread across his greasy chops. 'We used to fart in the chemistry lessons, pretend her experiment was going wrong and stinking the place out, see?'

'You were a regular laugh a minute, weren't you, Terry?'

'Then another time, and this was really the best one ever . . .' He jabbed at me with a piece of chop speared on a fork; I could see that in his head he was a thirteen-year-old kid again. 'She had to take us up the swimming pool because one of the regular teachers was off. A few of us swam under, got hold of her legs and pulled her down to the bottom. She was wriggling all over the place and her eyes were popping out like a frog's. It was just a joke like? But you should have seen her when we let her up. She was screaming that we'd tried to kill her and telling the pool-guard to call the police.'

'Did he?'

'Nah. Once they'd got her dried off, she calmed down. Fact she even saw the joke. Apologized to us for over-reacting.'

Which was the vacillating approach to discipline that Gillian Anderson had described. It was exactly the wrong way to handle a class of thirteen-year-olds.

'Do you remember the teacher she shared a cottage with?'

'Miss Gibbs. She was *fit*. Great tits. She did these plays, in French. I was in one once. Had to do this love scene with her. Tongues and everything. I could tell she really fancied me.'

Not only had Terry's mind slipped back twenty years. His delusions had too.

'Did you know she got married?'

'Did she? Yeah, I remember. She left after that. Teachers were always leaving.' He shovelled in more food, slurped down with tea.

Either he'd forgotten her married surname or, more likely, she'd continued to use her maiden name at St

Martin's and the kids had never known she was Mrs Pennington. I decided to keep the fact that Miss Gibbs was now Mrs Assistant Chief Constable for another time. 'What did you think when you heard Trudy Hepburn had been murdered?'

He wiped his plate with a chunk of pork. 'Far out. Who'd want to kill *her*. She was pathetic.'

'What about the girl who did it?'

'Never noticed her.'

'You must have talked about it afterwards. Was anyone else in the frame? One of the other kids?'

'No, none of the others would have sorted Heartburn after . . .' He stopped.

'After?' I prompted.

'Nothing.' The old aggressive Terry materialized. 'What's it got to do with you anyhow?'

'A client asked me to look into the case.'

'An amateur like you shouldn't be sticking her nose in a murder case. Leave it to us professionals.'

'Us professionals have been off the case for the past twenty years, Terry.' I leant across the table and coaxed. 'Come on, talk. I'm all that's standing between you and a night in the beach shelter remember.'

'Nothing. There's nothing. Lay off, Smithie.'

The expression in his eyes was hard to read for once. Embarrassment was there. But there was something else. For a second, I could have sworn he was terrified.

13

Three freaky things hit me when I reached Vetch's offices the following morning. The front door was unlocked, the air inside was a few degrees above Siberian winter and Jan had actually got into work early when there was no one who mattered (in her opinion) to clock her time-keeping.

Today the outfit of choice was dominatrix vampire: black polo-neck sweater, chain jewellery, a black leather metal-studded mini-skirt, black knitted tights and black patent thigh-high boots with spike heels. I got the full effect because she was perched on the front edge of her desk painting her talons dark green.

'What d'you reckon to this shade? It's called Poison Ivy.'

'It could have been brewed for you.'

The basement door at the far end of the reception area creaked open and a stocky bloke in blue overalls carrying a huge metal toolbox came through. He was followed by a younger, thinner version of himself.

'I've done the best I can, Jan love, but I reckon they stopped making that boiler the year the *Titanic* sailed.'

My heart gave a little hop and skip. A plumber. A real live plumber.

'Thanks for trying, Uncle Walter.'

'No problem, love. This the lady who's in charge?'

'No, she just thinks she is.'

'Cheers, Jan. I'm very grateful Mr . . . ?'

'Just call me Walter.'

'You have made me a very happy woman, Walter. And probably saved this parrot's life.' I swung the cage on to

Jan's desk. Tallulah fluffed, sneezed and launched into a half-hearted chorus from *South Pacific.*

Young and Thin sniggered. His eyes were fixed on Jan. He looked like a lovesick ferret.

'You've heat and hot water.' Walter informed me. 'But this whole system needs an overhaul.' As confirmation, the reception radiator rattled and banged so hard it nearly ripped itself off the wall. 'You need new valves on the rads and a couple of new bits on the boiler. I haven't got them but I've rung a mate who thinks he's got some in his salvage scrap. He'll bring them round later if he can get them cleaned up. Let's be having you, Eric.' The ferret was in a world of his own. 'Eric!'

He jumped. 'Yeah, OK. Coming, Dad. See you then, Jan.'

'See ya.' Not bothering to look up, Jan started on the second coat of polish.

I parked my bum on the radiator and asked how long she and Eric had been an item.

'We aren't. I've told him, it will never work.'

'How come?'

Jan swung round to stare at me. 'Well, I'm gonna be famous, aren't I? It never works. You see it all the time. Some girl is going out with an ordinary bloke from a factory or something and then she gets famous. What does she do? Dump him so she can pull an actor or a footballer. I said to Eric, it's best we don't get it together, that way you won't get hurt when I have to dump you.'

Jan was convinced she would be famous one day. Quite how she was going to achieve this none of us knew, since she had no discernible talent for anything, so far as we could see.

'You're all heart, Jan.'

'I know.' Trying not to smudge her nails, she opened the cage. Tallulah waddled out and nibbled at a stapler. 'This bird's bald. I'm gonna report you to the RSPCA.'

'No, she's not. Not very,' I amended. The featherless patches did seem to be speading.

‘Poor birdie.’ Jan stroked the bald head with one talon. I’d noticed before that she seemed fonder of dumb creatures than humans. ‘Don’t you worry, I’ll stop nasty Grace from torturing you.’

It occurred to me I’d found a place to dump the feathered pest. I’d already enjoyed a relatively peaceful night – broken only by the occasional scream of ‘Shut up, you noisy sod’ – by allowing Terry to occupy the spare cupboard again on condition he slept with the light on and shared space with the bird.

‘When can I have me case?’ Jan asked.

‘What case?’

‘You said I could work on cases when you rang me.’

‘No, I didn’t.’ Did I?

Compromise was called for if I was going to get her to petsit. ‘Let me get some neighbourhood survey files sorted, then you can give one a go.’

‘Knew you did.’ She flounced back to her chair with a clash of jewellery, settled herself comfortably with her boots crossed on the desk and took out a bar of chocolate.

‘The Neighbourhood Survey’ was a new service that Annie had set up a few months ago. The idea was you commissioned someone to snoop around the street where you were planning to buy your new home and dig up any dirt. It was a steady income and the clients seemed happy with their glitzy reports in specially designed binders and a lot of words inside that basically just said no one in sniffing distance keeps pigs, the neighbours aren’t bunny boilers and the heavy-metal fan hasn’t been seen since he went for a motorbike ride with those nice boys with tattoos six years ago.

I made up a file for a property on the newish estate out by the golf club and told Jan what she was to look out for and – more specifically – what she wasn’t to do. ‘You don’t ask the neighbours whether anyone pongs or sorts out rows over parking spaces with the aid of a chain-saw. Be subtle.’

‘I *know*. I’ve watched you lot do it, haven’t I?’ Jan

shrugged on a puffa jacket that barely covered her belt-skirt. 'I'm moving out now. You want to log my exit time so you can despatch back-up if I fail to make contact in my Estimated Return Zone?'

'You're walking around the North Bay Estate, not parachuting into Columbia. Now push off.'

Once she'd gone, I took the 'to do' list from the pink plastic file and considered my next move. I still needed to talk to Alison's parents. I hadn't got very far finding out about the 'forensic evidence' that had convicted Alison. I hesitated at item number five. I'd certainly located Gina Gibbs, but we'd hardly exchanged confidences on her years with the late, and apparently totally unlamented, Trudy Hepburn. I stuck a question mark against that item, rang the Jacksons' house and left a message on their answering machine asking if they had a home number for the Penningtons.

The next stop was a website Annie had recommended. When I'd emailed that damn WAP phone of hers to ask how I could locate past pupils at St Martin's Comp, she'd pointed me in the direction of Classbuddies, a site listing every school in the country, where you could locate all those with whom you'd shared double-maths and detention, providing they'd signed up for the service. I duly signed up as a past pupil of St Martin's Comp. (One of the joys of being called 'Smith' is there's always one or more in every class and who the heck remembers the name of everyone they went to school with?). I calculated the year Alison would have left and entered that as my own leaving year.

There were thirty pupils listed for that year. Some were just names but others had added little CVs of their life after St Martin's. A large number of ex-pupils seemed to have emigrated to the other side of the world. (Seatoun can have that effect on you).

There were none of the names that Gillian Anderson had mentioned, but I estimated there would have been about a hundred pupils in the year, so access to one third wasn't bad; a lot were probably still in contact with some of the non-registered ones. More experimentation got me another list of pupils who'd left in the year before Alison, and then the year after her. By the time I'd finished I had near enough a hundred names. With probably several hundred more waiting to be called up if I went through every year that had been at St Martin's at the time of the murder. I knew I was about to canoe into one of those mind-numbing, bum-numbing canyons of tedious research that form the basis of most investigation work.

'Crap time,' I informed Tallulah who was perched on the in-tray.

She took it as an instruction, and then launched herself into the air. It was a shock. I'd got so used to her walking I'd forgotten she could fly. So had she apparently. She crash-landed on the stairs. With a squawk of annoyance she let go a whole thesaurus of expletives then started pulling herself up the treads, using her beak and claws. There was nowhere she could go on the upper landings so I left her to it.

Wiping up the souvenir she'd left behind, I drafted an email for all the potential sources of information. After a few over-long efforts, I settled on:

> Hi, I'm a private investigator looking into the murder of Trudy Hepburn by Alison Wynne-Ellis. Do you remember Alison or Trudy? What were your impressions of them? Did you ever hear anything in school that explained why Alison did it? Did you hear anything that might mean Alison wasn't guilty? Did anything happen at the school around that time that struck you as strange or odd? Who was Alison's boyfriend?

By the time I'd typed it out ninety-seven times, the back of my neck was stiff and my shoulder blades were aching from being held in an unaccustomed position for so long. Way above my head a ghostly, echoing voice telling me there was nothing like a dame was swirling around the stairwell.

I needed a break. A free cappuccino at Pepi's with a large custard slice appealed. Should I go and round up the parrot? Or sneak out and hope she wouldn't notice? I looked up. A small bald head was poking through the bannister rails. Yep, she'd notice. I reached under the desk to snag her travel cage and go bird wrangling. The phone trilled in my ear making me jump. With my head still under the desk I located the receiver and pulled it down to ear level. 'Vetch's Investigations.'

'Keep your nose out of the Wynne-Ellis case, bitch, or you'll be dealt with.'

14

I dialled one-four-seven-one. The robotic female confirmed I'd received a call a minute ago and that the caller had withheld their number.

I'll bet they did. The voice had been hoarse and muffled, I couldn't even be sure whether it was male or female. How many people knew I was investigating the case? About ninety-seven at the last count, I realized, not to mention the people I'd spoken to. I'd been using the office email address which contained the name of the business. It didn't mention we were in Seatoun but a quick call to Directory Enquiries would have located us.

Looking on the bright side, it suggested there was something to find out. Looking on the not-so-bright side, somebody with acute laryngitis wanted to thump me.

The phone rang again. I whipped it up ready with a few zippy responses to the next batch of threats. It was Kathy Jackson with the Penningtons' telephone number. It looked like a London exchange to me. Kathy confirmed it was. 'They decided not to move back down here. You don't really need to live in the county if you're an assistant chief constable. They have large cars and drivers to rush them up and down motorways to important meetings. Look, I must go, Max breaks up early today, half-term.'

I rang Frosty Georgie immediately. Once more it was an answering service. I left a message asking if she'd mind ringing me back.

Feeling the virtuous glow of one who has achieved a reasonable morning's work, I decided I'd really earned that custard slice. I'd been discarding layers as I emailed. Now I struggled into the sweaters, coat and Peruvian cap again and dived under the desk once more for Tallulah's cage.

This time the front door slammed open, crashing back into the wall. I straightened up to find a stranger striding into the reception toting a large canvas bag. At the same moment the hall was rocked by a series of loud explosions. It took me a moment to separate the two incidents and realize that the bangs were coming from the hall radiator. I could hear the ones on the upper floors joining in in a kind of overture to lousy plumbing.

'Those valves need sorting,' my visitor said. 'Should take a look at the boiler too.'

I'd forgotten Walter's mate. 'Hang on a minute.'

Locking the front door, I led him down to the basement. I saw him take in the bizarre decoration. During a short-lived attempt to rent it out, the tenant had painted scenes of ghosts, ghoulies and all things undead on the walls.

'We lease it out to the Ladies' Knitting and Embroidery Circle; satanic rituals sub-division.' I opened a side door. 'This is the boiler.'

'So it is.'

We both stood listening to the huge cylinder sounding like an asthmatic warthog. 'Do you want to see the radiators as well?'

'Why not?'

We returned to the hall and I took the keys from the desk, opening up Vetch's office so he could see the double radiators. This room had been the residents' lounge during the time Grannie Vetch had run the place as a boarding house, and it was larger and warmer than the others. 'There's a couple more rooms out back, but we don't use them, so they're aren't heated.'

'OK.'

We went up to the first floor and I opened up the two offices that were in use and pointed out the rooms that weren't. On our way up the second flight we passed

Tallulah, who had resumed her mountaineering and was beaking and clawing it up the carpet.

'Another tenant?' the plumber enquired.

'Monk's tottie. This is my office.'

I gave him a quick glimpse of the bare boards and eclectic collection of junk yard salvage with its single radiator before unlocking Annie's beautifully decorated and furnished domain opposite – with its large notice on the phone: 'Grace – don't try to make calls on this phone. It's programmed to deliver ten thousand volts.'

'There's a bathroom at the end of the landing.' I let him take in the glory of the original copper piping and free-standing bath. 'And a room that we don't use. Although I guess it's on the same heating circuit or whatever you call it.'

'I see.'

We were interrupted by a loud and sustained ringing on the front door, followed by several loud rat-tats.

'I'd better get that.'

On my way down I scooped up Tallulah and stuck her in the travel cage. The delay caused the visitor to deliver another assault on the door. When I finally got it open, he was just climbing back into a white van parked at the kerb. The side was inscribed: 'Randall & Co. Plumbers and Central Heating Engineers'.

'Got the parts for your system, love.'

'Sorry?'

'You are the lady Walter phoned me about?'

I swung back. My other visitor was lounging against the stairpost with his hands thrust in his pockets. The bag was resting at his feet.

'You said you were the plumber!'

'No, I didn't.'

I tried to remember. OK, so he hadn't actually *said* he was a plumber but . . . 'What did you think I was showing you the boiler and radiators for?'

'For all I knew it might be your idea of foreplay. It seemed rude to interrupt you.'

His face was dead-pan. I desperately wanted to come back with some witty retort, but the best I could manage was, 'Well, now I've introduced you to every valve in the place, maybe you could introduce yourself to me?'

He levered himself off the bannisters with one shoulder and gave a small bow. 'D. O'Hara at your service. I hear you've been wanting a word.'

The other police constable who'd discovered Trudy's body. Rosie Wilmott must have tracked him down. I'd expected a phone call, rather than the man in person.

The plumber was still hovering. I pointed him towards the basement door. 'The boiler's down there.'

'I could show you if you like?' Declan O'Hara offered. There still wasn't so much as a twitch on the corners of his mouth.

'I'll find it, mate.' Hauling two heavy bags, the plumber clanked his way into the depths.

O'Hara and I stared at each other. 'I appreciate you coming in Mr O'Hara—'

'Call me O'Hara, everyone does. And you'd be?'

'Grace Smith. A lot of people call me Smithie. I'd rather you didn't. Didn't Rosie tell you my name?'

'All I heard was an investigator was digging into the old Wynne-Ellis case. That would be you, would it?'

'Yes. Can we fix up a time to talk?'

'How about now? Or are you going out?'

'I was going for a coffee. But I can't leave the plumber alone in the building.'

That problem was solved by the reappearance of the receptionist from hell. I left Tallulah with her and headed round to Pepi's with O'Hara striding easily beside me. He made no attempt at conversation. We managed to bag a seat by the window where I could rub a porthole in the condensation on the glass and watch the sea if I pressed my cheek to the window and craned around at an angle.

O'Hara stretched his legs under the table, leant back and watched me struggling out of the layers of clothing again. When I was finally back in just the trousers and flannel shirt, he said, 'Pity. I kind of liked the hat. I knew a duchess once who always wore a hat like that.'

At a charitable estimate, if he'd been in his early twenties when that newspaper picture was taken, he had to be in his mid-forties now. He carried his years well on one of those tall, rangy frames that didn't hold any extra fat. His face was thin with a narrow nose, but his mouth was wide enough to stop any suggestion of meanness. The eyes that had looked near enough black in the old photo were actually navy-blue and contrasted with his skin, which was lightly tanned. The dark hair had gone iron grey but it didn't add age, just interest. If I hadn't known better, I'd have guessed him to be in his thirties.

I expected him to ask me questions. But he just sat, apparently unbothered by my sizing him up.

'Do you live locally?'

'No.'

That was it? No? 'Why *did* you come?'

'Because there was something off-kilter about that case.'

'Really!' Maybe this was my lucky break. 'What?'

'I haven't the faintest idea.'

We were interrupted by the delivery of the coffees and Shane's duet with Elvis, as they both crooned that that Hound Dog weren't no friend of theirs.

O'Hara added sugar to his cup. 'What's your interest in the case?'

'Did you know Alison had a daughter? While she was on remand?'

'There were rumours. Judge sat on them, I think. Protecting a minor, not prejudicing the case, that kind of thing. She your client?'

'She wants me to prove her mum was innocent. Do you think I can?'

'Well, you seem sharp enough. Except when it comes to plumbing. And possibly pet care.'

'The parrot suffers from stress. And I wasn't asking if you thought I was bright enough . . .' I stopped, seeing the gleam in the navy-blue eyes. 'Tell me about the night of the murder. What can you remember?'

'That night?' Resting his elbows on the table, he stared through the steam porthole, then refocused on me and repeated, 'That night. All right, I need you to picture the scene. It's nine-thirty on an April evening. Thirty minutes to the end of the shift. A bloody boring shift so far. Now in the patrol car we have the driver, one of the brightest, handsomest, most charming officers ever stationed in this area. And in the passenger seat we have Clever Clive; graduate entry officer and one of the biggest pains in the arse ever stationed in this area. Clive has the serious hump; there's been too much routine work for him. Anything half decent and CID swarm all over it. Strangely enough, they don't invite Clive to share his insights. Clive's been bitching it for the entire shift and the handsome and charming driver is just about ready to stick it to him in the most painful place he can think of. So the patrol car swings out the back of the Downs Estate and takes a turn up Millrun Lane.'

'Why?' I interrupted the handsome and charming one. 'I mean, there's not much up there apart from a few cottages.'

'Some break-ins in the local farms recently; theft and arson mostly. Anyway, the car passes this kid walking the other way, towards the estate. Now, as you rightly point out, duchy, there's not much along that road to be walking *from*. But the really odd thing is that most everybody, when walking past a big white car with a big blue light on the top, either looks at the car – or looks away, as if hoping not to get noticed. But this kid just doesn't react at all. Just walks. One foot in front of the other: plod-plod-plod. So there's a row in the car. The driver, being not only handsome and charming, but also perceptive, wants to turn round and take another look. Clever Clive, however, is cheesed off with teenage vandals. It's only thirty minutes to clocking off and he doesn't fancy writing up the paperwork. Then, while they're having a frank and fearless exchange of views, the call comes through; some female's dialled nine-nine-nine, says she wants to report a murder at Abbot's Cottage. It's a few hundred yards from the patrol car's position. No danger that anyone was going to get there before Clever Clive. He was practically salivating at the thought of his very own murder case.'

'Surely he must have realized it would go straight to CID?'

'I think you under-estimate the power of Clive's ability to delude himself. He took charge as soon as the car pulled in. The house-mate, Gina Gibbs—'

'I've met Gina. Now Mrs Clever Clive.'

'Yes indeed. Married within four months of setting eyes on each other. Ain't love grand? Anyway, at the moment they *did* set eyes on each other – which was on the patio at the back incidentally – Clive clasped her to his manly bosom and assured her all would be well.'

'Did she show any sign of needing his manly bosom?'

'No. A very cool customer. And I was speaking figuratively about the clasping. Clive was way too cute to take a lunge at an attractive blonde.'

'She wasn't hysterical? In shock?'

'No. She'd even had the presence of mind to use her scarf to lift the telephone receiver to avoid smudging fingerprints.'

'Were there any?'

'Only the ones you'd expect. But back to that night. The incident was called in as a suspicious death. And that was when the major row started. Clever Clive wanted to stay and secure the crime scene.'

'Which is what you should have done.'

'But there was the girl, you see. The girl who was walking away from the crime scene, whose reactions weren't right, and would soon be lost amongst the streets of the Downs Estate. Not to mention months of Clive lecturing on "the correct procedure". So in the end, only Clive stayed to secure the scene and comfort the ice maiden.'

'While you went after Alison.'

Custard slices were delivered with a pelvis-gyrating chorus of 'Great Balls of Fire'. '*Goodness gracious* . . . more coffees?'

O'Hara asked if he could get a lager.

'Sure you can, mate. Pub's just along the promenade.'

O'Hara settled for bottled water.

'Alison,' I prompted. 'You picked her up before she reached the estate?'

'Didn't even react when the car pulled in front of her. Just kept staring. Straight ahead.'

'Was *she* in shock?'

'Defence tried to make out she was. I don't know. She was "contained" is the best description. Her clothes were soaked in blood.'

'Didn't you notice that when you drove past her?'

'No street lighting out that way and she was wearing dark clothing, black jacket and skirt. She was clutching the knife. And before you ask, that wasn't easy to see from the car either. She was holding it the opposite side to the road and the skirt was a long loose one; the knife was lost in the folds.'

'Did she say anything?'

'"She's dead. It's my fault." It was never admitted into evidence. No witnesses. And it was before the caution.'

'Did she say why she'd done it?'

'Never said another thing about the case, far as I know. Listened to the caution and then stood there calm as you please, like she was waiting for a bus, until they sent another car up to collect her.'

'You didn't take her in yourself?'

'Teenage girl, alone in car . . .' He shrugged and took a swig of the water.

I recalled Rosie's comment that he'd often got into trouble for thinking with his todger. 'Did you sit in on the interviews?'

'No. The super at the time – Frank Broughton – snapped it up.'

'Did you hear anything about the investigation?'

'Mostly that there wasn't much to investigate. Victim's blood all over Alison; only Alison's prints on the knife; her footprints in the blood; fingerprints throughout the cottage. No other suspects.'

'I'm not saying she wasn't *there*. But what if she got to the cottage and found Trudy dead or dying?'

'And didn't ring for help?'

'She could have been in shock. You said yourself she was acting weird when you drove past. How long had Trudy been dead?'

'No more than thirty minutes before she was found, the pathologist said.'

'So, time for someone else to slip out before Alison arrived. Did the knife belong to Alison or Trudy?'

'Neither. Ms Gibbs and Mrs Wynne-Ellis both failed to identify it.'

'So somebody else could have brought it to the cottage.'

'So could Alison.' He laced his fingers together and stared straight into my eyes with those deep, navy-blue irises. 'Not what you want to hear, is it, duchess?'

Of course it wasn't what I wanted to hear. But more to the point. 'What the hell did you say the case was out of kilter for? Sounds to me like you'd made up your mind Alison did it before you'd even found the damn body!'

'It was the girl, Alison. Have you ever looked into someone's eyes and seen they're in hell?'

'Well, she'd either just found her teacher stabbed, or she'd done the stabbing. Either way, she's going to be pretty shook up, unless she's a complete psychopath.'

'No, I'm not talking about shock. This was somebody who'd been inside that hell for a lot longer than thirty minutes.' He took a fork from his plate and set it on the table surface. And then carefully balanced a knife on the curved section of the handle. It rocked slightly, like a see-saw, and then hung horizontal. 'That's how a case should be. Perfectly balanced: crime on one side.' He touched the blade. 'Evidence on the other.' He tapped the handle. 'But the Wynne-Ellis case never felt like that. It was light on this side.' He indicated the handle end.

'They missed some evidence?'

'I'd say so.'

'Evidence that would convict Alison? Or clear her?'

'That's what we have to find out, isn't it?'

'*We?*'

'Definitely – partner.'

'I don't need a partner.'

'You don't think you're going to solve this case without me, do you?'

'As a matter of fact, yes I do.'

'Well you may be right, duchy. But either way, I'm going to be looking into this case. I figured it would be cosier if we rubbed along together?'

'Why are you looking into it?'

'Private reasons.' His tone was dismissive.

'You mean I shouldn't bother my pretty little head about it?'

'Don't get all defensive on me, duchy. I've a hunch we'll be good together.'

15

When I arrived back at the office, the radiators had stopped making like a percussion band. Unfortunately they'd also stopped making like a heating system. The temperature had dropped far enough for Jan to be wearing her puffa jacket as she lounged in front of the computer using one finger to nudge the keyboard.

'Has the boiler packed up again?'

'Uncle Unwin turned it off while he fixes the radiators.'

'Is your entire family in plumbing?'

'He's not a real uncle. I call all my mum's friends uncle. There aren't half some funny emails on here.'

I looked over her shoulder. It was a reply to my generalized trawl of the ex-pupils of St Martin's Comp. 'That's for me. Can I take a look?'

'Yeah, if you like.'

Jan continued to lounge, flicking her way through the inbox. I carried a visitors' chair over and set it down next to her. Sixteen people had already responded to my pleas for information on Alison/Trudy. It was really encouraging. Until I read the first one.

This is a wind-up isn't it Mickie. I know it's you.

The next one read:

Dear Vetch's Investigations, my name is Julian Selleck. I am currently working as a credit controller in Norfolk but becoming a private detective has always been an ambition of mine. Perhaps you would consider giving me a trial? I think I would make an excellent investigator because I have always been interested in working with people and, as I expect you already know, Selleck is the name of the actor who played Magnum PI.

There were sixteen like that; tributes to years of enforced education at St Martin's.

Uncle Unwin's efforts with the radiators were echoing around the heating system like a poltergeist trapped in the pipes. And as counterpoint a small voice was singing about raindrops on roses. It was coming from above our heads. Looking up, I found Tallulah pacing down the bannister rail. She looked . . .

'What the hell have you done to the parrot?'

'I picked up some of me old dolls' clothes when I was out on me case. I cut slits for her wings. Neat, eh?'

Neat wasn't how I'd have described it. Tallulah was now wearing a red and blue padded jacket with a big gold 'S' on the chest. And a matching peaked cap in shiny, royal-blue polyester that tied under her chin.

'She looks daft. And she can't fly with that lot on.'

'She can't fly anyway. She's got no feathers. Have you ever seen a plucked chicken flying?'

'No. But that's probably because the only ones I've ever seen are deep frozen and have a plastic bag full of giblets stuffed up their jacksies. Which reminds me, I found this great recipe for roast parrot. It's a delicacy in New Guinea.'

It had the effect I was hoping for. Lifting Tallulah off the bannister, Jan assured the partially feathered bundle that she wasn't to worry. 'I won't let nasty Gracie take you. You can come home with me.'

'There's a bigger cage at my place.'

'I'll send Eric round in the van for it.'

After a night free of parrots or homeless Roscos, I returned to Vetch's on Saturday morning and wallowed in a huge bath full of free hot water before checking out the emails again. The St Martin's trawl had hauled in another bunch of weirdos (including one who had a theory that Alison was being controlled by voices from the Andromeda Galaxy at the time – apparently they frequently told him to take ladies underwear from laundrettes). There was one possible contact who sounded as if it might lead somewhere other than the door marked 'Fruitcake Academy': 'RE YOUR REQUEST FOR INFO ON ALISON WYNNE-ELLIS AND MISS HEPBURN. I THINK I MIGHT KNOW SOMETHING THAT MOST PEOPLE DON'T KNOW.'

The 'From' line said it had been sent by Betterman@Adami .com. The Classbuddies website didn't list email addresses; you had to send all messages via their site initially so I couldn't tell who this response had come from.

I sent back: 'WHO ARE YOU? WHERE ARE YOU BASED?'

In my Miss Efficiency mode I rang the Penningtons' number again. Georgie answered. And it was clear from the tone of her voice that she'd been expecting someone else to be on the other end. Hard luck, lady. Now pretend to be out.

'I was hoping to have another chat with you about the Wynne-Ellis case.'

'I thought I'd explained, Miss Smith, that I don't think it's a good idea to rake over that particular business.'

'Indeed you did. However, you didn't mention that you'd been living with Trudy. Or that you were the one that found her body.'

'It's not something I care to dwell on.'

If she'd had that prissy manner of speaking when she'd taught at St Martin's, the kids would have taken the mick in spades. I'd have bet that Georgie's tones had become a little posher with each new rank that Clever Clive achieved. 'I'd really like to speak to you about those days. You never know, you might remember something now that hadn't seemed important at the time. If Alison was innocent, you'd surely want to help clear her name?'

I let the 'how is it going to look if the wife of the Chief

Constable in Waiting can't be bothered to co-operate in investigating a miscarriage of justice' hang in the air.

Georgie got the message. 'Very well. I really can't imagine I have anything to contribute but if you insist . . .'

'I could come up to town this evening?'

'This evening Clive and I are attending a charity ball at The Dorchester in aid of landmine charities.'

Of course they were. All that brown-nosing doesn't come cheap. 'Tomorrow?'

'I suppose I could accommodate that. Do you have our address?'

We fixed a time and I rang off. In the time that had taken, three more emails had arrived. None for me. And none from Annie.

I sent her: 'WHAT'S THE MATTER, HAVE YOU RUN OUT OF SCENERY TO GLOAT ABOUT?'

I wrapped things up at the office, intending to head down to Pepi's for a quick lunch and then check out the murder scene again. I wanted to walk the route between Alison's home and Trudy's cottage.

As a last task I checked the mailbox. Since the husband of a former client had reciprocated our interest in him via flammable liquid and a match through the letterbox, Vetch's post is held in a big fire-proof container fixed to the inside of the door. There was the usual collection of junk mail in there, plus a couple of letters for Vetch and Annie marked 'private', what looked like some kind of credit check from a French *Banque* for the other two and a small, fat, brown padded envelope addressed to 'Vetch's'.

I ripped and tipped at the same time. I was aware of a bang and a brilliant flash immediately. A nanosecond later my shocked senses picked up other sensations. The smell of burning tickling my nose. Pain and wetness in my hands.

I looked down. Blood was pouring from my fingers and dripping to the floor.

16

Snivelling on the floor, I counted fingers. Four on each hand, plus two thumbs. The numbed brain cells debated this total for a moment before sending back the message 'all present and correct'. Anger started to replace nausea and shock. Try to blow me up, would you, you rotten bastards? Then another thought kicked in: how did I know the package was for me? It could have been for any of us.

The thing was lying under the desk where I'd flung it in panic. Crawling across, I left red handprints on the tiles. The envelope was lightly charred at the open end and soaked in blood, which it was sucking up from the pool it was sitting in. There was something else caught against the leg of the desk.

I nudged it cautiously with a ruler. It slowly uncoiled. It was one of those labels designed for use in the freezer – the sort that don't smear if they get wet. Which is why the printed message on it hadn't been affected by the blood: 'THIS IS YOUR LAST WARNING, BITCH. KEEP YOUR NOSE OUT OF THE TEACHER'S BUSINESS.'

Yep. It was definitely for me.

I decided to stick to my original plan to check out the murder site again. The 'bomb' had turned out to be a kind of super party-popper that was triggered by a piece of tape attached to the inside of the envelope. The blood had been contained in a small plastic bag that had ripped when I opened the envelope.

I wanted to prove to my sub-conscious that I wasn't the kind of girl who can be intimidated by a party-popper. (My sub-conscious has long known I'm a rotten liar.) Leaving the car parked up near the Wynne-Ellises' old house in Hinton Road, I set out to walk to Abbot's Cottage. Before I'd got to the end of Hinton Road, I'd confirmed the sub-conscious's opinion of my nerves. Each time I passed a tall hedge or concealed entrance where someone could be hiding, I found my stomach tensing. Ideally I'd have preferred to be toting a large axe or an exceptionally heavy crowbar – but I'd settled for the big pink plastic file. It made me feel professional. I was a kick-ass PI on a case.

It took just over thirty minutes to walk to Abbot's Cottage. O'Hara was leaning against the fencing on the opposite side of the lane.

Once again, he stayed silent, forcing me to open the conversation.

'What are you doing here?'

'Just checking out a few things. You?'

'Same here.'

I just wished I could think *what* to check. I stared at the thick cottage walls, willing them to give up some kind of clue. Out of the corner of my eye I could see O'Hara watching me with a half-smile on his lips. What was so funny, buster? To prove how professional I could be, I eased a sheet of paper from the folder and scribbled notes.

'Have you learnt anything new?' I asked him casually.

'Fly fishing last year; tap dancing this.'

'OK, don't share information. I guess I'm managing fine without your input. Someone just tried to warn me off the case with a letter bomb.' (All right – a party popper bomb.)

O'Hara nodded. 'Had a poisonous snake slipped in my bed once by a couple of bad dudes.'

'Yeah? Well, a while back someone tied me up and tried to burn me to death.'

'Imagine a metal box . . . this size . . .' He held his hands a few feet apart. 'No air holes. Locked tight. Dropped in forty feet of water . . .'

'Are you telling me you got out of that?'

'Me? God no. Shouldn't think anyone could.'

'Then why did you . . . ?' I caught the glint in his eye. 'Right. So if you haven't learnt anything new, what about remembering something old? Like the night you discovered the body?'

'Technically speaking, Gina Gibbs discovered it.'

'I'm seeing to her tomorrow. Pennington's an assistant chief constable now, but he's planning to bag the chief constable's job.' I wanted to show off my inside knowledge of local police politics. 'Was there any sign of a break-in at the cottage?'

'Nope.'

'What about the body. Where was it?'

'Kitchen. It was lying half through the door into the hall.'

'Which half?'

'Top.'

'So she was probably heading out of the room when she fell?'

'Probably. She had cuts everywhere. Post-mortem listed twenty-two. Most fairly superficial. Along her arms.'

He'd started to walk back towards Seatoun. I tagged along beside him.

'The pathologist pegged the first strike as going in here . . .' He touched a spot high on the left side of his chest.

'So she was facing her attacker, who was right-handed, and she wasn't expecting the blow.'

'That's the way they read it, duchy. It wasn't deep. She put her arms up and starts backing away, taking a whole load of superficial blows on her forearms. Then they think she turned round to try to run away. Maybe Alison – or whoever – had stopped lashing out for a moment. Anyway, she doesn't make it. Next couple of blows go into her back, still quite high, they scored the shoulder blade. And then the next blow . . . here . . .' He touched his back. 'Into the liver. The killer twisted the blade. Big wound, heavy blood loss. They reckon that was the one that killed her.'

'Then couldn't Alison have arrived at the cottage, found Trudy and tried to help her? That would explain why she was covered in Trudy's blood. And why she thought it was her fault when she couldn't save her.'

'It wouldn't explain why she failed to dial nine-nine-nine.'

'Deep shock.'

'For twenty years? That shock isn't so much deep, as subterranean.'

'Do you have to be so damn negative?'

'Heh, don't blame me if you can't find the happy-ever-after ending.'

I picked up the pace. He strode easily, the heavy canvas bag slung over one shoulder. Back at Hinton Road, I unlocked my car, climbed into the driver's seat and re-locked the door. Leaning on the pink folder, I wrote up my notes. From the corner of my eye I could see O'Hara lounging against the gate-post of the Wynne-Ellises' old house writing in a small notebook. Ignoring him, I threw the pink folder on to the back seat and turned on the ignition. He tapped on the kerbside window.

'Can I cadge a lift?'

My pride said no. My head said he might have more information on Alison's case, despite his off-hand manner. I didn't know what to make of it – or him. I flicked the lock off.

He folded himself into the passenger seat, adjusting it to accommodate his longer legs, and heaved the bag into the back. It dislodged something, which fell to the floor with a soft flutter. Twisting around, O'Hara scrabbled up the Quixsilver Autos brochure and tucked the loose papers back into their flap.

'Orlando Roles,' he read from the business card. 'Relative of the better-known Billy?'

'Is he? Better known?'

'Used to be years back. Better known to the police computers.'

'He's got a record?'

'Billy was way too savvy. Nothing stuck to Billy. They used to call him the Handyman. Whatever you wanted fixed, Billy was your man. Anything strictly illegal undertaken. A clean car stolen for a job. A hot one disposed of. Temporary storage for any weapons you might not want lying around your own place. Cash loans to induce a little amnesia in truck drivers, security guards, witnesses and the like.'

'Versatile guy.' I tried to tie up the picture O'Hara was drawing with the drunk I'd encountered at the used car lot – and failed. 'So, how come I never heard his name when I was in the job?'

'He retired, according to some accounts. Or the tide retreated and left Billy out to dry. Whichever you choose to believe, he's not been doing any fixing for the last ten years or so.'

'How do you know? You also being on the beach?'

'I still have contacts.'

'With the good guys or the bad?'

'Both.'

I told him I was surprised he didn't remember Orlando. 'According to the school, he was a shining example to any teenager going for a career as a troublemaker in those years.'

'One teenage git is much like another. You don't remember the names. Billy was a serious player. The kids were just minor irritations.' He indicated a turn. 'Hang a right here, will you, and drop me at the station.'

'Are you leaving?'

'Don't fret, I'll be back. I have to pick up some fresh clothes and my car. I came here straight from the boat.'

'Where'd you sail from?'

'Egypt.'

'Holiday?'

'No.' He opened the car door and unhooked the seat

belt, jumping out before I came to a stop. 'I'm going to check the timetable. Don't go away.'

The bag was still on the back seat. As soon as he'd disappeared into the waiting room, I leant over and casually tugged at the zip. It slid back a few inches. The black notebook was sitting on the top of a pile of clothes. With one eye on the station, I flicked the pages. They were all blank – apart from the first one. He'd written: 'I quite like her but it's a pity she's ditched the hat.'

I pushed it back quickly as O'Hara reappeared. 'There's a train in ten minutes so I'll say bye for now. Try not to miss me too much.'

He reached through the open front door to retrieve his bag. I caught the twinkle in those navy-blue orbs and knew he knew that I'd read the notebook. I also guessed he'd deliberately left the damn thing there as bait. Leaning over, I slammed the door a fraction of a millimetre from his fingers and hit the accelerator.

Pepi's was buzzing. I had to perch at a counter seat while Shane rustled up a bacon, egg and fried tomato triple-decker sandwich, and a comprehensive selection of Chuck Berry's greatest hits.

'Where's the parrot? . . . *Nadine* . . .'

'With her birdsitter. Just while I do some legwork,' I added hastily. Hopefully a period that would stretch to the point when Brother Monk reclaimed the feathered pest. I asked Shane when that would be exactly?

'Ah. There's been a slight hitch with the work on the monastery. The pool's sprung a leak.'

'Pool? You mean like a fish pond?'

'No. It's an indoor swimming pool. They've got a jacuzzi too. And a steam room and sauna. It's dead classy. You should go stay sometime.'

'Do they let females in?'

'Sure they do. They run all these courses. I've got one of the bruv's business cards somewhere.' He extracted a small square from the till drawer. 'Here you go.'

BROTHER LANCE
St Humphrey's Monastery
Personal Trainer for the Soul
Individual coaching to help you tone your spiritual muscles

I cut into the tower of fried bacon and runny egg and tomatoes. 'What's he do with Tallulah while he's working out them spiritual pecs?'

'They've got this ancient monk. The old boy's about a hundred and ten so he's not up to much, he just sits in his cell all day and night, and Tallulah keeps him company. They watch videos of films together. Musicals are their favourites.'

'Musicals are not their only favourites, I'd say.'

'Yeah . . . well . . .' Shane actually blushed. 'They found out the old boy was switching over to the Triple X-rated adult film channels.'

'How long is this pool refit business going to take?'

'Another week or so.' Before I could tell him that would be fine (or that it would be as soon as I broke the news to Jan), Shane pulled a twenty from the till. 'Will that cover the extra heating?'

My conscience woke up and started waving. Cadging a few meals was fine because Shane knew I was doing it; this felt like fraud. 'Look, Shane, I can't—'

He quickly slapped another tenner on top. 'Thirty do you?'

Very nicely, thank you.

I spent the rest of the afternoon working on other neighbourhood surveys and then dumped the car back at the flat before walking around to the office for another check of the emails. The bar told me one new message had been received. I clicked on the inbox. It was from Betterman: 'ASK THEM ABOUT 788.'

Ask who? I sent the question to Betterman and waited. After thirty minutes I guessed that was all I was getting for now. I closed us down for the night, reset the alarms, unbolted the front door and found myself gazing down on Hannah.

'Hi. You didn't phone, so I thought I'd come down.'

'There's not much to report yet, I'm afraid.'

Drawing the door closed behind me, I debated whether to head for my flat or Pepi's. I'm not keen on letting clients know where I live, but I figured I could handle Hannah in the unlikely event that she turned vicious. She seemed smaller than at our previous meeting. Glancing down, I found the reason below the swirling hem of the frock – the killer-heeled cream boots had been swapped for more practical flat lace-ups.

'Did you speak to . . . *her*?'

There was no point in trying to kid her. 'I did. She told me to get lost. Look, Hannah, I did warn you this might not work out the way you are hoping. I might end up proving she did it.'

'I know. But you'll still do it, won't you?'

'As long as you keep paying me to.'

17

We turned down my street, past the lit windows of the laundrette, convenience store and tool hire place. As we got nearer to my territory, I got a sudden sinking feeling. Something large and lumpy was huddled at the top of the metal staircase.

'Ish not fair . . . I've been a good husband . . . where's she going to gesh a better bloke than me?'

'Probably by turning over the nearest rock, now shift out of my way, Terry.'

It was impossible to get down the staircase without climbing over him. I tried tugging and just succeeded in leaving him at a 40-degree angle to the pavement.

'I love thosh kids. She's no right to shtop me sheeing my kidsh.' His angle was becoming acute. So was my irritation.

'Push off, will you? I want to get to the stairs.'

Terry struggled to his feet. Gravity and 40 per cent proof fought against him and won. Swaying, he started to topple backwards. He snatched out at the nearest thing. Which happened to be my arm. I could feel myself being pulled off balance. Out of the corner of my eye I saw Hannah reach forward to help. I tried to shout a warning to her. Terry was twice her weight and he had momentum on his side. It was too late. Just before we all pitched into the basement, I heard a car back-fire and felt something brush my cheek.

Terry went down the iron treads head-first. Hannah and I were on top of him. It was like riding a fifteen-stone snowboard. We ended up in a heap on the basement stones. I took stock as we untangled ourselves. An elbow and the back of one calf were throbbing after taking glancing blows from the railings during our toboggan ride. Something wet was dribbling down my cheek. I wiped it away and my fingers came away holding a small splinter of brick. Which was strange because my face had been buried in Terry's chest during the trip. I held it out to say something to Hannah and found her face had taken on a two-toned hue, one pale, the other dark, in the unlit basement, her eye glinting from the shadowed side. It took a while longer to realize – blood was pouring down the right side of her head.

Still slightly disorientated, I looked round for answers. And saw a paler circular patch in the grimy brickwork above the window. The sort of patch that would have been gouged by a projectile slamming into the wall. It hadn't been a car back-firing.

'Stay down! That was a shot!' Keeping low, I scooted to my front door and got it open, 'Come on. Keep down.'

Bent double, Hannah scuttled over and into the dark flat. Easing after her, I shut the door, keeping my hand on her arm. 'Stay on the floor for now.'

'Isn't there a light?' She was whispering. I realized I'd started to do the same. It was the effect of darkness, some remembered primeval instinct to stay hidden from night predators. In my case it was tempered with a strong desire to punch out the night predator's damn teeth.

'The switch is a few feet above your head,' I murmured back. 'I'm going to slip out again. Don't put it on until I'm clear of the basement, OK?'

'OK. But what if he's still out there?'

'Then I'll be coming back in real fast. But I doubt if he is. He'll have figured we're calling the police and he won't want to be hanging around when they turn up. As soon as I'm outside, close the door and don't open it again unless you're certain it's me. If I'm not back in five minutes, dial nine-nine-nine.'

'Shouldn't we do that anyway?'

'Maybe not such a great idea. I'll explain when I get back.'

I re-opened the door and dropped down on all fours. I kneaded into something soft and squashy. A low moan, carried on whisky-scented breath, was forced out of Terry as I planted hands, knees and feet in his stomach. Cautiously I went up the spiral iron staircase. The street was deserted. To the right the lights from the small parade of shops were spilling over the pavement. In front of them I'd be an easy target. But anyone running past would have been visible as well. If I'd been the shooter, I'd have headed left into the dark.

I trotted in a weaving pattern, checking out the possible hiding places, my ears straining for any sudden sounds. There was nothing. At the junction at the far end, I looked both ways. It was empty time on a Saturday night. None of the neighbours had reacted to the shot. Those who had heard it had probably put it down to a car back-firing, as I had.

Retracing my footsteps, I moved with more confidence. I was pretty certain the shooter had gone. Passing my own flat, I continued towards the seaward end of the road just in case. The grocery assistant was reading a newspaper. When I peered through the security-glass window of the empty shop, he raised bored eyes, identified me as a neighbour rather than a possible lager-pack nicker, and went back to the sports page. In the laundrette a dosser was sprawled over the bench in front of the driers, a hunched shoulder, the soles of worn trainers and the back of a red baseball cap pointed towards the street, a curtain of yellow hair providing a handy cushion on the wooden slats. A younger bloke with a baby in a pushchair was mesmerized by the sight of his laundry tumbling behind the soap-filled porthole of the washer. An old girl in the standard winter uniform of Seatoun pensioners – a shapeless nylon mac and peaked plastic rain-hat – was studying the instructions for obtaining soap from the wall dispenser. The tool hire shop had shut hours ago.

Having made the gesture, I returned to my flat. Once

inside the warmth and light, the stupidity of what I'd just done hit me. I'd actually charged down a dark street in pursuit of someone with a loaded gun! One bullet from a side street and . . . the world swirled in a grey mist. Quickly I sat down on the bed next to Hannah.

She swayed with the motion of my thumping on the mattress edge and bumped against me. Instead of righting herself, however, she continued to lean against my shoulder. She'd found one of my towels and had been holding it against her head. Her face was the colour of a dead fish's underbelly and her eyelids were fluttering. 'I feel . . . I f . . .'

I grabbed her and laid her down. Lifting her feet, I packed my pillows under them to raise her legs. She didn't actually pass out but her pulse was reedy and, despite looking fairly superficial to me, the head wound continued to pump gore at an impressive rate. It wasn't a bullet graze, she must have cracked it on the stair railings.

'I think you need to go to the hospital. Can you make it to the car?'

She nodded. With me hanging on around her waist with one arm, we made it outside to the basement area. I'd have stepped over Rosco again, but Hannah paused. 'Shouldn't you do something about him?'

'Probably. But my lobotomy reversal skills are very limited.'

Hannah refused to be urged over the comatose slob. 'He could get robbed.'

Which would serve the idiot right in my opinion. The temperature had risen far enough to make it unlikely he'd get hypothermia. But since Hannah wasn't moving, I reluctantly leant her against the wall, grabbed the big slob under his armpits and heaved him inside. I stuck him in the recovery position and threatened castration if he threw up in my living space.

The hospital's A & E department obeyed the rule for Saturday p.m. after the doctors' surgeries had closed; it was packed. We booked in and took our seat in line, sandwiched between a bloke who kept scratching and a mud-splattered rugby player with his two front teeth wrapped in his handkerchief.

Hannah had been very quiet in the car. I asked her if she was OK. 'Cracked skull aside, obviously?'

'I was wondering, who do you think did it? Is it something to do with *her*?'

'You do tend to make enemies in this job, Hannah. It could have been anyone with a grudge against the firm. Or no one at all. It could just be the way some kid is getting his jollies on a Saturday night.'

'Random, you mean?'

'Maybe.'

Or maybe not, given the earlier warnings I'd received, but I didn't want to worry Hannah more than necessary at present. My first impression, that she seemed smaller, had been reinforced by another sensation, that she also seemed younger and more vulnerable. It was a feeling strengthened by her clothing; underneath the cloak the cream temptress outfit had been ditched in favour of a patchwork pinafore dress over a white T-shirt. She looked like a kid on her way to kindergarten.

It dawned on me that our first meeting had been largely a big act. The whole thing had been set up to project a confidence veneer. Underneath she was just a very young girl who was scared of whatever nasty secrets were buried in her past. Which made my decision not to involve the police in our little adventure tonight the right choice.

'Listen,' I murmured, leaning away from Mr Itchy, 'I didn't ring nine-nine-nine after the shooting because police stations can be leaky places.' She turned a blank face to me. 'They'll ask for details,' I elaborated. 'About my case load. Anything juicy will somehow find its way to the press. And the daughter of a convicted murderer is a juice-jackpot. I know you said you didn't mind people knowing . . .'

'I wouldn't want it in the papers,' she said quickly. 'Not with pictures and everything.'

'That's what I figured. So as far as this lot are concerned, you tripped down the stairs, OK?'

I knew what I'd told Hannah was only part of the reason I was reluctant to involve the police in this – or any other – illegal incident. Apart from a few of the good guys like Jerry Jackson, a large section of the police still had a tendency to treat me like a nasty smell. I'd got into the habit of avoiding any contact with the official processes of the law.

Because it was a head injury, Hannah got bumped up the queue, but it still meant sitting around for a couple of hours while she was assessed. For some reason they decided to scan her and then she had to be X-rayed and cleaned up (I got a sticking plaster). I was waiting for Hannah to have her final dressing when a porter came through into reception to collect an empty wheelchair. There was something vaguely familiar about him, but I couldn't quite place it. He was heading through the swing doors into the main part of the hospital, when the receptionist shouted and waved an envelope.

'Mark, drop this into Oncology on your way, please.'

He came back with obvious bad grace, snatched it from her hand and retraced his route, using the wheelchair as a battering ram to open the doors.

Mark. Mark who? It was bugging me. Skirting a drunken kid, who was propped drooling below the counter, I asked the receptionist if she knew the porter's surname. 'I'm sure I used to know him.'

She frowned and said over her shoulder to a colleague, 'Nita, what's Mark's other name?'

'Boscombe.'

He was one of those kids in the picture of Trudy Hepburn's last school trip. 'Cheers.' Hannah emerged from the cubicle area as I charged past. 'Back in a tick, information to chase.'

I headed down the corridor he'd taken. It was empty, but

by asking everyone I passed if they'd seen a porter with a wheelchair, I managed to track him to a basement area that smelt of over-cooked potato and bleach. All the doors were locked and the corridors lit with the minimum lighting necessary, the space constricted by ranks of tall cages on wheels holding huge bags of dirty laundry waiting for pick-up.

I couldn't see Mark, but the squeak of an unoiled wheel coming closer was hopeful. Rounding a corner, I found him coming towards me, the wheelchair now transporting a green cylinder of oxygen.

'Mark Boscombe?'

'Who wants to know?'

'My name's Grace Smith. I'm a private investigator and—'

'Shit!'

The wheelchair crashed into my knees and the oxygen tank kept right on coming. I fell backwards hugging the weight to my chest and hit a laundry cage. It slid away from me on unlocked wheels and I sat down heavily with a jolt that ricocheted from my butt to my neck. Sprawled on my back, with the sound of all those laundry cages shunting into each other like falling dominoes, I watched Mark Boscombe sprinting into the darkness.

18

Scrambling out from under the oxygen canister and wheelchair, I ran after him.

He seized a laundry cage and slewed it around to block the corridor. He was slamming each one horizontally as he ran. Big mistake. It was taking him as much time to move them as it was me to remove them. Finally I heaved the last one out of my way in time to see him fumbling with an outside door.

He got it open and ran through with me a few yards behind. We were in a narrow space that encircled the basement area like a moat. Limping up the access steps to ground level, I found myself at the rear of the hospital in a tarmacked area that was used as a staff car park. Mark was ducking and weaving between the closely packed vehicles. Another daft move. I sprinted around the perimeter of the park and was waiting for him when he emerged between two wing mirrors.

'Hi! I'm sensing we have a communication problem here.'

'Get out of the way, bitch or I'll sort you.'

I wacked my trainer down *hard* on his instep.

My instincts were right. He backed off with a whimper. 'Look, I'm sorry, OK? I only just started here, all right? Tell Stacey I'll sort out her money soon.'

I began to see. 'Stacey would be your ex, right?'

'Yeah. Well, you know that.'

'And you haven't been entirely truthful when her solicitor asked about your income, have you?'

'She's got plenty. She got the bleeding house, didn't she?'

'And where is that?'

'Nottingham. Hang on, you ain't working for her, are you?'

'No.'

'Then what the hell do you want?'

'A little chat about St Martin's Comp.'

'You what?'

His mouth dropped open. It wasn't a good look for him. He had large brown, full-lashed eyes, but his face was the shape of a thin wedge and his fleshy ears hugged his face at their centre but stuck out at the top and bottom, giving the odd impression that they'd been inexpertly glued on. The sixteen-year-old in the old photo had had a Romantic Rock look of long curly brown hair, ruffled shirt and jewellery. All that thick dark hair would have disguised the oddities, but now it had been reduced to a closely-shaved stubble that was receding around a widow's peak.

'Do you remember Trudy Hepburn, the teacher who got murdered?'

'Yeah,' he admitted warily.

'I'm making some enquiries about her death.'

'Look, I ain't got time for this.' He tried to slide back between a couple of cars. And hooked his overalls on a wing mirror.

'Has your ex reverted to her maiden name?'

'No. Why?'

'So if I were to start looking in Nottingham for a Mrs Stacey Boscombe, who probably still thinks her husband is living on benefits—?'

'Yeah. All right. What d'yer want to know?' He released the overalls with a rip of tearing material.

'Tell me about Trudy Hepburn. Can you think of anyone, apart from Alison Wynne-Ellis, who might have had a motive for killing her?'

'No. She was a weed. Why would anyone bother to rub her out? You didn't need to. She wasn't going to give any bother, was she?'

He massaged his wrist-watch, twisting it as if the band was too tight. 'I got to get back. Just keep your nose out if you know what's good for you, get it?'

He pointed his finger at me. The wrist-strap slipped fractionally up his arm and I caught a glimpse of a tattoo: three numbers, a seven, an eight and another eight enclosed in a circlet of entwined leaves. And then he was fighting his way through the tightly packed vehicles back towards the hospital.

I recalled Betterman's advice. *Ask them about 788.*

I wandered around the easily walked perimeter, skirted the exterior of the building back to the A & E entrance, and retrieved Hannah and my car.

'How did you get to Seatoun?' I asked, turning right out of the main car park and heading along the sea road. 'Train?'

'A friend was driving down to see her bloke in Dover, so I hitched a lift with her. She's picking me up on the way back tomorrow.'

'Right. So you're planning to stop the night?' I did a mental assessment of my bedding. I hadn't changed the stuff in the cupboard room since Terry had crashed out in there. I didn't think I had any more sheets.

'I'll go to a hotel. They won't be full this time of year, will they?'

'They're generally not full any time of year. You're welcome to crash at my place.'

'No, honestly. The hotel will be fine. I'd just like to go to bed. My head's throbbing.' She touched the thick pad of gauze over her hair gingerly.

I drove her around to the Rock Hotel. It was the biggest and swishest hotel in town, but even with an inducement of booze-cruise packages and fan club reunions for geriatric rock bands, the place was only 20 per cent full at this tag end of winter. The receptionist had no problem booking in a guest with a bandaged head, blood-soaked hair and no luggage beyond a shoulder bag.

Taking her key, Hannah turned from the desk, swayed and grabbed the edge of the wooden counter. I hooked her under an armpit and sat her down in a chair.

'When did you last eat?'

She thought about it and decided it was breakfast. It was now nearly ten o'clock and she'd already suffered a mild concussion.

'You'd better grab some food.'

They'd given her a big twin-bedded room with a view over the beach at the rear of the hotel. We ordered hard-boiled egg sandwiches from room service and ate them lounging back on the beds watching the TV news. Once the final credits rolled I yawned loudly. 'Sorry, I'm bushed. I'll leave you to it.'

She stood to see me off. And swayed again.

'Maybe we should get you back to the hospital?'

'No, it's just when I stand up suddenly. It's happened before. Before tonight, I mean.'

I wasn't entirely convinced. I guess it showed.

'You can stay, if you like?' Hannah suggested.

It was only two minutes to my flat. Centrally heated room with cable TV, room service, mini-bar and a big bathroom with complimentary toiletries, or my basement?

'Bags the bed by the window.'

Her shoulder bag yielded a neatly rolled night-shirt, toothbrush, paste and deodorant. She used the bathroom first. There was a loud crash from inside but when I shouted through to see if she'd passed out on me she yelled back, 'It's OK. I knocked the glass over.' She came out in the night-shirt. The thin material clung to her shape, revealing what the pinafore dress and swirling cloak had hidden before.

'You're pregnant.'

'Four months.' She curved the slight swell with her palm, a self-satisfied smile playing on her lips.

'Are you OK?' I mean, going down the stairs like that?'

She scrambled under her duvet. 'That's what they took

the scans for. We're fine. It's one of the reasons why I want to find out about my birth parents. When the baby asks I want to be able to tell him everything.'

'And not have to say that his grandmother is a murderer?'

'Do you think she did it?'

'So far I haven't found anything to suggest she didn't,' I admitted.

She was sitting with the pillows propped behind her back, her knees hugged to her chest and her chin resting on them so that the curtain of Titian hair hung like rippled curtains, hiding her face from me.

'It honestly doesn't matter,' I began. 'It doesn't matter who . . . or what . . . your mother was—'

'It does, it *does*.' She swung blazing eyes in my direction. 'It *does* matter. And you have to prove she didn't do it.' Angrily she slammed off her bedside lamp and snuggled down under her duvet.

Right. So glad we got that sorted.

She was up before me and announced through the bathroom door that she'd ordered breakfast in the room. Plainly I could like it or lump it. As it happened I liked it. Although I was somewhat less pleased to discover it was only half past six.

I made some serious use of the complimentary bath toiletries, pocketed the ones we hadn't opened and then we ate watching the sun rise over the waves to reveal humps of grey rock speckled with white like a colony of stone seals pressed up against the wooden groynes. This time Hannah managed to send a cup flying. The girl must have some serious crockery bills. We were just finishing up when her mobile rang. I gathered that there was a problem with her mate in Dover.

'She's not going back to London today, I'll have to get the train.'

'I'm heading that way today, I can give you a lift.'

I arranged to pick her up from the hotel later. It was still only seven-thirty. Even allowing for the journey time to London, I had several hours to fill before heading out to keep my appointment with Georgie Pennington.

I used the office email to send a message to Betterman: 'Mark Boscombe is connected to the 788.'

He took the bait. After thirty minutes of flicking through Jan's pile of celebrity gossip magazines, the 'new message' icon appeared on screen: 'Did he tell you?'

'Let's say I read the signs. What is the 788? Does it have something to do with Trudy Hepburn's murder?'

He came back immediately: 'Perhaps.'

'Are you going to tell me what?'

'I'm not sure I have the right to do so.'

Then why the hell were we having this conversation? I put that to Betterman. There was no reply. Feeling somewhat cheesed off with all these cryptic clues, I fired off: 'Somebody got killed. What gives you the right not to say something?'

'You're right, of course. I do have a duty to tell what I know. But do I also have the right to prevent others from finding their own salvation?'

I typed back: 'Beats me. I'm just trying to find a murderer. Are you going to help? Can we meet?'

'Let's leave it to a better power to decide. If you can find me, we can talk.'

19

I was left wondering about the significance of 788. Had it been a lower number I'd have considered a house number. But there was nowhere in Seatoun that came anywhere close to that. In fact I doubted if there was a street anywhere in the British Isles that contained that many properties. An apartment number? There was nowhere locally that big. One of the larger cities might have a tower block that went into the seven hundreds. But I wouldn't even know which city to start in.

A telephone number was another possibility. Except it wasn't long enough to be an area code or line number. Not locally anyway. The old London area codes used to be three figures but why would Seatoun kids be connected to a London number? It was more likely to have some connection to the school. Locker number? Room number? Lesson number?

Since the freezing weather was still being held back by a weak spring sun, I decided to take a run before going home. I started at the tide's edge, sprinting along the hard sands with spurts of salt water springing from under my trainers, and salty winds battering at my skin and ripping at my hair. At the other end, I turned to climb up to the promenade and take the concrete pedestrian route to West Bay. Panting up the softer sands to the steps, I saw a familiar figure leaning on the prom railings watching me.

'Hello, Mr Darrowfield. How's Philip?'

He nodded back towards the nearest shelter. 'Wind's nippier than we thought. But he likes to watch the sea.'

Philip was strapped into a wheelchair. He was wearing

sunglasses, but as I came into his circle of focus, he started jerking his head violently and one earpiece slipped off. 'A'eee. a'eee. Find A'eee.'

'I'm afraid I haven't seen her yet, Philip. I'll give her your love when I do.'

'Yeth. L . . . A'eeee.'

His speech was harder to understand today. Spittle drooled out of the corner of his mouth. His father drew out a roll of kitchen paper from a bag on the back of the chair and cleaned the mess.

'Nice to see you again, Philip.' I was backing away. Philip reacted by grabbing at the blanket covering him and throwing it off. As I moved in to retrieve it, his hand locked on to my wrist.

'Let her go, Phil!'

'A'eee. See A'eee . . .'

We were both trying to pry his fingers off. The struggle pushed his jumper sleeve up his forearm. On the underside a row of ragged black symbols marched up the skin: 788. With a final twist I managed to wrench myself free. The imprint of his fingers was dug into my flesh in five vivid ovals.

'Sorry. He doesn't know his own strength. Slow breaths like the nurse taught you, Phil.'

'Mr Darrowfield, you don't happen to know the significance of those tattoos on Philip's arm, do you?'

'Significance? There's no blooming significance. Just some daft stunt the other kids put him up to. Don't breathe so fast, son. Slow . . . easy . . . in . . . out . . .'

I said goodbye and set off again at a comfortable trot. The hint of spring weather had brought everyone out. I passed half a dozen more joggers streaming past me the other way. We all exchanged the slightly smug half-smiles of those who are sweating it out while lesser mortals lazed in bed. Mid smug smirk, I recognized one of the other prom pounders just as I registered with him.

Orlando Roles swung round in a smooth half-arc and ran up next to me. 'Well, hello again. Where's your parrot?'

'Sleeping over at a friend's.'

'Did you look through the brochure?'

'Haven't really had much of a chance yet. Did you speak to any of your old school pals about the murder?'

'I caught up with one, but he said pretty much what I told you; Alison and Heartburn were a pair of losers. Have you picked up on anything new?'

'What do you know about seven eight eight?'

I was watching out for the guilty start of recognition they always give in books. I guess Orlando didn't read those particular books. 'Seven eight eight what?'

'No idea. It was just something I heard.'

'Do you want to do lunch?'

'Now? It's only . . .' I turned his wrist to read his watch.

'I didn't mean right this minute. I'll pick you up later. Drive in the country. Drinks. Lunch. I know several very pleasant hotels.'

'I'll have to take a raincheck, thanks. I have other plans for today.'

A slightly mulish expression flitted over his eyes and mouth, confirming my opinion that Orlando wasn't used to people saying no. 'Come on, Grace. We're both too old to play games. You fancy me, I fancy you. Ditch whatever plans you've got and come with me. It'll be worth it, I promise. I know how to treat a girl well.'

'Then treat this one well and understand that no means no.'

The pout was still there for a moment. Then the professional charm was back in place. 'No problem. Catch you later?'

'Could be. Did you remember to ask your mate about Alison's boyfriend?'

'It's like I said, she never had one. Maybe she wasn't interested in men. Have you considered that she and

Heartburn might have been dykes? It could have been a lovers' quarrel.'

'That theory is on my list, thanks.'

Pulling up, I ran through a series of warm-up stretches, culminating with reaching to the sky then dropping from the waist and putting my palms flat on the floor. Straightening with a grin, I said, 'Blokes can never manage that one. Something to do with shorter hamstrings.'

'Want to bet?' He stretched and dropped. The sleeves of the tracksuit jacket rode up. No tattoo on the inside of his forearms just like there had been none under his watch. There went another brilliant theory.

I hit the ground at a fast sprint. It took him thirty seconds to catch up with me and another couple of minutes to pull into a convincing lead. As soon as he was pounding it out, I reversed direction and went back to the beach. Three more laps scattering indignant black-headed gulls into flight and I was done.

Collecting the car from outside Vetch's, I drove it round to the flat, signalling I was pulling into my parking space as I approached the house. The dark blue Merc in front of me slid neatly into the gap. In summer it's a hazard of living in a seaside town; in winter it's a liberty. I hit the horn. The driver's window slid down and O'Hara waved. I leant across and lowered my passenger window. 'That's my space.'

'Sorry, duchy, I thought we'd be using your car.'

'For what?'

'Going detecting, of course – partner. Would you rather we used my car?'

'No. I mean ... *we* aren't going anywhere. *I* have an appointment in London.'

'Me too. So we're using your motor, right?'

I started to tell him what to do with his motor and was drowned out by the impatient blast of a flat-bed lorry behind wanting to get past. By the time I'd parked the Micra on the next corner and trotted back, O'Hara was in my basement, staring up at the raw gouge of brickwork above the window. 'Is that a bullet hole?'

'Yes.'

'Do you know what calibre it was?'

'No idea. Why?'

'Just curious. I had a neighbour used a thirty-eight. Looks like a similar entry size.'

'Your neighbour used to shoot at you?'

'It wasn't personal. He had a thing about pigeons. You just had to be careful walking past the windows.'

'Was this in Egypt?'

'Liverpool. Are we going in or are you ready to hit the road?'

I was relieved to find the floor unoccupied. Terry had taken himself off, leaving behind the scents of unwashed slob and stale beer. O'Hara helped himself to a chair and stretched out, apparently content to wait until I was ready to leave. He was one of the stillest people I'd ever met. Most people, especially when they're in strange surroundings, can't help fidgeting. Declan O'Hara just blended into the scene like a well-camouflaged predator. Today he was in grey; sweatshirt and soft trousers.

Pulling fresh clothes out of the pantry-wardrobe, I considered whether I wanted to get into a partnership. The answer to that was a definite no. However, if O'Hara was planning to dig into the case anyway, then I was quite happy to exploit whatever contacts or leads he might have. It also made some kind of sense to travel with him. If he wanted to keep an eye on me, for reasons of his own, then that plan could work in reverse; the more he was in my sights, the more likely it was I'd figure out this guy's real game plan. 'Why are you heading for London? Is it something to do with Alison's case?'

'I've an appointment with Peter Corbin, the prosecuting lawyer at the trial.'

OK, that was definitely a meeting I'd like to be in on.

'Wouldn't her defence lawyer have more information? His name was—'

'Vaughan Greives,' O'Hara supplied. 'And he probably would. But unless you know a particularly talented medium we ain't going to be hearing it.'

'He's dead?'

'Done to a crisp over ten years ago. The old boy was pretty much at the end of his career at the time of Alison's trial. Peter, on the other hand, was just starting out on his, and luckily for us, Greives was his godfather.'

'What about her solicitor, Indira Patel? Do you know her life story too?'

'Gave up the law to run a scuba-diving company in Alaska, married an Inuit and is now raising six children in Anchorage.'

'That's a no, then?'

'She seems to have dropped out of sight years back.'

'Do you think her disappearance is connected with the case?' I had visions of the bad guys kidnapping her to locate the one crucial piece of evidence that would clear Alison, and then disposing of her body in some remote woodland grave.

O'Hara dismissed my bad-crime-novel cliché. 'I shouldn't think so. I guess she just decided to take another path. People often end up very far from the place they were heading for at the beginning.'

I recalled Clive Pennington's comment that his ex-colleague had gone over to the dark side and wondered if O'Hara was talking about Ms Patel or himself?

'Make yourself a coffee, if you want. I think there's a jar in the top cupboard. If not, you can use these.' I emptied my pockets of sachets of coffee, decaffeinated coffee, teabags, herbal teabags, chocolate drink, brown sugar, white sugar and artificial sweetener, courtesy of the Rock Hotel.

'No biscuits?'

'I left them in the car.'

Bundling my outfit up, I took it into the bathroom to

change. By the time I returned, he'd switched on the television news, made two mugs of coffee and found half a bottle of milk that had decided to take a giant leap forward in evolution and become yogurt. We both opted for black.

I started to ask, 'What do we—' And then realized that O'Hara's eyes were no longer fixed on the TV screen but on something behind me.

20

The door to the spare cupboard room stood open. Terry's bloodshot eyes peered through a tangle of hair. 'What's the time?'

O'Hara consulted his watch. 'Half past nine.'

'Bollocks, I'm late for work.' He staggered into the bathroom. Giving us both an ample chance to admire his fleshy buttocks. It wasn't a pretty sight. But it was better than the front view – given that he was stark bloody naked.

The sounds that came out of the bathroom were a cross between the office plumbing and the birth pangs of a pregnant warthog. Two minutes later Terry burst out, rushed into the spare room and grabbed his clothes. Passing the counter, he snatched the milk bottle. Our last sight was of him tipping the stuff down his gullet as he tried to shuffle his shoes on and belt up his trousers.

The reverberations of the slammed front door had died away before O'Hara asked: 'Friend of yours?'

'Never seen him before. The squatter problem is really getting out of hand around here. Shall we go?'

He was retrieving a leather coat from the Merc's boot by the time I'd locked up. It was an old-fashioned style Mercedes. But it *was* a Merc. 'Maybe we could take your car. If you'd prefer?'

'Up to you, duchy.'

'I promised to give someone a lift.'

'I have four seats.'

'Let's roll then.' It was polished on the outside and gleamy clean and leather scented inside. 'Nice car.'

'I like Mercs. Solid bodywork, reliable mechanics. They

say you're more likely to survive a car bomb in a Merc.'

'I always think that's an essential feature in any car. Second only to the twelve-disc CD changer.'

'I have one of those too.'

Of course he did. I tried to sort out my feelings about this bloke while he drove us round to the Rock Hotel. There was a kind of quiet sexiness under that tranquil exterior. I knew he was sending me up a lot of the time – which I found extremely irritating. But on the other hand, I liked his laidback reaction to my bullet hole. Most people would have asked for details and started telling me to call in the police.

'Who are we collecting?' he asked.

'Hannah. My client. She's Alison's daughter.'

She was already on the front step looking out for me. She greeted O'Hara with one of those big, heart-stopping smiles as she settled into the back seat and unfastened her cloak. Even with the bandaged head she looked radiantly pretty. 'Hi! I'm Hannah.'

Before I could introduce him, O'Hara slewed round and offered a handshake over the seat back. 'Call me Dee. I like the outfit.'

'Do you?' Hannah exuded a few more watts of radiance. 'I designed and made most of it myself.'

'Dee is . . .' I began. A pair of strong fingers pincered the flesh above my knee. 'Going to drive us to London,' I finished.

'Mega. I like your outfit too, Dee. It's Italian, isn't it?'

'Picked it up in Milan.'

Would you believe they talked fashion most of the way? I discovered Hannah was studying design. O'Hara either read a lot of women's magazines or spent a lot of time shopping for frocks. I wondered who he bought them for? Hopefully not himself. I'd been down that route with a bloke before.

The house in Cricklewood to which Hannah directed us was an old brick terrace.

'Thanks for the lift. Would you like to come in for a coffee?'

I didn't particularly. But I did want to use their loo. So the three of us decanted ourselves from the Merc.

We all had to flatten ourselves against the wall to ease past a bicycle parked in the hall. 'The loo's at the top of the stairs,' Hannah informed me, opening the door at the rear of the hall which led to a kitchen overlooking an overgrown back garden. The cupboards were labelled 'Hannah', 'Shelby', 'Chloe' and 'Niall'.

'Student share?' I asked.

'Yes.'

'I'd assumed that this was your home address.'

'No. My parents live in Yorkshire.' She took a mug from her cupboard and just managed to field the second as she dropped it.

'I'll skip coffee, thanks. I'll just use your loo.'

When I came out again, the door to the opposite bedroom was open. Hannah was putting her outdoor clothes away. The room overlooked the back garden and beyond the fence there were apparently endless lines of weed-choked railway tracks. The vibration of two passing trains reverberated through my feet. 'Don't the trains get on your nerves?'

'You stop noticing them after a bit.'

Most of the room was occupied by a double bed covered in a patchwork quilt, which I guessed was her work. As were the framed shots from fashion magazines on the walls. The only out-of-place item was the cot. It was white with yellow rabbits gambolling over the base section and climbing the corner supports.

Hannah ran a loving hand over the top rail. 'I know some people think it's bad luck, buying stuff for the baby before it's born, but we saw it at a car boot sale and I just had to have it. I'm making a quilt for it.'

She didn't look old enough to have a kid. Curious, I asked how her family felt about it.

'They'll be fine.'

She shrugged a shade too casually. The 'when they know about it' hung unspoken in the air. The noise of the key in the front door carried up the stairs, followed by a muttered 'shit' as someone collided with the bicycle. The radiance lit her face again. 'There's Ni!' She ran downstairs.

He was one of those tall, lanky types and she only came up to his chin. He returned her hug and then held her at arm's length. 'What the hell happened, Han? Are you OK? Is the baby OK?'

'We're fine. It's not as bad as it looks. I'll tell you later. This is Dee, he gave me a lift back to London . . .'

O'Hara had strolled into the hall, sipping from his coffee mug. Even though I was looking down on his head from the first-floor landing, I could see Niall stiffen. 'I thought you were catching a ride with Chloe.'

'She's staying down in Dover for a few days. Man trouble. Dee has a Mercedes.'

Strange male with flashy car. Not good news from Niall's point of view. He slid an arm round Hannah's waist. 'Thanks for bringing her home.'

'My pleasure. We should get going. Ready, Grace?'

Niall noticed me at the top of the stairs for the first time. The tension visibly relaxed. Flashy bloke had a blonde in tow.

'He was ready to be jealous,' I said, as O'Hara and I settled back in the car.

'I'm flattered. Given I'm old enough to be her father. Is your boyfriend the jealous type?'

I started to ask what boyfriend, and then realized he meant Rosco. 'If you mean the lardy zombie who was squatting in my spare room, he is *not* my boyfriend and I'm not living with him. OK?'

'Whatever you say, duchy. Where to?'

'Sunbury. I've an appointment with Georgie Pennington. And why didn't you want Hannah to know your name?'

'She might have made the connection and wanted to talk

about her mother. And she'd have wanted me to say good things about Alison, which maybe I couldn't.' He started the engine, drove a couple of yards, and stopped. 'I think we're being followed.'

I glanced in the side mirror. Niall was sprinting along the pavement. Reaching the car, he bent and signalled for me to lower the window.

'You're the private 'tective, right? Did Hannie tell you about her mum? The one who brought her up, not this killer one.'

'What should she have told me?'

'She's dead. Died a couple of years back. And my mother is a bit, well she doesn't like Hannie much, and I reckon she's going to give her grief when she hears about the baby. I think Hannie's like ... you know ... looking to plug a gap.' He looked round at the house, signalling very clearly that Hannah didn't know we were having this conversation. 'I wanted to say, well, I can look after her, so you find out anything seriously bad about this other mother, you give me a ring first, OK?'

He shoved a piece of paper with a phone number at me and shambled back the way he'd come before I could ask what he rated worse than hacking a teacher to death.

I'd half expected O'Hara to try to muscle in on the meeting chez Pennington, but he pulled up a street away and jotted down his mobile number. 'Ring me when you're ready to roll again.'

Sunbury-on-Thames lies in the pashmina-belt that rings London; an area where the property prices reflect the easy commuting distance into the city. The avenue where the Penningtons lived was lined with large detached houses in the middle of big gardens planted with mature trees and double garages. Georgie must have been watching out for me; she had the door open as I reached it and ushered me inside quickly before I could lower the tone of the neighbourhood.

'Come through to the conservatory. Although as I told you, Grace, I really don't see how I can help your enquiries.'

She was in some kind of navy lounging suit today. It emphasized her Nordic blondeness. The doors were closed as she led me to the back of the house so I had no idea if Clever Clive was in residence or not.

The conservatory stretched out into a large garden where early bulbs were already pushing through an immaculate lawn. Georgie took a chair beside the coffee table and waved me to the opposite one.

'Lovely garden,' I said, trying for the bonding approach. 'Must be a bit of a hike for Clive to get to work from here.'

'He overnights near the office for part of the week. Is that relevant to your enquiry?'

'No. Just making conversation.'

'Perhaps you could stick to the point. Would you care for a drink?'

The invitation was unexpected. If she'd brought back a glass of tap water it wouldn't have surprised me, but she returned from a trip into the house with an open bottle of white wine and two glasses. 'Chablis, I hope that's acceptable.'

'Very. Thanks.'

Once we were both served, Georgie raised enquiring eyebrows. My turn to talk.

I laid the big pink folder on the table between us. I'd stuffed it out with some plain paper so it looked more impressive. Extracting the school photo I'd obtained from Gillian Anderson, I invited Georgie to tell me about Trudy Hepburn.

'She was dull, lacking in confidence. I barely knew her. We had nothing in common beyond teaching at St Martin's.'

'Yet you described her as "a dear friend" in the newspaper?'

Georgie sipped calmly; the wine barely wet her lips. 'It seemed kinder.'

I waited. She stayed silent. 'That's it?' I finally asked. 'All you can say about her?'

'There really isn't anything else *to* say. I did warn you this would be a wasted journey.'

'Oh, come on. There must be something else.' Slagging off murder victims probably wasn't politic if you're aiming high on the police promotion ladder. 'I'm not bugged, you know. No hidden tape recorders,' I joked.

Georgie's glass jerked, slopping wine over the table surface. 'Damn.' She busied herself mopping it up with a tissue extracted from her trouser pocket. And then topped my glass up rather than her own. 'Trudy was a mass of contradictions; she had an inferiority complex but at the same time thought she was better than other people, if that makes any sense.'

'Not really.'

Georgie visibly collected her thoughts before saying, 'She used to write letters complaining about everyone. She complained to the Education Department that the headmaster was unable to bring any discipline to the school; she complained to the headmaster that the caretaker was encouraging the pupils to behave badly; she complained to parents that their children were rude and unmanageable. The only problem was, she never posted any of the letters. She'd read them out endlessly to me, asking if I thought they sounded OK, but she never had the guts to post a single one. In the end I lost my temper and told her either to get some evidence of her grouses and post the damn letters, or just shut up.'

'Was that the only problem between you?'

'If only. Have you seen the film *Single White Female*?'

'Bridget Fonda and Jennifer Jason Leigh.'

'Trudy started to copy me. I had a big breakfast cup, the kind that the French use to serve café au lait. Trudy admired it and asked me where I'd bought it, so I gave her the name of the shop. Then a few weeks later, she bought some bed linen that was identical to that in my room. After that it was make-up; if I bought a new shade of lipstick, the same one appeared on Trudy's dressing table. Then it was my clothes, shoes, handbags. She even lost two stone for heaven's sake, so she could get into the same size as me. In the beginning, I was amused, even a little flattered. But after a while it started to get on my nerves. It was like being stalked.'

She twisted the newspaper photo and tapped the red and white jumper. 'I had a jumper exactly like that. And those jeans. It reached the stage where I'd be smuggling new things into the cottage just to avoid this . . . doppelgänger compulsion.'

'Is that why she changed her hairstyle? To match yours?' Her blonde locks were sleek and feathered now, but if flicks and curls had been in fashion twenty years ago, then Georgie would have worn them.

'That really was the last straw. People started mistaking me for her. Not when we were face to face obviously, but I remember one parents' evening some wretched woman started shouting at the back of my head about what a useless teacher I was. Of course, when I turned round she apologised, but by that time half the other parents who had overheard had moved on. It was embarrassing.'

'So why not get rid of her?' As I said it, I realized that she could have done just that.

Georgie did too. A wry smile twisted the perfectly lipsticked mouth. 'Did I snap and plunge a knife into her, do you mean? No, I didn't. We'd both signed the lease. I was planning to suggest we go our separate ways once that expired. Which would have been a couple of months after her death.' She refilled my wine glass again. She'd drunk barely more than a few sips from her own.

'What about Alison? Gillian Anderson said she and Trudy were friends. Did she often visit the cottage?'

'Gilly is still at St Martin's, is she?'

'She's the headteacher.'

'She would be,' Georgie said cryptically.

'You two weren't bosom buddies, I'm sensing?'

'I thought she was smug and self-righteous, since you ask.' The phone rang inside the house and she excused herself. It was two rooms away, but this job hones your hearing. I caught her tone first (snappy), and then the words 'She's here now.' By the time she returned, I was idly sipping wine and admiring the garden. She'd brought a wine cooler, a packet of cigarettes and an ashtray. 'Clive hates me doing this in the house.'

She opened a window before lighting up, then ground the partially empty wine bottle into the crush of ice-cubes in the bucket. 'Alison,' she said resuming the conversation, 'came to the cottage once or twice a week. Personally I was against the visits; it's a great mistake to get too close to one's students. It can lead to . . . misunderstandings.'

'Inappropriate bonking?'

'If you like. Or at least the accusation of such.'

'Was there anything like that between Trudy and Alison?'

'Heavens no. They were friends, that's all.'

'Didn't you find that a bit odd? I mean, Trudy was in her mid-twenties and Alison was ten years younger.'

'You wouldn't think so if you'd known Trudy. She was very immature in a lot of ways. I don't think she'd ever had a boyfriend, or even a quick tumble.'

If it was true, it rather ruled out sex as a motive. I asked what she'd made of Alison.

'Have you met Mr and Mrs Wynne-Ellis?'

'Not yet. They're on my list.'

'They were older parents, and they were absurdly strict. Alison was just starting to rebel against it. She and Trudy used to have these heart to hearts: should she defy her parents and wear nail varnish? Should she deliberately stay out half an hour later than her curfew? She was fifteen, for heaven's sake. Most of the parents were grateful if they knew where their children were, much less when they might deign to come home.'

'What was Trudy getting out of the relationship?' I asked.

Georgie blew out a cloud of smoke and said, 'A boost to her pathetic self-esteem, I should think. I doubt if anyone else had ever asked for her advice.'

'Did anything change in the last few weeks before the murder?'

Georgie screwed up her eyes against the smoke and appeared to be thinking about the question. 'Now you mention it, yes it did. Alison stopped coming to the cottage.'

'Why?'

'I've no idea. I didn't ask.'

That I could believe. I suggested it might have something to do with Trudy's increased self-confidence?

'Did Gillian tell you that?'

'Isn't it true?'

Another cigarette glowed into life from the butt of the previous one. Another inch was added to my wine glass. 'I suppose Trudy did seem a little different,' Georgie admitted. 'She was more relaxed. That photograph proves the point really. She actually looks like she's enjoying herself. I'd have expected her to look like a rabbit in a cage of rattlesnakes with that particular group. They really were some of the most unpleasant rabble I have ever had to teach.'

'And Alison, did she change?'

'I can't say I noticed. I took her for French, but she was always one of the quiet ones.' She looked at her watch. 'Is that all?'

'Tell me about the night of the murder. You'd gone to a restaurant, right? On your own?'

Georgie shrugged. 'I'm quite capable of dealing with any clumsy pick-ups. The truth is I couldn't face an evening stuck in the cottage with Trudy, so I rode for an hour or so, until it got too dark, and then I decided I felt like having a decent meal so I drove round to Winstanton. They were just starting to renovate the area then, some of the restaurants served quite acceptable food. Afterwards I drove home.'

'Tell me your first impression as you reached the cottage. Anything, no matter how silly it might sound.'

Georgie blew out another cloud of smoke on an impatient breath. I was overstaying my welcome. 'I was surprised that both the lights were on. It was one of those irritating habits Trudy had. Every time she left a room she'd switch the lights off, even if she was coming back in almost immediately. I think the great-aunt who brought her up must have been very frugal. Maybe she was poor. Whatever, she'd got Trudy trained: leave the room, flick the light switch.'

'But not that night?'

'No. The living-room curtains didn't quite meet so I could see the light was on as I drove in. We used to park on a track beside the house and go in through the side gate to the back garden. As soon as I opened it, I saw the kitchen light was on as well.'

'So that gate wasn't locked?'

'It didn't have a bolt.'

'What about the back door to the house?'

'Whoever was last in at night locked it. I saw her as soon as I stepped inside. I was fairly certain she was dead, but I checked her breathing and pulse, and then I dialled nine-nine-nine and waited for the police in the back garden. Fortunately they came very quickly.'

'And it was love at first sight?'

She gave an artificial little laugh. 'Not quite that. But Clive was marvellous. So decisive. There's no denying power can be an aphrodisiac.'

I asked her what she'd thought of the policeman who'd been riding with Clive that night.

Georgie looked blank. 'I really can't remember. I know Clive didn't have a very high opinion of him. Slapdash methods and a contempt for regulations. I believe he left the police some time ago. Under a cloud.'

Haven't we all?

Georgie asked, 'Have you managed to speak to him about your little enquiry?'

'He gave me a lift here today.'

'Then I expect he can fill you in on any more background that you might require.' She stood up.

I stayed seated. 'Did Trudy leave any money or property?'

'Hardly. She'd spent most of her salary copying me. There was just the car, which had a loan outstanding. And the things at the cottage.'

'What happened to those?'

'I dumped them.'

OK, so much for money as a motive. I started retrieving my papers and visible relief flowed over Frostie's features.

'There is one thing . . .' It had only just occurred to me. 'Where is Trudy buried?'

'At St John's in Seatoun. I got stuck with arranging the funeral. The staff at St Martin's held a collection to pay for a stone, and the pupils got press-ganged into providing a choir and flowers.'

I refastened the pink folder. 'Does the number seven eight eight mean anything to you?'

'In what connection?'

'St Martin's. Some of the pupils had it tattooed on their arms.'

'The pupils had all kinds of things tattooed on various parts of their anatomies. If the parents didn't object there was little we could do about it.'

I was being shepherded firmly down the polished corridor, past silver-framed photos of Clive and Georgie in various family poses with two blond boys who went from chubby toddlers to long-limbed teenagers. 'Can I use your loo?'

I hadn't spotted a downstairs cloakroom anywhere, so I was banking on her directing me upstairs. It's harder to lurk pointedly outside an upstairs loo for some reason. Georgie stayed at the foot of the stairs where she could have spotted me going along the landing into some of the bedrooms. Luckily there was a phone extension on the landing and out of her sight line. While I noisily opened the bathroom door and called down loud compliments on her décor, I quietly lifted the receiver and dialled one-four-seven-one. The last caller had rung from an area code that covered the Seatoun district. Possibly Clive from work? Flushing and running taps, I jotted the number down on my arm.

I was over the front step before I remembered I'd meant to use their phone to summon up my personal chauffeur. When I rang the bell again, Georgie ignored it.

It took me nearly half an hour to find a working public phone. As I waited for O'Hara to arrive, I dialled the number of Georgie's last caller. It was picked up on the third ring.

'Roles Motors. Hello? Anybody there? Hel*lo?*' Orlando's smooth tones were becoming more irritated at the silence. I hung up on him as the Mercedes came gliding round the corner. Surreptitiously I rubbed the number off my arm with a wet thumb; a girl has to protect her sources.

'How did you make out?' O'Hara asked.

'OK. I made Georgie nervous. And she tried to make me drunk.'

'Did she succeed?'

'On one bottle of wine. No chance.'

'What does it take?'

'Why, you planning a bit of alcoholic seduction?'

'Darling, I have never had to resort to alcohol to get a woman into bed.'

Somehow I had a feeling he was telling the truth there. 'Can we go to Thamesmead now, please?'

'Another hot lead?'

'I'm going to see Alison's parents. Do you want to tag along?'

'No, thanks. I think I know all I need to about that pair.'

There was something about his tone that made me look more closely at him. He was half turned away from me, watching his wing mirror as he signalled to ease out into traffic.

'So far I've found out that the Wynne-Ellises are older than your average parent, heavy-handed disciplinarians and would rather cut out their own tongues than draw attention to themselves. Is there something I've missed?'

'Ask me again after you've met them, duchy.'

21

The Wynne-Ellises could have been anywhere between sixty and ninety. They were a pair of matching grey twigs: stick-thin, narrow-faced, dry-skinned and (I'd have bet) with tightly clenched buttocks lest an emotion decided to make a dash for freedom via that route.

Moira wore a grey and pink cardigan that buttoned to her neck and a tweed skirt that came to the bottom of her calves. She was barely five feet tall and wore her hair in an oddly juvenile pageboy style. Viewed from behind she could have been taken for a young teenager dressed in her granny's clothes. Emlyn didn't even have the splash of pink to relieve the unrelenting greyness between carpet slippers and tie.

Moira had carried with her the conviction that cleanliness was next to godliness. The windows shone, the nets were gleamy white, furniture was polished, even the pile on all the carpets lay in the same direction.

They hadn't wanted to let me in. But I'd sort of expected that, given the reception Hannah had received. So I told Moira Wynne-Ellis the deal. Either she let me in and talked to me, or I was going to go round the entire street asking all their neighbours if they knew they had a murderer's parents living in the neighbourhood.

They sat on the sofa facing me. There was something inherently unlikable about them. No wonder Alison preferred to confide in her teacher.

'So, do you see much of Alison?' I asked.

'We never see Alison,' Emlyn said.

'Moira nodded her head in wordless agreement. She took

her husband's hand, pulled it into her lap and fastened his shirt cuff.

'Right.' I was left floundering, but then I guess it didn't really matter that much. It was the fifteen-year-old Alison I wanted to know, not the present-day Alison. 'So do you think you could kind of paddle back to the night that Trudy Hepburn was killed?'

'The Lord called her to Him. Praise be the name of the Lord,' Moira said.

'Yeah, well, the Lord had a bit of help there. About two dozen whacks with a carving knife. Did you know that Alison had gone to the cottage that night?'

'No, we did not.' This was from Moira.

'So where did you think she was?'

'In her bedroom.'

The houses in Hinton Road weren't that large. I asked if they hadn't heard her go out.

'We had gone out ourselves.' Moira brushed more invisible fluff from her husband's clothes and straightened his collar at the back. 'We assumed she was in her room when we returned as she had been when we left. She had homework.'

'On the last day of term?'

'The school often set course work to be done during the holidays.'

And Alison dived straight in, rather than leaving it until the last day like the rest of us? Boy, that girl's home life must have been dull. I asked if it was possible that Alison had gone to Abbot's Cottage to ask Trudy for help with her homework? The Wynne-Ellises looked blank.

'When did you realize she'd gone?'

'The police came?' Moira said it almost as a question. She looked at Emlyn for confirmation. He nodded. She stroked back a strand of his hair and brushed an invisible speck off his shoulder before adding, 'We had to go to the police station.'

'What did Alison say?' It was the first opportunity I'd had to hear Alison's version of events.

'We don't know,' Moira said. 'She didn't want us to witness her testimony.'

'Then when did you talk about what happened?'

Once more they exchanged looks. 'We didn't,' Emlyn explained. 'Alison asked that we not visit her at that place they took her to. The solicitor came and fetched clothes for her.'

'So you didn't see Alison again until . . . ?'

'The trial,' Moira said. 'The barrister said we must go to that. To create a good impression.'

'What about when Hannah was born? Didn't you take pink bootees along or something?'

'A child conceived in sin is an abomination in the sight of the Lord,' Moira said calmly.

'Right. Talking of conceiving, have you any idea who was in on that? Did Alison have a boyfriend?'

'No.' Emlyn shook his head firmly. 'She was a child. Untouched by lust.'

'Well, somebody touched her. Assuming she didn't find Hannah under a gooseberry bush, when did you actually realize Alison was pregnant?'

'Her solicitor told us,' Moira replied.

'What about the murder? Do you think she did it?'

'The jury found her guilty,' Moira said.

'I know. But what do *you* both think?'

'The truth,' Moira announced, 'will be revealed when all are called to judgement.'

Quite possibly. But that was going to be a bit late for me to collect my fee. 'Has Alison never said anything – written anything – to you about that night?'

They denied it in unison. Another suspicion unfurled.

'Have you actually spoken to Alison since that night?'

'We did try,' Emlyn said, displaying some emotion for the first time. 'We presented ourselves at each of the places where she was incarcerated, but each time she sent word that she would not see us.'

'Why do you figure she did that?'

'How would we know, when she would not speak with us?' Moira enquired.

'So you haven't seen her for twenty years?'

'Yes, we have,' Emlyn said unexpectedly. 'At Chelsea Flower Show three years ago. I asked if we could share her table at the refreshment area. I didn't recognize her, until she looked directly at us.'

'What did she say?'

Moira said: 'That chair is taken.'

I thought Moira might have developed a sense of humour. But no, she'd taken the question literally. 'And after that? What did you talk about? Did you ask about the murder? You must have been curious?'

Emlyn said, 'No. I told her about the new jobs we'd obtained after we moved here. Retired now, of course. And about the house. She asked us about the neighbours in Seatoun, but we were unable to answer her.'

Pink flushes coloured Moira's cheekbones. 'They did not wish to know us after a sinner came into our midst.'

Unexpectedly Emlyn contradicted her. 'Well, that's not entirely true, Ken and Lucia had been acting strangely before that.'

'About what?' I asked. I'd assumed from what Ken Darrowfield had said that the falling out between the two families had been *after* the murder. But if it was before, was it possible Lucia Darrowfield had seen something in Alison that had frightened her enough to want to keep her away from their house?

'We don't know,' Emlyn said. 'We never knew.'

'And this is what you spoke to Alison about? Nothing else?'

Moira said: 'She gave us her address and said we might direct others to it in the case of emergency, but she did not wish us to contact her. We have respected her wishes. We cannot help you with your enquiries, Miss Smith. We have put that life behind us. We have no daughter now. We pray for the soul of that poor unfortunate woman who was killed. We shall pray for yours as well.' Her tone implied that she thought I was in desperate need of divine intervention.

I couldn't resist asking if they prayed for Hannah as well.

'Of course,' Moira agreed calmly.

'Well, instead of all that chatting with higher powers, couldn't you have a nice chat with Hannah? All she wanted was a bit of family background.'

Once again Emlyn displayed some independent spirit. 'Perhaps we were harsh. If the girl just wanted to talk for a little while, Moira, it would be a charitable gesture.'

Moira plainly wasn't into charity. 'The way of transgressors is hard and the past is best left in the past.'

'That would be a no then, would it?' I clarified. They both went for a synchronized head-bob. 'Tell me, did the fact that Alison had stabbed someone to death surprise you? Did she ever display any signs of aggressive behaviour at home? Pulling the wings off flies?' I prompted when they still remained silent. 'Breaking rabbits' legs? Flying into violent rages?'

'She had a pet rabbit,' Emlyn said. 'It died. Alison cried, didn't she, Moira?'

'Doesn't sound like a potential murderer, does she?' I directed the question to Moira. I was hoping she might open a bit now her husband had.

'Alison was not a violent girl. She had a meekness that was proper.'

'What about just before the murder? Was there anything unusual? Did she seem angrier? Quieter? Meeker?'

Emlyn said: 'She seemed to stay in her room more, don't you think, Moira?'

'Alison enjoyed her own company. Her strengths were sufficient unto herself. I do not think we can be of help to you or the girl, Miss Smith.' Moira stood up.

I let myself be manouevred towards the door. To be honest, I was as keen to get out as they were to be rid of me. The house was tiny by comparison to the one in Seatoun. We all had to march single-file to the front door, with Moira in the lead and me forming the filling in the sandwich. When she opened the door, I stepped back to give her room and cannoned into Emlyn. He put a hand on my upper arm to steady me. Wordlessly Moira reached over and removed it. She stepped outside and waited.

'Goodbye, Miss Smith. We shall not speak again.'

Amen to that. It had grown dark outside while I'd been interviewing the holy duo. This time I didn't have to find a phone box to ring O'Hara. He was parked up at the end of the road and attracted my attention with a blast on the horn. I scrambled into the passenger seat, fastened my seat belt and let out my breath with a gasp.

'Those people are unreal. I bet Alison found a high security prison light relief after home.'

He started the engine. 'Where to?'

'Take the fastest route back to Planet Earth. If I'm ever adrift in a lifeboat, I definitely want the rest of the passengers to be atheists.'

'I think you'll find somebody pointed out there are no atheists in a lifeboat. What did you make of Pa Wynne-Ellis?'

'He seemed slightly less up his own orifice than Mummy Wynne-Ellis. Am I missing something here?'

'He's a kiddy fiddler – allegedly.' I shot him a suspicious look, wondering whether this was the start of another wind-up. Lights from the shops threw an illumination over a grim mouth and intense eyes. 'The Wynne-Ellises used to be the plain old Ellises. Wynne is her maiden name. They tagged them together when they moved from South Wales to Seatoun. Thereby ensuring a cursory search under the letter "E" in any records wouldn't turn them up. Ellis is supposed to have had it away with a couple of local girls.'

'How old?'

'Thirteen and fourteen. Local legend had it that it wasn't exactly a novel experience for either of them. They specialized in dirty old men. Between them they'd seen more grubby raincoats than Sketchley.'

'Did it come to trial?'

'No. Both girls refused to make statements.'

'So how come you know about it?'

'D . . . determined digging by the original investigating team. It was just a punt into Alison's family background. The local police still had their notes in the files. Someone had complained about the girls' activities. They never got any evidence.'

'Did it come up at Alison's trial?'

'Considered irrelevant.'

Maybe by the courts. But it was the kind of thing the press loved. And if a humble uniformed PC like O'Hara had heard about it, it must have been pretty well known in the police station. How come nobody had sold that juicy rumour to the papers, I asked O'Hara.

'The families claimed their daughters were angels who went to Sunday school, helped old ladies across the road and played with their Sindy dolls. Even the most reckless editor is going to see a fat libel case looming if he starts hinting sweet, innocent underage girls have been having sex with a dirty old man.'

'Why do you think the families wouldn't talk? Protecting the kids?'

'You'd like to think so. However, before the move the Wynne-Ellises-owned their own house. When they moved to Seatoun, they went into Council property.'

'They paid the girls off.'

'I'd say so, wouldn't you?'

'Why? I mean, if it was their career of choice, they weren't going to report him to the police, were they?'

'I rather think the families had a nice little sideline going in blackmail. My guess is they didn't talk to the press because they were scared someone would make them pay back not just the Wynne-Ellises' fat little hush money packet, but all the others as well. By all accounts they weren't exactly the hottest synchronized swimmers in the gene pool.'

So Emlyn liked young teenage girls. There was one obvious route to go from there. 'Alison's baby . . . do you think?'

'Found any other candidates for the daddy?'

'No. Oh hell.' I imagined trying to tell Hannah that her granddad was also her dad. And then something else hit me. 'I've got it!'

'Is it catching or would you like me to pull over at the nearest chemist's?'

'Shut up. Listen, I know who killed Trudy.'

22

'Alison used to confide in Trudy. Suppose she told Trudy what her dad was doing to her? And Emlyn realized what she'd done? Or even both of them? Moira must have been in on the pay-off to the girls in Wales. The headteacher at St Martin's told me that Moira had been assaulted once by another parent but she refused to call in the police. It wasn't because they didn't want any fuss, it was because they didn't want the local police digging into their own background. Supposing Emlyn went to Abbot's Cottage that night . . .' I broke off. In the headlights from the on-coming cars, I could see a distinct twitch on the corner of O'Hara's mouth. 'And I'm amusing you this time because?'

'Hey, don't get all uptight on me, duchy. Your enthusiasm is one of the things I like about you. But even the most bone-headed investigation team are going to have considered that one.'

'And?'

'The Wynne-Ellises went to some church event every Friday evening: games and fish and chip supper. Alison sometimes went as well, but that evening she claimed to have schoolwork to do. Which she didn't incidentally. The team checked. The school hadn't set any project work for that holiday.'

'Maybe she just wanted a few hours away from Mummy and Daddy. I would have. Couldn't they have killed Trudy before – or after – supper?'

'Trudy's body was discovered at nine-thirty and the pathologist considered she couldn't have been killed more than half an hour prior to that and probably far less. The Wynne-Ellises didn't leave the social until gone nine.'

'Where was this religious shindig?'

'Couple of rooms above a shop in St John's Road. Owner used to let them out for kids' parties, wedding receptions, that kind of thing.'

'They could have made it to Abbot's Cottage by nine thirty. Did they have a car?'

'Yes. But it was searched thoroughly at the time. So was the house. Whoever killed Trudy Hepburn was going to be trailing her blood. And the only sign of that was splattered all over Alison.'

'Maybe they cleaned up. How long between picking up Alison and the officers going to her house?'

'A couple of hours. It took a while to identify her. She wouldn't, or couldn't, tell them her name.'

'So her parents could have had time to destroy evidence.'

'It's not that easy to get rid of bloodstains. And even if they did, it means they kept their mouths shut and let their daughter take the blame. Is that likely?'

'Who knows. Maybe Alison hadn't measured up to what they wanted in a child. Maybe they just didn't want a child. They obviously hadn't bothered to check on her when they came home. Do you know which church it was?'

'Some sect. Apparently this particular church don't have regular premises. You hungry?'

'If you need to ask, you don't know me at all well.'

He took his eyes from the road for a moment to look at me. 'I'm hoping to fix that situation.'

Normally I'd have brushed that off as a bog-standard try-on. But something made me say: 'Why?'

'Because you're a good looking blonde with great legs.'

'You've never seen my legs.'

'That's another situation I'm planning to fix. The Waldorf Hotel suit you?'

For a second I thought he was planning a couple of hours

in a double bedroom. He let the moment hang and then added: 'For dinner?'

'I thought we were going to see the barrister who prosecuted Alison, Peter Corbin?'

'He can't see us until later this evening.'

We were seated surrounded by tourists who were 'doing London' and who were already dressed for an evening of after-dark fun.

'Why did you want to eat here?' I asked after the waiter had whisked a napkin the size of a pillowcase on to my lap and oozed away to collect our drinks order.

'The room's big enough to talk without having to share your conversation with the next table.'

'You come here a lot?'

'Off and on, when I'm in London.'

'Which is how often?'

He slipped on a pair of gold rimmed spectacles and looked at me over the menu. 'Depends on my plans. They tend to be fluid.'

Rosie Wilmott had said he'd 'dropped out of sight' and Clive Pennington had claimed his former patrol-car-buddy had 'gone over to the dark side'. How do you ask someone if they're bent, or if they've joined a hit squad of warlocks?

The arrival of another waiter to take our food order put off the moment. Once the waiter had taken himself off again, O'Hara removed his specs and shrugged his way out of his leather coat, leaving him in a T-shirt the same shade as his wool/silk mix trousers. I'm sure Hannah could have told me which Italian designer had created it. Over his shoulder I saw several of the female diners checking him out. He was . . . checkable.

I dumped my own jacket; revealing shirt and jeans by some Far East sweat shop with a tadge of Oxfam influence.

The waiter came back and started shifting cutlery around. There was no chance of having a private conversation about just how dark and dirty O'Hara had got since he'd left the police, so I asked him about Egypt instead. 'What's it like?'

He took a sip of the iced mineral water he'd ordered as an aperitif, and then said: 'Hot. Amazing. Constantly surprising – and contradictory. What do you think about when you hear the word "Egypt"?'

'The pyramids I guess.'

'Describe the picture you've got in your mind.'

'Enormous triangular-shaped buildings set in the middle of an endless desert of sand. With a few camels and bedouins kind of drifting around the bottom.'

'That's the picture that everyone retains. Because it's the one that's been sold to you in all the books and brochures and post-cards. And on one level it's true, stand on one side of the pyramids and that's what you'll see.'

'And if I stand on the other side?'

'You'll find yourself in downtown Cairo. If the pyramids were in London, they'd be on Hampstead Heath.'

He talked about Egypt all through dinner; it was all fascinating, but I started to know how the sheep felt when the dog was herding them into that pen. In my case I sensed O'Hara was steering me away from things he didn't want to talk about. There's nothing like a challenge to make my nosiness perk up and strap on the turbo-charged booster. He gave me an opening when he mentioned some ancient Egyptian who'd married a woman old enough to be his mother.

'Georgina Pennington is older than her husband, isn't she?'

'Few years I guess.'

'Did it surprise you when she and Clive got it together?'

'Nope, can't say it did.' He signalled the waiter for coffee and the bill.

'How come you haven't asked me anything else about my visit chez Pennington?'

'I figured you'd get around to telling me sooner rather than later. How did it go?'

I told him about Georgie's claims that Trudy had been trying to turn herself into a clone, plus what she'd said about Alison's visits to the cottage. 'According to her, Clive described you as slapdash. Any comments?'

'Bollocks springs to mind. Clever Clive's idea of professionalism was to stick to the book. If the book had said throw petrol over a burning man, he'd have done it.'

'So how do you account for his rise to assistant chief constable. Witchcraft?'

'He had some lucky breaks early on. He transferred to CID, had a few solid gold tip-offs, was in the wrong place at the right time, made some good arrests. It doesn't take much. You get the reputation for being lucky. You can feed on it for the next few rungs up the ladder. People even make allowances for the failures: *It's just a miscalculation this time, he'll get lucky again.* And when the legend started to wear a bit thin, he transferred to the Met and rode up on reputation for another ten years or so.'

'Clive reckons you went over to the dark side after you left the police. Did you?'

'Depends where you think the light finishes and the dark begins, I guess.'

Lots of the other tables had had a simultaneous meal-finish. All around they were scraping back chairs, collecting up bags, finding room keys, arranging meeting points in the lobby. I expected O'Hara to use the racket to slide into a safer conversational topic.

Instead he said abruptly, 'Sometimes you take a wrong turning and then when you try to go back, you find the path behind you has disappeared. The only way is forward, down whatever route is open to you. Haven't you ever made choices in your life, duchy, that you'd undo if you could?'

'One big one.'

I told him about the time keen-as-mustard PC Grace Smith had answered a call to a domestic incident and found the wife of a small-time villain bruised and bleeding. It was a regular occurrence. Each time she'd bring charges against him and then withdraw her statement after a little 'persuasion' from her husband. This time she'd sworn she'd go through with it if I'd back her up and say I'd seen him do it. It had seemed like a lie in a good cause. Unfortunately at the time I'd put hubby and his flying fists in the marital home, a combined police and customs drugs bust further down the coast had gone down and one of the policemen had been run over by someone that bore a strong resemblance to Mr Wife-Beater. Initially his injuries hadn't appeared to be too serious, so I'd panicked and stuck to my original statement. When his condition had taken a turn for the worst, it had been too late to change my mind. I'd been 'invited' to sign my resignation letter.

'Shortly afterwards, several thousand pounds appeared in my bank account.'

'Did you keep it?'

'Natch.'

O'Hara grinned, his teeth very white against the tanned face. 'Atta girl!' He folded a wad of notes on to the bill holder and signalled to the waiter. 'You ready to go or do you want to do something about that cream around your mouth?' Without waiting for a reply, he took one corner of the napkin and wiped it off. 'In case I don't mention it later, the way you don't keep checking your appearance like most women is another thing I like about you.'

'Gee, all these compliments could go to a poor girl's head.'

'I can't help noticing that they all seem to be one-way.'

'Yeah, I noticed that too. You fit?'

I hooked my jacket back on and headed for the doors. He caught up with me as I reached the pavement.

'We're meeting Peter over on the South Bank.'

Concentrating on dashing across the roads between the traffic made conversation difficult until we reached the broad stretch of the Embankment. The touch of spring in the weather over the last couple of days plus the protection of the closely packed building in London had driven the fact it was only February from my mind. Down by the Thames the reality hit me with an icy blast. I gave an involuntary shiver and O'Hara tucked the jacket of my collar up around my neck.

'This way.' He turned left. I fell into step beside him. We walked beside the river until we came to the next bridge. O'Hara ran up the steps to road level and turned across it. On the opposite bank a small flight of steps between the buildings fronting the river led into an open space surrounded by tall blocks of flats and offices. The central section was a paved pedestrian area planted with a dozen trees (currently leafless), wooden benches, black and gold rubbish bins, and a red postbox. It seemed a popular place to hang out judging by the number of people here.

Most of them were dressed in layers of clothing, supplemented by the odd blanket worn poncho-style, and several were clutching the leads of skinny mongrels. There were a lot of unshaved whiskers out there and an equal number of white, pinched faces. We got enough dossers on the beach in Seatoun during the summer seasons for me to recognize that these people could be found tucked up on a nice warm pavement slab most nights.

'This is where Peter said he'd meet us,' O'Hara said.

A barrister on the skids. Was this guy going to remember the details of a case from twenty years ago. Was he actually going to remember his own name?

'What's he into?' I asked O'Hara. 'Drink? Drugs?'

'I didn't ask. Hang on here a second.'

He went over to talk to a group. Two men and a girl. All huddled in long coats, the girl in a woolly hat pulled to her eyebrows. Even from this distance I could read their body language. Suspicion. Fear masquerading as aggression. Acceptance. Something was passed over. O'Hara flicked his lighter on and the girl dipped her face into the flame, cupping her hands. Her nose jewellery flared in the light.

They said something to O'Hara and he nodded, moving into the crowd. The grey hair and black leather coat were swallowed in the murkiness beyond the street light.

23

There was a change of dynamics amongst the street dwellers. They started shifting and rearranging themselves, almost as if they were forming an audience around something. Their behaviour was explained when a van pulled into the 'stage' area. It was a food run for the homeless.

Some disappeared as soon as they'd collected their suppers. Others found a seat nearby and tucked straight in. The air started to fill with the smells of curry and coffee. Looking over the blokes shovelling in rice with plastic forks it was hard to picture any of them standing on their hind legs in a courtroom trotting out the legal arguments. How were we supposed to recognize Peter Corbin?

The crowd around the van back was thinning out. I edged a bit nearer. The woman distributing the food gave me a big smile. 'Hello, haven't seen you before, have I? I'm Milly. I've got chicken curry or macaroni cheese, which would you like?'

I caught a soft chuckle and knew it was O'Hara.

'I've eaten thanks. At the Waldorf.'

She smiled a let's-humour-her kind of smile. 'Well, would you like a hot drink?' She indicated the big vacuum jugs.

'No, I'd like a Peter Corbin. Do you happen to know one?'

She leant back into the van and called through. 'Pete. Someone to talk to you.'

The driver slewed round. 'You want me?'

O'Hara had moved to the front of the van while I was

fending off the offers of refreshment. 'O'Hara, we spoke on the phone.'

'Step inside the office.' He leant across and opened the passenger door.

I wasn't being left out on this interview. I scooted round and scrambled after O'Hara. The front was designed to carry three, providing one of them was on the thin side. I found myself squeezed thigh to thigh with O'Hara. He moved an arm and lay it along the seat behind my neck to give me more room.

'Thanks for seeing us, Pete.' They had one of those manly hand-shaking eye-to-eye bonding moments. 'This is Grace, she's an associate.'

'Actually, she's the private investigator hired to look into the Trudy Hepburn killing. Nice to meet you, Pete.'

'Same here. Hope you don't mind the location, but I needed to prepare a case this morning and then we had to drive down to my son's school to pick him up. This is really the only time I could fit you in.'

'This isn't a full-time career, then?'

'No. It's just me salving my social conscience by doing my bit one night a month. So, Trudy Hepburn, that was a lifetime ago.'

'Not for her,' I pointed out.

'No. It's always sadder somehow when someone dies before they've really done anything with their life. One of the duller murder cases I've worked on. No unexpected surprises. No fireworks. No passion.'

'You find murder passionate?'

'In my experience the reasons that provoke it are generally very passionate. What feeling could be more extreme than the desire to deliberately snuff out someone else's life?'

He shifted his weight fractionally to avoid twisting his neck to look at me. I guess if he was prosecuting a murder case twenty years ago, he must be at least fifty now, but he looked a lot younger. He had one of those slight, boyish figures and a Peter Pan face to go with it under a neat crop of light-brown hair that didn't appear to have a single grey strand in it. I asked him what he'd made of Alison.

'You have to remember that I wasn't her counsel, so my contact was limited. You know my godfather Vaughan Greives led for the defence?'

'O'Hara mentioned it.' It was an opening for O'Hara to join the discussion. He didn't take it. Once again he'd gone into Sphinx mode. He lounged back, letting me make all the running. 'Did your godfather talk about Alison?'

'Some time later. After it was decided there were no grounds for appeal. According to Uncle Vaughan, Alison claimed to have no memory of being at Abbot's Cottage that night. She said that the period between being in her bedroom at home and being in the back of the police car was a complete blank.'

'Really? Because that would rather tie in with a theory I had.' I described my scenario where Alison found Trudy dying and wandered from the cottage in shock.

'Possibly.'

'I get the sense I haven't sold you on it, Pete.'

He looked forward through the windscreen where a couple of dossers were tucking in. 'Alison underwent several psychiatric examinations before her trial.'

'And the shrinks didn't buy the amnesia act?'

'Opinions were divided. Uncle Vaughan decided that in order to make the psychiatric evidence credible he would have to put Alison on the stand. There was no point in telling the jury about Alison's loss of memory if they weren't going to be allowed to hear about it for themselves. It would simply raise doubts as to whether it was true – or a story cooked up by the defence team.'

'Do you know why he didn't put her up?'

'He didn't think she'd make the right impression on the jury. She was very self-contained. Almost detached. It's not what juries want to see. Particularly in a young girl. If she had been weepy, scared, vulnerable, something that could make them feel warm and protective towards her, she'd probably have got off, frankly.'

O'Hara made his first contribution to the conversation. 'Didn't Uncle Vaughan try to coach her into this winning mindset?'

Corbin's eyes twinkled, taking a few more years off his age. 'Naturally he did. But she wouldn't, or couldn't, play ball.'

'Were you surprised at the guilty verdict?' I asked. O'Hara's hand had dropped fractionally behind me and he'd started to move the tip of his thumb up and down the nape of my neck in what seemed to be an unconscious gesture. I was getting tingles in funny places.

'Could have gone either way. The case really rested on the forensic evidence. There wasn't a lot else. The police had never managed to link the knife to Alison but the jury didn't seem overly concerned by that. The lack of any motive was a big stumbling block in my case. Uncle Vaughan made a big production of that fact. If Alison had worn her school uniform and done a bit of weeping and wailing, I'm sure the verdict would have gone for her.'

'Did you know she'd recently had a baby?'

'Yes. The trial was arranged so that she'd be over the pregnancy by the time she appeared in court. I think the Social Services had obtained an order to prevent any mention of the baby in court or the press. It was going up for adoption and they felt the less attention, the better chance it had in the future. Pity really, from Uncle Vaughan's point of view; a cute baby crying for its mummy would have been a real jury swayer.'

I was rather warming to Corbin's cynicism on the importance of evidence in jury trials. 'Did you hear if the police ever had any other suspects for the murder?'

'Nary the one that I know of. Well, you'd know that better than me, O'Hara.'

Of course, I'd almost forgotten that they'd have met

before when PCs Pennington and O'Hara gave evidence at the trial.

'Uncle Vaughan did try to put forward your theory,' Corbin added. 'The unknown intruder and Alison stumbling on the scene, but the jury didn't go for it. Juries don't really like unknown intruders, they like a name and face to pin the guilt on. And there just wasn't anyone in Miss Hepburn's life for Uncle to point an underhand slander at. The dear lady appears to have led a blameless, and spectacularly dull, existence. Sorry I can't be of more help but as I said, most of what I'm telling you is coming second-hand from conversations I had with Uncle years ago.'

The two other helpers were packing up behind us. It was time to go. Slipping back to the ground, I asked Peter, as an after-thought, if he happened to know what had happened to Alison's solicitor, Indira Patel.

'Moved to Mauritius. She inherited a rather good portfolio of stocks and bonds and a town house in Chelsea from a . . . much older man ten years ago.'

'Uncle Vaughan,' I guessed.

'Uncle Vaughan.' Peter Corbin grinned. 'It's ironic really. Everybody had always assumed the old boy was gay. Well, must be going, we have to pick up another load of food and do another run. Nice to have met you, Grace. O'Hara.'

By the time we'd retrieved the car from the NCP where we'd left it and driven back to Seatoun, it was tomorrow. The journey back had been weird. O'Hara had played classical CDs. He seemed to have retreated to somewhere inside himself. Either he was deep or an Olympic class sulker.

That suited me since I was tired and full of white wine. I spent a lot of time in a near hypnotic state, lulled by the road lights and the rhythms of whichever dead composer was filling the leather-scented interior of the Merc. I was wondering whether O'Hara was going to try to follow through on what had felt like the beginnings of a pass in the van. And how I was going to react if he did.

'Where do you want dropping? Your place?'

His voice jerked me awake. The lit tower of Seatoun's only high-rise block was ahead of me, and out on the horizon the riding lights of a couple of oil tankers were winking. 'The office. I want to check something.'

He obediently negotiated the near-deserted streets and drew up outside Vetch's. I asked him where he was staying. 'Or do you live locally?'

'I got a place.' He didn't elaborate.

It was annoying when he had my address, not something I give out to just anyone. The red tail lights of the Merc were pulling away around the corner before something hit me. I *hadn't* given him my home address! I quickly re-ran all the conversations I'd had with him. No, I definitely hadn't mentioned it. So how come he'd turned up outside this morning?

I'd wanted to check for further emails from Betterman, perhaps a few clues as to where I could find him as he'd challenged me to do. But the inbox proved to be a Betterman-free zone.

Locking up again, I walked back to my flat. A large lump was sprawled face down before the door. Flaming Rosco.

Scooting down the metal steps, I kicked the drunken slob's legs. 'You aren't sleeping it off there, Terry. Push off and annoy someone else.'

He gave another deep-belly groan. If he'd thrown up on the step I was definitely going to castrate him. I played the beam of the pencil torch on my key-ring on to the base of the door. No vomit. The light flickered over Terry's head, and glinted on something on his hair. I moved closer, subconsciously registering the lack of alcohol stink tonight. The 'something' was a wet stickiness. I touched one finger to it and smelt. Blood. He wasn't drunk; someone had coshed him.

I quickly played the light around the rest of the basement

area. There was something wrong with the door; a dark central shadow where there had never been a shadow before. I let the illumination slide upwards and . . . yeuk!

24

With another groan Rosco pushed himself on to all fours, thereby greatly increasing his resemblance to a fifteen-stone porker. All he needed was the twirly tail on his rear. 'I'll kill him when I get my hands on the scroat.'

'A bloke, was it?'

'Bound to be. A bird couldn't put me down.' Ironman tried to stand, swayed and reached out to grab something. What he grabbed was the tub of razor-sharp exotic succulents that lived outside my front door – and which stubbornly refused to get themselves stolen. 'Ow!' He stuffed a fistful of fingers into his mouth. 'D'ertumdr.'

'I don't speak idiot, Terry.'

'I said there's something on your door. I was just taking a look when they jumped me.'

'Had accomplices too, did he?'

'Yeah. Probably.'

The torch was flickering. I located the keyhole before the light disappeared completely and opened the door, turning on the room light. It was now clear what the 'something' was.

A dead rat attached to the door by a nail in its tail. Somebody had slashed its throat and a white freezer label was protruding from the raw, red-rimmed gash like a stuck-out tongue. Trying not to touch Ratty, I twisted the label out: 'THIS IS HOW YOU WILL END UP IF YOU DON'T DROP THE TEACHERS BUSINESS, BITCH.'

'What's it say?'

Rosco tried to read over my shoulder. I palmed the message.

'The butcher. He's sorry I was out when he delivered, but he's left the usual. Well, 'night, Terry.'

'Heh, hang on!' He blocked the door with a foot. 'I've been attacked. I need first aid.'

'Try the hospital.'

'Ah come on, Smithie, let me in. I feel bad. And this hand hurts like shit.'

If I shut him out, he'd probably pass out on the step just to annoy me, and I'd end up down the nick explaining how he was assaulted by an unseen somebody and a tub of plants. 'Get inside then before anyone sees you.'

After I'd washed off rat, I sorted out some disinfectant, a box of plasters and a pair of tweezers. 'Here, you can pull the spines out of your hand while I sort out the head. Have you got any other symptoms? Nausea? Splitting headache?'

'Yeah, I have.'

'Oh good. Hold still.' The wound had bled copiously, but then head wounds tend to do that because there are a lot of blood vessels in that area. 'You're going to have a big lump here but I don't think it's done any serious damage. Did you pass out completely?'

'I don't think so. I heard him . . . them . . . legging it and then you came.'

'I'll have to cut off some hair to get to this.' I snipped off the blood-soaked bits. And then a little above. Plus a tad of straightening . . . 'Disinfectant coming up.'

He gave a heart-warming scream of pain. I cleaned out the wound and applied a large strip of plaster. 'Has Linda let you back in the house?'

'Heh, nobody tells Terry Rosco where to go. I'm still letting her sweat.'

'Fine. This is done, so snuffle off now. I'm tired and I want to get to bed.'

'Yeah, well, the thing is . . .'

'You are not spending another night here.'

'I feel really ropey. I could have concussion.'

His colour was getting better all the time and he'd had no

co-ordination problems extracting the spines. I was sure he didn't have concussion. On the other hand the wine and early start this (or rather yesterday) morning were kicking in in a serious way. I just wanted to lie down. And I couldn't be bothered to argue with Terry any longer.

'Get rid of the rat before you go to bed.'

The morning started well. Terry had gone.

It got worse. Terry came back.

'Left the door on the latch so I wouldn't have to wake you up,' he announced, crashing in just as I was coming round. 'I bought this.' He presented me with a carton of milk. 'You can make breakfast now.'

'I'm going round to Shane's place for breakfast.'

'Isn't he closed on a Monday?'

He was. Damn. Scrambling out of bed, I checked the stocks. Half a loaf that was a bit on the stale side, a tin of sardines and half a jar of peanut butter.

I slung the loaf on a plate. The plate broke.

Rosco was exploring the top of his head with his fingers. 'You reckon this plaster could come off now? It makes me look like a plonker.'

'I think you're crediting it with too much influence. Let's have a look.' Tweaking up a corner of the plaster, I peered underneath. 'The bleeding's stopped, it should be fine.' I grabbed a section and ripped.

Terry screamed. 'Hell . . . that *hurt*.'

'I thought it might.'

I plugged in the kettle and headed into the bathroom. There was no way I was getting into a bath with Terry Rosco the other side of an unlockable door but I needed the loo and a quick splash of cold water over my face. When I re-emerged, Terry was engaged in the tricky chore of pouring water on teabags. We had toast topped with the peanut butter and sardines. It's an acquired tase.

I retrieved the pink file from my coat pocket and jotted down notes while I ate.

'You still on that schoolgirl case?' Terry asked.

'I am.' I tipped out some of the envelope contents so I could disentangle my notes to date and pin the new ones to them. The photocopied picture of Trudy on the field trip was on top. 'Last time we spoke, Terry, you said none of the kids at St Martin's would have killed Trudy because ... Time to sing for your breakfast and finish that sentence.'

'Dunno what you're talking about.'

'Yes, you do.' I glared at the shifty slab of blubber. 'What did you do, swear a blood oath in the playground? It was twenty years ago, for heaven's sake, and you're a police officer. If you know something about a murder, cough it up.'

'I don't. It's nothing to do with her getting done. It's just he ...' He tapped a blob of sardine on to Orlando Roles's face. 'He said we were to lay off her.'

'And you always did what Orlando Roles said?'

'Yeah ... well ... some kids did. I could handle myself, but them that couldn't ...'

'Orlando was a bully?'

'Yeah ... no. He was like ... *The* Man.'

'And this lot?' I indicated the boys grouped around the smiling Trudy Hepburn.

'They were his mates.'

His enforcers, I guessed.

Terry pointed his greasy digit along the line, reeling off the names. 'That's Bossy, Knightie, Mick, Larry, Inchie, Andy and Spastic.'

'Spastic would be Philip Darrowfield?'

'Yeah.'

'Equal bullying opportunities for the mobility challenged. Very pc. What was Philip's contribution – breaking toes with his wheelchair?'

Terry looked blank. 'He didn't have a wheelchair.'

'Why the nickname then? Spastic?'

'Cos he was thick.' Rosco drew out the other picture Gillian had given me, of Alison Wynne-Ellis's year. 'See her?' He jabbed at a blonde girl in the front row. 'I gave her one. Back of the ghost ride at the amusement park.'

'When was this? Befriend a Dork Week?'

'Nah, it was a couple of years back.'

While he drained the teapot, I checked the spare cupboard-room. And reeled back. 'Bloody hell, Terry, why didn't you chuck the rat outside?'

'I did. I think the bedding needs washing. You want to think about that next time you got guests. It could put some people off staying with you. Got to take a slash.'

I pulled on some clothes while he was in there. Now that Vetch's plumbing was firing on all cylinders, I could have a bath at the office. I'd just finished when there was a knock on the front door.

O'Hara was in grey and leather again. He smelt of fresh soap and warm sugary dough. The latter was explained when he extended a paper bag and two carryout cups from Seatoun's latest coffee chain franchise.

'Breakfast. Croissants and coffee.'

'I already ate. Sardines and peanut butter.'

'Are you pregnant?'

'Not unless it's the longest gestation period in history.'

'Lean period in the romance stakes, duchy?'

'No. I'm just very selective.'

'I'll bear that in mind. Lucky I'm such a remarkable catch.' He put the coffee down and examined a silver-framed photo of a mutt I'd dog-sat last year. 'Yours?'

'No. Just a friend.'

'I too have known the love of a good dog.'

Rosco erupted from the bathroom. At least this time he had his clothes on. And he'd been eavesdropping. 'I went out with a dog once. Nothing wrong with dogs. Ugly birds have got their place. They don't expect none of this I love you bollocks. And they're dead grateful.'

He disappeared into the spare room again. We both listened to the sounds of grunting and cursing.

'Prune?' O'Hara said.

'I've heard him called worse.'

He held out the open bag. 'Prune, almond, plain, or warm chocolate croissant?'

Rosco barrelled out again. He was holding something bundled up in one of my sheets. He barged between me and the bakery bag. 'Oh cheers, mate!' The warm chocolate croissant left the flat clutched in Terry's mitt.

I gave O'Hara a big smile. 'So, apart from the breakfast delivery, was there any other reason for this visit?'

He took a chair and stretched out easily, levering the lid from his coffee. 'I came to compare notes, see where we were with case.'

I could sense a change in him. The dark moody stranger who'd driven me home last night had gone and the easy-going charmer was back. On the surface at least.

'I'm not sure *we* are anywhere. How did you know where I live? I never told you.'

'Traced you through your phone number.'

'I didn't give you my phone number. And I'm ex-directory.'

'I know someone who can hack into the telephone subscribers' database. You're the only G. Smith on this area code that lives in Seatoun.'

'Wouldn't it have been easier to ask me?'

'I had a hunch you might not tell me. Do we have any other problems in this partnership?'

'I don't know anything about you. You spent the entire meal last night talking, and you didn't give out one personal fact that I can remember.'

'It takes me a long time to decide who I want to let inside my life. I'm sort of guessing you're the same, duchy.' He gestured around the room with his cup. 'The only photograph you have on display is of a dog that isn't even yours. Not a lot of clues in here to point to the real Grace Smith.'

I could feel myself getting defensive. Mostly because I knew he was right. And I didn't like it being pointed out to me. I took a few deep breaths before saying, 'I told you about my reasons for leaving the police. That's one more fact than you gave me.'

'So are you going to ditch the partnership because I haven't given you my complete CV?'

No, I wasn't. He might have information or connections that I needed. On the other hand, I wasn't going to tell him everything either. 'Someone nailed a dead rat to my door last night.'

'Is that usual?'

'No, they usually post it through the letterbox. Of course it's not bloody usual! It was another warning to drop this case. So I'm obviously rattling someone's cage. Possibly the real murderer is scared of what I'm going to uncover.'

'Possibly. However, that would seem to rule out your theory that the Wynne-Ellises did it. Unless you're theorizing that they popped down while we were eating dinner in order to deliver a rodent?'

'No, I'm not. They might have had an accomplice. Someone who still lives in the area.' He lifted an eyebrow.

OK, even I could hear that my theories were getting wilder by the minute.

'Any other theories?' he asked.

The mysterious 788 perhaps? Only I was keeping that nugget to myself. I tried to dredge up some excuse to get rid of him.

He lobbed the empty cup across the room into the bin and stood up. 'I have to go.' He scrawled a number on the croissant bag. 'That's my mobile number if you need me.'

'Should I get my tame hacker to trace it?'

'Cash purchase. Pay As You Go. How about yours?'

'I don't have a mobile. The dog ate it.'

'Right.' His tone was sceptical. 'How about dinner tonight? What do you fancy? French? Italian? Polish? Chinese?'

I elected for French. O'Hara headed out for wherever. And I headed for Vetch's.

As soon as I stepped through the office door I knew something was wrong. Several somethings.

25

After nearly two weeks of empty, echoing spookiness, Vetch's had a lived-in feel again.

'Vetch is back,' Jan announced. 'And the other two came in to collect their messages. They're catching the Eurostar into Lille if anyone wants them.'

Right at that moment I didn't really care about the re-population of Vetch's Investigations. Lurking in the middle of the waiting area was Tallulah's larger cage. I tried very hard to believe that Jan had brought it in so the bird didn't go walkabout around the office.

'Is the parrot OK?'

'Course she's not. She's bald, she's scared of being on her own and she never stops yapping. I reckon she needs therapy. Mum says she can't stay at our house any more. She says the racket is driving her mental. She drank a load of tequila.'

'Your mum or Tallulah?'

'The parrot.'

The cage was empty. 'Where is she now?'

'Up there.'

I found her on the first-floor landing, watching the reception area through the bannister rails. Today the outfit was red polyester with a spiderweb pattern.

'How's life, kid?'

Tallulah's large eyes and beak stared reproachfully from her red hood. '*I'm ready for my close-up.*'

I bent down to examine her. Jan was right. She didn't seem to have many feathers left under there. On the other hand, she was lively enough and her vocal chords were still going non-stop. I went back down to Jan and asked if she couldn't bird-sit in the office.

'Suppose. Only Vetch don't know she's here. I told him you were keeping the cage for a client. And I ain't staying overnight.'

'I'll do nights. And I'll handle Vetch if he cuts up.'

I popped into the ground-floor office to say 'hi' to our esteemed leader. The little gnome was huddled behind his over-large, leather-finished, wooden executive-style desk. The tips of his nose and pointy gnome ears were red and most of the desk top was covered with cold remedies and boxes of paper hankies.

'Sweet thing. How dovely to see you again.'

'Can't say the same, Vetch. You look awful. Are you sure you should have come in?'

'Must show willing, sweet thing. I look worse than I feel. Although if you habben to be passing a chemist, I'd be grateful for another shot of the hard stuff.' He waved a bottle of Day Nurse cold remedy. 'Pull ub a chair and tell me what's been going on. Starting with why our receptionist is writing a neighbourhood survey report?'

I brought him up to date with what had been happening in the office (minus Tallulah).

'Letter bombs and shootings? I don't like the sound of that, sweet thing. Why haben't you brought the police in?'

'To tell them what?' Somebody sent me a giant party popper? I'm not even certain that the shooting was connected. There's been no other attempt since. It could just have been some kid trying out his new shiny toy that he bought in the pub car park. Random shootings aren't exactly unknown in Seatoun.'

'True.' Vetch steepled his fingers. Increasing his resemblance to the gnome with the fishing rod, the one that's always perched by the pond edge. 'But normally they tend to be our happy summer trippers who've mistaken the amusement arcade bindows for a row of plastic ducks. And they use air rifles.'

'Life moves on, Vetch. And so do the moronically challenged. Last year was air rifles and text messaging. This year it's converted replicas and video messaging. We shouldn't stand in the way of progress.'

'We certainly shouldn't if it's got a firing pin behind it. Keep in regular touch with the office and if anything else habbens on these premises, I want it reported to the police regardless of your personal feelings. Agreed?'

'Whatever you say.'

'In fact, for your own safety, sweet thing, it might be as well to get every incident checked out from now. Even those with charmed lives eventually reach the bottom of the luck bucket. And for heaven's sake, make sure you check Jan's report before it goes to the client. I don't want the company sued for libel.'

I assured him I was monitoring Jan closely and that giving her a little responsibility had worked wonders on her job motivation. Luckily he didn't follow me back into reception, so he missed the sight of Jan with her black-booted and fishnet legs crossed up on the desk while she nibbled a peppermint cream bar and browsed the latest copy of *Wannabee* (the magazine for those who want to be famous).

I asked her if she could send some emails for me.

'Yeah, I suppose so. After I've sent for me entry forms.'

I set her up to send another message to all the ex St Martin's pupils, both those who'd replied to the first trawl and those who'd ignored me.

'Just send: "What can you tell me about seven eight eight?" '

'What's seven eight eight?'

'That's what I'm trying to find out. And while you're doing that, I shall be taking a bath and then calling on another source of information – your Mr Root.'

'He's not my Mr Root. He's a creep. He used to stand under the stairs looking up the girls' knickers . . .'

Vetch's door opened and his little bald head popped out.

'By the way, Jan, don't open any bulky letters or parcels. If there are any in the bostbox, leave them where they are and call me. Grace had a letter bomb.'

'Really! Wow! Can I have a case like that?'

'No. Unless you bish to be famous as the fingerless typist.'

'Anyway it was a party popper bomb,' I corrected. Loudly. Above my head Tallulah's voice was rising. 'How are the rehearsals for the musical going, Jan? *Oklahoma*, isn't it?' Taking a deep breath, I sang the first word at the top of my voice. She caught on and joined in. Together we bawled about wind rushing over the plains.

'Good bod,' Vetch said faintly. He retreated behind a shut door.

St Martin's school appeared to be deserted. And there was no answer from the caretaker's (sorry – premises manager's) house. A situation that was explained when I knocked at a neighbour's house.

'Half-term. All week.'

'Do you know when Mr Root is due back?'

After a scrutiny from my newly-washed hair to my second-best trainers, Root's neighbour admitted that he was planning to be back sometime today.

The warmer weather had retreated with a vengeance. When I got back to the promenade, sand grains were blowing in undulating waves over the contours of the beach and ragged-topped grey waves were being torn into fragments of spume as they roared towards the shore. On an impulse I turned right and walked up to St John's Road. It was one of the longest streets in Seatoun, stretching from the seafront right through the town and out into farm fields beyond.

The church of St John the Baptist stood on a small natural rise of land and was surrounded by the grass field of the churchyard, which was bounded by stone walling on the road side. I wove my way through the gravestones, stepping carefully to avoid the slush of last year's fallen leaves that had decomposed into a slippery mass.

Those tombs nearest the church and St John's Road were large decorated monuments – mostly dedicated to long-forgotten church officials and the odd local nob who'd owned land hereabouts. Round the back the grave markers were simpler. Many of them were standing at drunken angles, the grasses at their base overgrown and the flower containers all empty. At the furthest point from the main road, I found the cremation stones. Small square slabs and raised wedges in all shades from pink speckled marble to gleaming black granite.

Trudy's stone was near the end of the last line. It had probably been plain white once; now it had aged to a dirty grey covered with green mildew and the muck of twenty years' decomposing vegetation. I scraped some off with my trainer to make out the dedication:

TRUDY HEPBURN
aged 25 years
This stone is dedicated to her memory
by her friends and pupils at St Martin's School

She was five years younger than me and this was all that was left of her. A shiver went through my soul.

Returning to the street, I caught sight of a chemist across the road and remembered Vetch's cold remedy. A couple of squabbling magpies landed on the roof and skidded down the tiles. Following their descent, I found my eyes being drawn to the golden lettering on a dark red background: Sorrenson's. One of the boys in Orlando Roles's gang of thugs had been a Laurence Sorrenson. It was an unusual name for this area; there had to be a connection.

It turned out there was. His parents had owned the pharmacy, but they'd sold it to the present owners five years ago when they'd moved to Australia to be near their son and grandchildren.

'Laurence?' I queried.

The pharmacist nodded. 'He was their only child. They sent me a photo last Christmas. I keep it in the shop because customers are always asking after them. See?' He handed me a glossy shot of a family group enjoying Christmas on the beach. One couple in their seventies, the other in their thirties and, perched amongst the adults, three little girls. Both the men and all the children had the near white-blonde hair of their Scandinavian ancestry. Laurence was wearing a short-sleeved T-shirt, his tanned right wrist apparently ringed by a chain tattoo until I borrowed a magnifying glass from the pharmacist and checked it out. The 'chain' was made up of the interlinked figures 7 and 8 constantly repeated.

Since I was on a roll, I asked the pharmacist if he knew of a shop in this road who rented out their upper rooms for social functions.

'You mean Inchbeck's Bakery. It's the Chinese takeaway now.'

I took a logical guess and said, 'And their son, Sean . . . I don't suppose you happen to know . . . ?'

He did. Sean and Laurence had taken off for Australia together. Sean was now a proud father of four little girls and living in Sydney. As I said, Seatoun does tend to breed a desire to put half a planet between you and it.

Mr Root still hadn't returned home, so I headed back down to the office to see if there had been any replies to my emails regarding 788.

Jan shook her head, setting a large pair of silver earrings shaped like daggers swinging in opposite directions. 'I'm only just finishing sending them.' She clicked on a bit of text, did something else and the text suddenly appeared in a fresh email.

'How'd you do that?'

'It's called cut and paste. Annie showed me how.' Her voice sounded a little husky.

'You're not getting the bug back, are you?'

'I have to keep singing, don't I, every time Vetch opens his door.'

I looked up. A small head was staring through the railings on the first floor. 'She doesn't seem to be making as much noise as usual.'

'I've put sunflower seeds over the stairs and landings up there. It gives her gob something else to do.'

26

The gates of Roles Motors were standing wide open. Cleopatra, the hybrid werewolf, was thrilled to see nine stone of fresh meat arriving. She danced on her hind legs, straining against the ship's anchor cable and howling like a canine banshee.

The racket attracted Billy Roles out of the cabin office again. 'Shut up. Bitch. What do you want?'

I wasn't entirely sure which one of us was the 'bitch'. Billy looked tidier and soberer and meaner than at our last meeting. Perhaps he'd remembered I'd walked off with his bottle of vodka.

'Hi. Grace Smith. We met a few nights ago.'

'I know who you are. You're a private snooper, Orlando reckons. So you can sling your hook from here, darling.'

'Have you got anything to drink in the cabin, Mr Roles?'

'Why?'

'Because I much prefer you drunk.'

His thin face creased, narrowing his grey eyes into slits. And then suddenly his features relaxed and he chuckled. 'Ay, you may be right, darling. I like me drunk better too. Come in and have a glass with me.'

Instead of heading up the stairs, he walked round the back of the cabin. I followed, keeping well out of the werewolf's fang range. The chain was bolted to a metal post at the rear of the building. Bending down near it, Billy scuffed the ground. Cleopatra bounded over and scrabbled with her front paws. Carelessly, Billy punched her muzzle. She retreated with a whimper. Billy exposed a hinged metal lid. Taking a key from his pocket, he unlocked it, reached inside and drew out a litre bottle of vodka.

Looking at me over his shoulder, as we returned to the office, he winked. 'Safer than Fort Knox, darling. Cleo will rip the throat out of anyone who tries to get near.'

Ever since my inglorious departure from the police, I've had to be wary of giving them any excuse to pick me up. On the other hand, the most enthusiastic wielder of the breathalyser was currently trying to bum a free bed at my flat. I reckoned I could risk a small vodka. Billy interpreted this as half a glass. He filled his own to the top.

'Cheers, darling.' His Adam's apple bobbed frantically as most of the contents slid down. With a contented sigh, he wiped his hand over his wet lips and refilled. 'First one today. The docs reckon I should lay off the booze. Doesn't go with me medicine.'

I sipped. 'What's wrong with you?'

Billy eased his tie knot undone. His eyes had a moist glaze. It didn't seem to take much to get him boozed up. 'Nosy little bitch, aren't you?'

'Goes with being a snooper.'

'I'm dying, darling.' Billy tapped the trilby. 'Got a tumour up here. Docs say they can't cut it out. So who gives a shit if the medicine don't like the vodka. *I* like it.'

He proceeded to prove it by knocking back another shot. 'Never used to drink. Had to be careful. Keep my wits about me. Making up for lost time now.' The folder he'd been using last time appeared on his desk again. 'I've got it all planned out, you know. Me funeral. All me old mates will be there. Some of me old enemies too.' He chuckled at a private joke, then pulled out another load of brochures and stroked the covers. 'Formal dress. I'm not having anyone turning up at my funeral in jeans. And I've marked out the procession route I want to the graveyard. To be followed by a champagne reception; swanky country club, none of your sandwiches in the front room for Billy Roles. All the old firms will be sending a representative. Billy's not been forgotten. Going to be a do they'll be talking about for years. If Al Capone had lived in Seatoun, this is the funeral he'd have had.'

'Sounds like a hot ticket.'

'I've put it all in my will so if I don't get what I want, Orlando won't get my cash. What you doing up here then? Not looking for a car, are you?'

'I was looking for Orlando. I wanted to ask him something, but maybe you can help instead. Has he got any tattoos?'

'Got some numbers on his backside. Had 'em done when he was a kid. Sure he'll be happy to show 'em to you.' He helped himself to more vodka. 'I always reckoned he'd do something important; surgeon or a judge, or running one of them big companies that pay you millions for bollocking the job up. That's why I called him Orlando. Can't spend your life tossing hamburgers with a name like that. So what's he ever done? Start bloody useless businesses that I had to bail out.'

'The Internet car business not doing well?'

Billy spat accurately into the wastepaper bin. 'I made more from this place than he ever did with his stuck-up plans.'

'Legally?'

'What?'

'I was talking to an ex-copper the other day about your other career – as the Handyman, the villains' fixer of choice.'

An expression settled on Billy's face – pride. 'I was a good 'un back then, darling. Everyone knew they could trust Billy Roles. The coppers never proved anything neither. I had *respect*.'

I raised my glass to him. 'Respect.'

He beamed. 'Cheers, darling.' He whacked back another triple shot. 'Kept thinking he'd make good, you know.' His eyes moistened further. Billy was plainly a maudlin drunk rather than a fighting drunk. 'When he was eighteen, twenty-five, thirty ... kept thinking he'll get himself a proper career, make me proud. But I've got to face facts, he's thirty-six and the only ambition my Orlando's got is to see me drop dead, so he can flog this place to some builder who wants to build a block of flats, and buy himself some more fancy suits. Be a bit of a shock for 'em when they start digging the bodies out of the foundations.' He saw my reaction and burst into loud laughs. 'Just a joke, darling. I've got more sense than to dirty my own doorstep.' He sighed and stared into his vodka as if it were a crystal ball.

'Did Orlando ever talk about the murder at St Martin's?' I asked.

'What's to say? Some teacher got stuck.' Billy lifted indifferent shoulders, still looking for his future in the vodka.

'Did you know her?'

I was expecting a no. But surprisingly Billy said, 'Lumpy, dark-haired bitch. She come up here once. Complaining about my boy. Reckoned he was giving her grief. Wanted me to "reason" with him. Stupid cow. She was the teacher, she wanted respect, she should have earned it. Not come whining to me.'

I asked Billy if he'd told Orlando about the visit. 'Probably. Can't remember. He wouldn't have cared. Thought he was cock of the walk at that school. He probably was. Had a few shocks when he got out into the real world; they soon sussed him for the useless prat he really is. I made sacrifices for that boy, you know? He wasted them. I wanted him to make me proud.'

He stretched out in the chair. His head fell back and his mouth fell open. I was debating whether to creep out or wake him, when Cleopatra solved my problem by launching into an intruder-alert howl. It brought Billy to life with a grunting snort just as his son-and-heir entered the cabin.

'Grace. We must stop meeting like this.'

'She's interested in your arse.' Billy gave a snort of

laughter and grabbed the vodka before Orlando could reach it.

'You know the doctors said—'

'Stuff the bloody docs. Now leave me alone or I'll change me will. Leave the lot to Cleopatra.'

Orlando apparently decided to let his dad drink himself senseless. 'So what was it you wanted? Taking me up on that drink?'

'Raincheck again. Sorry. I really am interested in your butt.'

'Well, great. I like a girl who makes the running.' He hitched the trouser leg of one of those fancy suits and sat himself next to me in the other visitors' chair.

I let him preen for a few more moments before adding. 'Or to be exact, the tattoo on your butt. Seven eight eight.'

'Who told you I had that tattooed on my butt?'

'I have my sources. So what's it mean?'

'It was the name of our band. Me and some friends formed a rock band. We were going to be the next UB40.'

'So how come you didn't mention that the first time I asked you about that number?'

'Truthfully? I don't really know. Because it was embarrassing I guess. Even thinking about it now makes me cringe. We must have looked like total wusses. Why'd you want to know anyway?'

'Just a few leads I'm following up on a case.'

'You follow butts for a living? Sounds fun. Maybe I should consider a career change.'

'Bit sodding late for that,' Billy muttered behind him.

'Is that all? Only my father is unwell—'

'I'm pissed.'

'– and I should be getting him home.'

'Well, since you're in such an informative mood, do you mind telling me where you were on Saturday night?'

'Rugby Club dinner. Got there about seven-thirty, left when they closed the bar at one. Would you like the names and addresses of the other guests?'

So that put him out of the frame for the shooting. 'What about Sunday night?'

'Drinks and dinner in Winstanton and then off to bed. Not on my own.'

'Have you got a name and address for her too?'

'I don't think she's your type. Strictly AC – no DC.'

Could be true. In which case he hadn't been the rat delivery either.

'Is that it?'

'There are a couple of other things. Why did you call the dogs off Trudy Hepburn a few weeks before she died?'

'Because the younger kids had nearly drowned her. Even I could see that was taking the game too far.'

'How warm and caring of you.'

He laughed. 'It wasn't concern, well, not for her anyway. We had a sweet deal going at the school. The headmaster was a muppet. You could do pretty much anything you liked. But if we'd actually managed to kill one of the teachers, then it was a pretty safe guess that the old fart would have been replaced by someone with a less relaxed attitude, shall we say, to school discipline. Anything else I can do for you?'

He reached out and stroked the back of his hand down my cheek. I daresay someone had once told him it was a sensual gesture. I leant in a little closer and watched the certainty start to glow in his eyes. 'Actually, Orlando, I was wondering . . . why are you and Gina Gibbs discussing my movements?' He looked confused. 'You called yesterday when I was there.'

He lied and denied it. We both heard the thud of the bottle just before the puddle of vodka trickled under the desk towards our feet. Billy's chin had sunk to his chest and, as we watched, Billy sunk under the desk.

I left Orlando to it. I needed to make a couple of calls.

I went back to the flat to avoid any parrot problems should Vetch have detected the featherless one. Parking up,

I bounced down the basement steps, side-stepped the succulent exotics and opened the front door.

My stomach flipped.

27

I edged inside, ready to fight or flee if anything nasty popped out of the woodwork. My ears picked up that alien sound again. It was the faintest metallic '*thrump*'. Rather like a door closing quietly. I moved to the side slightly where I could see the bathroom and spare room doors. They both appeared closed. Listening hard, I tried to detect sound from one of the rooms. If I chose the wrong one, whoever or whatever was in the other would have a fraction of time to dash out and make the front door. Which, on the whole, might be a plan that suited us both pretty well.

I took another step and my heart jumped into my mouth. The sound had come again. Only this time it was behind me. I whirled round. *Thrump*. It was over to my right, by the cooker. As I watched, the lid of the large saucepan lifted and settled again with a soft '*thrump*', releasing a cloud of cooking smells and steam.

I didn't have a large saucepan. At least, I hadn't when I left this morning. A vision of the dead rat pinned to the door swam in front of my eyes. Was this another warning? We can get into your flat?

The saucepan was still letting off little pops of steam. I detected a meaty, alcoholic aroma. Rat au vin perhaps? I eased off the lid. Gravy was bubbling like a volcanic mud pool. I cut the heat and wondered what to do with the contents of the saucepan. It smelt wonderful, but even I drew the line at eating rat. Finding a spoon, I fished around for a lump of meat. It didn't look like rat. It looked more like beef.

In the end I left it where it was. Since I'd promised Vetch

to be a responsible little investigator in future, I'd get a sample packed up later and send it off to see if it had any extra added ingredients not recommended by *The Good Food Guide.*

I gulped down a couple of glasses of water to dilute the effects of the vodka and looked up G. Knight in the phone book. There were three and I got the postman on the third attempt. This time I was a promoter putting together tribute bands for a nostalgia weekend at the local holiday camp. 'Someone gave me your name. I hear you and Orlando Roles played in a wicked band about twenty years back?'

'Not me. Never been in a band in my life. You must have the wrong number.'

No, I had the right number: 788. What I had was the wrong explanation for its existence. Thanks to Orlando Roles, whose nose should be as long as he plainly thought his dick was.

I re-locked the front door, heaved the tub of succulents across it and scratched an inch-long mark on the flagstone at the back with my ballpoint pen. If my intruder came back with dessert, at least I'd have some warning.

The lights were on in the premises manager's house. As I lifted my hand to ring the bell, the door opened and Gillian Anderson came out. She looked like a woman on duty.

'I thought it was half-term?'

'It is. But school business doesn't stop because there are no pupils in it. Are you any further forward with your enquiries on Alison and Trudy?'

'Some. Does the number seven eight eight mean anything to you in connection with St Martin's?'

She shook her head. 'No, it doesn't. But after you left I did remember one other small incident concerning Alison. I don't suppose it's of any consequence, but since it is one of the few times I can recall her clearly, I thought I'd mention it. About a week before the end of that term, I saw Alison in the corridor. She was talking to a couple of the boys. She seemed upset.'

'Could you hear why?'

'No. I was too far away. The only reason I noticed was because she was edging along the wall, as if she was trying to get away and one of the boys put his arm out, as a barrier. I assumed it was just part of the normal bullying culture that went on in the school at that time. But . . .' She frowned slightly, her eyes focused on something twenty years in the past. 'I'm not sure it was. The boys didn't look threatening. They were almost . . . pleading.'

'Which boys?'

'It was two of Orlando Roles's little clique. One was Andrew Lee, and I think the other was Michael Forbes. I was going to go down there and intervene, but Orlando beat me to it. He went for Andrew, and Alison shot off while I was breaking up the fight. That was unusual in itself. Orlando didn't normally get involved in rough stuff. He preferred psychological torture. The physical side was usually delegated to one of the others.'

'Do you know what the fight was about?'

'I remember Orlando saying something like, "Where is it?" And Andrew telling him to get lost. I left them to it. It must have been fairly serious because now I think about it, I remember that Andrew wasn't part of that gang for the last term of the year. But don't ask me why, because I haven't a clue.'

'Can I ask you about Philip Darrowfield instead? You said something about him needing special schooling, but I keep hearing he wasn't in a wheelchair then?'

'He wasn't. It wasn't a physical problem. Philip had learning difficulties. When the others were at the intellectual and emotional levels of sixteen-year-olds, Philip was at the level of a ten-year-old, consequently he was either neglected or he was disrupting the entire class. He was a very large boy, physically strong, and if he became frustrated because he couldn't understand the lesson, he had a tendency to throw furniture or punch out windows. It wasn't deliberate violence, more that he was incapable of making the connection between throwing the chair and the fact that if it hit someone, it was going to hurt them. Was that all?'

'Yes. No.' It wasn't any of my business probably, but I couldn't resist asking what had gone down between her and Georgina Pennington.

'Who said anything had? Gina?'

'It's more your tone of voice when you talk about each other.' That and the fact Georgie had described her as smug and self-righteous. I was curious to hear the adjectives Gillian would apply to Georgie.

'Well, it's no secret. Shortly after she joined the school, there was a major outbreak of graffiti. It was plainly first-years; lots of badly spelt crude references to sex that they thought would shock us. Anyway, one day Gina marched a boy into the head's office and announced he'd owned up and volunteered to clean off all the graffiti and pick rubbish up in the playground for a month. We were all impressed; until we found out how she'd done it.' She pushed the collar of her jacket into her throat to counteract the cold wind. 'She'd hidden a tape recorder in their classroom. She had a recording of the culprit boasting about what he'd done and, fortunately from her point of view, also boasting about taking money from his mother's purse, so he didn't dare complain to his parent when Gina told him what she'd done. The headmaster, and indeed most of the staff, couldn't see anything wrong with what she'd done. I thought it was underhand and not the way for a responsible teacher to behave. She thought I was a prig.'

Lights from the hallway slid over her glossy bob as the door was pulled wider open behind her. 'Is everything all right, Mrs Anderson?'

'Yes thank you, Brian. This is the private investigator I spoke about. I'll be in Friday to check how you're getting on with the graffiti removal. It needs to be finished before lessons start. Goodnight.'

She clicked away on high heels. The expression on Brian Root's face suggested Friday wasn't going to be the high spot of his week.

'Hi! Grace Smith. Can I come in?'

Brian stepped back. His house was freshly decorated in bland colour schemes that you forgot as soon as you'd seen them. He showed me into a sitting room where a couple of small beige sofas were arranged to corral a low coffee table and face a widescreen TV and DVD player. Shuffling together some sheets of handwritten notes and balancing two dirty cups and saucers on top of them, he offered tea or coffee.

I went for tea. It would take him longer. While he was clattering around in the kitchen at the rear, I checked out the stack of DVDs in the rack. They were all hot porno triple XXX and the latest pop music promos.

He came back with two cups balanced on a tray. 'You didn't say whether you took sugar, so I brought the bowl. Or are you sweet enough already?'

I smiled at the ancient joke and spooned in a couple of shots. Brian perched opposite. He was one of those thin, round-faced, nondescript blokes that can stand in an empty room and make it look unoccupied. I'd recognized him as the bloke in the pea-green blazer who'd been holding the hospice appeal bucket in that old photo, but he reminded me of someone else as well. It took a few moments to remember who. He was a dead spit for a picture of Dr Crippen I'd seen in *True Crimes.*

'So how can I help you, Gracie? The head said you were investigating that teacher's murder? Bit of a while ago now.'

'Twenty years. Do you remember that time, Mr Root?'

'Call me Beattie. All the kids do. We don't stand on formality around here. I remember everything, me. Got a retentive memory. She was a funny one, that Miss Hepburn. Heartburn we used to call her.'

'Who's "we"?'

'Me and the kids. I've always got on with the kids. They see me as more of a mate. I keep up with things, me. I can talk to them in their own language. I can tell you all the bands in the charts this week.'

'Did any of the kids talk about the murder after Alison's arrest? Suggest someone else might have done it?'

'Can't say they did, Gracie.' And he put forward the same reaction that I'd had from everyone who was around St Martin's at that time. 'Can't see any reason why anyone else would *want* to kill Heartburn.'

'You never saw Trudy arguing with anyone? Or anyone threatening her?'

'One or two of the kids might have said something in the heat of the moment. But they don't mean it. It's just the juice talking. None of them would have really bothered to work up a sweat about Heartburn. She didn't have anything about her. Not like the other one. You know she used to share with another teacher here?'

'Gina Gibbs.'

'Yeah.' Crippen ran the thin tip of his tongue over his lips. 'Now *she* was a good-looking woman. And strict. Knew how to keep control. None of the kids messed with her a second time. She knew how to discipline them.' His voice caressed the words 'strict' and 'discipline'. 'She's an old mucker of mine too. Think she fancied me a bit, know what I mean, Gracie?' He gave me a big wink. 'Often used to drop round for a drink after school, Gina did.'

I grappled with the idea of Gina Pennington getting it on with Brian Root. It was an impossible scenario. 'Are you still in touch?'

'No. Love 'em and leave 'em, that's my motto. She's a happy memory, my Gina. Even these lads didn't mess her about.' I'd taken the group photo of Trudy and the boys from the file. He picked it up. 'They were a good bunch, but high-spirited, know what I mean?'

'Mates of yours, were they?'

'Oh yes.' Beattie's pigeon chest swelled. 'Practically one of the crew, me.'

Did he have a 788 tattoo? There was just no way I was asking to see it.

'That's Orlando Roles. Of Roles Motors. Got me a good deal on a second-hand motor. Do anything for me, Orlando. He was a case. Always had to have the best gear. Looked like one of them models in the expensive magazines; the ones with the posh girls in little tight dresses. I remember once, this kid ran his bike through a puddle, splashed Orly's trousers with mud. The kid was terrified, but Orly was cool about it. He said something like, "That was rather unfortunate, wasn't it? You *will* remember not to do it again?" and you can see them all thinking, What's he going to do to make that kid remember? And then a week later, I come back here one evening and there's this kid locked in the cellar, stark naked, with his bits painted green. They'd used that neon paint on him. His willy must have glowed in the dark for days.'

'Did you call the police?'

'Course I didn't. It was just a joke, wasn't it? Even the kid said it was cool. It's being heavy-handed that gets these kids' backs up. You've got to learn to talk their language . . . roll with the rap, you know . . .' He mimed what might have been a dance movement. Or perhaps his bum itched.

'Tell me, Beattie, does the number seven eight eight mean anything to you? Something to do with St Martin's?'

'No. Can't say I can bring anything to mind, Gracie.'

I *hate* being called Gracie. 'It's not a classroom number? Or a locker number?'

'No. There are no classrooms that high. And the lockers only went up to a hundred on each colour. You'd have Red one to Red one hundred, and then Blue one to Blue one hundred—'

I interrupted quickly before he could run through the entire spectrum. 'Mrs Anderson thought the gang had sent

Andrew Lee to Coventry during their final term. Do you know what that was about?'

'Well, it's a question of loyalty, isn't it, Gracie?'

'In what way?'

'My lips are sealed. Can't help you. But apart from that, drop in anytime. I'm cool. Anything you want to talk about, Beattie Root's the man for you.'

Only if he was the last one left on earth. And not even then if there was a single sheep left alive on the planet.

Jan was applying the finishing touches to a full face of slap. She tended to go for deep greys and purples and layer them on. With the black clothing and gothic jewellery she generally looked like a vampire hooker. In her cage Tallulah was warbling her *Grease* selection ('*lightning . . . lightning . . . lightning . . . big boy*'). She was wearing a fetching little red velvet cape and a matching bonnet.

Catching my look towards Vetch's door, Jan said, 'It's OK, he's gone. And now I'm outta here too. I changed her outfit, and here's her spare ones. You need to change them regularly because she poops on them.' She handed me a carrier full of dolls' clothes, all slashed to accommodate wings.

'Is this really necessary?'

'How would you like having to walk around naked in this weather? Birds are dead sensitive to temperature. See ya.'

'Hang on. What about the big cage? I can't get it in my car. Can Eric use the van again?'

'Suppose. I'll ask him.'

Setting the alarm, I toted Tallulah out to the car in her travel case and drove home. The tub outside the front door had been moved back into its original position and the flat lights were on.

28

I locked Tallulah in the car and took the jack out of the boot. Keeping to one side where I'd be shielded by the wall, I nudged the front door open.

'Are you coming in?'

I peered round the door. O'Hara was calmly stirring the contents of the saucepan. The gold-rimmed spectacles were back. He waved a dripping spoon at me. 'Dinner will be a bit longer than I'd planned, duchy. Someone turned the heat off under it.'

'Someone! What do you mean bloody someone! How many people do you think regularly break into my flat?'

'I assumed your boyfriend had a key.'

'Terry is not my bodyfriend. He doesn't live here and anyway he's gone. And why the hell am I explaining all this to you? What are you doing here?'

'Dinner. French, remember?' He put a half-empty bottle of red wine on the table beside two full bottles. '*Vin ordinaire.*'

'Let me rephrase that. You are in my flat. My locked flat. For the second time today apparently. How did you get inside?'

'I picked the locks.'

'Most visitors knock and wait for me to let them in. Have you ever tried that approach?'

'You weren't here. The stew needed to simmer. Are you planning to stand out there all night or are you coming in?'

'I have to get Tallulah.'

As soon as I let her out she made for the curtains and started hauling herself up with beak and claw.

'I had a dog I used to dress up once,' O'Hara remarked, adding pepper to the saucepan. 'Of course, I was six years old at the time.'

'She's bald. She needs to be kept warm.' I was getting madder with the bloke by the minute. First he breaks in (twice) and then he starts implying I'm a few anchovies short of the full pizza. I took out my frying pan.

'Are you planning to belt me with that?' O'Hara enquired. 'Or don't you trust my cooking?'

'It's for Tallulah. She has to have protein.'

I cooked her a single fishfinger and put it on the table with a dish of water. Detaching the sherpa parrot from her drapes, I put her down and told her to get stuck in.

'I'm sensing antagonism here, duchy. You're mad at me for breaking in, right?'

'Wouldn't you be if I broke into your home?'

'You'd be welcomed with open arms, I promise. Not least because you would have demonstrated that my security system has some serious flaws.'

'You mean mine has.'

'Obviously, I'd say.'

'You're right, I've just got to get some decent locks fitted. Seatoun is swarming with psychos trying to break in and rustle up a lemon meringue pie.' I was grumpy because I knew he was right.

O'Hara peered over his steamed-up spectacles at me. 'I'd heard that. By the way, your parrot is drinking the wine.'

Tallulah had got the partially used bottle on its side, dragged out the cork, and was just clamping her beak over the neck. I grabbed the bottle. The action tilted more of the wine down the neck. Tallulah hung on and glugged. By the time I'd detached her, the bottle contents were evenly distributed between the parrot's stomach and my clothes.

I dumped Tallulah and her dinner on the floor. 'I'm going to change.'

'Not too much I trust. I like a touch of eccentricity.'

'I am *not* . . .' I caught the twinkle behind the specs. It was bloody irritating and kind of stomach-tingling at the same time. Pulling an armful of clothes and a packet of tights grabbed from the 20p bin at Save the Children from the pantry-wardrobe, I shut myself in the bathroom and ran the bath.

I'd been planning on wearing a short black skirt with one of my skimpier tops for tonight. But that was when I thought it was going to be at a French restaurant rather than a cheap date. It occurred to me that O'Hara might be skint. His clothes might be classy but looked to me to be as old as his car. Dinner at the Waldorf could have cleaned him out. Cooking up a storm with stuff from the local supermarket might be all he could afford. I could relate to that.

I untangled the heap of clothes I'd grabbed at random. The skimpy top was in there but the other half was going to have to be a floor-length skirt. Since the tights turned out to be black stockings with lacy 'stay-up' tops, that was probably a good thing.

Adding a large dollop of carnation bubble bath to the swirling water, I jumped in and lay back. On the other side of the door I could hear Tallulah giving a rendition of her *West Side Story* selection with slightly slurred overtones and O'Hara moving around, accompanied by the sounds of metallic clinks and china rattles. I guessed he was laying up the table. It all felt kind of cosy. I shouted through, asking if he could find everything he needed.

'We're cool out here, thanks. Do you want a drink before the meal? It's red wine or red wine.'

'I'll have red wine then, thanks.'

I lifted a leg and watched a large blob of bubbles slip from ankle towards the thigh. And . . . bloody hell! O'Hara wandered through the door, carrying a glass of wine.

'I didn't mean right now!' I slid under the water, my knees protruded from the bubbles like two pink islands. I checked the bubbles. There seemed to be gaps at strategic places.

'Dinner will be about twenty minutes.' He sat the glass on the edge of the bath and walked out. As he was closing the door, he said, 'I was right about the legs.'

By the time I'd dressed, applied some eyeshadow and mascara and gulped down the wine, I'd calmed down sufficiently to be able to wander back into the living room like I regularly entertained while in the bath.

It was years since a man had cooked for me. (Not since my inglorious departure from the police had been followed by my ex ending our relationship by locking me out and flying off to a new job in the Far East.) I took one of the laid-up places. It looked directly across to the other major feature of the room: the double bed.

O'Hara lifted a plate from the oven, where I assume it had been warming (it was news to me that the oven worked, I don't remember ever using it), and held it with a padded towel. He lifted the lid on the saucepan and released more clouds of that meaty steam. The serving spoon was just dipping in, when someone rapped on the door.

'Do you want to get that?' he asked.

'No. If it's important they'll break in.'

Whoever it was knocked again. And again. Tallulah started screeching and bobbing around.

The visitor wasn't taking the hint. Between the racket in here and the racket out there, the din was impossible to ignore. O'Hara replaced the lid. I opened the door.

Rosco pushed a large bundle of bedding forward. 'I washed it at the laundrette. I'll put 'em back on the bed.'

'Don't bother.' I yanked the massive bundle away from him.

Terry grabbed it back. 'I can't sleep on a bare mattress, can I?'

'You can't sleep here at all! Push off!'

'I just spent a bloody fortune getting these blankets dry.'

We both paused at the sound of the spoon tapping on the saucepan lid.

'I was just wondering if this bloke that you don't live with would be joining us for dinner?'

'Yeah, great. I'll just dump this lot.' Terry shoved past me into the spare room.

O'Hara grinned at my glare.

The pig from the pit trundled back and plonked himself down in my chair. 'I'm bloody starving. What we having?'

O'Hara resumed serving. 'It's beef. And local vegetables. Braised in a red wine sauce.'

'You one of them chefs?' Terry asked.

'No.'

'You're not a poofter, are you?'

'No.'

'What you doing the cooking for then? That's not a bloke's job.'

'I find it impresses women.'

'Yeah?' Terry's brain cell chewed that over, while his chops chewed the stewed beef. 'Take my tip, mate, there's other things to impress 'em with. I guess if you haven't got the equipment, then you need a few gimmicks, but you look like you'd be pretty well set up in that department.'

'I've never had any complaints. Wine?'

'Mmm . . .' Rosco raised his trotter.

Conversation was off the menu; sound effects were provided by Terry's slurping and Tallulah's off-key warbling. As soon as I'd finished eating, I excused myself to go to the loo. I didn't want to pee, I wanted to kick something very hard. But common sense set in before I'd done any serious damage to my toe bones. I splashed cold water over my face, scrubbed off the make-up and went back.

And Rosco was feeding Tallulah *vin ordinaire* from his glass. 'Heh, look at that, this bird likes a drink.'

'Don't all your birds, Terry? I'd always assumed blind drunkenness was the secret of your pulling technique.' I grabbed the glass.

'I used to give my first girlfriend's brother a fiver to go

out and let us have the house to ourselves,' O'Hara said. 'Do you think it would work in this situation?'

Terry looked up immediately. 'Make it a tenner, mate and I'll go to the pub. Give you a couple of hours to get down to it, eh?' He smirked.

O'Hara extracted a note from his jacket and passed it over.

Terry beamed. 'Don't do anything I wouldn't do.'

He barrelled out into the cold dark night. I tried to stare O'Hara down. If he seriously thought I was up for a couple of hours of hot passion after that evening, he was in for a few home truths.

He smiled blandly. 'Do you want to finish off the wine first?'

'And what do you think is coming second?'

'Coffee.'

Relaxing was another problem. I only had the upright chairs at the table. Normally I sat on the floor – or the bed. I propped my floor cushions against the sideboard and stretched out my legs.

O'Hara leant back beside me. 'Tell me,' he said. 'Why does that bloke you don't live with have a large shaved patch on the back of his head in the shape of a V sign?'

'Beats me. Can I ask you something?'

'Anything you like, duchy.'

'Why have you decided to dig into Alison's case now? If you felt there was something dodgy about the verdict, you've had twenty years to do something about it.'

I thought for a moment he wasn't going to answer me. Then he said, 'It's that path we talked about. Sometimes you get to the point where you know you can't keep going forward, that it's time to take stock, to undo some of the mess you left behind.'

'Alison isn't your mess. Not your case. And the jury convicted her, not you.'

'Maybe.' He stared across the room at his own reflection

in the TV screen. I sensed he was slipping away into that dark place he seemed to inhabit sometimes.

The room was silent apart from the sounds of water pipes in the upstairs flat and Tallulah's attempts at *Oklahoma* ('*homa . . . homa . . . homa . . . homa . . . oh bugger, hot arse*'). She was wandering around the floor dragging the cape; the bonnet had slipped over one eye, giving her the appearance of a demented little old lady. I watched as she walked straight into the table leg, fell over sideways and continued a zigzag course.

'I think the baby's drunk, dear.'

I glanced back. O'Hara had returned from the dark place.

Scrambling up, I refilled her saucer with water and put it on the floor. When I returned to the cushions, O'Hara's arm had somehow stretched along the pillow at my back. Oh well, hardly worth asking him to move it. Shifting brought us hip to hip. I could feel the heat of his leg all the way down mine.

'How are you getting on with the case?' he asked. 'Any progress?'

I gave him a quick resume of my meetings with Gillian Anderson and Brian Root. I left out the Roleses – senior and junior – because that would have led to an explanation of the 788 clue. And I still intended to hang on to that lead until – and if – O'Hara contributed something significant to this investigation. I was sure there was important information that he was holding back.

'So you think Root's a creep who keeps the kids on his side with mucky DVDs and turning a blind eye to bullying in his house,' he summarized. 'Does that help the investigation?'

'I don't know. What I don't get is what Gina Gibbs was doing hanging out with him. If it's true she was. Can you see her fancying a grubby little caretaker?'

'No. But even if he'd been a Tom Cruise clone, she wouldn't have fancied him if he was a caretaker. Gina was someone who wanted a high-flyer.'

'She picked on an ordinary police constable.'

'And look how high Clever Clive soared. She bagged a winner and hung on.'

His arm had slipped to waist level. I leant into him and he tightened his grip. Shifting my position let me put my head on his shoulder. 'Tell me about the knife?'

'I love it when you talk cutlery. The knife, let's see. It was about twelve inches long. A chef's knife of some kind, they thought. And it was old, probably nineteen twenties or thirties. Razor sharp but well-worn. The shaft was all cracked and chipped. It had a very distinctive handle: dark green with a red star. They think it was made for a commercial customer; hotel, shipping line, public school, something of that kind. The Sheffield firm that manufactured it went out of business in the sixties, along with all its records.'

'And you couldn't link it to Alison?'

'Moira and Emlyn Wynne-Ellis both denied it had ever been in their house. They checked next door with Mrs Darrowfield since Alison was in and out regularly, but it wasn't theirs either. Ditto it didn't come from her school.'

'You're certain the murderer brought it with them?'

'The owners of Abbot's Cottage had restocked the place with chain-store cutlery before they rented it out. I suppose the lovely Gina, or even Trudy herself, could have brought it with them, but Gina swore she'd never set eyes on it.'

'Did it occur to anyone that Gina might have done it?'

'No motive. No forensic evidence. You have gorgeous skin.'

'You can remember a lot of detail. Considering it was twenty years ago.'

'I checked out my files.' He found my lips.

I ducked out. 'Tell me about being a copper in Seatoun twenty years ago?'

'Ah, the golden age just before PACE.'

'Beating confessions out of suspects? Illegal searches? Fit-ups to make the clear-up rate look good?'

'Happy days.' He grinned.

It was probably a joke. Probably. 'Rosie Wilmott reckoned you had some weird cases back then.'

'Who?'

'Sergeant. On temporary placement at Seatoun just before the murder? Wasn't she the one who told you I was looking for you?'

'Like I said. I picked up the word on the grapevine. I know who you mean though. 'S funny how sometimes you can see a face clearly but can't put a name to it to save your life. How is she?'

'Good. She's retired. I ran into her at a christening. Apparently every police officer who worked on the case has been reduced to crispy copper crumbs, with the exception of you and Pennington.'

'My ma always said I was born under a lucky star.'

'So what was Seatoun like back then? Rosie said you had a genuine highwayman? Did he have the full kit? Mask? Horse? Pistols?'

'Handguns rather than pistols, but yes, he had the full monty. Sounds funny, doesn't it?'

'It wasn't?'

He refilled our glasses before answering. 'Couple of pensioners driving home late. Stopped because someone was lying in the road and they weren't the sort to go past someone in trouble. Next thing they know there's a masked bloke on a horse pointing guns at them and ordering them to stand and deliver – everything. He made them strip. Took the lot, even the wife's wedding ring. They had to walk like that for half a mile. The wife was devastated, had a nervous breakdown. The car was abandoned in a back street. Everything in it, apart from the wedding ring.'

'Kids?'

'You'd think so. Couple never gave a coherent description, probably warned not to. But sonny fired a shot into the ground when the husband tried to stand up to him. They recovered the bullet. Few months later that gun was recovered after a security van ambush in North London. And the guys who did that were definitely not kids. Sadly, they weren't caught either so nobody ever got to ask about the Dick Turpin stunt. As Rosie said, there was a lot of weird stuff going on back then. Some had amusement value; like goats left in the mayoral car. Others were more serious. Several arson attacks for one. Mostly farm buildings; no danger to life. Except that once the farmer went to investigate and got hit by falling debris. When he came round he'd been dragged outside, but his watch had been stolen. Another time someone broke into a pregnant woman's home when she was alone, locked her in the bedroom and trashed the place. Husband found her when he came home from a night shift. She'd gone into premature labour. Only things missing were about twenty quid in cash and a little fishing trophy that wasn't worth a dime. Lots of stuff like that went down. Bit of cash nicked but plenty of portable valuables left behind.'

'It sounds like kids.' And I was beginning to have a fair idea which kids. Could Trudy's killing have been another nasty prank that had gone too far? I really wanted to talk about it with O'Hara, but once again something made me hold back. I didn't buy all that taking wrong turnings on the path and running out of choices. This was a man who'd hack a path through the jungle if he fancied taking a detour.

O'Hara seemed to have lost interest in conversation anyway. He was nibbling at my ear. Somehow we slid down the cushions and I ended up flat on the floor. I could feel his excitement growing against my thigh. This was the moment to cool it. A quick snog was fine, but I wasn't about to go full on with a bloke I barely knew after one date. He got the blouse off one shoulder. Oh wow! Everything was on fire. Over his shoulder the room was rocking. Actually no. It was just the curtains.

O'Hara grunted with surprise as my knee connected with his solar plexus. 'Sorry.' I threw myself over him and dived, arms outstretched. I just managed to catch Tallulah as she tumbled backwards from the top of the curtains. The stupid bird hadn't realized she couldn't fly any more.

I stuffed Tallulah into her travelling cage. She didn't want to go and in the process I got several scratches and she lost her bonnet. I put her on the sideboard above us and sat down beside O'Hara. 'Sorry,' I repeated.

'*Love*,' Tallulah informed us, '*means never having to say you're sorry.*'

'We were about here, I think.' He twitched down both straps.

This was definitely the moment to suggest we back off. I unbuttoned his shirt instead. His chest was the colour of pale toffee. A thin silvery snake of scarring ran from the left collarbone to his breastbone. Another circled under one rib. I traced it with one finger. In doing so I somehow ended up pressing bare skin against his. We rolled over with him on top.

'*Fasten your seatbelts. It's going to be a bumpy night. Oooooooo . . . OOOOF.*'

O'Hara pushed himself onto his hands. 'OK, what just happened back there?'

'The parrot barfed on your back.'

It was an impressive chuck. Who'd have thought a small bird could hold that much red wine? Plus sunflower seeds. And mashed up fishfinger. And little gritty bits.

I made him lie still while I got a wet towel and cleaned him off a bit. Luckily a lot of it had hit bare skin. 'There's some on the bottom of your shirt, if you want to take it off . . .'

'I'll fix it in the bathroom, thanks.'

She'd thrown it over the cage bars too, plus some on the floor and the sideboard. I wet more cloths. By the time I'd put the towel, dirty cloths and mini-cloak in the washing machine with my wine-stained clothes from earlier, sponged down Tallulah and re-dressed her in a fetching jacket of yellow and white stripes, O'Hara still hadn't reappeared. There was a lot of water being run in there. I guessed Tallulah had hit a wider area than I'd thought. I noticed several spots of parrot sick on my skirt. I peeled it off and stuck it in with rest of the load.

Before I could get another one from the wardrobe, O'Hara came out of the bathroom, pulling on a damp shirt. I was standing in a pair of designer briefs that had been a present from a client and those black lacy stay-up stockings. It had been a long time. I'd forgotten the effect black stockings have on some men.

'Have you got anything . . . ?' I managed to ask.

'Jacket.' It was on the chair. He pushed me back on the table, leaning over me to grope in the pocket, drag a condom out and fumble with the packaging. Somebody knocked loudly on the front door.

'Leave it.'

'I'm going to.'

The visitor banged again. Tallulah started shrieking. Apparently door knockers were another one of her hang-ups.

'Push off, Terry!' I bawled.

'It's me. Open the door, will yer? It's freezing out here.'

'It's Jan. She never comes here.'

'I know how she feels,' O'Hara said.

By the time I'd pulled on a pair of tracksuit bottoms and got the door open, he was shrugging his way into his leather jacket. Jan and Eric were delivering the large cage.

While they lugged it inside, O'Hara headed out. 'I'll ring you tomorrow?'

'OK.' I watched him climbing the iron stairway from the basement. The night wind felt bitingly cold on my bare flesh, which was still tingling with inner heat.

He paused to look over the street level railings, the light behind him. 'Maybe I'll cook dinner again.'

'Feel free to let yourself in if I'm not here.'

His teeth flashed white in the dark. 'Goodnight, duchy.'

29

I had to let Terry stay in the end. It was that or share the room with Tallulah who'd found a new lease of life now she'd heaved up and was raring to sing her way through her entire repertoire.

'Bloody thing never shut up all night,' Terry grumbled next morning, heading for the bathroom, clutching a disposable razor.

'Shave at the station,' I ordered him. 'I'm locking up now and I want you the other side of the door.'

'What about breakfast?'

'I'm going to Pepi's.' Having missed so many free meals, I was intending to make up for lost time.

The café was sizzling with the aromas of frying bacon, sausages and eggs, and rocking to Elvis Vivaring Las Vegas. It was a little corner of paradise spoiled only by the sight of Rosco, who'd got there before me, stuffing in a full English fry-up at the far table.

Shane was not pleased to see Tallulah. I could sympathize. I'd been sick of the sight (and sound) of her for some time.

'I can't take her back yet, Smithie, the monastery's not fixed. They've got to re-lay the surface on the squash courts. Just a couple more days, I swear.'

'Don't worry, it's just a flying visit . . . well, in her case, a walking visit. I'll take a full fry-up and a large tea.'

'Coming up. Viva!' Shane hand-jived his way to his back burners.

I plonked myself opposite Terry and dumped the cage on

a spare chair. The bloke on the next table checked out the contents.

'Blimey, what an ugly bird.'

'Heh, she's not that bad. Show a bit of respect, mate.'

'He was talking about the parrot, Terry.'

'Oh.' He pushed in another forkful of runny egg.

'Terry, it is time you got this problem with Linda sorted. I can't believe I've let you con your way into my flat for so long. It's not as if I even like you. And you spend most of your time telling everyone I was a bent cop.'

'Yeah well . . . I was joshing. You know that, Smithie.'

'No. I don't. Go home, Terry. Grovel. Tell Linda you'll never look at another woman. Promise her a second honeymoon in Alicante. Just *go*.'

'I can't do that. It's down to her.' A mulish look settled on his fat chops.

'Please yourself. Just get used to sleeping on the beach. Because you are not getting into my flat again.'

I swung round to see what had happened to my breakfast. There was a small queue at the counter collecting take-away coffees, teas and bacon sandwiches, as people headed into work or came off night shift. The one at the tail end, directly behind my chair, was Mark Boscombe.

'Hi, doesn't the hospital have a canteen?'

He shrugged and mumbled something, his face turned away from me.

'How about the number seven eight eight? Mean anything?'

'It were a band.'

'Nice try. But I've already found out from one of its so-called members that it didn't exist. You'll be the one that Orlando managed to contact then?'

'Look, bitch.' He swung round. His left eye was swollen and half closed. 'Keep your nose out if you know what's good for you.'

'Oi!' Terry whipped out his warrant card. 'You threatening this lady?'

Lady! Wow, Terry really didn't want to doss down on that beach.

'No. I never meant . . . look, forget it, OK?' Mark had lost his appetite. He shot out of the café.

Terry squared his shoulders, threw out his chest and checked that the rest of the customers had noticed his heroic rescue. 'Who was that?'

'Mark Boscombe. Didn't you recognize him?'

'*That* was Bossy?' An odd expression joined the grease flowing over Rosco's face. 'I'm bigger than him.'

'You're bigger than most people. I'd lay off the triple-cheeseburgers when you and Linda hit Alicante.' He missed the hint. He was too busy charging for the door.

'What's his problem?' Shane said.

'At a guess, it's connected to a thirteen-year-old kid locked in a cellar with his todger painted luminous green.'

I'd left the Micra parked down the road because someone had already pinched the spot outside my flat. I walked back to it, intending to collect it and move it to outside the office.

During the night someone had poured yellow paint over the windows and slashed all the tyres. A small white freezer label wound round the extended aerial was flapping like a pennant. There was no message on it. But there didn't need to be really.

I did the only thing I could do. I walked to the office.

There was an email from Betterman waiting: 'Cracked 788 yet?'

I sent back: 'Found some of the arms and arses it decorates. Any clues?'

I had to wait until Jan turned up then leave Tallulah with her while I got a pick-up service to take the car to the tyre replacement place, and then hang around while they fitted four new ones.

I got back to the office to find no new emails and a

ready-boxed parrot waiting for my attention. Vetch had discovered the featherless one.

'You are, of course, quite welcome to keep it in your own office, sweet thing,' he murmured. 'But I can't have potential clients entering reception to be greeted by invitations to shake their arse and a demented receptionist singing "Oklahoma".'

'That was just to drown out the parrot. I can't leave her upstairs, she goes bananas if she's left on her own. Think of her as interior decoration for the hall.'

'I'd rather think of her as somewhere else.'

Jan gave me a 'sorry' shrug. The surface of her desk was littered with books.

'What's with all the literature?'

'They're for me report. I got dictionaries, report writing manuals, thesaurus and one on how to draw pictures on the computer. I'm gonna make it really artistic. Did you find your phone message?'

I picked up the wastepaper bin. Scrabbling through a pile of torn sheets, I found a post-it stuck to the bottom. 'This would be it, would it?'

'Yeah. She phoned yesterday.'

Rosie Wilmott with a telephone number asking me to ring because she'd finally found some news about Declan O'Hara. Damn, I'd forgotten to call and tell her he'd found me. I pushed it into my jeans pocket, intending to call and apologize later.

Jan answered the reception phone and nudged me with the receiver. 'For you.'

I put it to my ear, my mind already on what I was going to do once I was mobile again.

'That was your final warning, bitch. Next time it won't be the car that gets hurt. Stop asking questions about the teachers or you get to disappear.'

I punched in 1471 quickly. Number withheld. Big surprise. The voice had been hoarse and disguised. Maybe they hadn't been so careful when speaking to the receptionist. 'What did that last caller say *exactly* when you answered the phone?'

Jan puckered a mouth lipsticked the colour of aubergines and thought about it. ' "Can I speak to the lippy blonde bitch that's always sticking her nose in." Knew it was you right away.'

I was running out of lines of investigation. But at least there was one alibi for that night of Trudy's murder that I might be able to check out.

December Drysdale lived on the edge of Seatoun. Behind his house was the stable block that housed the donkeys several generations of Drysdales had trotted along the beach each summer with kids hanging on to the high saddles. Each stable door had a soft muzzle and large ears turned inquisitively in my direction. Having duly patted my way around from Lana (Turner) to Errol (Flynn) via Clark (Gable) and fed a quarter of an apple to each, I followed December indoors. His house was well-worn and gave no clue to the fact that he was probably one of the wealthiest blokes in Seatoun. Settling in a squashy armchair, I accepted a coffee mug shaped like a grinning donkey's head and asked December if his church lot had ever used rooms in St John's Road.

'Years back. Used to have a social above the Inchbeck's old bakery every Friday. Why?'

'Do you remember a couple called Wynne-Ellis?'

'Kiddie killed a teacher. Course I remember.'

'They have a granddaughter who was adopted at birth. Hannah, the granddaughter, is convinced her mother didn't do it. What did you make of Alison? She came to the socials sometimes, didn't she?'

'Not so much once she was old enough to be left on her own. It was just board games and then a fish and chip supper. The older members organized it. It died a death years ago. The girl was a quiet little thing. Polite enough. But not . . .'

'The kind of girl you noticed?' I finished for him. It was hard to reconcile that docile child with the hard-faced woman I'd met at the garden centre. 'What about the parents?'

'Odd couple. Always had the feeling they were hiding something.' There wasn't much that got past December. 'You know they say that in any marriage there's one who loves and the other who is loved? Well with the Wynne-Ellises it was her who did the loving. She was always fussing over him. Fetching and carrying food and drink to the table; running round getting the vinegar and the salt for him. Some of the members said she used to lose games deliberately if it meant him winning. It was different with the other couple. He was the one did the loving there. She doted on that lump of a son.'

'The Darrowfields came? I thought they were Catholics? They've got crucifixes and Madonna statues.'

December raised eyebrows thick as scouring pads. 'I don't think Catholics have a monopoly on those. You really should consider becoming a little more godly, Grace. But we don't preach at people. Everyone's welcome. We had a lot of members who converted Friday evening and rescinded on Saturday morning.'

'Did Philip come too?'

'Sometimes. Not the full shilling, that one. He didn't come so much either as he got older.'

'Did he come on the night of the murder?'

'No. The Darrowfields hadn't been for several weeks. Some of the ladies decided Mrs Darrowfield must have taken a turn for the worse. You know she was disabled?'

'I heard. Philip is now.'

'Anyway when the ladies went round with their fruit baskets and bunches of flowers, they found Lucia Darrowfield was no worse than she'd ever been. They reckoned the two families had had a falling out.'

'About what?'

'No idea. The Darrowfields never came back to the

socials. Does Jerry Jackson know you're poking around in an old murder case?'

I blanked the question. 'Thanks for the coffee and the chat.'

Picking up the cage knocked Tallulah's needle out of the *West Side Story* groove. '*Oooh hot . . . hot . . . baby. Shake that sexy bootie.*'

'She lives in a monastery,' I explained in response to a raise of the scouring-pad eyebrows. 'With personal spiritual trainers.'

'No wonder the board games lost popularity.'

I parked the car up near the harbour, bonnet pointing towards the sea. In the summer this was a no-parking zone. Actually in the winter it was too, but with less traffic around you could see the wardens coming. Leaning my arms on the wheel, I watched the gulls strutting around the few boats resting at an angle on the mud.

'I'm running out of ideas here,' I informed Tallulah. 'The trouble is, there is just no motive. Trudy sure as hell wasn't killed for money. She didn't have any. She didn't appear to have a sex life either, so I guess we can rule that out. So what's left? Revenge? For what?' I emptied the pink folder on to the passenger seat and sorted through, trying to get some kind of order into my notes. I'd written numerous lists and memos to myself; there must be something in there to point me in another direction. After half an hour, I summarized what I'd achieved. 'Basically what I've got to show my client for her money is a whole load of totally useless lists.'

'*Sometimes nothing is a real cool hand.*'

'Not in this case, baldy.'

I started scrabbling papers back into the folder. I'd had one eye on the mirrors all the time in case a warden tried to creep up under cover of the ubiquitous rain-coated early-season pensioners struggling along the promenade. A familiar figure slid across the square of wing-mirror glass.

Keeping down, I twisted and peered through the back window. O'Hara was striding up the hill, a carrier bag from the local supermarket swinging from one hand. That suggested to me he was heading for whatever he called home. Well, the guy had invited me to break in anytime . . .

He was fly enough to notice a car idling along behind him. And if I tried anticipating and driving on ahead, he'd probably notice if I did more than one pass. It was going to have to be by foot.

By the time I'd shifted the car to a side street where it wouldn't end up clamped, retrieved my lock-picking kit from the hidden compartment, and improvised a cage cover with my jumper, O'Hara was out of sight. Hugging the travel case, I picked up the pace to a trot, eyes scanning down the side streets to the right. The road was climbing steadily towards the higher cliffs of North Bay.

I was just beginning to think I'd lost O'Hara, when I spotted him turning into a house on Marine Crescent.

The terrace had – inevitably – started life as boarding houses. At various times they'd been divided into bedsits, joined together to form a single hotel and now, it appeared from a board fixed halfway up one, some optimistic developer was converting them into luxury flats.

O'Hara had gone into one midway down the circular sweep. I trotted past at a brisk pace, checking the number as I went. The Mercedes was parked two houses down. At the end of the terrace I weighed up the next step. I was going to have to get O'Hara out of the way so I could get in there and prove he wasn't the only one who knew how to spring a surprise. I needed a phonebox close enough to be able to check that he actually left the flat when I rang his mobile. Unfortunately the only thing in front of the terrace was a wide sweep of mown lawn, which was used by the bowls club in summer, and a couple of council shelters used by dossers, desperate lovers and druggies at any time of the year.

O'Hara solved my problem by emerging, minus carrier,

and walking back downhill. I gave him three minutes to make sure he wasn't coming back and walked quickly up the shallow flight of steps to his front door.

If you're going to pick a lock in plain view it's best to be open about it. Skulking around looking furtive attracts attention. If you look like you're meant to be there, most people will assume you are. Of course, having a parrot warbling that we're off to see the wizard is something of a handicap when you're trying to be inconspicuous. Finally I got the locks off and opened the door cautiously, ready to run if there was any sign of an audible alarm.

There was no noise at all. The place had the echoing quality of an empty building. There were three doors leading off the front reception area. The one on the right was slightly open. Walking over quietly, I nudged it a little further. Directly ahead of me an inner door stood wide open. The room beyond it was bare. I edged inside. There was a fitted kitchen on the left; the units in place but the gaps where the electrical appliances should be trailing wires. The faint aroma of wood-dust and paint clung to the place.

Both the other flats on this level were in the same condition and both equally empty. The other floors were exactly the same. The catches on the outer doors were set to prevent the locks engaging. Probably been left like that to allow the builders free access as they moved around. Which was great from my point of view, but hardly the state-of-the-art security system O'Hara had been boasting about.

I was conscious of the noise I was making. In addition to Tallulah's efforts, with bare floorboards everywhere and uncarpeted stairs it was impossible to move totally quietly. But on the bright side, it meant no one was going to be able to sneak up on me. I'd get plenty of warning if O'Hara came back.

On the top floor, two of the flats were as open as those below, but the third door refused to budge. I shoved hard in case it was just stuck. Nope it was definitely locked. Had to be this one. Taking out the tension tool and pick I got to work. 'Five minutes max,' I murmured to Tallulah. 'Time me.'

It was all very *Style* magazine: polished wood floor, big couches, rugs, plain dining table and chairs, low lighters and arty objects like a stone bowl holding polished marble eggs, big steel comb sculptures that looked like they were melting and a chess set carved from ebony and crystal or something. The bedroom was furnished in a similar style, but with softer shades in the furnishings. I opened the wardrobe. A couple of pairs of trousers, three shirts and a sweatshirt swung gently on the hangers. All grey. The drawers underneath were equally sparse: a dozen pairs of white pants and half a dozen of grey socks. A battered hold-all on the floor held a pair of shoes. There was no sign of the canvas bag he'd been toting the first time I'd met him. So this was just a flop, his regular haunt was elsewhere. I suppose that made sense since he'd been catching the train to somewhere else when I dropped him at the station. But it was kind of disappointing not to find some clue to the guy behind the sphinx-act.

The kitchen was all stainless steel and the electrical appliances had been connected. The carrier O'Hara had been carrying was lying on the counter. I took a peek. Meat, vegetables, milk and two bottles of Italian wine. There were a couple of saucepans sitting on the hob, which looked to be a matching set for the one I'd acquired the other evening.

I wandered back into the seating area and my heart bounced off my tonsils and rebounded back into my stomach. O'Hara was sitting on the sofa.

30

He gave me a round of applause. 'Not bad. It was five minutes, ten seconds by the way. I timed you.'

'And you were where, exactly?'

'Flat to your right. Sloppy search, duchy, you missed me.'

'I wasn't looking for you. In fact, I can't think of any reason why I'd ever be looking for you, O'Hara.'

'Heh, put the prickles down. I'm glad you're here. I'd like to repay your hospitality and cook you dinner here this time. What do you say?'

My inclination was to tell him where to put his largest cooking pot. But I knew I was reacting irrationally. I was mad because he'd obviously spotted me scoping the place out and slipped back just to prove to me how bloody clever he was. On the other hand, it was my own fault for not checking properly as I searched. If something nastier than O'Hara had been lurking I could have been in really serious trouble: empty house, no one knowing I was here, no knowing when the builders were coming in again. Yep, definitely not a smart move.

'What are we having?'

'Italian.'

'*Si*, then.'

'Great. Come and help me cook.' Dumping the leather coat in the bedroom, he led the way to the stainless steel enclave and sorted out a chopping board and knife. I was handed a carrot. 'Peel that and chop it into small chunks.'

We chopped our way through all the veg in the bag, then O'Hara diced up the meat. 'Chicken. I was going to get veal but then I remembered some females get girlie over eating the cute little calves.'

'I do not get girlie. Although,' I admitted, 'I don't like eating veal. But it's not because I'm girlie. It's simply a personal preference.'

'If you say so. Can you pass the pepper?' I swung back with the mill. He came round the other way with the salt. Before I quite knew how he'd done it, I was locked in a tonsil-tasting snog.

'Cut that out,' I gasped when I came up for air. 'I haven't decided whether we have that kind of relationship yet.'

'We seemed to have the other night.'

'I got a bit carried away by the moment. Moments. I think we should cool it. See how it goes for a while.'

'You do?'

Actually now I was pressed up here against a kitchen counter and an Italian silk/wool mix sweater . . . 'Er, yes. I don't like rushing into things.' I pushed him away and asked what was next. 'On the cooking side?'

'We just dump this lot in here . . .' Everything went into a saucepan. 'Add a bit of seasoning. Crumble an instant gravy cube. Add a dash of water and, of course . . . the most important ingredient . . .' He poured in half a bottle of red wine. 'And now it goes on to simmer for a couple of hours.'

The truth about his culinary skills finally dawned on me. 'Can you actually cook anything but stew?'

'Never felt the need to. I've never understood why people make such a song and dance about cookery. Just cut it up and add the appropriate brew.'

'So if I'd have chosen Polish as a meal option, this lot would have been soaking in vodka?'

'That's the idea. So what are we going to do for the next couple of hours?'

'I could go back to the office. Come back later.'

'You could. But why would you want to?'

Good question. It wasn't like I had anything urgent

waiting for me back there. But if I stayed here, I could end up doing something I'd probably regret.

'Do you play chess?' O'Hara asked.

'Yes. I used to play my dad.'

'No more?'

'We aren't currently on speaking terms.'

'Want a game?'

'OK.'

We released Tallulah in the kitchen, with those weird steel sculptures blocking the entrance. We left her with a saucer of water and a couple of marbled eggs to play with. Since she could see us through the bars, she was happy with that arrangement. O'Hara drew a low coffee table in front of the French windows where we could look through to a small balcony and the bare upper branches of trees in the garden below.

He was a good player. But so was I. I asked him how come he was the only tenant in the building.

'People renovating ran into a bit of financial trouble. It's on hold until they get some new backers. This was supposed to be the show flat. I'd have gone for one at the front with a sea view myself. Check.'

'So? What? They asked you to flatsit so the place wasn't left empty?'

'I'm sure that would have occurred to them eventually.'

'They don't know you're here, do they?'

'Is that a problem for you, duchy?'

I wasn't exactly in a position to bag the moral high ground when it came to squatting. On the other hand nobody had seen the owner of my flat for years; this place still smelt of paint and wood-shavings. 'What are you going to do if they come back?'

'Grab my stuff and bail out. There's a very handy drainpipe by the balcony.' He conceded the game and untangled himself from the floor. It was growing dark. He moved round putting on lights.

'We've time for another game before we eat. Fancy making it strip chess?'

'No, thanks.'

'Windy.'

It was one game. One item either way. 'Rack 'em up and prepare to be creamed, O'Hara.'

We managed two fast games before dinner. He lost his sweater and I lost my shoes.

Piling stew on two plates, he brought them through to the sitting room together with the wine. 'How are you getting on with the murder case? Any new leads?'

'No. Not really. I just keep coming up with the fact that nobody had any reason to kill Trudy. Maybe that's the whole point.' I forked up booze-soaked stew. 'Perhaps this was a totally random killing. Those other things you told me about . . . the highwayman . . . the farmer who was caught in the barn fire . . . was there any evidence that those victims were targeted in particular? Or were they just in the wrong place at the wrong time?'

'The latter, I'd say.' He topped my glass. 'You think someone decided that was the night for a knifing, and Trudy just happened to be the unlucky choice?'

'I'm not sure it was even that. Gina said Trudy had a habit of turning lights off. If you came at that cottage from the back all you'd see was an apparently uninhabited property. The back gate and door are open. Good opportunity to grab any spare cash lying around . . . and then suddenly there's Trudy in the doorway. And you panic.'

As I said it, I could see how much sense that made. It was on the tip of my tongue to tell him about Orlando's little band, but I bit back the words. It was me doing all the talking again, while he contributed nothing.

O'Hara gave a straight look. 'I have the feeling there're things you're not telling me, duchy.'

Well, ditto with knobs on, mate.

'Of course,' O'Hara remarked, 'if you did happen to turn

up some new evidence, the murderer, or indeed murderers, would probably be prepared to resort to pretty much anything to stop you telling what you know. One life sentence or two, no difference to them. You need to take care, duchy. Another game?'

This time he lost his shoes and shirt. I lost my shoes, trousers and shirt. And then I lost the next game. If I took my bra off there was no going back. I could hardly kid myself that sitting there in just my panties came under the heading of 'cooling it' unless I was some kind of gigantic tease. And I'd never known how to play those kind of games.

I reached for the bra hook.

And a loud wailing howled outside. O'Hara swore.

'What's that?'

'My car alarm.' He grabbed his sweater and shoes. 'Don't go away.'

Sitting on the floor in your underwear isn't quite so seductive when you're on your own. I got up and carried my clothes into the bedroom. As I stood, considering whether to get dressed, a piece of paper drifted from a pocket – Jan's scrawled message from Rosie Wilmott. I'd forgotten to call her.

There was no phone in the flat. I checked the pockets of O'Hara's leather coat. Bingo, his mobile was in the pocket and switched on. Rosie answered on the first ring.

'Sorry not to get back to you earlier, Rosie. I should have told you, I didn't need Declan O'Hara's details any more.'

'You heard then. Can't say I'm surprised, but I would have liked to share one more shot of Glenfiddich with the charmer.'

'Sorry, I think we're on crossed wires here. What about Declan O'Hara?'

'He's dead. I was right about the pension; he left it in the police fund. They paid out death benefits last month.'

I felt sick. 'You're quite certain he's dead?'

'Trust me, they wouldn't pay out unless they'd seen the death certificate. How's the parrot?'

'She's fine. I've, er, got to go, Rosie.'

I broke the connection. If I hadn't been about to jump into bed with Declan O'Hara, then who was he? Someone with a vested interest in this case was the obvious answer. Like the members of Orlando's little 788 gang. Orlando had told me he was in touch with some of his former mates at St Martin's hadn't he? Hell, he'd even told me he'd contact them for me.

The pink file was locked in my car. I tried to picture that old school photo. Two faces on the end lost in shadow: Andrew Lee and Michael Forbes. Tall and dark with blue eyes, Gillian Anderson had said. The whole of the last weeks flickered past my eyes, like a slide show with my own personal demon providing the commentary for each slide.

The first anonymous telephone warning?

'*Came just before O'Hara appeared on the doorstep at Vetch's.*'

The party-popper bomb?

'*Hand-delivered to Vetch's on a day you know O'Hara (or whoever he is) was in the area because you met him outside Abbot's Cottage.*'

The evening someone took a shot at me, he wasn't in Seatoun. I saw him catch a train earlier.

'*No, you didn't. You saw him walk into the station. He even told you what calibre the bullet was, remember?*'

He hadn't recognized Rosie Wilmott's name. And after our trip to London, I'd asked him to drop me at the office. Leaving him time to nip round to my place, cosh Terry and pin a dead rat to my door before I went home.

An awful lot of things started to make a horrible kind of sense. Like the way he'd never wanted to sit in when I interviewed any witnesses despite his supposed desire to re-investigate this case. The Penningtons would have spotted him as a phoney immediately. I didn't know how much contact he'd had with the Wynne-Ellises after Alison's arrest – enough for him not to want to risk it obviously. He'd spoken to Peter Corbin though. But perhaps that hadn't been such a risk. Corbin must have interrogated thousands of witnesses in the past twenty years. What were the chances of him recalling the features of a young policeman he'd have seen in the witness box for ten minutes? Particularly when said copper would have supposedly aged from mid-twenties to mid-forties. O'Hara (or whoever) must have needed to know if Alison had said anything incriminating to her barrister.

I recalled that my first impression of O'Hara was that he looked younger than he ought to be have been. Why the hell couldn't I have listened to my instincts? Now I was stuck in a flat . . .

The notes of someone whistling 'Mac the Knife' carried very clearly in this unfurnished building. I fled across the living room and out on to the landing. The lights were on out here. 'Time switch' the small part of my brain that was unfrozen decided. I looked down the stairs. A foreshortened O'Hara was just climbing the first flight. Something whirled in his hand and spun in the air. Light glinted from the blade. He caught the knife handle easily and twirled it again. A few more treads and he'd disappeared from my sight. The thin strains of 'Mac' drifted up the stairwell.

The demon helpfully replayed that final anonymous phone message in my head: '*That was your final warning, bitch. Next time it won't be the car that gets hurt. Stop asking questions about the teachers or you get to disappear.*' Hell, he'd just told me the murderer would have nothing to lose by killing me.

I reviewed my situation: empty house, no one knowing I was here, no clue when the builders were coming in again. Yep, definitely not a smart move. Why didn't I learn to listen to myself? All O'Hara (or whoever) had to do was clean up after himself and it would be like we'd never been here.

I sped back to the flat and picked up a chair, intending to

get in with the first blow. And knew it was no good. He was seriously fit. I'd seen (and felt) the muscles. If he incapacitated me, I'd had it. There was no one to hear whatever he did afterwards. I needed to attract attention or get away fast. The phone! I turned for the bedroom just as I caught the unmistakeable sound of O'Hara on the landing outside. I was out of time.

'*Be afraid. Be very afraid.*' Tallulah hissed.

Tallulah or the phone?

Leaping the steel barricade into the kitchen I scooped her up, pushed her into the supermarket carrier and hooked it over my arm. At least having no tail feathers streamlined the shape. Taking another high jump, I flew across to the living-room windows. The front door of the flat was opening as I scrambled behind the blinds and opened the doors to the balcony.

The drainpipe he'd mentioned was just reachable. Sitting on the balcony rail, I leant out and grabbed.

My hands slipped on the shiny paintwork of the pipe. I pushed harder to get a purchase. For a moment I was still, clinging to the metal, with my feet braced against the wall and tiny fragments of stone falling into my face. I took a deep breath to steady myself. Just clamp your knees around the pipe and slide, I told myself. And do it quick. You need to reach ground before him. Once I was amongst the bushes, I'd have a chance to get over the garden wall and into the street. Where I had every intention of running like mad and screaming at the top of my voice.

I moved, ready to hug the pipe. And the significance of those stone fragments hit me. The fixings were wrenching from the brick.

There was one almighty crack and then I was falling backwards fifty feet to the ground.

31

'Everything OK, duchess?'

'Just fine, thanks.'

'Only I couldn't help noticing that you're sitting up an oak. Naked.'

'I'm not. I've got my knickers on.'

'My mistake. Are you planning to perch up there all night? I was leaning towards eggs for breakfast, but I could probably get a piece of cuttlefish or a handful of peanuts if you'd prefer?'

His arms were resting on the balcony, his whole attitude relaxed. I couldn't see his face properly because the light was behind him and I was looking up through a mist of tears. The drainpipe had fallen into the branches of the tallest tree in the garden. Crashing through with things snapping all around me, I'd just grabbed out blindly and ended up straddling a large bough. My bra was hooked on another branch just out of reach. The pipe had kept on going and was now lying amongst a bed of demolished bushes below. So far nobody had come to find out what all the racket was about.

'You're not Declan O'Hara.'

'I know that.' He moved fractionally. The moonlight caught the metallic glint in his hand.

Tallulah stirred and croaked. It was a relief to hear her. I'd lost track during our backward arrival in the tree and I wasn't certain whether the momentum had carried the carrier's swing into the trunk and reduced her to parrot pâté.

'Can you shin down? Or do you want me to climb up and rescue you?'

'No! Don't you come near me, you bastard!'

'Well, whatever you say, duchess. I guess you could be a selling point when they put the property on the market. There can't be that many luxury flats with a view of a naked blonde.'

'I am *not* na . . .' A beak hooked over the carrier rim, as Tallulah tried to haul herself out. A rip started to slowly travel down the plastic like a ladder in tights.

'Stop that, you stupid bald bird. You can't fly.'

'Sure about that rescue?'

I had to know what I was dealing with. Was this a member of Orlando's merry band or not? I'd already examined the top half pretty thoroughly and there was no 788 tattoo up there. 'I need you to do something for me first.'

'And that would be?'

'Take your trousers off.'

'I'm flattered. But that's at least ten feet.'

'I didn't mean . . . I want to see if you have a tattoo.'

'Why?'

'Because if you do, I think I can figure out who you are. And if you come anywhere near me I'm going to start screaming my head off.'

'I see. Don't go away.' He disappeared inside the room and reappeared a moment later – fully dressed. 'Catch!'

I had visions of a knife thudding into my heart. The thing whirled directly at my chest. I slapped my palms together and wobbled to the left before I managed to re-balance myself. The object was a pillow case wrapped around something. Inside was a pocket torch and a single-fold leather wallet. I shone the light over the document inside and O'Hara's picture stared back at me from an international driver's licence.

'Who the hell is Dane O'Hara?'

He gave me a bow.

'You said you were Declan O'Hara!'

'No, I didn't. I said I was D. O'Hara. Declan was my big brother.'

'You know damn well I thought you were Declan. All that rubbish you've been feeding me about being involved in the Wynne-Ellis case was just a pack of lies.'

'If you think back, you'll find I never said *I* was at any of those incidents.'

'You're being pedantic.'

'At least I'm not being naked and stuck up a tree.'

'I'm *not* . . . Why were you carrying a knife?'

'Took it off some little scroat trying to break into my car. Must be getting kind of nippy up there, isn't it?'

It was damn freezing. I was beginning to appreciate how Tallulah must feel without her feathers.

'So, are you coming down?' O'Hara enquired. 'Or have you got the hots for an owl?'

'I c . . . can't. I'm sort of stuck on something.' And it was hurting like hell.

'Don't you dare laugh.'

'Would I do that, duchy?' Choking back something that sounded suspiciously like a laugh, O'Hara leant casually back against the wall in the A & E waiting room.

There were plenty of spare chairs but we were both standing to one side. In my case I had no choice. When I'd hit the branch, I'd managed to impale myself on a splinter of bark. It was (according to O'Hara), shaped like a kid's drawing of a Christmas tree. It went in just fine, but the spiky barbs prevented it being drawn out. O'Hara had had to climb up and saw through the section attaching it to the tree with a penknife to release me. Getting my jeans back on was impossible. I'd had to improvise a skirt with two pillow cases and my belt and lie face down on the rear seat of the Merc while he drove me to hospital.

'Why didn't you tell me you were Declan's brother?' I hissed.

'Wasn't sure if I could trust you. Lot easier for me to drop out of sight, if you didn't know who I was.'

'*You* didn't trust *me*!'

'You find that hard to believe?'

I guess there was no reason why he should trust me. He barely knew me. And I'd told him myself about my dodgy police past. But I was still determined to hold a grudge against him for it. I leant against the wall too and jumped off with a shriek that brought a lot of startled looks in our direction.

'It was still a lousy trick. Feeding me all that bullshit about Alison's arrest when you weren't there. Were you?'

'Hardly. I was still at school. But it wasn't bullshit. Everything I've told you was true. Well, apart from the bit about learning tap dancing.' He shifted so one shoulder was propped on the wall and he could look at me directly. 'Declan was dying. That's why we went to Egypt. He liked the heat. It took him nearly a year to go, and it wasn't easy. Especially not in the last months.'

'I'm sorry. Were you close?'

'He was my big brother. When I was a kid, he was my hero. Anything he did was OK with me. And when I got older, well .. what they said about him going over to the dark side, I guess that wasn't far off. He did some bad shit in his life.'

'The path that wasn't there when he tried to go back?' He hadn't been talking about himself in the Waldorf.

'Yeah. Something like that. He regretted a lot of it. I guess he figured he'd go back and do something about it later. Like we all do. There's always tomorrow to fix it. It never occurs to us that the sand will all run through the timer one day. In a way Dec was lucky. He knew he was dying. He had time to try to fix some of the mistakes. We talked the whole time. At least, Dec talked and I listened, took notes, re-created files. He had a photographic memory. He could remember events, places, conversations from twenty years ago like they happened yesterday. Believe me, whatever I told you about this case, was how it happened.'

'And your brother thought Alison's conviction was a mistake?'

He spread his hands palms upward and mimed scales balancing. 'Out of sync. There was something missing. He said it was as if Alison was imprisoned in a glass, soundproofed cage. He could see her shouting for help but couldn't hear her or work out what was wrong. It bothered him that he'd ignored it.'

'It wasn't his case. What could he have done?'

'Looked harder maybe. I don't know. I just promised I'd take a look at all the bad stuff and try to put it right if I could. So when he died, I scattered his ashes, packed up the files and headed home.'

I recalled his arrival in Seatoun. 'Is that what was in your bag the day you arrived? Files?'

'Pretty much.'

'That was one big bag.'

'As I said . . . there was a lot of bad karma in Dec's life. Lot of wrong choices.'

'And you're going to sort them?'

'If I can.'

'Starting with Alison?'

'I was kind of figuring which case I'd start on when I picked up a message some PI wanted to ask Dec about Alison's case. Seemed as good a place to start as any.'

'Was it?'

'It's had its moments.'

He grinned. I didn't smile back. I was still smarting. Partly from the fact he'd found it so easy to deceive me and partly from the injuries sustained in my attempt to fly. In addition to the massive splinter in my butt, I had scraped skin and grazes all over the place from being fired backwards through all those branches. I hadn't noticed them when the adrenaline was pumping from a mixture of fright and anger. But now they were starting to throb like crazy.

Tallulah was back in full concert mode. A fact I only realized when the receptionist stalked towards us and demanded: 'Is that a parrot?'

O'Hara raised the singing one's cage to eye level. 'Certainly not. As you can see, she is a rare featherless Tibetan dwarf turkey.'

'She still can't stay in here.'

'We'll wait for you in the car, duchy.'

I had no idea just standing was so tiring. Despite the pain I had to walk around. I shuffled a few steps to the drinks machine. And then back the other way. On my sixth circuit, I recognized the head bending to retrieve a cup from the delivery slot. He straightened at the same time and saw me.

'Evening, Mr Darrowfield.'

'Good evening. Are you . . . er, all right?'

Sure I was. I always wore pillowcases and walked like Donald Duck with constipation. 'Just fine. You?'

'They've admitted Philip. Couldn't clear his lungs.' He sounded defeated.

It was one of those empathizing moments when I was supposed to say the right thing. The best I could come up with was, 'Well, I'm sure they'll soon sort him.'

'I'm not sure I want them to. Might be best if he goes now. I don't want him to linger like Lucia. Only I gave her my word I'd look after him, see?' He was almost talking to himself. He slumped into one of the waiting-room chairs and stared at the back of another. 'She always refused to have him tested. But I reckon she knew. Made me promise to keep him at home. Don't let him go away. Always so close they were, him and his mum.'

He drank some instant tea as if he wasn't tasting it. Which – given the standard of drinks in this place – was probably something of a blessing. I asked him what had been wrong with his wife.

'Huntington's. Reckon she might have got it from her father. We never knew much about him. Came from Malta. Died in an accident when she was a baby. She'd never admit it, the Huntington's, I mean. Used to say it was nerve damage brought on by an accident. It was as if she was ashamed. Like she was touched by plague.'

'Gosh, I'm really sorry I . . .' I nearly sat down next to him. And remembered just in time. He looked a bit startled as I leapt away. 'Is that why Philip is, er . . .'

'Slow? No. Huntington's can affect the mind in the later stages, but sufferers are born as intelligent as you or me. Philip was just dealt a doubly lousy hand in life, the poor little sod.'

'I was talking about you and your wife to someone the other day. December Drysdale?'

'The donkey man.'

'Yep. He was telling me about the church socials in St John's Road.'

'Lucia enjoyed those. They were good about carrying her up the stairs. And they didn't have smoking. Smoke irritated her lungs.'

'Why did you stop going? December thought it was because you'd fallen out with the Wynne-Ellises. Had you?'

'Lucia had.' He frowned. 'I never knew why. They had a key, in case Lucia needed help when I was at work. They were good like that. And then one day, she just tells me to go ask for our key and give them theirs back. Told me I was not to talk to them again. And to see that Philip didn't. Couldn't understand it. We'd always been so close.'

'Didn't you ask the Wynne-Ellises?'

'They couldn't understand either. Said there'd been no quarrel. But I had to do as she said. She'd have known if I lied. And I knew it was her illness talking, not her. Same as it made her take against my birds.'

A lot of odd things seemed to have happened a few weeks *before* the murder. The Darrowfields and Wynne-Ellises had fallen out – but none of the surviving participants had the faintest idea why. Ken Darrowfield had had to get rid of his parrots. Alison had stopped going to Abbot's Cottage so frequently. Trudy Hepburn's confidence had blossomed. But I just couldn't see how any of that tied into the murder.

When I came out from the treatment area, Ken had gone. So had O'Hara. There was no sign of the Merc in the parking area. I limped around the bays, thinking perhaps he'd had to move. Just as I was about to go inside and call a minicab, the Merc drew up beside me.

O'Hara held up a paper bag. 'Tallulah and I have been late-night shopping. We bought you a present. Ready to roll?'

The local anaesthetic hadn't completely worn off, making it just about bearable to sit in the passenger seat on the way back to the flat.

'How did the docs make out?' O'Hara enquired sliding into the traffic stream. 'You gonna live?'

'I'm fine.' Apart from a large cut in my bottom, a whole hem of stitches, a tetanus shot and pains in places I didn't have places, I was just *fine.*

He carried Tallulah's cage down the basement steps behind me. When he tried to step through the door after me, I grabbed the cage and put my trainer into his shin. 'Don't. Do not – in any circumstance – come near me again.'

'Heh, it wasn't my fault you decided to make with the pigeon impression.'

'Yes. It was.'

'Whatever you say. Here's your present.'

I slammed the door in his face. Turned the lights on. And sniffed back tears. I was exhausted and in pain. My life stank. It couldn't get any worse. I sat down on the bed – and discovered it could. The anaesthetic had worn off.

32

'Why are you carrying that thing around?'

'I'm eccentric, Jan.' Her desk was once again covered with a small library of books. 'Any messages?'

'Not for you.'

Vetch's office door opened. And O'Hara strolled out. 'Catch you later, Vetch. We'll do that drink.'

'Look forward to it, Dane. Morning, sweet thing.'

One meeting and he was on first-name terms with the boss. I couldn't run for my own office. I'd already discovered that stairs were agony. Each tread pulled on the stitches. Jan picked up Tallulah and disappeared up the stairs.

Trapped, I snarled at the cause of my pain. 'What the hell are you doing here?'

'Look, duchy, if you think I owe you an apology, then you've got it. In my life I've got used to being cautious. I need to know before I trust. I see that's not everyone's way, but it's mine. And yours too, I'm guessing.'

I couldn't exactly deny that. I *was* wary of trusting people I didn't know well. 'But I don't set out to make fools of people, O'Hara.'

'I never intended to do that. I just needed to stay close to you.'

He ran a finger around my mouth. I got those tingling feelings again. Time for a bit of decisive line-drawing. 'Forget it. This relationship is staying on a strictly professional basis from now on.'

'We've still got one then?'

I was getting nowhere with the case. I was going to have

to get some help. And I didn't think I'd have any scruples about doing the dirty on O'Hara if I needed to later. 'As I said. Strictly professional.'

'Fine. Now tell me what you've been holding out on, duchess. Because I know there's something.'

So I told him about Betterman, Orlando Roles and the 788 gang. Taking a pen from Jan's desk, he scrawled the details. 'Don't do anything more on this until I come back to you, OK?'

I crossed my fingers behind my back. 'If you say so.'

'Is there anything else?'

'Just the one thing.' I held up his 'present', an inflatable red and white rubber beach ring with a grinning duck's head. 'You couldn't get one without the duck?'

'Only one in the shop. Catch up with you later. Don't do anything I wouldn't.'

'Lying? Cheating? Breaking and entering? Stealing? Yep, figure I can work within those parameters.'

Jan still hadn't reappeared. Putting the ring on her seat, I lowered myself cautiously and checked that there really hadn't been any emails for me. There were books open all over the place. Jan was really going overboard on this neighbourhood report. I'd probably have to edit most of it out. Idly I scanned to see what she was looking up. A paragraph jumped from the page and waved at me. Yee . . . ha! I'd cracked it!

Grabbing the keyboard, I banged off a message to Betterman, signing off with: 'Do I get a prize? How about the truth?'

There was no immediate response. But the strains of '*Maria . . . maria*' announced Jan's return from the upper regions. 'I think she's growing feathers. I changed her outfit and she's got little fluffy bits on her chest.'

'Life just gets better and better. Watch her while I go to the loo.'

It was an operation that took a lot of delicate handling and careful manoeuvring of clothing. When I finally got everything assembled and stepped out into the reception area, I heard myself.

'Forget it. This relationship is staying on a strictly professional basis from now on.'

Jan took a sip of coffee and smirked. 'I knew you'd been at it with that bloke.'

'How the hell did you do that?'

She dived under the desk and pulled out a mike on a thin cable. 'You can record on this computer. Neat, eh? I wish I'd found that out before.'

'Magic.' I shot over, ripped the cable out and rolled it into my pocket. The action jerked the table and Jan's coffee mug fell over, sending a milky tide over the desk.

Grabbing a couple of paper tissues, she blotted up the mess. 'If this goes in the computer, I'm blaming you . . . You OK? You look like you've just had an electric shock.'

I'd had a déjà vu moment: a casual joke about not taping our interview; Gina wiping up spilt wine. '*She recorded them.* That's what she was doing at Beattie Root's house. Setting up recorders and then retrieving them. No, not recorders. It was probably a wire, with a pick-up outside. Then she tried to use it against them. It was never Trudy. Trudy had no money, no sex life, no spunk. But she turned herself into Jennifer Jason Leigh. The kitchen lights were out. Orlando would just have seen the silhouette.'

'You aren't half rambling.'

'Not to me. To me, Jan, I am making perfect sense. I'm going to fetch my car, I left it parked up by the harbour.'

I nearly made the front door before Vetch's door opened. I'd swear Jan wasn't the only one who had the reception area bugged. 'Haven't you forgotten something, sweet thing?'

'Half an hour max, I promise.'

'I'm not concerned with your speed, just with the impression our clients receive as they step into reception. Take Polly walkies, please, sweet thing.'

'*Tallulah . . . deadwood.*'

'Understands every word we say, Vetch.' I grabbed the cage and nicked one of Jan's books.

I limped along the promenade, lugging the cage covered with an improvised woolly cover in one hand, and keeping the duck-head rubber ring anchored to my chest with the other. The wind kept tugging at it, trying to drag it from me. The near-empty arcades flashed neon lights and thumped out electronic music and the occasional clink-kerchunk of whirling slot machine drums. I was wading up the hill with discarded greasy polystyrene burger and fish trays, fizzy drinks cups and straws and chip cartons blowing around my ankles. I should have felt depressed, but I felt *great*!

I'd cracked it. And I'd done it without Mr Smug-faced O'Hara's help. Retrieving the big pink file from the boot, I slung it on the passenger seat before edging in very carefully on to the rubber ring. What now?

'It's not very likely Orlando's going to admit the truth, is it? Nor's Gina if it comes to that. She might have found something at the cottage linking the killing to him – or one of the others, I guess – before the patrol car turned up. She may even be blackmailing him still. That could explain why Orlando's businesses fail. Blackmail payments probably aren't tax deductible.'

'*Elementary, my dear Watson.*'

I realized I didn't even know where Orlando lived. If there was anything linking him to Gina, he surely wouldn't keep it at the office where his dad might find it?

'Whither now, partner?'

'*O-o-oklahoma.*'

'Tempting. But Roles Motors might be more practical. If I can convince Billy I fancy his son, he might tell me where I can locate my designer-clad hottie.'

The rubber ring pushed me up into the steering wheel. I had to adjust the chair position and stretch arms and legs to reach the wheel and pedals. In addition to throbbing grazes and bruises and collateral splinter damage, my back and neck muscles were aching by the time I hobbled out of the car in the yard of Roles Motors. I felt about a hundred and five.

The werewolf was nowhere to be seen – or heard. Tallulah and I edged warily towards the cabin, ready to break into a fast limp if she was planning an ambush. There was no response to my knock. When I tried the handle, it opened.

'*I don't like it, Sergeant. It's too quiet,*' Tallulah hissed.

'Hello? Billy?'

Given Billy's drinking habits, there was every chance he wouldn't have heard me if I'd marched in with the Philharmonic Orchestra in tow. I checked behind the desk in case he'd crashed out down there. Nothing but cord carpet. The funeral folder was on the desk with a dozen or so engraved invitations dealt out over the surface. It would seem that Billy couldn't decide between the traditional black-rimmed or the funkier gold-edged designs. I tried the door behind the desk. Loo and washbasin; no drunks.

Billy's trilby was on top of one of the filing cabinets, so he couldn't be far away. It was sitting on a furry rug of some kind. Curious as to what it was, I went over and lifted the trilby. Billy's grey curls came with it and hung like a curtain below the rim. Turning it upside down, I found they were attached like a fringe to the hat band. Neat. One of the filing drawers was partially open. I glimpsed another hat and couldn't resist. It was a tweed cap and this one had a fringing of straight chestnut. It must be his country pursuits look. Underneath was a stetson with a black pigtail; country and western? I delved in again and my heart gave a lurch into my mouth.

'Couldn't get on with the wigs, darling.' The heart bounced off the inside of my skull this time. He'd come up the outside steps without making a sound. 'Too hot. So I had these made up. Have a bit of fun like.'

He came across to me. His head gleamed whitely above the tanned face so that he resembled a partially shelled boiled egg. Collecting up the hats, he started to return them to the drawer. And saw the one I'd reached: a red baseball cap with a fringe of long yellow hair.

There was no point in trying to talk my way out. He read the truth in my eyes at the same time as I found it in his. 'The dosser in the laundrette, it was you. It was you who tried to shoot me!'

'If I'd been trying to shoot you, darling, I'd have hit you. Old Billy hasn't forgotten how to handle a shooter. It was just a little warning. Keep your nose out. But you didn't take it, did you? You've bottle, I'll give you that. But you should have taken notice. Don't meddle where you're not wanted. It can be dangerous. Fatal even.'

'I take it the phone calls and the letter bomb were you too?'

'You can't say I didn't give you fair warning.'

Normally I could out-kick and out-sprint someone Billy's age without problem. But normally I hadn't just had a close encounter with an oak tree.

'And my car?'

'I could have torched it. But I like you, darling. I decided to give you one last chance to get out.'

'Thanks for nothing.'

Tallulah's cage was on the desk. I wandered casually towards it. Billy made no attempt to stop me. I lifted the cage and wandered doorwards.

'*Unleash hell*!' Tallulah screamed.

Billy whistled sharply. There was a scrabble of paws on the metal treads outside. The werewolf peered round the open door.

'Can you keep your big beak *shut* in the future,' I snarled at the featherless pest.

It was the closest I'd ever been to Cleo. I hadn't appreciated quite how large she was. The head was cow-sized. She walked forward, giving me the chance to see the powerful neck under the metal ring collar. And to notice that there was no anchor chain attached to it. Her ears and eyes were fixed on Billy, but when I moved she turned the head towards me and bared a set of fangs that looked like they'd been borrowed from a Great White. A low growl rumbled deep inside the shaggy black coat.

'She'll have you if I tell her to. Best guard dog I ever had.'

I believed him. I'd babysat a dog last year. He could put out with the bovver-boy rumble if needed, but he was capable of some kind of reasoning. When I looked into this animal's eyes, they'd flared red with pure madness. I was facing the canine equivalent of a psychopath.

Keeping him talking was my only chance. 'What did Gina get on your beloved son and heir and his mates?'

Before Billy could answer, we both caught the sound of a car turning into the lot. Any hope of rescue was squashed by the arrival of Orlando.

Even a self-obsessed prat like Orlando couldn't fail to pick up the vibrations in here. 'What's wrong?'

I told him. 'We were just discussing Gina Gibbs's blackmail. After she recorded you and the rest of the seven eight eight gang discussing your alternative career in crime. Or was it just you shooting your mouth off?'

Orlando looked from me. To his father. To the werewolf. And back to me. 'What are you talking about?'

It was my turn to do the puzzled circular look. I missed the dog out and ended up with Billy.

He sneered. 'Think she'd go to him? She knew to come to the organ grinder, not the monkey. She had it all on tape. Mr Bigman here planning the jobs, giving the orders, describing how clever he'd been when he shot at a pensioner and terrorized a pregnant woman. Oh, he's a brave boy, my lad. He made them take souvenirs too, you know? Lots of identifiable bits and pieces, and all with Mr Bigman's fingerprints over them. Kept them hidden out back. Secret hiding place. So bloody secret, he told his mates about it. She shinned over the fence one night. Drugged the dog. Took the lot. Taught me a lesson that; trained all my dogs since not to eat anything unless I give it to them. I use cayenne pepper and mustard. Makes 'em sick as a dog.' He laughed loudly at his own joke.

'She phoned me. Told me what she'd got. I had to do it, don't you see? He was going to be something important . . . have respect. I couldn't let him get a criminal record. I had to do it.'

Had to do what? Pay up? Or stop the blackmailer for ever by stabbing her to death? He'd told me himself that his dad had worked on a liner and the investigating team thought the murder knife had been made in the thirties for a shipping line. Why hadn't I made that connection earlier – before I'd charged into the werewolf's lair, for instance? Had Gina realized they'd killed the wrong woman immediately? She'd plainly kept her head well enough to set up some kind of arrangement that ensured Billy would never try it again.

'Gibbsy took the box?' What his father was saying finally dented Orlando's stunned expression. 'I thought somebody else had . . .'

'Andrew Lee.'

'How'd you know that?'

'Because she's smart, son. She digs. She gets under the skin of things. And that makes her dangerous.'

'It was you who phoned Gina Pennington when I was there, wasn't it? Not Orlando.'

Billy spat. The dog quivered. 'Told me to stop you meddling, the ice queen did. Scared what you'll turn up. Scared I might give a statement. Testimony of a dying man. Can't ignore that, can they?'

'You could do that. Wipe that superior expression off her face?' I suggested.

'I could, couldn't I?' Billy's face lit up. I held my breath. The light died. 'But I can't. Too much to lose.'

'Dad, I didn't know, I swear. What you did for me, it was . . . brilliant.'

'It was bloody stupid. If I'd known how you were going to turn out, I'd not have bothered. I'd have let you clear up your own mess. He took a gun, you know?' He complained to me. It was almost as if Billy and I were on the same side and Orlando was the outsider. Hang on to that illusion, Grace.

'One you were minding?'

'Keep 'em safe, keep 'em virgins. Untraceable,' he elaborated. 'And what does the bonehead do, eh? Play Dick Turpin and leave bullets behind.' He slapped Orlando's cheek. Orlando's fist bunched but he kept his mouth shut. 'I didn't know until I heard it on the tapes. I'd already passed the guns along the line by then. Used goods. How would it have looked if that team had been picked up and they'd traced the guns back to some prat prancing around on a horse in Seatoun.'

'Don't suppose they'd have got a lot of respect inside, would they?'

'Exactly, darling. That's what it's all about – respect. Surgeon!' He slapped Orlando again. 'Judge!' Slap. 'I wouldn't give you a job sucking out sump oil.'

We both looked sadly at the loser. I risked another doorward shuffle. Cleopatra made a keening sound in her throat.

'Don't be doing anything silly now, darling. Billy wouldn't want to see you getting hurt.'

Billy and I had so much in common we were practically soulmates. 'Look at it this way, Billy: Gina would have a bit of trouble explaining why she sat on this evidence for twenty years. She's got a lot more to lose now. Even if it did surface, Orlando's changed. Head of his own business. Could be a suspended sentence.'

'Get this into your head, you bitch, there's no way I'm going to court. We have to deal with her, Dad.'

'*We* don't have to do anything. I'd trust Cleo to sort her out before I'd trust you.'

That was kind of what I was afraid of.

'If this was just about you ending up in court, I'd let you

take your chances. But there's something much bigger at stake than your sorry life.'

He made me give him my car keys. I tried reasoning with him. 'Billy, look this is stupid, this isn't going to help ... mmmmmm ...' Reasoning is tough when you've got duct tape over your mouth. More went around my wrists. Cleopatra whimpered. I felt like joining her.

'Stick her in the washroom,' Billy ordered. 'She'll keep in there until I make some arrangements. I'm going to move her car out of sight.'

Billy strode out and Orlando dug his fingers into my shoulder: 'Up.'

I expected to be marched in the direction of the bathroom cubicle. Instead he pushed me into the desk seat and stood behind me. I could feel his breath on my neck. 'Now, you little prick teaser, let's give you what you really want.'

He pushed a hand into the collar of my jumper and slid it downwards. His fingers dug inside my bra and found my nipple. He rubbed it between his thumb and forefinger. 'Not a lot here to get excited about, is there? I like a woman with big tits myself.' His wet tongue rasped my cheek as he licked my skin. His hand moved lower. Down across my stomach. I tried to stand, but he locked his other arm around my chest, pinning me against the chair back. I squirmed; Cleo growled a warning. My waistband was tight. For a moment, I thought he was going to give up, then he was inside my panties, groping in the hair, finding his way between my legs. He was leaning so far over me now I could see his tongue flicking in and out in sync with his short, fast breaths. 'Nice. Very nice. Shall I show you what I've got for you, bitch?'

Cleo's massive head swung towards the door. Her ears pricked. I caught the sound of Billy's footsteps on the gravel.

I was hauled to my feet and pushed towards the bathroom. A shove sent me inside. I felt behind me with taped hands and put the bolt across. A totally useless gesture. It wasn't designed for security, just modesty. One hard kick would deal with it. But it made me feel better. I pressed an ear to the door crack.

'What are you going to do with her?' Orlando asked.

'I'll have to think. Might have to torch the car after all. Best to wait until dark.'

'*Suicide is painless* . . .' warbled Tallulah.

'Fetch that cage. At least I can shut that bird up.'

I heard the outer door open and close and a moment later an engine started outside. The car noise roared into life and moved away. There was another noise. Ungreased hinges. Something heavy shifting. I guessed they were shutting the gates. As soon as I was sure they'd gone, I looked round for something to cut the duct tape.

Low-level loo. Washbasin. Plastic wastepaper basket. Packet of paper towels (half used) on top of the cistern. Toilet roll on plastic holder. Slimy bar of soap. Tiny window so high up that I couldn't reach it. There's never a razor blade around when you want one.

I figured the washbasin was the only possibility. Backing up, I leant over it and located a tap. The rim of the spout was rough metal. Pushing the tape into it, I started sawing. Back and forth, back and forth. There was a slight lessening of the tightness of the binding. I pushed harder and gasped as the raw metal rasped down my skin instead. Wait until dark, Billy had said. But I didn't know whether that meant they weren't coming back until this evening, or they'd be returning as soon as Billy had put whatever plans he had for me in motion. My mouth was dry and I couldn't swallow properly. The glue on the tape over my lips was making me want to heave.

There was one final section. I tried snapping it. The plasticized tape stretched but held. I used both thumbs to hold it tight against the tap rim and sawed frantically. It gave, and my arms were free. Ripping off the mouth tape, I ran the tap and scooped water gratefully with cupped hands, rinsing and spitting. There was wetness on my cheek, probably from the basin, but it was where Orlando had licked me. I lathered soap over my face and splashed, rubbing until the skin squeaked. I knew I should get out of there immediately, but I couldn't stop. I dragged off my top clothes and pulled my trousers down. I went through the entire stack of paper towels, scrubbing off the feel of Orlando's hand, not caring about the raw grazes that stung under the onslaught. Finally I re-dressed over damp skin, slid the bolt back and pushed the door.

Something huge and evil lunged at my throat.

33

In situations like this, it's helpful to be shut in a lavatory. All facilities were available to let me throw up hygienically and rinse out afterwards. Shakily, I sat on the loo. Outside Cleo was keening and snuffling. Her claws scraped with fast shish-shish-shish sounds. She was actually trying to dig her way under the door.

Closing my eyes, I tried to picture the brief glimpse I'd had of the office, before my mind had been concentrated on imminent dismemberment. I was pretty sure the outer door had been shut. Which meant there was no chance of Cleo getting bored and wandering off to check out the yard. All she had to keep herself amused was figuring how to get dinner out of the can.

Closing the seat, I stood on the loo and examined the window. It wasn't locked but the opening was less than ten inches square, way too small to get through. From my position all I could see was the yard's blue fence. Which meant anyone over the other side wasn't going to be able to see this window so signalling from it was useless.

I screamed and bawled for an hour before giving up. This was a road people drove not walked. If there was the odd pedestrian passing out there, all they were going to hear was the normal sound of Billy Roles's guard dog going berserk.

Slumping back down, I weighed up other possibilities. It was a short exercise. There didn't seem to be any. Now I was quiet, Cleo had shut up too and re-channelled her energies into trying to dig under the door again.

Dig! Floor! It was covered in some kind of easy-clean material. I found a corner and pulled. It came back easily to reveal a metal surface with no obvious signs of fixings or joints. I crawled over the surface with my nose two inches from it. The only places it had fixings were where they'd bolted the toilet and sink pedestals in place. Even if I could have got them out, the gap I'd have been left with would have been smaller than the window.

OK, think laterally. Or even vertically. If not the floor, what about the ceiling? Standing on the loo again, I stretched up and found I could place my hands flat on the ceiling. It was definitely lower than the height of the cabin and, better yet, it yielded to slight pressure.

Pulling off the cistern cover, I used some brute force on the ballcock arm to wrench it free. Scrambling back up, I hit the ceiling with a series of fast jabs. Bits of ceiling material crumbled and fell into my mouth and eyes. Cleo went berserk. A tiny hole appeared. Forcing the rod into it, I rocked it back and forth, breaking sections from the rim and widening the gap. It fell into the open cistern and swirled around in the sheet of liquid spreading over the floor.

I wasn't high enough to pull myself through. Looking around for extra height, the only thing available was the wastepaper basket. Up-ending it on the loo seat, I climbed. The flimsy material bent and distorted under my weight. Thrusting both hands into the gap, I hauled myself up quickly and lay flat to distribute my weight.

There was no light apart from the tiny amount coming from my excavation. The false ceiling was no more than large panels of some kind of compressed polystyrene nailed to some equally insubstantial wooden battens. I bet the whole thing was an illegal fire-hazard. Cautiously, I tried to pull myself forward a few inches. Everything creaked and groaned (me included).

There was no obvious way out. I'd been vaguely hoping they'd covered over a ventilation grille or something up here. But there was no variation in the darkness to indicate light seeping around the edge of an opening. Logically (and belatedly) I guessed a grille was unlikely to be any bigger than the bathroom window, and equally useless as an exit. But doing something felt better than doing nothing. I eased along a little further. The ceiling protested but Cleo didn't. Building noises didn't seem to register with her.

There was a loud cracking sound in the darkness to my left. I lay very still. It didn't help. Crack . . . crack . . . crack. It was too late to squirm back to my hole. The ceiling lurched underneath me and I was sliding forward. I bowled down a slope and slammed to a stop against something hard. Since it was my bottom that had made first contact, the pain was enough to make me scream loudly. Cleo snarled. She sounded about two inches from my ear, but I couldn't see her. In fact, all I could see was ceiling.

I tried to make sense of the scene in front of me. The entire false ceiling had been wrenched off its fixings. At the bathroom end it was still being held up by the partition wall, but in the main office it had fallen until its progress had been stopped by something underneath. Which meant that it was balanced on the filing cabinets over on the back wall and then tilted towards the door side until its progress was halted by the desk. That would have been it, if my weight hadn't rolled down the length. The extra load had snapped battens at impact points so that a large section had dipped floorwards like a broken wing. I'd ended up on top of this section in the far corner of the cabin – and Cleo was trapped underneath it up at the bathroom end. Unfortunately so was the phone. Cleo's barking sounded confused rather than aggressive – however, as soon as I tried to stand she attacked the portion nearest the sound. More wood splintered and tiles crunched. Levering myself up with my back against the wall and my feet on the sloping ceiling, I considered the door. The fake ceiling was lying diagonally across it. No chance there. It would have to be the window.

I had to edge up the slope to reach it. I put my weight on a wooden strut. It bent and dipped. I tried to lean my shoulders against the outer wall and let that take some of the weight. Cleo continued to attack from the other side. Her charges lifted the ground under my feet. I trod on a tile trying to regain my balance. One foot went through. With a squeak of fear, I drew it up before Cleo could enjoy toe tasties. She charged again and a piece of polystyrene tile smashed outwards. Her muzzle appeared in the hole, nostrils widening as she scented victim. I was conscious that if the window was locked, I had nothing this side of the partition with which to smash it.

It was hinged in the centre and designed to open outwards and . . . oh joy . . . it did!

I went through head first, tucking in and somersaulting as I hit the ground. Normally a good move. Unless you happen to have a butt full of stitches.

The gate was the best option, I figured. The diagonal strengthening struts of wood and the metal handles would provide the best footholds for climbing out. I hobbled forwards, then stopped. A car engine roared outside and then dulled to the throb of an idling motor. Customer? There was the sound of chains rattling as they were withdrawn from the outer handles.

I hobbled fast into the ranks of cars and tried to crouch down out of sight. Not a good position for me. Eyes watering, I got as near to the gates as I dared. Orlando drove the Lexus into the yard and got out to rechain the gates on the inside. That was a bummer. I'd hoped to be able to slip out while they were busy at the cabin.

My options weren't great. I could still try to make the climb, but I wasn't exactly in shape to clear tall buildings at a single bound. They could pull me back long before I got to the top and that would be my one chance of getting away blown. Under cover of an ancient Capri, I watched father and son arrive at the cabin. Billy's explosion of swearing was answered by a whine from Cleo. Orlando jumped back into the car and switched the engine on. Brilliant. Go, boy, go.

'What do you think you're doing?' his father shouted.

'She's escaped. She'll have gone for the coppers. Let's get out of here.'

'Bollocks. She could still be in there. Now come here and help me shift this.'

Any hopes I had of getting over the fence while they were busy trying to reach the bathroom to see if I was still inside, were squashed when Billy stayed outside, his eyes scanning the car parking area, as Orlando climbed in.

Eventually Orlando must have managed to smash up enough ceiling to get the bathroom and outer doors open. He reappeared in the doorway, his hair and clothes covered in lumps of greyish-white ceiling. 'She's gone.'

'Damn. Where's that bloody dog?'

Billy had turned to talk to his son and heir. I tried the Capri's door. It opened. Watching through the windscreen for any sign they'd spotted the movement, I squeezed inside and drew the door to. Lying across the front seats, I eased myself up to watch their next move. It turned out to be turning the werewolf loose into the yard.

Cleo got her nose to the ground and started circling: the wrong way. It would seem that the great hairy mutt relied on seeing or hearing intruders. She wasn't a great tracker. Allelujah!

I stayed watching as long as I dared, and then lay flat, listening.

'What if she's already gone?' Orlando shouted from across the yard.

'Then I'm stuffed. Which means you are too.' Billy sounded as if he was so close, he could have been in the back seat. I scrunched smaller and the stitches felt like red hot needles in my butt.

'She can't prove anything. Not without Gibbsy squealing.'

'She can talk,' Billy growled. 'Start people thinking. There's people out there smart enough to work out the way it was. Work out what I did.'

He sounded like he'd moved away. I risked sitting up

slightly. There was no sign of Billy, but Orlando was working his way along the cars on the far side, stooping to peer into each window as he went past. I calculated distances. If I could work my way round to the cars he'd already searched, I could hide inside one and they might decide I'd already legged it out of the yard before they returned. All I had to do was avoid Billy and the werewolf. And if I pulled that one off, I might try juggling custard.

I opened the driver's door a fraction to see if I could spot either. My heart somersaulted. Billy was lying flat under the car ahead with just his legs showing. Any hope that he'd had a convenient heart attack was squashed as he drew the grey trousers in and squirmed out clutching something. The brief glimpse I got was enough to tell me O'Hara had been right about the calibre. That was definitely a thirty-eight; I'd seen one once on the police firing range.

Ducking as Billy straightened, I held the Capri's door shut. It's times like this I appreciate how important it is for an investigator to go out properly equipped: mobile phone, Uzi machine gun, partner with knack of arriving in nick of time.

'Hello, inside. Will you be opening the gates now?'

O'Hara seemed to have picked up an accent thick enough to smother a leprechaun. The chains rattled as he shook the gates. Cleo erupted into a furious onslaught of barking and charged over the yard to confront the new threat.

'Are ye there?'

'We're closed. Come back later.' Orlando. Loudly.

'Shut up, you fool, he didn't need to know there was anyone here.' Billy. Much softer.

'I've come t' buy a motor. Will you be letting me in now?'

'Are you deaf? We're closed,' Orlando bawled back. His tone upped Cleo's aggression a few notches.

'Ah, there yer are.'

Billy's shadow passed over me. He didn't look inside the

Capri. I peeked up to see what had got his attention. O'Hara was perched on top of the gates.

Orlando and Billy were staring up at him. Both had their backs to me, which meant I could see the gun Billy was tucking into his trouser waistband and O'Hara couldn't. Cleo was taking running jumps at the gates, her jaws snapping closed over empty air at each abortive attempt to reach her tormentor.

'Will you call the dog off now?'

'Are you stupid? We're *closed*,' Orlando shouted.

'Sure now it doesn't say closed outside.'

'Could you read it if it did, you moron? Why do you think the gates are locked?'

'To keep the dog in. That's a lively beast. Does she bite?'

'Of course she bloody bites, now shove off.'

'But I want a motor. Oi've money, see?' He held up a wodge of folded notes.

He had their full attention. Should I try to run for the side fence and hope one of the cars was parked close enough to give me a leg-up, or stay put and see if O'Hara had a plan beyond acting the idiot? I decided to risk letting him know where I was. Sliding my legs out of the door, I stood far enough up for him to see me.

I'd intended to duck back inside fast. Billy moved even faster. From having his full attention on O'Hara, he spun. The gun was pointing straight at my head.

'There you are, darling. I thought you'd pop up sooner or later, while your mate here was acting the goat.'

'Who are you calling a goat?' The 'Oirish' had disappeared. And a small black gun had appeared. 'Now which will be it? The hound?' The muzzle pointed at Cleo. 'Or the man?' It swung towards Orlando. Which is worth more to you?'

'Hard to say. You've made your point. What do you want to do?'

'How about I lose my gun, and you lose yours?'

'Sounds fair enough to me. You first.'

'Get rid of the dog.'

Billy whistled. Cleo bounded over. Still keeping the gun directed at my head, he felt for the door handle of the nearest car. 'In!'

Once she was shut inside, he turned expectantly to O'Hara. Who said, 'Leave your gun on top and move away.'

'What about yours?'

O'Hara twisted his own weapon sideways and laid it on the gate post. He kept his hand on it. Billy put his gun on the car roof. He moved a few inches away. O'Hara responded by edging a few inches along the top of the gates. Billy moved. O'Hara edged. Move. Edge. I found I was holding my stomach and butt clenched tight with tension. I relaxed. And wished I hadn't as the stitches made themselves felt again.

Move. Edge. EEEEEE . . . HAAAAAAA.

The blare of the horn filled the car lot. Cleo had jumped on the steering wheel and set it off. The distraction hit O'Hara mid-edge. He fumbled it, rocked on top of the gate and dropped to the ground inside the gates. Billy ran for his gun. Orlando ran for O'Hara. I just ran.

When we'd all finished sprinting, O'Hara and Orlando were struggling on the ground and Billy had the gun pointed at them. 'Get out of the way, Orlando.'

'I don't think that's going to be possible, Billy-boy.' O'Hara climbed to his feet holding Orlando in front of him. One arm was clamped around his neck and the other had Orlando's arm twisted behind his back. 'Now, you do anything stupid and I might have to snap something. Arm?' Orlando yelped. 'Neck?' This time Orlando made choking sounds. 'Or maybe you'd just rather shoot through him?'

'For two bloody pins I would.'

'Dad! Please.'

'Dad, please,' Billy mimicked. 'That's all I ever heard from you. Money please, Dad. Bail me out of this mess please, Dad. Make this bit of bother go away please, Dad.' He lifted the gun fractionally. I was sure all he intended was to frighten Orlando as a little payback for being a big disappointment. But we never found out. As they were talking, O'Hara had been walking forward, forcing Orlando to move in front of him. Billy was backing to maintain the distance between them. I'd been watching crouched behind the tail of a Ford. I had one end of the mike wire I'd confiscated from Jan clutched in my hand. As Billy came backwards towards me, I jerked the wire taut. The other end was tied to the bumper of the next car. The trip caught him behind the calves. He fell backwards and his gun soared into the air.

I leapt and fielded it by instinct. Unfortunately what I grabbed was the trigger. The crash of the shot even shut Cleo up. We all stared at the Lexus. The bonnet had popped and something was dribbling on the ground. Orlando looked sick.

'Nice shooting, duchy. Definitely a serious flesh wound.'

A tiny flame licked from the gap under the bonnet. 'Somebody get that fire before the lot goes up!' Billy yelled.

I looked at O'Hara. 'You want to get that? I've got them covered.' I swung the gun. All three men flung themselves to the floor.

'Point it the other way, duchy.' O'Hara shouted.

We watched O'Hara drag the fire extinguisher from the cabin wall and empty it over the engine before we all trooped back inside. The cabin was full of smashed ceiling tiles and battens and the floor was covered with a pool of water. The photos of gravestones were trodden and pulped into the mess. It wasn't a good look. O'Hara took the gun off me, hooked out the desk chair with his foot and pushed Orlando into it. Billy got the visitor's chair. I wasn't jealous. Right at the moment, I wasn't planning to sit down ever again. The roll of duct tape was amongst the crumbled debris on the desk top. O'Hara swiftly bound both the Roleses wrists to the chair arms.

'How did you find me?' I asked.

'Worked it out after listening to your ramblings on the

office computer. That odd receptionist of yours played me your theories re Gina blackmailing Orlando. So the lovely Gina taped Orlando and his mates shooting their mouths off, did she?'

'Yep. And not just that. She broke in here and took all the souvenirs they'd stolen from the victims. With Orlando's prints all over them.'

O'Hara tutted. 'Very clumsy, Orlando. Hardly living up to your dad's reputation, were you?'

Orlando scowled. So did Billy. At Orlando.

'Then she threatened to send everything to the police unless Billy came across. So he killed her. Or thought he had. Only Trudy had morphed into a Gina-clone by then. I guess he didn't know that. She was still the dark-haired frump when she came up here to moan about Orlando's behaviour at school. It must have been a nasty shock when he put the light on and found he'd stabbed the wrong woman.'

'Heh, hold up there, darling! I never killed anyone.'

'Yes, you did.'

'I swear to God I didn't.'

'It couldn't have been Orlando, he didn't know anything about the blackmail until now. So what did you do? Pay someone? I hope you got a refund. He definitely didn't fulfil his job description.'

'I never had anything to do with it!'

'Like hell! You said yourself this was about more than Orlando's little crime career being found out. Like you being done for murder, for instance?'

'No. It wasn't *that.* I never meant that.'

'What else was important enough to tie me up, threaten me with a werewolf and discuss making me part of the whole torched car scene?'

'My funeral.'

I couldn't believe he was serious. But he looked serious. In fact he looked desperate.

'Funeral?' O'Hara enquired. As usual he'd been letting me do all the talking.

'Billy's planning an event that will go down in crime folklore. Right up there with the St Valentine's Day Massacre, the Great Train Robbery, Jack the Ripper. But without the unpleasant consequences obviously.' I picked up a soggy sheet from the floor and held it up. 'This is the headstone he's going for.'

'Classy.'

'There's no need for you two to be sarcastic. A man's funeral is a sacred thing.'

'So's a woman's. And you were planning to bring mine forward, remember?'

'You didn't take that seriously, did you, darling? I was just trying to frighten you off the case. You wouldn't do old Billy out of his funeral, would you?'

'If you killed Trudy Hepburn—'

'I never.'

'And why should I believe you? Orlando had a fight with Andrew Lee a week before the end of the Easter term and after that Andrew was out of the gang. Because, I assume, Orlando thought Andrew had the box of souvenirs?' Orlando gave a sullen shrug. 'So that means Gina must have stolen them around that time and contacted you within that last week to ask for a payoff. And bingo – a few days later, Trudy gets stabbed after being mistaken for Gina. It fits.'

'No, it doesn't,' Billy insisted. 'That teacher got stabbed Easter time, right? The other one never let me know she had the tapes until the summer. The cold bitch sat on them for four months.'

'Why would she do that?'

'Because she didn't want money. You think all this is for money? I'd have *given* her money. I've paid out enough for that useless lump over the years. One more bloody bill wouldn't have made any difference. She wanted information.'

'On what?'

'Everything. All the jobs.'

'Why on earth would Gina want . . .' The answer struck me and O'Hara simultaneously. 'Clever Clive.'

'That'll be it,' O'Hara agreed. 'The secret of Clive's remarkable detection rate. He had his own private informer.'

It made sense. She'd started out trying to record something that would either keep Orlando and his pals in line or even get them expelled, then fate dropped Clever Clive into her arms; an ambitious policeman who was hacked off because he wasn't climbing the promotion ladder as fast as he felt he should. How long had it taken for them to put her incriminating tapes together with the rumours about Billy's criminal connections that Clive would have picked up from the police grapevine? 'And she made sure he married her before she handed over the tapes,' I guessed.

'How long did this arrangement last?' I asked Billy.

'Regularly – five or six years. They moved on. She called sometimes after that. But I didn't have the contacts like I used to.'

'And she didn't need them,' O'Hara said. 'Clive's reputation had been established. He was hot. On his way up the promotion ladder.'

'You won't tell, will you?' Billy pleaded. 'If the old firms find out I was a grass they'll not come to me funeral. I'll pay you. Give me a price?'

That got Orlando's attention. 'Don't give them my money, you bloody grass.'

O'Hara's dark-blue eyes swivelled in his direction. Orlando went quiet.

'How do we know you're telling the truth?' I asked. 'You think Gina's going to confirm it?'

'No. Look, I swear, that's how it was.'

I was inclined to believe him. But I didn't believe he'd only intended to frighten me this afternoon. If O'Hara hadn't shown up, I could have ended up as crispy fried investigator.

'Please, darling. The docs say I've only got a few months left.'

I looked at O'Hara. He did the slight shoulder lift thing.

'He shot at me. And sent me a dead rat and a letter bomb. And trashed my car. And tried to kill me. And that's not counting all the shitty things Orlando did twenty years ago.'

'They're never going to prove any of that now,' Orlando said.

'How about this for a plan,' O'Hara addressed Billy. 'We keep quiet about your career as a police informer and Orlando here has a sudden conversion to truth and justice and makes a full written confession to the police?'

'Drop dead,' Orlando snarled.

'Before you come to any hasty decisions, let me draw your attention to this pen. At one end, it writes.' He scribbled on a leaflet to prove it. 'While inside . . .' A fast snap pulled the bottom section apart. And revealed some kind of miniature electronic gadget. 'Records up to thirty minutes of speech. Now if I were to play our conversation back to the right people, Billy, or more accurately the wrong people . . .'

'He'll do it.'

'Like hell I will!'

'Shut up, Orlando. You'll get a few years at most. Might even be a suspended sentence. It's that or find yourself a job, because you won't be living off your inheritance. I'll leave the damn lot to charity.'

'So we have a deal then. Orlando talks. We don't. Suit you, duchy?'

'No.'

'No?'

I shook my head. While the idea of Orlando and Mark Boscombe spending a few years inside was appealing, I had a mental pictures of two sets of little girls in Australia whose lives would be destroyed. And who knows what family Andrew Lee and Michael Forbes had? I knew the responsibility for any bad stuff that happened was ultimately with the ex-members of the 788 crew, but I just didn't want to be the one that set all that in motion. If one of their victims chose to do so, that was their right, but I didn't want it to be mine. I never could get my head around the idea that if the fall-out from catching the bad guys hits others, then that's their fault, not mine. Maybe that's why I never made it as a copper.

'This stays between us. But that doesn't mean I'm not totally hacked off by what you did to me.'

'Grace is right. She deserves compensation,' O'Hara said.

'Course she does,' Billy agreed eagerly. 'You know where I keep the vodka, darling. There's another box underneath. You go help yourself.'

'Go ahead,' O'Hara instructed. 'I'll watch these two.'

I took a couple of the wads of notes. When I returned to the cabin there was a change in the atmosphere that I couldn't pin down. The gun had gone.

'I don't think these two will be bothering you again. Ready to head out?' O'Hara enquired.

'Hang on a minute. Orlando promised me something special. I just want to check it out.' He tried to kick out at me. I stepped to one side, reached down, found what I was looking for, and squeezed hard. I reckon they heard his scream in France.

Unexpectedly Billy laughed. Before asking, 'Aren't you going to untie us?'

'You'll figure it out,' O'Hara said.

As soon as we were outside, I asked, 'I know why I didn't want to report Orlando, but how come you were willing to let Billy off? Fellowship of the Dark Side?'

'Three reasons. One: that pen recorder doesn't work. Two: there's no other evidence. Gina Pennington's tapes and goody box will have gone up in smoke the minute Billy agreed to do the dirty. She's way too smart to keep that kind of incriminating material around. And three: this was never about Billy and Orlando for me. Declan had no history with them.'

We were passing the foamed drenched Lexus. Idly I glanced inside. And stopped. The cage was on the back seat. Tallulah, how could I have forgotten her! I eased the box out. Tallulah lay unmoving on the bottom; her body swaddled in a clown costume and a bobbled hat nearly touching her beak. 'He's killed her, the creep! That's it. All deals are off. Where's the gun?'

Tallulah's eyelids flickered. She raised one. Her eyeball swivelled taking in the wrecked cabin and trashed car. '*You were only supposed to blow the bloody doors off.*'

O'Hara retrieved an empty can of lager from the car floor. 'She's smashed. You can take her with you. She's not chucking up in my motor. By the way, wouldn't you like to know why I was looking for you at the office?'

Right at the moment, it wasn't top of my agenda. I was battered in more places than a fishfinger and now the adrenaline was wearing off, the reality of the situation I'd just got out of was starting to kick in. I wanted to go home. Soak in a hot bath. Snivel a bit. And count my money. 'OK. Tell me.'

O'Hara removed a bit of paper from his jacket and passed it over. 'Meet Betterman.'

I read the name. Three times. 'You're kidding?'

34

'*Deadwood ... Maria ... luscious bod ... ooooooooo ...*'

Swaying on the inflated duck-ring, I checked out the cage on the back seat via the rear-view mirror. 'Don't expect any sympathy from me, you lush. Serves you right.'

If Shane's brother didn't reclaim this parrot soon, she'd either be dead or collecting her season ticket to AA. I had a mental picture of a roomful of exotic birds, swaying on perches, croaking, 'My name's Tweetie. And I'm an alcoholic.'

Tallulah gave another heartfelt groan. She didn't sound too good at all. Maybe I ought to get her checked over by the vet. Ken Darrowfield might know one that specialized in parrots.

He let me into the living room/sick room. The bed was empty. 'Philip still in hospital?' I asked.

'He died. His heart gave up in the end. He never woke up, so at least he knew nothing about it.'

'Oh heck. I'm really sorry. I wouldn't have bothered you if I'd known.'

'I'll miss him, even though it was for the best. For him, I mean.'

'*I have often been forced to rely on the kindness of strangers*,' Tallulah cooed.

A smile cracked Ken Darrowfield's drawn face. 'That your parrot? Can I take a look?'

'Sure. In fact, I was going to ask if you could recommend a vet? She's got a hangover. Big time.'

He put the cage on a chair and crouched. 'She's stressed

as well. But she's getting her coat back. Would you like me to take her? Sort her out?'

'Could you? I've a big cage. At home.'

'Not to worry, I've got my old ones in the attic.' He opened Tallulah's cage. 'Let's see what we can do for you, shall we, old girl?'

I guess when you've been a carer for half a lifetime, the habit dies hard. But at least it meant I wouldn't have to lug her along tomorrow. O'Hara and I had a date with Betterman and the truth about Trudy Hepburn's murder.

'I can't tell you about the murder,' Betterman said.

You mean we'd just driven over two hundred miles for damn all?

'I wasn't there. But I can tell you what led up to it.'

Andrew Lee was still lean and dark-haired. His blue eyes were a fraction lighter than O'Hara's and he was an inch shorter, but if they couldn't pass for twins, they could definitely have claimed brotherhood. I'd known him as soon as he'd walked on to the stone bridge where we'd arranged to meet. He led the way down to the river bank.

We wound along the bank away from the city centre. Andrew and I were shoulder to shoulder. O'Hara dogged us a few paces behind. Close enough to hear, too far to have to join in the conversation.

The footpath was muddy but bearable, the trees were leafless but showing promise, and the silver-tinged water of the River Wye carried frantically paddling ducks along on its current. Upstream were the arches of the medieval bridge where we'd met, and soaring beyond and above it was the tower of Hereford Cathedral.

'It reminds me of Canterbury,' I said.

'Me too,' Andrew agreed.

'Is that why you moved here?'

'It wasn't my choice. It was the job. I was transferred here five years ago.'

'You never went back to Seatoun?'

'No.'

'What about Michael Forbes? I never traced him. He's your cousin, isn't he?'

'Mike's dead. Celebrated our graduation by taking off for the Greek Islands. Cheap booze, plenty of sex and more cheap booze. We decided to go for a swim one day. Dived off one of those inter-island ferries. Mike broke his neck. I'd like to claim it was a wake-up call, but if I'm honest it took a few more years to get my life together.'

OK, big family tragedy, but not my problem. Stick to the point, Grace, because he's trying not to. 'You two got over the big bust-up then, when you were black-balled from Orlando's gang?'

'Mike was family. And Orlando was history once we got to sixth form college.'

I paused in front of a carved wooden statue of a strangely ugly bulldog that was sitting on the river bank.

Andrew wiped mud from his shoes on to the grass. They were black and polished. Not really footpath gear. Neither was the formal suit he was wearing under the light raincoat. He'd told me when I telephoned yesterday that he was due at a wedding this afternoon.

'I think we'd better walk while we talk. It wouldn't do for the main man to be both late and covered in mud.'

'Is the wedding at the Cathedral?'

'No way. I'm not that grand.' We retraced our route back to the bridge, with O'Hara still making up the tag. Once we were at street level again, Andrew said, 'This girl you spoke about, Alison's daughter, will you tell her what I'm about to tell you?'

'I don't know. I'll decide when I hear it. Shoot, Andy.'

'You know about seven eight eight?'

I whipped one of Jan's books from the poacher's pocket of my jacket. *Roget's Thesaurus* is (according to its introduction) a collection of words and phrases that allows the reader to find the most apt, elegant and accurate phrase. Item number 788 came under Section Four: Possessive

Relations. Not over-protective parents as you might expect, but in the case of clause 788, over a hundred definitions of illegality. Everything from thieving, through bag snatches, cattle-rustling, highway robbery and tax evasion. A crime for all tastes. 'Have you still got your tattoo?'

Andrew unbuttoned his left cuff and rolled it back. 'It was Orlando's idea. He felt our gang lacked purpose. A mission statement. He found this in the library. We were going to work our way through the entire list. We were going to be the baddest guys in Seatoun. I got burglary the first time. I broke into someone's house and stole a silly little bracelet. We had to take something each time and bring it to the next meeting.'

'And give it to Orlando.'

'He held the treasure chest. He accused me of stealing it. I'd had a couple of run-ins with him about him always giving the orders. He thought I'd taken the box as the precursor to some kind of coup. I told him that was bullshit. I don't know what happened to it.'

'We do. Go on.'

'Well, originally we weren't going to steal anything else, it wasn't about theft, it was about showing we were in control. That we were untouchable. Then Mark Boscombe snatched a bag and it had a wallet full of money in it. We decided that if we dumped it, someone else would probably steal it – our morals were remarkably adaptable – so after that money was fair game.'

We were climbing up a pedestrianized street bounded by small terraced houses covered in some kind of climbing plant. Andrew stopped and pointed to an even older-looking grey wall opposite with a round blue plaque affixed to it. 'Nell Gwynne was born there.'

'Halfway up a wall?' O'Hara enquired. His footsteps behind us had been so quiet that I'd forgotten he was there.

'If only I had a pound for every time I've heard that one.'

'OK, I'll stop being a smart-arse. You go on with what you were telling Grace.'

'Orlando gave out the assignments. Whoever got it had to draw up a proper plan and they could press-gang others in as accomplices if needed. You had to do whatever task you were assigned, or you were out.'

'Orlando really had you lot soaring when he shouted "jump", didn't he?' I said.

'Orlando had money. And he had keys to the car lot. We just took any motor we fancied. We'd all pile in, drive out and party.'

'Set fire to barns. Terrorize pensioners.'

'Yes. I'm not trying to excuse what we did. I'm just trying to explain what it was like back then. How we were all thinking. We thought we were invincible. If they weren't clever enough to stop us, they deserved what they got. It's over here.'

He led us into the main shopping area. We were weaving in and out of shoppers, dodging into the road because the pavements were too narrow. When we could walk together again, I asked about Trudy's murder. 'Who did Orlando dish that out to?'

'Nobody. It wasn't like that. See there'd always been just the seven of us in the seven eight eight.'

'You, Orlando, Michael, Mark Boscombe, Sean Inchbeck, Larry Sorensson and Graham Knight.'

'You found that out. I'm glad. I'm not sure I'd have wanted to tell you the others. The magnificent seven. We ruled St Martin's. No one else was allowed in.'

'But somehow Philip Darrowfield managed to gate-crash the set-up.'

'He found out about the gang. And he decided he wanted to join. He had that kind of dumb stupidity that gets hold of an idea and won't let go. We tried threatening him to get rid of him. With everybody else at the school, just the hint that our crowd were thinking of sorting them out was enough to make them back off. We were premier league bullies. But it didn't frighten Philip, it just made him angry. Have you ever met him?'

'Yes.'

'Then you'll know, he's big. And very strong.'

'Was. He died. Heart failure.'

Andrew stopped dead. O'Hara had to do a fast double-step to avoid cannoning into us. 'I didn't ... in the circumstances ... perhaps I shouldn't say ...'

'Listen, mate, you definitely should say. It's not like it's going to hurt Philip now. And if you didn't *want* to say, you wouldn't have sent me those emails.'

'Yes, you're right. My life has been a lie for far too long.'

He re-started into motion so quickly that I had to trot several steps before I caught up. We were well out of the city centre now and striding downhill past industrial units and newer housing. Andrew's pace didn't slacken. His face was set, the mouth grim. 'Are you late for this wedding?'

'No. Besides they can hardly start without me.'

'Then could you slow down a bit? I'm finding it a bit difficult to stride out at present.'

'Sorry.' He dropped back to a stroll. 'I was just ...' He made a helpless gesture. 'Anyway Philip. He was determined to be in the gang. He was always hanging round us. And if we tried to shake him off, he'd lose it. He could do serious damage if he landed a hit. And he didn't seem to register any pain we inflicted on him. So Orlando decided if we were stuck with him, he'd make his first seven eight eight something really special. Something we hadn't done before.'

'Murder?'

'No. Not even Orlando had the stomach for that one. He asked Phil if there was a girl he liked better than any of the others. Philip said Alison Wynne-Ellis. That suited Orlando. He didn't like Alison. She'd reported him for setting a teacher's car on fire. Orlando wasn't used to people reporting him. He took it very personally.'

'What did the rest of you think of her?'

'We thought she was whatever the female equivalent of a dork is. Anyway Orlando told Philip that he had to pass an initiation test to get in. He said we'd all had sex with our girlfriends, and Philip would have to do the same if he wanted in.'

I looked sideways at Andrew. His jaw was clenched so tightly, the lines at the corners appeared gouged with a knife. 'The crime you chose . . . ?'

'Rape,' he said shortly. Still not looking at me, he said, 'Course, we didn't tell Philip that. I doubt if he'd have known what it meant. Orlando told Philip he'd fix up a date with Alison. All Philip had to do was turn up at the next meeting. And not mention this plan to anyone. Ever.'

'These meetings, you held them at the caretaker's house, right?'

'Yes. How did you know that?'

Because that's where Gina Gibbs recorded them. Had she got the details of Philip's 'initiation' on tape? I decided to give her the benefit of the doubt and assume she'd taken her recordings either before or after that meeting.

Andrew hadn't expected an answer. 'Beattie Root. What a creep. He was always trying to ingratiate himself with the pupils. Whenever we needed the house, Orlando would tell him to make himself scarce.'

'And Mr Root trotted off like a good little creep?'

'He even left out the booze and porn videos. Orlando showed Philip some. Give him an idea what he was supposed to do. Orlando drew up the plan and handed out the assignments.'

'And yours was?'

'To lure Alison.' He came to another stop in the middle of the pavement. 'I didn't know her. Not really. I didn't think of her as a person. But I was good at chatting up people. The connection man, Orlando called me. Alison was too shy to make friends easily, but she became more relaxed around me. I actually started to like her.'

'But you still went through with it, didn't you?'

'The gang was everything. It's hard to explain our mindset back then. It was as if everything outside the gang was happening in a film; we saw it and heard it, but it didn't affect us. It wasn't until we left St Martin's that reality kicked in. Anyway, I found out Alison liked animals; she nursed sick ones in her back garden. We already knew her parents went to the church social in St John's Road on Fridays because they used the rooms above Sean Inchbeck's parents' bakery. So we watched until they left, and then I rang Alison. I told her I'd spotted an injured fox crawling into the shrubbery around the school grounds and I wasn't sure what to do. She came up there. She had some mince, I remember. I followed her in. Like I'd just come from home. I'd brought a thermos of coffee because it was cold and we might have to wait a long time. Larry Sorensson's father was a chemist.'

'You drugged the coffee.'

'I don't know what it was; but she was all over the place by the time I got her to the house. I managed to get her undressed and put her on Beattie's bed. The rest of them were in the main room pouring drink into Philip and watching videos. Soon as I gave Orlando the signal, he told Philip his girl was waiting for him upstairs and it was time for him to prove how much he loved her. To be honest, I don't think any of us thought he'd go through with it. I guess we didn't think he could get it up.'

'But he did.'

'A couple of times. And he'd memorized all the dialogue – such as it was – from the porno films. The others . . . we . . . were all laughing and cheering him on.'

'And Alison? Was she unconscious?'

'Yes. No. Some moments she appeared to be lucid, and then she'd drift out again. Afterwards, when Phil couldn't perform any more, we got out of there. Only I started to feel bad about leaving Alison there . . . like *that*.'

'Caring of you.'

'I'm not making excuses. I'm just telling you how it was. Mike and I took my father's van. He was always at the pub on Friday nights. We went back to Root's, got her dressed, found her key, drove her home and carried her up to her room. Then we got out of there.'

'When was this? How long before Trudy's murder?'

'About six weeks.' Further down the road a car drew into the kerb. Two passengers in pastel-shaded frocks got out, hands clamped on large hats to prevent them blowing away. One raised her hand. Andrew waved back. 'We weren't sure what to expect when we went into school the next Monday. We'd all spent the weekend expecting the police to turn up. We had our alibis fixed up to prove we weren't even there. Alison came into class as if nothing had changed. She was quiet. But she always was. There were no accusations. No tears. It was as if that night had never happened. I started to think perhaps whatever Larry had put in the coffee wiped out the memories. And then I tried to talk to her. Really talk, I mean, not just *hi*. And when I looked into her eyes . . . they were . . . dead. It was as if everything that had been Alison had died inside her.'

We were directly outside the church now. The porch was crowded with guests in clothes that were too flimsy for the weather.

'Normally we went over and over the jobs at each meeting. But none of us ever talked about that night again. It was as though, if we didn't speak of it, it hadn't really happened. And then, five weeks later, Orlando and I had that fight about the missing treasure chest, and I never went to any more meetings.'

'Here he is. Here's Andrew now.' All faces turned in our direction. A black-robed clergyman hurried down the path.

Andrew Lee spoke quickly. 'I don't know why – or if – Alison killed Trudy Hepburn, but I do know that she was deeply traumatized from that night on and not responsible for her actions.'

'And had you told her defence team this at the time, she would never have been convicted of murder.'

'I know. I was a coward. And the further the memory slid into the past, the more I told myself it wasn't important, and what I'd done since had cancelled out the bad stuff I'd done back then. But it doesn't work like that. It's not up to me. When you see Alison, tell her I'm sorry and I'll do whatever she wishes. If she wants me to go to the police and sign a confession, I'll do it.'

I asked him something that had been puzzling me. 'How did you know I was looking into Trudy's death? You weren't on the list I emailed.'

'My wife, Sue, is a member of Classbuddies. She was the year under me at St Martin's.'

'Does she know about . . . ?'

'No.'

Black-robe had reached us. Andrew smiled at him. 'Sorry, am I late?'

'Not at all. We've just heard the bride's car has left the hotel. I'm so pleased you'll be able to conduct the service today, Reverend Lee.'

35

'Speak to me, duchy.'

'What do you want me to say?'

'How about finishing this sentence: I've spent the last three hours staring at a wooden dog because . . . ?'

'I like this dog.' The truth was the carved dog on the bank of the Wye reminded me of a previous case last year. Before I'd taken Hannah's case. When I knew nothing about Alison Wynne-Ellis and her baby's father. 'Anyway, I haven't spent the entire three hours looking at this dog. I've walked up the river. And looked round the Cathedral.' And I'd visited the medical section of the bookshop.

'You have been the perfect tourist,' O'Hara agreed. 'It's just that if you're planning to spend any more time with the pooch, perhaps we should consider booking a hotel room for the night?'

'It's not that late. Let's go.'

'Home?'

'Alison.'

While I'd been pacing restlessly around Hereford, trying to decide what the hell to do now, O'Hara had been a silent presence at my side. He seemed to understand that I didn't want any chit-chat. He asked, 'You going to tell me?'

'Let's get going first.'

We were snarled in jams as soon as we tried to leave the city.

'How long do you think this is going to take us?' I asked.

'Should be about three hours. Longer if we keep hitting roads that think they're car parks like this one. Are we in a hurry?'

'I'm not sure if Alison lives at the garden centre. If it's closed, I might not be able to find her tonight. But maybe that's for the best. I mean, maybe it would be good if I didn't speak to her at all. It's not like she really needs to know, is it?'

'If I knew what you were talking about, I might be able to give you the benefit of my brilliant and insightful mind. Something to do with the visit to the bookshop?'

'I was looking up Huntington's. It's a progressive muscle-wasting disease. And it can be inherited from either parent. Philip got it from his mother. She got hers from her father, they think.'

'Aaah.'

'Very brilliant and insightful.'

Telling Alison would be tough, but how was I going to tell Hannah? I kept having visions of her knocking over cups and glasses.

'She should know so she can get herself tested,' O'Hara offered.

'Would you want to?'

'Probably not.'

We made the garden centre as David Wright was padlocking the gates shut. His initial pleasant regretful wave changed as I stepped from the car and into the headlights.

'You shouldn't have come back. Unless you've good news?'

By which he meant proof of Alison's innocence. 'No. Sorry. But I have to speak to Alison. It's really important. Tell her it's about an injured fox in the shrubbery at St Martin's. Please.'

He came back in a few minutes. I figured since she'd sent him out as the messenger it was a no. Which was totally OK with me. I was already composing my weasley-worded report for Hannah on the lines of 'father's identity can't be confirmed'.

David unchained the gates. Damn.

He led us through the centre and towards the restaurant.

I assumed Alison was working, but he swerved to a door marked 'Private' near the lavatories and inserted a key. Behind was a carpeted staircase. 'Go up. She's waiting for you.'

We both moved forwards. David stepped in front of O'Hara. 'Just Grace.'

The top floor of the farmhouse had been converted into a flat. It smelt of polish, wet dog and simmering cooking. Alison met me at the top of the stairs and led me into a sitting room. The low plaster ceiling had exposed beams and there was a real fire burning in the brick fireplace, coaxing gleams of reflection from the copper coal scuttle beside it. Gardening magazines were sliding off a low table in a gentle waterfall to the floor, a stack of paperbacks had collapsed in one corner, a vase of flowers had dropped leaves in a pool of light under a low lamp. The whole room had a messy cosiness that had been lacking in her parents' home. Alison pointed to a large squishy sofa covered in pale yellow fabric. Once I'd taken a seat at one end, she settled at the other, curling her legs up under her and hugging a cushion to her stomach. The lamp-light turned her hair to the colour of the fire-burnished coal scuttle. Her resemblance to Hannah was extremely strong tonight. A Jack Russell came scampering into the room, leapt up beside her and made himself comfortable in the deep cushions.

'So you know. How?'

'Andrew Lee told me. He said to tell you that he's prepared to go to the police and sign a full confession, if that's what you want.'

'Is he?' She stroked the terrier with a rhythmic mechanical movement. Its stub of a tail thumped the cushion. 'What about the others? Did you find them too?'

'Sean and Larry are abroad. Graham, Orlando and Mark are still in Seatoun. Michael Forbes and Philip Darrowfield are dead.'

'Philip's dead!'

'Heart failure. He'd been ill for some time.' Now was my

chance to lead into the reasons for Philip's illness. I flunked it. 'Why didn't you tell anyone?' I amended the question. 'Did you tell anyone?'

'What the hell business is it of yours?'

'You're right. It's not. Sorry.'

I waited to see if she'd take it further. She hugged the cushion tighter. The dog whined uneasily. She spoke to the back of the terrier's head rather than looking directly at me. 'The next morning, when I woke up in bed in my room, I couldn't remember what had happened. I had this sense of something awful, but that was all. I thought I'd had a bad dream. Then I tried to get up – and I had my clothes on. And I hurt – down there. When I looked, there was bruising and blood, and I couldn't *think*.' She drew her legs up to her chest, crushing the cushion even harder as if the square of feathers was all that stood between her and the pain.

'They'd drugged you.'

'I guessed that. Later. Not then. I just couldn't understand what was happening. Then I heard Philip outside in his garden with Uncle Ken and I started to get all these terrible pictures in my head. I'd known Philip for ever. We used to play together, like brother and sister. And now I was getting all these images of Philip doing things to me. And saying these filthy words. And I couldn't stop him. I didn't try to stop him.'

She paused, her eyes looking far away down twenty years of memories. I thought she wasn't going to say anything more on the subject, then she continued.

'I was extremely naive. My parents never talked about sex. I thought I must be having some kind of breakdown. Imagining it all. But the pictures just kept coming. All that day, more and more of what had happened came back. Not all at once, like a continual film, but more like flashes of scenes. I saw Andrew taking my clothes off. And I remembered thinking I shouldn't be like this, but I don't mind being like this with Andrew. In fact, I quite like it.'

She frowned. 'I suppose I was sexually attracted to Andrew, although I didn't recognize the signs then. And then there were all the other faces watching me from the bottom of the bed and the landing. They were laughing and cheering. And when I tried to get up, Orlando was holding me down by the shoulders. Afterwards, when it finally stopped, I think I must have passed out. I don't remember getting home at all. I still don't know how I got there.'

'Andrew and Michael brought you back in his dad's van. If it's any consolation, I think Andrew has been beating himself up ever since.'

'Good.'

Yeah, I could go with that feeling. 'Didn't your parents notice something was wrong?'

'No. I spent a lot of time in my room or out with the animals anyway. I guess part of me thought they'd know. That something that bad couldn't happen to me without my parents somehow seeing the difference. That Saturday I sat in the bath all afternoon and just washed and washed. I told my mother I had period pains. And then I started to really realize what had happened.' She raised her blue eyes and looked directly at me. 'And I knew reporting it was the right thing to do. But I couldn't. I just couldn't walk into a police station and *tell* them what they'd done to me. Next day I was helping my mother prepare Sunday lunch – our kitchen window looked out over the back garden – and Philip came round to help my dad fix the back fence. Everything was just – normal. Phil actually waved and smiled at me. I remember thinking, This is how it's going to be. I'll have to see him every day, talk to him, be alone in rooms with him. I panicked. I couldn't say what they'd done. Not everything. So I said: "He tried to make me have sex with him." Maybe I was subconsciously thinking she'd say, "What do you mean", and we'd start talking. And I could tell her bit by bit. I was never close to my parents. Especially my mother. But I couldn't talk to my father – to any man – about it. And she *was* my mum. You expect your mother to love you, even if you don't particularly love her. Do you know what she said?'

I shook my head, afraid to break the flow of speech.

'Scrape the carrots while I mix up the Yorkshire pud.'

The fire in the grate collapsed in a shower of sparks. Fragments of ash drifted into the air. The terrior jumped from the sofa and chased them with snapping jaws.

'Wilf!' A vigorous patting of the sofa brought the dog bounding back. 'I always wanted a dog. My mother wouldn't allow it. Too much mess in the house. Just the wild animals I could keep outside where she didn't go.' There was another silence and then she returned to that Sunday morning. 'I thought she hadn't heard me. So I said, "*He touched me, down there.*" She hit me across the face.' Unconsciously Alison rubbed her cheek. 'My parents didn't believe in corporal punishment. They'd never so much as smacked me. And now my mother had hit me so hard that it made me cry. She called me a little liar. Said if I ever repeated my filthy lies to anyone, she'd throw me out of the house.'

'She thought you were talking about your father. Did he ever try it on with you?'

'Of course he didn't. He was my *dad*. How could she think that!'

'Your father was involved with a couple of underage prostitutes in Wales. It's the reason you moved to Seatoun.'

'*Dad* was? I didn't know.'

If Moira had confided in her daughter, just how much of this mess could have been avoided?

'So I told Auntie Lucia,' she said blankly. 'Not everything. Just that Philip had made me. I thought she'd stop him coming near me. And she didn't believe me either. She called me a wicked, foul-mouthed little slut. I couldn't understand why nobody believed me. I started to think I was mad.'

'She did believe you. She was scared for Philip.' She'd made Ken give up his parrots so there would be no reason for Alison to come round to the house any more. Pushed into a choice, Lucia had chosen to protect her son and sacrifice Alison. When the police car turned up to collect Emlyn and Moira the night of the killing, Lucia must have thought her worst nightmare had come true.

'I know that now. All the Darrowfields stopped talking to us. They even asked for their spare key back and gave us ours. I was glad about that. It meant Philip couldn't get at me in the house. I didn't know what else to *do*. But I thought Trudy would. Trudy would know I wasn't lying about what those boys did to me.'

'Because she was your friend.'

'Because she was *there*.'

36

We both stared at each other.

Alison spoke first. 'That's what I remember most about that night. Not the boys' faces but hers, watching through the gap on the hinge side of the door. I didn't remember at first. It was one of the last scenes to come back. I was packing my science homework up on the Monday morning . . .'

'You were actually going into school? After that?'

'I think I'd slipped into some kind of auto-mode. It was easier to do familiar things; I didn't have to think, I just did. But when I saw the science books, I got another flashback. And I could see Trudy's eyes in that gap. Do you know the silly thing? I was actually *pleased.* I thought, Trudy will tell my mother and Auntie Lucia that I wasn't lying. And she can tell the police too so I won't have to talk to them. It didn't occur to me to wonder why the police hadn't already come to the house to find me.'

'What was she doing at the caretaker's house?'

'I think she was trying to catch Beattie Root out. Everyone knew he let kids use his house for drinking and porno videos. She used to talk about finding evidence and getting him sacked. She had these crusading periods. Sometimes she was really down and talking about finding a job somewhere else, and then she'd give herself a sort of mental shake-down and announce they weren't going to beat her, and she was going to take that job by the scruff of the neck and show them all. Everyone despised her. Not just the pupils, but the staff too. I suppose that's why we drifted together. We were both outsiders.'

She threw away the cushion and pulled Wilf into its place. His tail-thumping became frantic. 'She blanked me. I don't mean she didn't want to talk about that night, it was like looking at a stranger. We had a chemistry class first period that Monday. Normally it was chaos. Everyone messed around: they ignored her, chatted, had fights, brought music in and listened to it. Trudy used to try being strict some days. And then the next she'd be keeping her head down, pretending there was nothing wrong. Only that day it was all different. Everyone listened. They all worked properly. And when somebody threw a book across to another table, Orlando picked it up, took it back to the owner and whispered something in his ear, and the thrower apologized to Trudy. It was like that through the whole school. I watched her teaching a third year class, and they were the perfect pupils.'

'Orlando knew she'd been a witness that night?'

'He probably saw her. The rest of the boys were facing me, but Orlando was holding me down at the shoulders, so he was looking the same way as me. She must have run the instant she realized he'd seen her, I think. We never actually discussed it, you understand.' The irony was thick in her voice.

So Trudy had made a pact with the devil. Orlando had called the dogs off not because he was worried they'd kill her and bring the police down on the school, but in return for her silence.

'I waited,' Alison said, 'all the rest of that term. I was sure Trudy was going to help me. She was my friend and when she told the truth, everyone would believe her. They'd arrest the boys and all the pain would go away. But she wouldn't even speak to me. And at school she was talking and laughing with those frigging boys. I just didn't understand.'

Of course she didn't. But Alison had been strong enough to stand by her principles and report Orlando for setting fire to a car because it was the right thing to do. Whereas the weak and frightened Trudy Hepburn had sold out to her tormentors.

'Did you kill her?'

'What I told the police was the truth. I remembered my parents going out to the church social that night. I remember going down to the shed to feed a rabbit I was nursing. And thinking how much I hated everyone: those boys, my parents, Auntie Lucia, and most of all Trudy. It was all I could think about, ever since that night.'

'You were in a deep trauma.' In a livelier girl it would have been noticed, but in the quiet, reserved Alison, it had gone undetected.

'Wow, and there was me thinking I was in a really bad mood.' She caught her breath and her temper, and continued in a calmer tone. 'I realize now that I was behaving irrationally, but at the time it seemed perfectly normal. In an odd kind of way I think it saved my life. If I hadn't had the hate to hold on to, I think I might have killed myself. But as for what happened that evening at Trudy's, I just couldn't remember. I was at home and then I was sitting in the policeman's car and he'd taken a knife from me.'

'Was it your knife?'

'I didn't remember it. They said they asked my mother and it wasn't from home. In prison I became something of a guinea pig for all psychiatrists and psychologists who were interested in amnesiacs. I had a parcel of experts trying to retrieve those lost hours.'

'Did you tell them about the rape?'

'No. If the people who I thought were closest to me didn't believe me, why should they? Later on, as I got older and talked to other women inside, I realized that a lot of victims feel like that. But I also heard how they felt after they reported attacks. They said the court case was like being raped again. I couldn't go through that.'

'But it could have formed the basis for a plea of

temporary insanity. It still could. The sentence could be quashed. You'd be free, not out on licence.'

'That won't give me back the twelve years I served in prison, will it?'

'Don't you care that someone else may have been the murderer?'

'Refer to my previous answer.' Alison stretched, dislodging the terrier who wandered over to explore the fireplace again. 'It took me a long time to forgive Trudy. Ten years to be exact.' She smiled and I saw where Hannah had inherited hers. 'I turned twenty-five, the age Trudy was when she died. And I realized you didn't always feel grown-up at that age. Sometimes you still feel like a scared little girl. She was a coward, but I could understand why.'

'What about the boys? Did you forgive them?'

'No!' The single syllable was emphatic. 'I'll never forgive them. Or Auntie Lucia. Philip, I can almost. He really didn't understand what he'd done. He thought it meant I was his girlfriend. He actually tried to give me presents afterwards, sweets. But the others . . . and Auntie Lucia. No!'

'Lucia Darrowfield died years ago.'

'Really?' Alison was quiet for a moment. I could see her assessing how this news made her feel. 'I'm glad. She knew what Philip had done. Was it from her accident? She was in a car crash that gave her some kind of nerve damage.'

She must have seen Lucia Darrowfield deteriorating over the years, but she'd been too close or too young to realize the degeneration couldn't possibly have been from a car crash. Now was my cue to tell her the truth.

'Yeah. That was pretty much it, I think.'

'I see.' Alison stood. 'Well, dinner smells as if it's cooked and David will be starving.'

'How long have you two been together?'

'I'm not sure how to answer that. Cheryl married and moved to Ireland. It made prison visiting far more difficult. So David took over. I'd known him for ages, of course. But as for when it turned into something more than friendship,

I'm not sure. It rather crept up on both of us. David's been an absolute rock. He's never doubted my innocence for a moment.'

'Does David know about the rape?'

'I told him a few years ago. He wanted to find the boys and kill them. But I've had enough of frigging prison. I'm not going back even as a visitor. I truly do not want us to go backwards, just forwards. David finally understands that. And accepts it.'

'What about Andrew Lee's offer to sign a confession?'

'I'll think about it. It won't hurt him to stew. Well, it probably will,' she corrected herself. 'But that's fine by me.'

'And Hannah? What do I tell her?'

'She's your client. So I suppose you must tell her what you think is right. Just make it clear it doesn't make any difference to what I told her. I don't want to see her ever again.' She tried to move me towards the door.

'When did you realize you were pregnant?'

'When they remanded me into the Secure Training Centre. I had a medical examination and they asked me all these questions – like when did I last have a period. I wasn't totally naive, you know, I did know about the symptoms of pregnancy, it was just that where I'd been, in the dream world, I hadn't registered I'd missed one.'

'So you were well inside the limits for a termination.'

Alison sighed heavily. 'Please, if you're nursing some pissing stupid fantasy about my secretly wanting the baby, can you dump it now? I told you before. I don't agree with abortion, but that doesn't mean I *wanted* her. I hated having that thing growing inside me. And that is how I thought of her, as a thing. When she was born I made them take her away immediately. I wouldn't hold her. I wouldn't even look at her. I never expected to have to. Are you finally getting the pissing message?'

'I got it ages ago. But I'm not sure Hannah will. She's very stubborn. And she lost her adoptive mum a couple of years ago. Plus she's pregnant. I'm guessing that nineteen years old isn't feeling all that grown up right now.'

And she might have an inherited degenerative disease. This might be a good moment to mention that.

I dug a pen out of my pocket and jotted a phone number down. 'This is where you can find Andrew Lee once you've decided what you want to do about his offer.'

'You realize that if she decides not to report the rape, the entire seven eight eight gang will get away scot-free with everything. I should have reported them for all the other stuff – the bag-snatching, burglary, highway robbery. I daresay Andrew would be up for a blanket confession.'

'You wouldn't get a conviction on a single confession,' O'Hara said. He pushed his seat back to stretch his legs under the restaurant table and extended his arms, linking his fingers above his head. He'd flung the leather coat on the next chair and was sitting in his grey T-shirt. Four teenage girls at another table checked out the shoulder muscles flexing and abdomen tautening. O'Hara was a hottie for all generations. I wondered how old he really was. It was one of the million things I didn't know about him.

He finished the stretch as the waitress brought our order to the table. I'd made him stop at a roadside restaurant on the way home. Its neon signs had promised an American Dining Experience. That meant burgers to me. I'd ordered the triple-deluxe cheeseburger with extra fries and a full-cream-supersmooth-chocolate shake. Burying misery under a mountain of fat, sugar and artificial additives has always worked for me.

'And,' O'Hara continued, cutting into a rump steak, 'Billy Roles would ask for a refund. How much did you get from his stash?'

'Enough.' Holding the burger two-handed, I considered where to launch my first bite. 'All those little girls in Australia, and maybe any little Lees up in Hereford, will be devastated if Alison does decide to report the rape. I don't know whether to hope she does or she doesn't.'

'It's not your problem, duchy. We can't make the world a happy smiley place for everyone.'

'We don't seem to have made it happier or smilier for anyone – except the bad guys. Even the Penningtons are going to get away with it.'

'Word has a way of getting around. Maybe we've stopped Clive climbing any further up the promotional ladder.'

'With our form to date, O'Hara, we've probably got him a medal for initiative.'

With my elbows resting on the table and the burger bleeding fried onions and ketchup from its base, I chomped steadily. O'Hara finished first. Instead of laying his cutlery together, he placed the fork on the table and balanced the knife across it. We watched it swaying until it steadied and settled in a horizontal line.

'Now we know what she was seeing behind those eyes. Not Trudy's body, but the hell of that earlier night . . . Well, here's to the conclusion of our first case, Dec.' He lifted his cup in a toast to his absent brother, Declan.

'Does that mean you're leaving?' The lurch of disappointment in my stomach took me by surprise. 'But we don't know for certain she did it.'

'This was never about her innocence for me. Just about that look haunting Declan. He was right that someone should have dug further. It was mitigating circumstances. To tell you the truth, duchy, Dec reckoned she *had* done it.'

'Well, screw Declan.'

'You've missed your chance. Pity. He'd have fancied you. We always had similar tastes.'

I buried myself in my shake. It was so thick it hurt my ribs trying to suck it up the straw. 'Where will you go?'

'Wherever brother Dec's memories take me next.'

'Seriously?'

'I'm always serious.'

'Seriously irritating.'

'And I love you too, duchy.'

'Do you?'

'No, but you can't deny I've made several serious attempts do so. Want to try again?'

Did I? He was sex on legs and I got hot in places I'd forgotten I had places when he kissed me. I liked his self-confidence and the way the silences weren't awkward when I was with him. On the other hand, there were those million things I didn't know: Where had he come from? Where did he learn to pick a lock and fire a gun? What was he doing with a gun anyway? What had he done before he became brother Declan's retrospective conscience? Was there a Mrs Dane O'Hara out there somewhere?

'Lets stick to friends.'

He drove me back to the flat. Since we'd established the boundaries, I invited him in for coffee. At some point between boiling the kettle and discovering I was out of milk again, I started crying.

'What?' O'Hara asked.

I tried to identify the lump inside my chest that wasn't undigested cheeseburger. 'I wish I'd never taken this damn case.'

Putting his arm round my shoulder, he sat me down next to him on the bed. 'You didn't tell Alison about the Huntington's, did you?'

'No. It doesn't really affect her, does it? But I've got to tell Hannah.'

I buried my face in the soft section between the arm and shoulder blade and wept for the girl with the bright copper hair, the mega-watt smile and the white cot with yellow bunnies. O'Hara cuddled me without comment. After a while we fell back on the bed and he reached over and put the light out.

So in the end I did get to go to bed with O'Hara – fully dressed and blubbing myself to sleep. When I woke up in the morning, he was gone.

37

I called the locksmith and had the back and front locks at the flat changed, since you just never know who might decide to drop in and cook – or worse. After that I decided to use the office phone to ring Hannah. I figured while I was there I might as well use the upstairs bath. In fact, I decided I might as well do that first. It would give me a chance to rehearse the best way to frame: 'Hi, kid, still don't know if your mum is definitely a murderer. Oh and by the way, you and the sprog have about a fifty-fifty chance of inheriting a fatally crippling disease with no cure.'

I didn't really *need* to ring her immediately. It wasn't as if every minute counted with this disease. I might get breakfast first. And go for a jog. Yep, I definitely needed some exercise. Cuts, bruises and butt stitches were no excuse to neglect my workouts.

The ocean was noisy, driven inland by a fierce wind and slapping against wooden groynes and piles of boulders and erupting into fountains of crashing spray. The air had that scent of salt and iodine that you only get on the coast. The skin on my face and lips tingled and then grew numb. Feeling rejuvenated (and knackered), I limped back towards Pepi's.

'Smithie! We were just talking about you. Come meet the brothers. This is the *actual* brother . . .'

One of the people sitting at the table nearest the counter stood and offered a hand. The resemblance to Shane was obvious: round face, big stomach and hair follicles that were no longer challenged – they'd waved the white flag.

'Brother Lance. Pleasure to meet someone with such a

beautiful name. *Amazing Grace . . .*' He crooned the first verse. Shane joined in. So did half the customers. I just hate it when that happens.

'I thought you'd be in a robe, with a big dressing-gown cord?' He was actually wearing dark-brown trousers and a three-quarter-length hooded tunic.

'This is our travelling outfit. Isn't that so, Brother Samson?'

I'd assumed the second person at the table was a kid. He was tiny, lengthwise and widthwise. The hood of his tunic was up, but when he raised his face in response to his name, it slipped back slightly. A small, shrivelled head, topped with a few wisps of white hair, peered up. Brother Samson regarded us from two bright black eyes set either side of the biggest hooter I'd ever seen. The guy was a dead spit for Tallulah.

'This is the lady who has been taking care of Tallulah for us, Brother.'

Brother Samson smiled and nodded. 'Hot totty.'

'Brother Samson cares for our parrot.'

'I'd kind of figured that. She's with a parrot expert at the moment. I was a bit concerned about her ready-plucked look.'

'Been shedding again, has she? It's stress. She'll soon pick up. Tallulah's been losing her feathers again, Brother Samson.'

'Great jugs, sister.'

I sat down – very carefully – opposite Brother Samson and ordered breakfast. He promptly started singing 'Oklahoma'. Except he stuck on the first word. '*Homa, homa, homa . . .*'

Lance was going down memory lane with Shane, so I was stuck with the human parrot.

'So,' I asked Samson, 'was being a monk a lifelong ambition or did you used to have a proper job?'

I ate to a chorus of hit tunes from the great musicals – or at least the one word of them that Brother Samson jammed on. He swayed from side to side as he warbled. Had he climbed on the seat and headed a little bell I wouldn't have been surprised. Midway through his one word performance of 'Greased Lightning', he suddenly fell silent. I signalled his fellow monk.

Lance leant over and whispered. 'He's nodded off. Don't worry, he does it all the time.'

Who was worried? I spread butter and marmalade on the toast and munched in peace apart from the background babble and the jukebox until the shrill ring of the wall phone cut through the hum of noise. I leapt half out of my seat and shouted: 'Tell her I'm not here!'

Shane and Lance weren't the only ones who stared.

'Tell who?' Shane asked.

'Er . . . nobody. That is, if it is for me. I'm not here.' It was ridiculous to imagine Hannah would track me down here. She'd leave a message on the office phone.

The racket hadn't disturbed Brother Samson. He was still snoozing happily. I looked harder. 'Er . . . Lance.' I moved my head fractionally, indicating he should huddle closer. 'I don't think Brother Samson is asleep, I think he could be what we technically call . . . dead.'

Lance slid a hand inside the tunic hood and found the scrawny neck, waited a moment and then withdrew, pulling the hood a little further over the face. 'What a pity. He was looking forward to seeing Tallulah again. Rest in peace, Brother.'

I looked round. Nobody else seemed to have noticed that Samson had fallen off his perch. 'What now?'

'Act naturally,' Shane hissed. 'They may think it was something he ate.'

'Shouldn't we call an ambulance?'

'Better not.' Lance sat next to his dead colleague. 'He specifically asked for no resuscitation attempts. Let's leave him in peace for a while.'

Shane walked over to the door, turned the sign to 'closed' and put the catch on. 'No hurry, folks,' he beamed at the other customers. 'Finish your meals. I'm shutting for a few hours. Family party.' Coming back via the jukebox, he inserted a handful of shillings. As he sat down, it started playing 'Three Steps to Heaven'.

'Very nice, bruv,' Lance murmured.

'Seemed the least I could do. It's Jerry Lee next – "When the Saints Go Marching In". Repertoire's a bit limited. We don't do death a lot.'

'I wish I didn't,' I said. 'I seem to be surrounded by dead people and religion at present. It's enough to make you become a vampire.'

Lance took a mobile phone from his tunic pocket. 'I'll ring the monastery and tell them to prepare for our Brother's return. I'll drive him home myself. Lucky we brought the estate. I can lay him out in the back.'

'Will there be room for Tallulah's cage?'

'Tallulah? Well, em, er . . . the thing is, Grace, we don't really *want* Tallulah. She was company for Brother Samson, but now he's gone . . . if you've grown fond of her . . . ?'

'I haven't.'

Lance's eyes drifted in Shane's direction. 'Forget it, bruv. Marlene would divorce me.'

I suggested Ken Darrowfield might like to keep her. Once the last customer had left, Lance drove me round to Hinton Drive. On the way, we picked up all the rest of Tallulah's things from my flat. If this didn't work out, there was no way she was getting a claw-hold back in my place. Luckily Ken was thrilled with the idea of being lumbered with Baldy, who was currently in full sing-a-longa-mode.

'All that singing doesn't get on your nerves?'

'I like it,' he admitted. He stroked the end of Philip's bed, which was still in situ in the specially adapted room. 'It's too quiet here, now they've both left me.'

It was an empathizing moment. I wished I'd brought Lance in instead of leaving him outside in the van. 'How long, I mean . . . how long were they ill?'

'Lucia was thirty when she was diagnosed. Her symptoms

were aggressive – came on fast. Philip must have been twenty-five. I suppose he was showing signs earlier. But he was such a clumsy big lump anyway – I put all those dropped cups and plates down to that.'

'Right. Oh good. No, I don't mean good. It's awful.' I was babbling. I got a grip and asked if Ken had realized Tallulah couldn't be left on her own.

'Another bird will sort that out.'

'You mean I could have just got her a budgie?' Rather than lug that flaming travel cage everywhere?

'A larger bird. I was thinking of an Amazon. And I might get a few parakeets if I can afford them. I had to pay for part of Philip's care, see, since I insisted on having him at home. In fact, there's something I wanted to show you . . .' He opened the sideboard and took out several large photo albums. 'Found these upstairs with the cages. All me birds. See . . .' He turned the pages, pointing out Amazons, cockatoos and parakeets. Lots of the birds were posing by cups or rosettes. 'We always took awards at all the caged bird shows. But this is what I really wanted to show you.' He turned to a picture at the end. It was Alison. A happy, laughing Alison standing in a garden beside a stack of wire-fronted cages. Inside you could just make out a pink nose or a small beak. She'd been preparing their meals and there was an array of dishes, water bottles, and chopped fruit and vegetables across the trestle table in front of her. That was probably what had attracted the parrot. It was perched on her hair, its wings stretched high and wide as it fought to keep its balance. Alison's eyes and mouth were wide with delight. 'That was in her back garden. Taken the summer before, well, you know. I was wondering, if you're still in touch with that girl, perhaps she'd like to have it? Don't suppose she's got any pictures of her mum?'

'I'm sure she would. Thanks. I'll just get the rest of Tallulah's stuff.' I pocketed the picture, marched out to Lance in the van and rapped on the window. 'He'd love to keep her, but he's a bit strapped for cash.'

'I'll give the abbot a bell. I'm sure St Humphrey's will want to contribute. In memory of Brother Samson.'

'I thought they might.'

With Tallulah settled and Brother Samson loaded for his last-but-one journey, I was freed up to ring Hannah. And I did intend to – eventually.

I walked all day. North Bay, West Bay, the promenade. I wandered around the flashing lights of the arcades and I walked on the wet sands of the beach, getting soaked by spray until it became too dark to see what I was doing. Twice I picked up a phone intending to call Hannah. But I kept seeing a white cot with yellow bunnies. And then the symptoms of Huntington's: involuntary jerking movements of the head and limbs, difficulty in swallowing, unconscious twisting movements . . . no cure . . . death from pneumonia or heart failure . . . I hung up each time. Why spoil her weekend?

I found myself in Marine Drive. There was no sign of O'Hara's Mercedes. I walked down a side street where I could see the backs of the properties. Weak moonlight playing on the windows of the show-flat showed me the blinds weren't drawn and the rooms were unlit. I guess he'd already moved on to right whatever wrongs brother Declan had wrought.

I spent the rest of the evening hunkered down on the floor of my flat with the curtains drawn and the television sound down low. If I didn't speak to Hannah soon I was going to have to change my name and leave Seatoun. On that thought I found the bottle of vodka that I'd nicked from Billy Roles and sunk what Tallulah had left. When the door knocker was rapped at midnight, I was too sloshed to care if it was the tooth fairy, Freddy Kruger or Hannah Conti.

It was Rosco. 'Any chance I could—?'

'No noise. No milk. No funny business.'

Letting go of the door handle, I aimed for the bed. I guess I made it.

Next morning my eyeballs hurt, my teeth itched and my tongue was glued to the roof of my mouth. Levering myself off the bed, I drank a couple of pints of water, ran a bath and dived underneath. Lying full-length I examined the view; what wasn't black was yellow, or purple or red. I looked like an illustration for a particularly virulent strain of plague. And that was without the butt stitches. Heaving myself up, I stood in the water and tried to twist round, looking over my shoulder.

The bathroom door burst open. 'Here, you know you're out of milk again?'

I dropped, sending a tidal wave over the bath sides, and slung the bubble-bath bottle. I had two choices. Put a bolt on the bathroom door. Or get rid of Terry.

It was Sunday morning breakfast chez Rosco. Like feeding time in the ape enclosure, but without the sophisticated manners.

'Brad! Justin! Break*fast*!' Linda Rosco shouted up the stairs.

'Are you bleedin' deaf? I told you, I've got the killer frog on the ninth grid, this is like crucial.'

'Oh dear, is it?' Linda said. She led the way to the kitchen. One of the twin mutants was clamped to her hip. The other was in his highchair drawing patterns in spilt cereal. 'Oh no, they promised that dish was tip-proof.' She thrust the other twin at me and grabbed a dishcloth.

I looked round for another highchair. There didn't seem to be one.

'He has to be on your lap to eat,' Linda said. 'Here.' A bowl and spoon were pushed at me.

It looked like wallpaper paste. I could relate to Linda's desire to glue the kids' lips together. They were both screaming their heads off. It was like trying to control an octopus on steroids; every time you got a grip on one limb, another shot out and hit the table. They were coming up for one year, and already enormous. They were also plug-ugly. They reminded me of Terry with their fleshy faces and hint of a double-jaw.

There was the sound of footsteps drumming down the stairs and Justin hurtled into the kitchen, sloshed milk and sugar over two bowls of cereal and flew out again, leaving a trail of Ricicles and milk along the hall. 'The frog's mutated. It's awesome.'

Linda said. 'They're not really supposed to have food in the bedrooms.'

'They need a father's hand.' (Or better still, stranding on an orbiting space station.)

'I know,' Linda sighed. She pushed more wallpaper paste into twin number one. He spat it over her.

'So, don't you think it's time you forgave Terry? I mean, OK, he had a little fling, but it's you he loves, you he's had kids with. This experience could strengthen your marriage.' (I'd read all the cheesy advice columns.)

Linda's mouth dropped open. 'Terry had a fling?'

Ah? 'Well that's why I . . . everyone . . . assumed you'd thrown him out?'

'No! No, no, no. My Terry would never be unfaithful to me.'

OK, I owed Terry an apology. The mutants hadn't inherited their dumbness from him. Half those genes had come from their mum.

I retrieved my own jaw from where it had hit my chest. 'Right. Good. Well that's good to know, Linda. You six make such a lovely family.'

'I know.' She smiled fondly at the twin fighting its way off my lap. I considered up-ending it and clamping the arms between my knees. 'But you see, Grace, the twins are a mistake.'

Well, what did she expect if she chose Terry Rosco as a sperm donor? She was never going to get prize winners from that source.

'I've always had problems with the Pill. It makes me chuck. And the coil was in when . . .' She gestured at the squirming mutants. 'So I told Terry it's as much his responsibility as mine to make sure we don't get caught out again.'

A light went 'ping' in my head. 'You want him to have the snip!'

'And he's not getting back in this house until he does.'

'Linda, I think you may be talking to the woman who can make all your dreams come true. Where do you stand on blackmail?'

'If it's in a good cause.'

She wasn't that dumb then.

I had to park a few houses from my flat again. Walking back, I started down the stairs to the basement. And realized too late there were two people at the front door.

38

A frown replaced the huge smile on Hannah's face. 'Are you all right?'

'Fine. Just fine.' My voice sounded as if I'd been breathing pure helium.

'You screamed.'

'Accident. Stitches. The pain. Catches me by surprise.'

'I hope you don't mind me and Ni coming here. I have something I've just got to tell you.'

Me too – unfortunately. I let us all inside and checked Terry had taken himself off. They perched side by side on the edge of the bed. Arms linked and shiny faces glowing with health and a buffeting from the seaside air. I sent out a silent prayer for someone to beam me out of there. It didn't work. I swung one of the chairs out from the table so I could face them.

'You'll never guess who came to see me yesterday?' Hannah said. 'My mother. Not my real mum, of course. But, her, Alison. She was really nice to me, wasn't she, Ni? She explained how it was a big shock me turning up like that, when she'd never expected to hear from me again. Which I can totally relate to. Anyway, now she's had time to think, she doesn't mind keeping in touch, if that's what I'd like. And you'll never guess? She's getting married too.'

'Too?'

'Oh, of course, you don't know.' She extracted her hand from Ni's and pulled the glove off. A small diamond was sparkling on the third finger. 'I said we should save the cash for baby stuff, but Ni wouldn't. And guess what?' She ploughed on again before I could join in the guessing. 'Alison is having a baby as well.'

'She is?' Maybe that's why she seemed so like Hannah on that last visit.

'She's not as far on as me. So my baby will have a half-uncle or aunt who's younger than him. Isn't that freaky? I'm going to make christening gowns for both of them.'

'And Alison's OK with that, is she?'

'She's looking forward to seeing it. Of course, we won't be able to get together too often. What with us both being busy with babies and careers. But we'll keep in touch by phone and email.'

'Right. Did you and Alison discuss anything else? Like your father?' It seemed unlikely given Hannah's bright perkiness.

'Yes,' she said. Her face became serious, as if she wanted me to understand something important. 'He was a boy called Gary she met at the amusement arcade. Her mother was very strict about sex and stuff, so she didn't know a lot. She decided to experiment, only things went too far. And she never saw him again. She doesn't even know his surname. And I'm totally cool about that. I mean, everyone makes mistakes. But I guess I'll never know who he was now.'

'I guess not.' I should have told Alison about Philip and Lucia's inherited disease. Now the only way I could warn Hannah about the Huntington's was to reveal Alison's well-meant lie.

'But the thing is, Grace, I want you to stop looking for the real murderer. I'm sorry to mess you about after all the work you've done . . .'

'Heh, consider it done. I do what I'm paid to do. I don't take it personally.'

'Oh good. I thought you might be pissed off with me.'

'Is that why Ni's here? Bodyguard duties in case I turn violent with disappointment?'

'No,' she giggled. 'We're going for a walk after this. I love to walk by the sea. And then we're getting another train and going to tell Ni's parents about . . .' She patted her swelling stomach.

Plainly Alison's visit had set a lot decisions in motion. But I was curious why abandoning the hunt for Trudy's killer was one of them.

'Alison asked me to. You see she feels that by keeping the hope of discovering the true killer alive, it forces her to look back all the time. And she doesn't want to be in that place. The marriage and the baby is a fresh start. She want to enjoy it and she feels the best way to do that is to look forward. Finding the real killer won't give her all those years back. And she's not interested in compensation. She and David – that's her fiancé's name, David – she and David have more than enough to live on.' She recited the words as if she'd been taught them. And then added with more directness, 'I don't want to make her life more miserable. I never wanted that. I still know she didn't do it, of course, but I respect her right to choose to put it in the past. I hope you understand?'

And I did. Her innocence had been a big glittering gift she'd wanted to give her mother by way of showing she was a daughter who deserved to be loved. But now Alison was prepared to cosy up and be a surrogate mum, proving she wasn't a murderer was no longer so important.

'Could I have some water?' Hannah asked.

Ni stuck his arm round her back as a support. 'You OK? You feel faint?'

'No. I feel thirsty. Quit fussing, Ni.'

I ran her a glass and handed it over. She reached for it, fumbled the hold, and half dropped it, slopping water over herself and the bed. 'Oh shit. Sorry.'

'For Pete's sake, Hannie.' Ni opened her bag and fished around inside. 'Put them on, will you?' He threaded the arms of a pair of spectacles over her ears. 'She thinks I don't fancy her in specs.'

Hannah flushed. 'I'm long-sighted. I'm always knocking over things near me.'

'Thank heavens! Er . . . thank heavens someone else is as clumsy as me.' Not that it proved Hannah didn't have Huntington's. But at least she wasn't showing symptoms. Yet. This was the moment. At least Ni was there to help her cope. 'There's something I ought to mention . . .'

'Oh sure. I brought my cheque-book. If you tell me how much more I owe you?'

'Nothing. That is, let's say what you've already advanced covers it, OK?'

'Are you sure?'

'Totally.' The notes I'd taken from Billy's strongbox had amounted to just over five thousand tax-free(ish) pounds. I could afford to be generous.

'Thanks ever so much.' Hannah pushed her chequebook back into the bag. It snagged on a paper bag. Wriggling it free, she took out a small fluffy yellow rabbit. 'Isn't it cute? It was in that gift shop on the front. I don't think one tiny toy is tempting fate, do you? Are you sure you're OK? You've gone a really minging colour.'

'Low blood pressure. I just need to lie down for a while.'

'Oh sorry!' She sprang up from the bed, pulling Ni with her. 'We'll be going then. I'll let you know when the baby's born, if you like?'

'Great.'

'Oh, I nearly forgot.' She extracted an envelope from her bag. 'Alison asked me to give you this. Bye then. And thanks for everything.'

I let them walk away. I just couldn't get the words out. How do doctors manage that sort of thing every day?

I opened Alison's letter.

Dear Grace

As I expect Hannah has told you (or is about to do so), I've asked her to call off the search for the truth about Trudy's killer. I find now I've spent time in her company, I don't experience the feelings of panic or disgust that I thought I would. (I lied when I said I'd never imagined what she looked like. In my head she'd always been large and dark and clumsy like her father.) I can't say I felt any affection for her. She didn't feel like my child at all. But she seems like a nice kid and I daresay I can cope with being a surrogate mum, providing it is at a distance. Who knows, perhaps I'll even become fond of her in time. David doesn't have many relatives on his side of the family so it may be that my baby will be grateful for a half-sister in the future.

I have also decided not to take up Andrew Lee's offer to confess for much the same reasons. It took me a long time not to forget, but to control the memories. For years I suffered from panic attacks and nightmares about that night. If I have to relive it in a trial, then I'm afraid they will start again. I don't want to bring that to my marriage or my baby's life. I want the future, not the past. I daresay some people would think that's just an excuse for cowardice and it was my duty to report them and ensure that it never happens again to someone else. But I'm afraid my reaction to 'some people' is stuff them. It's my life, and my choice. I shan't tell Andrew (I never want to speak to him again) but if you are in touch with him, or any of the others, you can hint that I'm thinking over his offer. I rather like the idea that they'll spend the rest of their lives waiting for the other shoe to fall.

Alison

I rang O'Hara's mobile to tell him about Alison's decision. I got the voicemail service.

Monday morning, I ran off fifty copies of the Terry-as-a-fairy picture and stuck them through Linda Rosco's door before heading into work.

'Annie's back,' Jan said. 'She got me a present.' She shook out a T-shirt in her favourite shade – black – with 'I know someone who went to Barbados and all she got me was this lousy T-shirt' printed over the chest in silver. 'Neat, eh? And these.' These were earrings shaped like tiny silver porpoises.

'Were there any messages for me?'

'No.'

Plainly O'Hara wasn't a guy who liked lingering goodbyes.

Jan asked, 'What have you done with Tallulah?'

'She's gone to a better place.'

'You pig, you've eaten her!'

'I have not.'

'I don't believe you. You'd eat anything if it was free.'

'Untrue, Jan. I draw the line at sprouts.'

I dragged myself upstairs and slung the big pink folder on my desk. I'd have to write up a proper report on Hannah's case for my files and send her a formal invoice.

Annie's office oozed in-your-face efficiency. Her fingers were flashing over the keyboard of her newly acquired laptop. The only signs that she'd ever left the place were a deep golden tan and blonde streaks in her normally mousy-brown hair. Plus the style was even more frizzily wide than usual.

I sat on the visitor's chair, trying to keep my weight off the stitched side. 'Hi. How was Barbados? No come to think of it, scrub that question. I already know. You kept sending me pictures of it. How are you?'

Annie stopped typing and looked at me through huge gold-rimmed spectacles. 'I'm fine. You look awful. What the hell have you been doing? And why are you sitting like that?'

'You first. I couldn't help noticing that the gloating messages stopped kind of suddenly? Any special reason for that?'

With a sigh, she logged off. 'Take my advice, Grace, *never* commit to a relationship until you've been on holiday with the guy. We wanted to do completely different things. It was a beach. I wanted to go diving. Try out the watersports – water-skiing, jet-skis, sailing. You know?'

I did. Annie was always hefting an extra couple of stones, but she was very fit. 'And Stuart didn't?'

'He was more into relaxing in the shade and reading. I did try. But I got fidgety. And then I could see him getting anxious because I wasn't having a good time. So then he'd try watersports. Only he didn't enjoy himself because he burnt so easily no matter how much sunblock he lathered on. You know how he's got that red hair and that very pale skin that goes with . . .'

She broke off startled as I leapt to my feet and flew into my own office. Grabbing something from the big pink file, I belted down the stairs as fast as bruising and stitching permitted. Annie's voice drifted down the stair-well as I hurtled into reception.

'Am I boring you?'

39

Beattie Root had been checking out the racing results. The teletext page was still on the television screen and betting slips were scattered over the sofa.

'Bit of a gambler, are you, Mr Root?'

'I like a flutter, Gracie. And I told you, call me Beattie.'

'I've got a little bet I'd like to put to you, Beattie.' I used the remote to switch off the TV. 'I've been talking to Alison Wynne-Ellis. Did you know she had a daughter?'

'No. Why would I? Let her out of prison, did they? Life ought to mean life, that's what I say. 'Stead they do a few years and they're free to go off, live with someone, have kids, same as us law-abiding people. Where's the deterrent in that?'

'I'm not talking about after her release. Alison's baby was born while she was waiting to be tried. A few months after her sixteenth birthday in fact.'

'That so?' Beattie licked his lips. 'Can I get you a drink?'

'No thanks.' I followed him into the kitchen. Beattie fussed with the kettle and coffee mugs.

'Alison always assumed the baby's father was Philip Darrowfield.'

'Big stupid kid. We called him Spastic. I wouldn't be surprised if she's right there. He didn't know his own strength. Could easily have forced himself on her.'

'Interesting the way you assumed it was rape.'

'Well, nobody would go with him would they? I mean the kid was . . .' He tapped his bald scalp.

'Did you ever meet his parents?'

'Could have done. Yes, I remember now. His mum had something wrong. Couldn't walk properly.'

'She was also from an eastern Mediterranean family. She inherited the dark hair and eyes, and olive skin that's typical of that region. She passed it on to Philip, see?'

I unfolded the old photo of the 788 gang grouped around Trudy Hepburn.

'Alison, now ... you remember Alison, I'm sure ... Alison had light brown hair.' It was there in the original report and photo of the trial. The short copper style was dyed. 'And she has blue eyes. So to return to the gambling ... Brian ... what do you think the odds are of those two producing a child with hazel eyes and red hair?'

'I dunno.'

'Slim to snowball in hell, I'd have said. But you were right on there with Alison's baby being the result of an assault. It took place right here in fact. During one of Orlando's little gang meetings for which you so kindly provided the venue. I did consider the others as a possible daddy, but you see, they're all dark-haired too, with the exception of Larry Sorensson, and he's almost white-haired.'

'Look, I've got work to be getting on with, Gracie, you'll have to go.'

'I'm sure it's not so urgent you can't spare me a few more minutes. Let's talk nicknames. See I'd always assumed you'd got yours from your initials – B.T.'

'I did. It's just a bit of fun.'

'It's not the only reason though, is it?' I produced the framed photo I'd just nicked from the school wall. The 'old' dark-haired Trudy Hepburn lurked in the background while Beattie and the former headmaster clutched the handle of the Hospice Appeal bucket; the head in his formal grey suit and Beattie Root in his pea-green blazer with its shiny brass buttons. Beattie Root before he'd completely lost his hair. 'It wasn't Beattie originally, was it? It was Beet Root. Because of your red hair.'

He picked up a knife. 'I don't want to start getting nasty, Grace.'

'I'd say you were well beyond the starting post on that, Beattie. You came back that night. You watched the boys leave and then you came in here and found Alison upstairs in your bedroom. And you raped her. And then what . . . you heard Andrew and Michael coming back so you scarpered?'

His eyes flickered, looking for a way out. 'I don't know what you're talking about. You're mad.'

'So I'm always being told. Luckily it's easy enough to prove these days. All Alison has to do is complain to the police and get a DNA test done on her daughter.'

His tone changed from belligerent to whiney. 'The little tart was in my bed and stark naked. It wasn't rape. She never said no. She enjoyed it.'

'She was drugged. She was in no position to say no. And I bet you knew that. But even if she was dancing around screaming, "Take me, big boy" it wouldn't make any difference. Alison was fifteen. Underage. Big trouble. I hear child molesters are way at the bottom of the food chain inside, Beattie.'

It was an empty threat. Alison would never make a formal statement to the police because I was never going to tell her. One rape was enough nightmare. There was no need to tell her about the second. I didn't know whether to kiss Beattie or kick him. He was a total shit, but a shit who didn't have Huntington's. Hannah and her baby were going to be all right.

I went for the kick. My toecap made contact with his fingers and the knife flew away across the counter with a clatter. Before he could recover, I closed in and brought my knee up hard into his crotch. With a scream he collapsed to the floor. I screamed and stayed upright. I'd forgotten and used the stitched side.

'What on earth's going on here?'

The synchronized screaming had covered the noise of

Gillian Anderson's arrival. 'I used the school key to let myself in, Brian.'

Beattie moaned and writhed on the tiles. Gillian gave me an enquiring look.

'I've just kneed him. I don't think he'll be wanting to make a formal complaint, will you, Beattie?'

'N–no.' Whimpering, Beattie used the lower unit handles to haul himself up. He stayed bent, using the counter as support.

'I wanted to be the first to show you this, Brian.' Gillian laid what looked like an article from a newspaper on the counter. 'I expect there will be a formal announcement in *The Times* later, but I picked this up off the Internet. It's wonderful how you can get news from all over the world these days just at the click of a mouse.'

Getting closer, I scan-read:

> Sir Percy Membourne (97) died last night at the home of his great-niece, Mrs Sherman Arlington-Wilson. Sir Percy and his third wife, the late Lady Emily, have been popular winter visitors to Florida for many years and were generous supporters of our local charities. It is believed that Sir Percy died in his sleep. A fuller report follows in our next edition.

'Let me help you up, Brian,' Gillian took his free arm and supported Beattie as he straightened painfully. 'Are you sure you won't be reporting Grace to the police?'

'Y–yes.'

She brought her own knee up. Beattie squealed and hit the floor again.

'I've always wanted to do that,' Gillian said in a conversational tone. 'I do hope whatever you've got on him covers me, Grace? Anyway I must be going. I have to liaise with the Education Department about drafting an advert for a new premises manager.'

'You c-can't do that,' Beattie managed to gasp out.

'Oh, I think she can,' I said. 'I mean, if I were to tell the authorities why it isn't a good idea to have you working with young girls . . . ?'

I followed Gillian out. 'Why isn't it a good idea?' she asked as we turned into the playground.

'Someone else's secret. I can't say, but he doesn't know that. Who's Sir Percy?'

'Sir Percy was knighted for services to glue or somesuch. He was a big philanthropist. He rented this land to the county for the sum of one pound a year in order that they could build a school. He also set up a fund to cover repairs and extensions. Percy could have sold it off for development years ago but he chose to carry on the good works. And he also specified in his will that the land and repair fund would go to the county, free and clear, on his death.'

'Nice. But what's this got to do with Beattie?'

'Lady Emily Membourne was the sister who married well. Another wasn't so lucky. She married a largely out-of-work actor called Felix Root.'

'Beattie's dad?'

'Exactly. Lady Emily promised that her nephew would always have a home and job during her lifetime. And Sir Percy carried on that pledge.'

'And now he's dead? Beattie's not coming into a fortune, is he?'

'No. Everything is going to charity and the Florida relatives. I know because Sir Percy told me years ago. He didn't like Brian, you see, he just felt obligated to his late wife's memory.'

'Promises to the dead can cause a hell of a lot of grief,' I said, thinking of Ken Darrowfield slaving away to nurse Philip at home.

'They can,' Gillian agreed. 'That's why I've told my two to scatter me over the roses and get on with spending anything they can find. Is that one of the school photos?'

'I borrowed it for a while. Mission accomplished, thanks.'

I gave her the framed photo. She wrinkled her nose and threw it into a handy wastebin.

40

Back at the office, I started tidying up the pink folder, preparatory to typing up the final report and sticking everything in a file. And then I remembered the photo of Alison with the parrot that Ken Darrowfield had given me. I'd completely forgotten to give it to Hannah. I'd have to post it on.

I looked into the fourteen-year-old Alison's eyes, searching for the woman I'd met at the garden centre. Something half hidden caught my attention. Opening a filing cabinet, I took out a small magnifying lens and found the focus length over the picture. A section leapt out.

The lack of background noise on the phone suggested Alison was in the flat rather than downstairs in the restaurant.

'I got your letter.'

'Good. I hope you understand my reasons for not wanting to report the rape?'

'Totally. It's your choice. And congrats on the baby.'

'Thank you. David and I are very happy.'

'I'm sure. I've dropped the murder investigation as Hannah asked, but can I ask you something?'

'I'd really rather not rake over it any more.'

'Last time, I promise. Did the memory of whether or not you stabbed Trudy really never come back?'

'I've already told you. It's blank.'

'No. You told me it was a blank when you were talking to the police. And you said the prison psychiatrists had tried to help you retrieve those memories. But you never actually said you didn't get the lost time back. But I suspect that may be because you're basically a very honest person who doesn't like lying.'

'And why would you think that?'

'Because when I asked you about the murder weapon, you said, "I didn't remember it" rather than "It wasn't mine" or "I don't remember it." '

'Is that significant?'

'I'd say so. Ken Darrowfield gave me a picture he'd just found. You and his parrot, by your shed, the summer before the murder. You're preparing food for your animals.'

'I remember him taking it. The Yellow-Fronted Amazon landed on my hair. He was always a greedy bird, that one. What have you done with the picture?'

'I was kind of planning to file it, in the Case Closed section. I daresay in time I might even forget I ever had it.'

'Yes. Memories can be a strange thing. One moment they're impossible to find, and then for no reason, they'll pop into your head. Goodbye, Grace. And thank you.'

It seemed a reasonable compromise. This way Alison had taken responsibility for her actions as she'd always believed it was right to do, and the people who cared about her, like David and Hannah, could go on believing the best about her.

I took a final look at the photo before filing it. Alison laughing into the camera; the parrot's wings spread wide to keep its balance as it eyed the spread of chopped goodies on the plastic table. And there, half hidden amongst the debris of chopped carrots, apples and cabbage stalks, a knife with a distinctive dark green handle, decorated with a red star.

41

I was packing up when Annie walked in carrying a large box, gift-wrapped, and tied with a red ribbon. At least it was too big to be a T-shirt.

'You shouldn't have.'

'I didn't. Your present is at home. I thought you could come round this evening and I'll demonstrate how to make banana daiquiris. This was on the floor out here. It seems to be yours. But according to Jan, nobody has been up here except you and me.'

The card read: 'Grace. The new locks are an improvement.'

Pulling the ribbon off, I unstuck and unwrapped. Inside was a big cardboard box. Removing the lid, I stared down at the contents. It appeared to be a large silver saucepan. But without the handle. And it smelt. Cautiously I lifted the lid. Chopped meat and vegetables huddled in a gravy that was giving off a strong smell of alcohol. A gift label was stuck to the side of the pot:

'Keep it warm.'

All Orion/Phoenix titles are available at your local bookshop or from the following address:

Mail Order Department
Littlehampton Book Services
FREEPOST BR535
Worthing, West Sussex, BN13 3BR
telephone 01903 828503, *facsimile* 01903 828802
e-mail MailOrders@lbsltd.co.uk
(Please ensure that you include full postal address details)

Payment can be made either by credit/debit card (Visa, Mastercard, Access and Switch accepted) or by sending a £ Sterling cheque or postal order made payable to *Littlehampton Book Services*.
DO NOT SEND CASH OR CURRENCY

Please add the following to cover postage and packing

UK and BFPO:
£1.50 for the first book, and 50p for each additional book to a maximum of £3.50

Overseas and Eire:
£2.50 for the first book plus £1.00 for the second book and 50p for each additional book ordered

---

BLOCK CAPITALS PLEASE

name of cardholder ....
....
address of cardholder ....
....
....
....
postcode ....

delivery address
(if different from cardholder)
....
....
....
....
postcode ....

☐ I enclose my remittance for £ ....

☐ please debit my Mastercard/Visa/Access/Switch (delete as appropriate)

card number ☐☐☐☐☐☐☐☐☐☐☐☐☐☐☐☐

expiry date ☐☐☐☐ Switch issue no. ☐☐

signature ....

prices and availability are subject to change without notice